Single Dad Needs Nanny

TERESA CARPENTER
ALISON ROBERTS
CINDY KIRK

Published in Great Britain 2014
by Mills & Boon, an imprint of Harlequin (UK) Limited,
Eton House, 18-24 Paradise Road, Richmond, Surrey, TW9 1SR

SINGLE DAD NEEDS NANNY © 2014 Harlequin Books S.A.

Sheriff Needs a Nanny, Nurse, Nanny...Bride! and *Romancing the Nanny* were first published in Great Britain by Harlequin (UK) Limited.

Sheriff Needs a Nanny © 2010 Teresa Carpenter
Nurse, Nanny...Bride! © 2010 Alison Roberts
Romancing the Nanny © 2007 Cynthia Rutledge

ISBN: 978 0 263 91186 2
eBook ISBN: 978 1 472 04481 5

05-0514

Harlequin (UK) Limited's policy is to use papers that are natural, renewable and recyclable products and made from wood grown in sustainable forests. The logging and manufacturing processes conform to the legal environmental regulations of the country of origin.

Printed and bound in Spain
by Blackprint CPI, Barcelona

Teresa Carpenter believes in the power of unconditional love, and that there's no better place to find it than between the pages of a romance novel. Reading is a passion for Teresa—a passion that led to a calling. She began writing more than twenty years ago, and marks the sale of her first book as one of her happiest memories. Teresa gives back to her craft by volunteering her time to Romance Writers of America on a local and national level. A fifth generation Californian, she lives in San Diego, within miles of her extensive family, and knows that with their help she can accomplish anything. She takes particular joy and pride in her nieces and nephews, who are all bright, fit, shining stars of the future. If she's not at a family event you'll usually find her at home—reading,

For Mom, who has always believed in me.
And for Yvonne, JD, Denise and all the Culversons
for their loving care of Mom this last year.
You guys are the best.
And for Rodney and Brandon, daddies extraordinaire!

CHAPTER ONE

"...everything." Nicole Rhodes arrived at the

glanced down at her navy ruffled vest, white tank and tailored khaki Capris. Together with her white sandals she felt she'd hit the right mark of cool and professional.

Two adjectives she rarely aspired to. She preferred to experience life.

Still, for today, going on her first job interview in five years, she needed all the confidence she could muster. Damn state budget cuts. She was one of a thousand teachers looking for alternative employment.

Pasting a smile on her face, she knocked on the door.

She needed a job and a place to stay ASAP. This nanny position offered both, with the added bonus of allowing her to stay close to her very pregnant sister, Amanda.

The door in front of her opened to frame a half-naked man. *Oh, mama.*

Her internal temperature spiked to match the hundred-degree heat as she admired six-pack abs, a strong chest dusted with dark hair attached to a corded neck, and a head buried in a gray cotton T-shirt.

"Hey, Russ." A deep voice came from within the depths of bunched-up material. "Thanks for coming over so quickly. I've been picking up before the nanny gets here. I've only got ten minutes to grab a quick shower."

Before she could respond, the shirt finished its journey, leaving mussed mink-brown hair in its wake. A myriad of emotions flowed over Sheriff Trace Oliver's sharp-edged features. Surprise, annoyance and finally resignation flashed through eyes the color of lush green grass.

"I suppose it's too much to hope you're Russ's older sister, come to help out in a crunch?"

She shook her head, felt the heavy weight of the long brunette mane hanging down her back and vaguely wished she'd pulled it up and off her neck. Smiling, and doing her best to ignore all the toned, tanned skin on display, she held out a hand.

"Nikki Rhodes, potential nanny," she introduced herself.

"You're early." The words were curt as he gripped her hand and let his intense gaze roam over her. Ever the optimist, she decided to take his comment as an observation rather than an admonishment.

"Yes. It's supposed to be an admirable trait."

In sheer self-preservation she broke away from his forceful gaze. Instead her glance fell to where her hand lay, cradled in his warm, strong grasp.

"Not always." He responded to her comment with a grimace, and motioned to his shorts and bare chest.

Oh, man. And she'd been trying so hard not to stare. She didn't want to think of her charge's father in a physical way. It just made for unwanted complications. She cleared her throat.

"I'll remember that for the future." She nodded her head toward her silver Camry at the curb. "Shall I wait in the car while you shower?"

"What? No." He stepped back, drawing her inside. "Please come in." He frowned at their clasped hands, as if surprised to find her hand still in his. Abruptly, he released her. "I'll adjust."

Nikki followed him inside; she took in the living room, small dining-room-kitchen combo, and wondered what he could possibly have had to pick up in anticipation of her visit. The rooms were buffed to a high gloss and lacked any form of clutter. The furniture, what there was of it, was all large and modern, all straight lines and muted blues and grays. Nothing in the room suggested a baby lived there. In fact, it had a military feel to it.

One glance around the everything-in-its-place interior and she recognized his need for control. Oh, yeah, she'd been there, lived with that and had no desire to repeat the experience. Reason number two why she should end this interview now.

Amanda, at home on bedrest, kept Nikki's feet planted right where she stood.

"Have a seat," he said. "I'm going to grab a clean shirt."

Yes, please. Cover up all that gorgeous toned skin.

"Girl, you are in so much trouble," she muttered under her breath, watching him disappear down a short hall.

She had no business noticing a prospective employer in that way. It said so right in her contract with the agency.

And she needed this job. She'd given up her apartment three months ago, and moved in with her sister while her brother-in-law was out to sea. Her intent was to save for a down payment on a condo. The timing had seemed perfect. Nikki would keep her sister company and help her to get ready for her first baby, then Nikki would move into her own place just before hubby and baby were due to arrive.

Instead Nikki had received a pink slip. And her brother-in-law had returned two weeks early. Yeah, perfect timing. She was very much the squeaky third wheel in the tiny two-bedroom house, but Amanda wouldn't hear about Nikki moving until she had a new job.

She had good credentials, so she didn't worry about being employable, but this was the only gig in Paradise Pines, and it was important to her that she stay close to her sister until she had the baby.

But Nikki's reluctance to walk away was about more than that. Since the day she'd left for college, and discovered a sense of freedom she'd never known at home, she'd vowed to live life—not hide from it.

Still, she needed to protect herself. She tended to give her heart easily. It was one of the reasons she'd chosen to work with young children. They thrived on her affection and were honest in their responses. She could trust them with her soft heart.

Sheriff Oliver didn't look as if he knew the definition of soft. He was all about neatness, control and schedules. She'd bet structure and discipline were two of his favorite words. Babies were messy, chaotic and unpredictable. Discipline and structure were important, but so was flexibility and creativity. A baby needed room to grow, to makes mistakes and messes in order to learn.

If she took this job, Nikki saw nothing but strife and loggerheads ahead, because she would fight for what was best for the baby. Maybe even harder than she needed to, because the situation hit so close to home.

When Sheriff Oliver returned, he wore blue jeans and a dark green shirt that did incredible things for his eyes. Eyes cooler now than when he'd left the room. As were his features.

He'd gathered his guard, something he wore with such ease she knew it was what he usually showed the world. They'd only stumbled into that moment of rare unease because she'd surprised him at the door.

"The agency said you're a kindergarten teacher," he said as he sat in the recliner adjacent to the couch she occupied. "You know this is a live-in position?"

Down to business. Good. Maybe they'd make it through this interview yet.

"Yes. I'm a victim of the recent state budget cuts." She gave a jaunty shrug, pretending to him—and herself—that losing her job was just a blip in life's journey. "But I was a nanny before; it helped pay my way through college."

"You juggled kids and school? Quite a feat. Most mothers don't even attempt it."

"I had the kids during the day, so I took most of my classes at night. The Hendersons knew I was in school, so they respected my hours. It worked out."

"How old were the kids in your care?"

"Two and four when I started with them."

He glanced down at the paper in front of him, which she could see was a copy of her résumé. "And you were with them for two and half years? Why'd you leave?"

"My parents were in an accident and killed." She could almost say it now without having her throat close up. "My sister needed me. She was in her senior year of high school. I took a semester off to settle my parents' affairs, and to be there for her until she graduated."

"It must have been tough." A gruffness in his voice reminded her he'd lost his wife just over a year ago.

"We had each other, which helped." But it had still been the toughest year of her life.

"Right." He cleared his throat. "So you haven't had care of a baby?"

"Not as young as thirteen months, no, but I'm sure I can manage. I have a master's in Child Development, and I love kids. In fact, my sister is expecting, so in six weeks I'll be an aunt for the first time."

He showed no change of expression at the mention of a pending birth. From mild to effusive, most people showed some form of acknowledgment. It made her wonder about the relationship between him and his son, and why Trace was only now taking custody of the boy.

She knew from the agency that he was a widower, that the baby had survived the accident that had killed his mother, and that Trace's mother-in-law had had care of the baby until a week ago.

"So what's the deal with you? Why are you just now getting custody of your son?" She put the question out there.

A dark eyebrow lifted at her bluntness.

She smiled and lifted one shoulder in a half-shrug. "I believe in open communication. Life is simpler that way." She kept her smile in place and waited. So sue her. She wanted to know, and she'd found asking usually netted answers.

After a moment he answered. "I've always had custody. My in-laws were just helping out until I got settled in a new location."

It took thirteen months? But she didn't voice the thought. Obviously there was something more involved than a simple move. And there would be, of course. A cop and a newborn were hardly a good fit on their own. Plus, something in his voice told her he hadn't been completely comfortable with the arrangement. She took an educated guess.

"I imagine it was a comfort to your in-laws to have their grandson close while they dealt with losing their daughter."

He leaned back in his seat, his brawny forearms

crossed over the wide expanse of his chest. He eyed her suspiciously. "Most people assume I was taking advantage of my in-laws. Not that it's any of their business."

From his defensive posture Nikki guessed "most people" weren't entirely wrong. But she also heard a note of hurt pride. Five years as a teacher had taught her to read people, be they little or big or somewhere in between. For a man of his control, who made duty a way of life, a shadow on his honor would bite big-time.

"Of course." She acknowledged his distancing comment, and then completely disregarded it. "Death is never easy on a family," she sympathized. "But from my experience once a grandmother has a baby in her care it takes a bomb and a crowbar to pry the child loose."

Sheriff Oliver choked on an indrawn breath.

"Oops." Nikki bit her lower lip. Her sister continually warned Nikki that some people didn't appreciate her chronic bluntness. "Not sensitive enough?"

Trace threw back his head and laughed out loud. Something he did all too rarely. He ran a hand over his face as he fought to regain his cool.

"You're very insightful," was all he said. Actually, the truth laid somewhere in the middle of what people thought and the need for a crowbar.

But, Lord, he did appreciate a little blunt honesty. The empathy was harder to accept. From the huskiness in her voice earlier, he had no doubt she still mourned her parents.

"Don't be so hard on yourself," she urged him in

earnest. "It couldn't have been easy handling a newborn on a sheriff's schedule."

"I wasn't a sheriff then. I transferred nine months ago. Before that I was a homicide detective, attached to a multinational task force."

"Sounds important."

"It was. And, as you said, difficult to juggle with a newborn. My mother-in-law offered to help out by taking Carmichael. I was grateful for her aid. But just over a week ago she had a stroke, and my father-in-law moved them back to Michigan, where her family could help with her care and support. It's just me and my son now."

Trace shifted in his chair. He didn't know why he felt the need to explain things to her he hadn't shared with anyone else.

Maybe talking was easier because of the understanding he saw in her intelligent amber eyes, or maybe her honesty called to something in him. Whatever it was, it needed to stop now.

"Carmichael?" she echoed. "I thought his name was Michael?"

"No, it's Carmichael. A family name on my mother-in-law's side."

"Oh. The agency has Michael on my paperwork."

"Then they have it wrong. He's been called Carmichael since he was born." Trace hated the name, but he'd agreed to it to make his wife happy. They probably would have shortened the name if she'd lived. But she'd died. "His mother chose the name."

"Right. Continuity is a fine family tradition." She carefully kept her tone even. He literally saw the struggle it cost her.

"But you don't like it?" He shouldn't test her when she'd made such an effort at politeness, but he couldn't resist.

She struggled for another moment, her smile both brave and patently false. Finally tact gave way to that refreshing honesty.

"It's just so much *name* for a baby," she said in a rush. "They have to learn to walk before they can run, and that's not just physically. Their little psyches need to grow and develop just like their bodies."

So much passion for his son, and she hadn't even met him. Just what any father would want in a nanny.

Right.

"Just be careful not to let guilt motivate your decisions."

The words hit him like a fist to the gut. This was what he got for sharing. "What are you talking about?"

"It's called survivor's guilt. And it causes rational people to make irrational choices. It's just something to be aware of. You think you're honoring her because she can't be here to raise Carmichael. But what she'd really want is for you to love him and raise him the best you can."

"Love the child, honor the mother?"

"Yes. It's that simple."

"Your life may be that easy, Ms. Rhodes, but you know nothing of mine. Don't presume you know my motive for anything." Hearing the harshness of his tone, he took a breath. But on this he needed to be clear. "Carmichael is the focus here. Never attempt to psycho-analyze me."

"Of course." She bit her lip. "I'm sorry. I only meant to help."

"Yeah, well, if there's one thing I've learned since becoming a father it's that nothing is simple anymore. Life has become one complication after another."

She nodded. "Families are complicated. Love is what makes it work."

Good Lord. If that were true, he was in a world of trouble. Rather than dwell on his emotional shortcomings, he switched back to her comments on Child Development.

"I thought you didn't work with infants."

"I don't. But in kindergarten they're still growing and learning when they get to me."

She shifted in her seat, smoothing a hand down a cotton-clad thigh, and then completely changed the subject on him. "I understand you've already had two nannies come and go in the past week. What was the problem with them?"

He frowned. "Why do you want to know?"

"It'll help me to know what you're looking for."

"Right. I guess that makes sense. The first couldn't handle the schedule. She was too concerned with disruptions to her time off and the distance from San Diego. The second seemed set in her ways. She had tried-and-true doctrines and regimens, and she made it clear it would be her way or no way. I chose no way."

"Good for you." Approval beamed at him from across the room, making him feel twelve feet tall. She was a pretty woman, with even features, a plump mouth and a peaches-and-cream complexion, but what really made her attractive was her animation. This woman lived life; it showed in her perpetual smile and those amazing amber eyes.

She lit the room with energy, just sitting on his slate-blue sofa. He watched as she tossed a flow of honey-brown hair over her shoulder. A slight frown created a furrow between slim dark brows.

"Sadly, a lot of parents want just such an arrangement. It's almost as if they prefer to be visitors in their children's lives rather than participants." Her tone made it clear what she thought of those misguided parents.

Must be nice to live in her merry little world. He knew the truth. "I'm in law enforcement, Ms. Rhodes. I can tell you parents often cause less damage to a kid just by virtue of their absence."

"You're right, of course. But that's not what I meant."

"I know what you meant. I've been a visitor in my son's life for more than a year. But that's over. I'm responsible for him now. I'll decide what's best for him."

And chatting up a kindergartener teacher, no matter how blunt and vivacious, wasn't going to get the job done.

Was she the nanny for him?

On the surface she was too young, too overqualified,

too inexperienced. It didn't take a master's degree to change a diaper, but it took someone who'd been around babies to know the difference between a fever due to teething or an illness. Something he'd learned just this week.

On the other hand it was a job, and the budget cuts did have a lot of teachers looking for employment.

"Ms. Rhodes—"

"Please," she interjected, "call me Nikki."

"Ms. Rhodes." It was better that way. Better to keep everything professional. "When can you start?"

CHAPTER TWO

"WHEN can you start?"

As soon as Trace said the words the cell phone on the coffee table rang and a cry echoed from down the hall. He stopped and reached for the phone.

"I'm sorry," he said. "I have to get this. Do you mind checking on the baby for me?"

"Right." Nikki surged to her feet and tugged on the short hem of her vest. She had the job! So she wasn't keen to be working for a control fiend—she'd get to stay close to Amanda, and that was what mattered. Nikki could hardly wait to tell her sister. "Which room?"

He nodded toward the hall. "Last door on the right."

Turned out Nikki needed the directions, because the crying had stopped. She found that odd. In her experience babies wanting attention usually got louder, not quieter.

She pushed open the half-closed door and peered inside. The room held only a crib and a dressing table/dresser set made of fine oak. The walls were white, the sheets and blankets a dark navy. There were no toys in sight.

A brown-haired, solemn-eyed baby sat quietly in the crib.

Nikki's heart wrenched. She'd never seen such a sad child in her life. Poor baby. He must really be missing his grandmother.

"Hello, Carmichael," she greeted him softly as she approached the crib. "I'm Nikki."

She rested her forearms on the wooden railing and smiled, prepared to chat for a moment before plucking him from his bed.

He watched her with those big sad eyes—green, like his father's—but made no move toward or away from her.

"Carmichael is a lot of name to live up to. Someday I'm sure you'll rate every syllable." Letting him get used to her, she reached out and wiggled his little nose. "In the meantime, you look more like a Mickey to me."

The corners of his mouth turned up in a tiny smile.

Pleased by his reaction, she asked, "You like that? You like the name Mickey? I like it, too." She gave his nose another wiggle. "Are you a fan of the mouse? He'd certainly bring a little color to the room, wouldn't he?"

The boy rolled over and crawled to the side of the crib, using the rails to climb up. Once he stood opposite her, he turned shy again, eying her warily. She kept her smile in place, showing him he had nothing to fear.

Her patience was rewarded when he suddenly poked her in the nose.

"Uh-oh," she said in mock alarm. "You got my nose."

He grinned and poked her again.

"Oh, look at you—you got me again. I'm going to get you back." She wiggled his nose one more time.

And he giggled.

The happy sound sent a buzz of triumph through Nikki. She'd made him laugh! The poor baby needed joy in his life, especially with a father ready to control his every move. Nikki readily admitted over-controlling parents were a hot button for her. If the location and the live-in facilities didn't make this the perfect job she'd be tempted to turn it down. She didn't look forward to working for a man with no *give* in his life.

Mickey raised his arms for her to pick him up, and her heart twisted in her chest. Here was another reason for her to stay. One smile made it worth her while.

She lifted him into a huge hug. One arm went around her neck and he laid his head on her shoulder. A lump grew in her throat. There was no feeling in the world like the soft weight of a baby cuddled trustingly in your arms.

She turned and found Trace framed in the open doorway.

Nikki met his green gaze over the baby's head. From the raw emotion in the jade depths she knew he'd heard Mickey's laughter.

"He likes you." Trace came no further than the threshold, his gaze locked on his son in her arms. "Good. That was Dispatch. There's been an accident. I have to go in. Can you start now? I tried Russ again, and he's still not answering, so I need a sitter."

When he raised his glance to her, his expression was closed again. For just a moment his guard had slipped. Now it was back in full force.

"Sure I can watch him. How long will you be?"

Mickey sat up in her arms and looked at his father, almost as if the baby understood what they were talking about. He couldn't, of course, but tone and undercurrents were strong in the air. He probably felt the tension pulsing through the room. She bounced him in her arms.

"I don't know. It could be late." Trace's shuttered expression didn't change.

"Okay, I'll call my sister and let her know I'll be late."

Trace gave one sharp nod. "Okay. I've got to change, then I'll show you where everything is."

"I'll change Mick—Carmichael's diaper and meet you in the living room."

Trace nodded and disappeared down the hall.

Nikki laid Mickey down on the changing table. He made no move to twist or turn away. He simply lay still and watched her. His listlessness tore at her soul.

She chatted to him as she cleaned him up. He took in every word she said, but showed no reaction.

She suspected his grandmother, in her love and loss, had wrapped him in Bubble Wrap, cared for him to the extent she'd smothered the life from him. And Nikki feared his father, obviously a man of discipline and control, would go too far in the opposite direction, until all sense of laughter and spontaneity were lost to this sad little boy.

As soon as Mickey had laughed she'd known she'd have to find a way to work with the father, because this baby needed her. Mickey needed joy and discovery, activity and a sense of adventure. She'd learned to embrace life, and she wanted to share the world with him.

"You went for an interview and you're starting now?" Her sister's droll response to Nikki's explanation of where she'd be for the evening restated the paradox of Nikki's unorthodox hiring process. "Sounds like a pretty desperate situation."

"It is. But it's in Paradise Pines, so I'll be close to you, and it's live-in so I can move out of your place. It's the perfect set-up for our needs right now." Nikki settled deeper into the corner of the couch, the phone tucked between her shoulder and her ear, Mickey in her lap. "And you should see this little boy. Mickey is so sweet, but so sad. I'm sure he misses his grandparents, but his despondency seems to be habitual more than incidental. He lost his mother; his grandparents lost their daughter. I don't think he's ever known happiness."

"Oh, Nikki, this does not sound good. You know you don't have to move out."

"You're being sweet, but we both know I do need to move out. You and Dan need this time together. Besides,

I'm a teacher. Morally and professionally it's my job to do something when I see a child in need."

There was a short telling silence. Then a sigh sounded down the line. "Nikki, do you really know what you're getting into?"

"Not at all." And yet Mickey's sadness had awakened all her protective instincts.

"Amanda, he's thirteen months old and can't walk." She ran her fingers through his silky brown hair, the curls so soft and fine they felt like down feathers. Mickey looked up at her with his solemn eyes. Her heart wrenched. "He doesn't even put his feet out when I set him down. His grandmother must have carried him all the time."

"Isn't all this his father's problem?"

"That's just it. Trace is new at all of this. I'm not sure he'll recognize the problems. In fact, he may make things worse. He's all about control and structure, and Mickey is well behaved so there's nothing for Trace to question."

"But, Nikki," Amanda calmly rationalized, "what can you do?"

"Trace Oliver is a good sheriff, which means he's dutiful and honorable. I'm sure he wants to do what's best for Mickey. He's just clueless what that is. I can teach him."

"Ha!" The rude exclamation tickled Nikki's ear. "I'm due in a month and a half, remember? I've read every book on the subject over the past seven months and I can tell you with little exaggeration that there are twelve thousand 'right ways.' Everyone has an opinion, and some of them are really out there."

"Yeah." Nikki smiled. Her sister did like to know what to expect. She took after Mom in that way. "But this is what I'm trained in. I know I can help Trace and Mickey."

"I have no doubt you can. I've never seen anyone better with kids than you. Because you care, and they can sense it. But that's the problem." Amanda's concern reached through the connection. "You give too much of yourself. This whole thing sounds like a heart-trap to me."

"So you don't think I should do it?"

Another sigh. "I know it will haunt you if you don't, but I'm worried about you getting hurt."

Yeah, that worried Nikki, too. But she'd promised herself on her eighteenth birthday she wouldn't live life afraid to feel. She gave herself to life, heart and soul. Sometimes that meant she got hurt, but it also meant her life was full of rich emotions and lasting memories.

"Life isn't meant to be pain-free."

"Nikki," Amanda said gently, "are you sure this isn't the backlash of your relationship with Mom?"

The question sent sharp pangs of sorrow and regret through Nikki. The frayed state of her relationship with her mother at the time of her death would forever eat at Nikki's soul. She hated, *hated* that her last conversation with Mom had been an argument.

"I can't say it doesn't strike a chord. At a time when he should be reaching for independence, Mickey is totally despondent. If he doesn't develop some spirit he'll never stand a chance."

"You mean, against his father?"

"No. Don't put words in my mouth." Was that how she really felt? Nikki shook her head. She didn't know. She hadn't spent enough time with either of them to make that call. "This is what I know—if I can bring them together now, then they'll have a foundation to build on that will hold them together when the times get rough."

After stating her concern one more time, Amanda ended the call. Nikki understood her sister's hesitation.

She'd defended him to Amanda, but Trace had barely looked at Mickey, much less touched him before leaving, which burned Nikki's hide. Somehow she needed to find a way to bring father and son alive, to teach them to love one another.

Two months. She'd give herself the summer to make a difference, then she'd re-evaluate her situation.

Mickey shyly petted her hair. She sighed and shifted him in her arms. She had a bad feeling she'd lose a part of her heart this summer.

Long after he'd expected to be home that night, Trace pulled into his driveway. The sight of a light inside sent an odd sense of warmth through him. He'd missed that sign of homecoming.

The thought of Ms. Rhodes waiting inside sent an altogether different type of heat surging through his blood. But he quickly blanked off the unruly attraction and pushed his way out of the SUV.

Ms. Rhodes was so far off-limits she might as well be on Mars.

The balmy night air flowed over him as the pine-scented breeze lifted the hair off his brow. Unlocking the front door, he stepped inside and traded fragrant pine for the savory aroma of roast chicken. His stomach growled, reminding him of the hours since his last meal.

He moved to the counter separating the kitchen from the living room to place his keys in their regulated dish, and found a note saying a plate was made up for him in the microwave.

She'd cooked for him.

He checked it out. Chicken, rice and a melody of mixed vegetables. It looked damn good. Again that mysterious warmth glowed in his depths. He cursed.

Hell, man, get a grip. What? Was he going soft at the ripe old age of thirty-five? How could a home-cooked meal and a baby in the house throw him so off-stride? So he had a son to raise. He'd do it like he did everything else—with discipline and structure.

Which in no way explained why he'd hired Ms. Rhodes.

With her short pants, flimsy sandals and figure-hugging navy vest, she'd looked more prepared for a day at the races than a job interview. And her cavalier "it worked out" attitude, along with her schedule with the Hendersons, spoke of a spontaneity he found untenable.

But she'd made Carmichael laugh.

Forking up a bite of chicken, Trace stood over the back of the couch and looked at Carmichael, asleep in Nikki Rhodes's arms. The four-car pile-up on the interstate freeway had taken hours to clear up and document. The Highway Patrol would do the forensics on the fatalities, but his men had been first on scene, so he'd been responsible for traffic control and dealing with the injured.

Death. There was no escaping it.

But then he was used to loss in one form or another. His wife to a car accident, much like the one tonight. His mother had just left—abandoning him and his dad when Trace was ten. And his dad had died two years before Trace married Donna.

Yeah, good old Mom and Dad. Never a demonstrative man, his father had taught Trace all about integrity and honor, but he'd frowned on any display of emotion. Which was why Trace's mom had left his dad. Left them. She'd used to say he was just like his dad.

He didn't know how to love.

Hell, he'd had no business marrying Donna. But she'd pushed for it and he'd found her companionable enough. Plus they'd been great in bed. He'd thought that was the best he was going to get.

Of course she'd wanted more from him than he could give. They'd fought. Often. Then Donna had landed on the idea of a baby. With his dad as an example of what kind of father Trace would make, he'd been against it. Especially when they were so often at odds with each other. She'd gotten pregnant anyway.

After his initial anger, he'd settled down. She'd been so excited, and he'd figured with a baby to focus her attention on she'd get off his case. God, she'd deserved better.

No, he should never have married. He wouldn't make the mistake again.

He pretended the thought had nothing to do with why his gaze sought out Nikki Rhodes. Seeing her and Carmichael cuddled together, Trace envied the peace on his son's face.

God, her porcelain skin looked as soft as the baby's. Trace fought the urge to touch, to test for himself. That was a no-go. As his employee she'd be strictly off-limits.

It shouldn't be a problem. He ruled his body; his hormones didn't. He rarely did anything without careful thought and planning.

The bottom line was he needed Ms. Rhodes.

She'd made Carmichael smile—giggle, even. For that alone she was worth any discomfort he felt. What kind of father would he be if he put his personal well-being above the very real needs of his son?

There'd have to be ground rules.

She was too much of a free spirit, and, where he appreciated the blunt honesty she'd displayed, her unpredictability would drive him nuts. His uncharacteristic openness with her spoke of how easily she'd twisted him up.

Love was not an automatic response. He didn't get all gooey-eyed or mushy inside when he looked at his son. He did feel a sense of duty. He'd made the decision to have a child and he'd do his best by him. Even if his best didn't include love. He'd survived without it. So would his son.

CHAPTER THREE

"YOU'RE home." The sleep husky voice came from the depths of the couch.

He looked down into honey-brown eyes, felt the warmth rising and turned away.

"Yeah, thanks for staying." Glancing at his empty plate, he saw he'd eaten every bite. He set the plate on the island countertop. "Let me take Carmichael to bed."

"Poor little guy missed you tonight." Nikki shifted around until she half sat, with Carmichael draped over her lap. "He wouldn't go to sleep in his crib. I think having a stranger here at bedtime threw him off."

"It wasn't you," Trace assured her grimly as he lifted his tiny son into his arms, careful not to wake him. "He hasn't slept well since he came here. Hang on, I'll be back in a minute."

He carried his light burden to the nursery and laid the boy down gently. He placed a toy giraffe next to the baby and tucked them both in with a soft navy blanket.

Carmichael stirred. Trace stood over him until he settled, then returned to the living room.

Trace thanked God he had the garage converted out back. At least he and Ms. Rhodes wouldn't have to share the house. He'd purposely looked for a property with a detached extra room or granny flat. The division of space served a couple of purposes. One, it preserved his reputation and that of any lady he hired, and two, it defined the barrier between employer and employee and established boundaries for personal space.

Nikki was in the kitchen, cleaning his dinner dishes. Quite the domestic picture.

"Leave them," he told her. "I'll get to them later."

She looked over her shoulder at him and smiled. "They're already done." She opened the cupboard to the left of the sink and placed the plate inside, then turned to face him as she dried her hands with a dishcloth. "It was no trouble."

"We have to talk."

She nodded, folded the cloth over the edge of the sink and followed him to the living room. "It's pretty late. It must have been bad tonight."

"Bad enough." He grimly dismissed the accident that had claimed two lives. A lawman couldn't afford to make it personal. "That's not what we need to talk about."

"Of course." She leaned forward. "Carmichael is such a sweet little boy, but so sad. He must miss his grandparents a lot."

"He asks after them, yes. They've been the constant in his life. He has to get past that."

"And he will, as you replace them in his affections."

He frowned, unnerved at being anyone's emotional stable. But this was his son, so he put steel in his backbone and strengthened his resolve.

"Bonding will take a bit of time," she continued, right through his moment of panic. "Especially with a schedule as erratic as yours."

That stung. "I'm doing the best I can."

"Are you?" She flushed and held up a placating hand. "I'm sorry. I understand yours isn't a nine-to-five job, but it'll really help if you can find some time during the day to spend together. That's usually easiest during a meal, or at bath or bedtime."

"I know the importance of an established schedule." How exactly had he become the one on the defense?

"I'm sure you do. And it's early days for the two of you together. I'm sure we'll find a system that works for all of us."

He appreciated her enthusiasm even as he resisted it. "Sit down, Ms. Rhodes. We have a few ground rules to discuss."

"Of course." The words were terse, reminding him that, as a teacher, she was more used to making rules than following them.

"First of all, there should be no touching."

Her brow furrowed and a question came into her eyes.

"You're an attractive woman," he clarified. "And I'm

a healthy adult male. I've noticed you're demonstrative. You talk with your hands and you express emotion by touching. We need to maintain a professional relationship, so no touching."

She inclined her head in acknowledgment. "That makes sense. What else?"

"I don't need or want you to cook for me. No getting cozy around the kitchen table or snoozing on the couch."

"Cozy?" She actually sounded offended by the notion. Perching on the arm of the couch, she crossed her arms over her chest. "I have to cook for the baby and me anyway. It's just as easy to include enough for you. In fact, it's harder to cook for one and a half than for three, so it's just plain wasteful not to include you. If you don't want me to leave it warming in the oven, fine. I'll tuck the food into the refrigerator and you can dig it out. As for snoozing on the couch—you were late. I fell asleep."

Frowning, she reached for the baby blanket she'd used as a throw and began to fold it. When she continued much of the defiance was missing. "From the sound of your schedule that's likely to happen again, so how do you suggest we handle the problem?"

Good question.

"I'll put a travel crib in your rooms out back. If you get sleepy, you can take Carmichael with you and I'll pick him up when I get home."

"That's disruptive for the baby."

"Yeah." His gaze roamed from her Blushed Rose toenails to her two-inch gold hoop earrings. "Well, I think it's best. I'd also like you to wear a uniform. It doesn't have to be formal, just keep to black and white."

Nikki shifted the blanket she'd folded from her lap to her chest and crossed her arms. "Maybe you should write down all these rules so I don't forget them."

He lifted a brow at her tone. "I'll let that slide, because it's late and we're both tired. But know this: I don't believe in ignoring problems. I believe in addressing the issue to prevent further problems from arising."

"Now, see, I have a different philosophy. Some problems, yes, need to be resolved right away. Others, if you ignore them, often go away."

"Or someone else handles them for you."

"Sometimes, and it's lovely when that happens. Other times new info comes to light which changes the situation so the original problem goes away." She stood and gathered her belongings on the way to the door, where she stopped and met his gaze straight-on. "I don't think you need to worry about us getting cozy around the dinner table." She hooked her purse over her shoulder. "See you tomorrow."

Nikki purposely timed her arrival for 7:00 a.m. the next morning. Not a minute before or a minute after. She'd learned her lesson about punctuality when it came to Sheriff Oliver.

As good as he looked in his skin, she was sure encountering him half-naked again would bend more than one of his rules.

She needn't have worried. He met her at the door fully dressed. He took her suitcase and set it inside the door.

"Carmichael is still sleeping," he told her. "And I got a call from Dispatch so I have to go." He grabbed his keys from the bowl on the counter and headed back to the door.

Oh, my, he did look fine in his uniform.

He wore it with an easy air of command that made the olive-green pants and khaki short-sleeved shirt—accessorized with holster and gun—downright sexy. The confidence and authority he projected made her nerves tingle.

She told herself it was in annoyance for his desertion even as she caught herself staring.

He met her gaze. "I'll show you your rooms tonight."

"Wait." She stepped into his path. "What about the time you're going to spend with Carmichael?"

"It'll have to be tonight." He walked around her. "I'll try to check in during the day. I left my numbers by the phone if there's an emergency."

The door closed behind him and Nikki found herself alone in the quiet house. That *so* had not gone how she'd expected.

That night, Nikki followed Trace Oliver's broad-shouldered, slim-hipped saunter to the garage behind his house. She eyed his chiseled profile, waiting for the right moment to address her concerns. She'd had all day to plot her course of action. She'd try to catch him in a good mood, but if that failed she'd have to risk the fallout. Mickey had needs and she meant to see them met.

"These will be your rooms." Trace opened the door and gestured her inside.

Head held high, she squeezed past him, inhaling soap, mint and man, an intoxicating combination. It was enough to distract her from her surroundings—until the wheels of her suitcase bumped up against the threshold and stopped. With a small tug, she proceeded into the room.

He'd been polite but distant since arriving home. Mickey was sleeping, so Trace was taking the opportunity to show her where she'd be staying.

The garage had been converted into a studio apartment. A large living area included a small kitchen in the far right corner. A full bath occupied the far left corner, with a closet dividing the two. Like the main house, the furnishings here were modern, simplistic, in dark gray and burgundy.

Yeah, a few feminine touches might bring it up to the level of an impersonal hotel room. Not a problem. She needed to clear out of her sister's place anyway. The infusion of her things would brighten this space, bring a warmth and hominess to the small suite.

She moved deeper into the room and caught her reflection in the full-length mirror on the closet door. Intent on fostering the professional relationship they'd agreed upon—and he'd outlined it in excruciating detail—she'd dressed in a pencil-slim skirt that ended two inches above her knees and a fitted vest both in black. For herself, she'd paired the severe clothing with a romantic white cotton shirt, ruffled at the scooped neck and capped sleeves. Black sandals completed the outfit.

Catching sight of his reflection behind her, she felt a punch to the gut. He looked as good now as he had this morning—better, actually. Being a little rumpled made him appear more approachable.

Not wanting to be caught staring, she quickly diverted her attention back to the room.

"This is really very nice. Is there wood for the fireplace?" Oh, great save. Like she needed a fire in late June.

"By the shed outside, to the left. But you probably won't be here long enough to use it."

"What do you mean?" Miffed, Nikki tried and failed to keep the bite out of the question. "I'm playing by the rules." She gestured to her uniform of black and white.

His intense gaze rolled over her until his eyes met hers. "Right. But we both know this is a temporary arrangement at best."

"Why do you say that?" she demanded. "I assure you I truly care about Mickey, and I'm committed to staying until—"

Whoa. She cut herself off as her mind caught up with her mouth. She couldn't tell him she intended staying until father and son bonded. Already she knew he'd take her interference as well as a cat took to water: with a whole lot of resistance and no discernible gratitude for the effort involved. He only accepted her presence now because Mickey liked her. That was where she needed to channel her efforts.

"Until what, Ms. Rhodes? He starts school? Can stay home alone? Begins to drive? You won't be here through the end of the year, let alone any of those milestones."

And there was a fine sample of opposition. Leaving her suitcase against the wall, she plopped into a soft gray armchair, planted her elbows on the arms, and got to the heart of the matter.

"Why did you hire me if you're ready to push me out the door?"

He surprised her when he gave up his position of power to sit across from her. "First of all, because you're a teacher, not a nanny. You're going to go back to teaching the first chance you get. It's obvious when you talk about it that you love your job. Second, I can see you do care about Carmichael. More important, he likes you. But let's not kid ourselves. You're a meddler, Ms. Rhodes. You can't help yourself. And I can't tolerate being manipulated. I have a high-pressure, high-exposure job. I need to know my child is being cared for to my specifications, and to find peace when I walk through my door at the end of my shift."

Okay, she gave him points for insightfulness and, yeah, she understood the whole peace-in-his-own-home thing. Her mother had always wanted peace. Nikki considered it overrated. Give her loud and loving every time. Laughter wasn't a quiet commodity.

As for meddling—he was right. She couldn't deny it. But the man had serious emotional issues. She intended to help him and Mickey find a connection. If he preferred for her to be up-front about it, she could do up-front.

"I prefer to think of it as caring about people." Earnest in her concern, she leaned forward. "I care about Carmichael. You didn't even stop to check on him this evening. So, yeah, I'm going to meddle. He needs you, so what's it going to take to get you to stand steady for him?"

Trace's dark brows slammed together. "You're out of line."

"Blame yourself." Nikki waved his irritation aside. "You hired me to take care of Carmichael. To me that means more than changing diapers and heating bottles. His emotional welfare is as important as his physical welfare. Why are you so afraid of emotion?"

He surprised her with an immediate response.

"I'm not afraid of emotion, Ms. Rhodes, I'm just not very good at it."

Nikki blinked at the unexpected reply. How sad if that was true. The total lack of feeling in his expression revealed he believed it.

"And it's easier to back away than try?" she guessed.

"I've tried." A shadow of pain came and went in his level gaze. The flash of vulnerability convinced her of his claim more than the stoic words. "That's how I know I'm no good at it."

She could tell it had cost him. Still, she had to press. For him and for Mickey. "Well, it's time to try again. Can I be frank with you? Mickey's development is stunted. You know I have a master's in Child Development. He's behind in speech, in walking, in his motor skills."

His eyes narrowed to slits. "You're saying my child is slow?"

"No. He's smart, and actually quick to catch on to new things. But he just sits, and he always wants to be held."

"His grandmother was very protective of him," he said slowly, his mind obviously at work. "Whenever I visited she held him all the time. I thought it was because she was afraid I would take him away. She must have coddled him to the extent he did little for himself."

"It's sad, isn't it?" she asked, compassion illuminating her features. "She'd lost her daughter. Her grandson was all she had left of her child. She hung on to him with all her might, and ended up impeding his progress instead of nurturing his growth."

"She held on so tight she may have irreparably damaged his ongoing development. That's not sad, that's negligent. And I let it happen."

"It's not necessary to place blame," Nikki assured him. "What matters is what you do now. Your son needs you. We talked about you setting time aside each day to spend with him. When would be best for you?"

"I've already explained my days are chaotic in the extreme. I keep a schedule, but I'm always on call. I can't give you a set time."

"Come on." She sighed, her understanding slipping. "That's a cop-out."

"Be careful, Ms. Rhodes." Dark color stained his cheeks and he fixed a fierce frown on her.

"Good parents make time for their kids."

"I'm aware of that, but—"

"No *buts*. Everyone's busy. We'll just work at it until we find a time. We'll start with breakfast. How does bacon and eggs sound?"

He shook his head. "I usually grab something at the station."

Now he was just being difficult.

"Good. You'll be able to focus all your attention on Mickey. You can have a cup of coffee while you feed him."

"I'm the employer, Ms. Rhodes. I make the rules."

"Yeah, I've noticed you're big on rules. It's all about structure and control for you, isn't it? So you'll understand the benefit of a regular schedule for your son."

He scowled, but she saw he was thinking about her comments. Good. She rose and went to the door.

"Thanks for showing me my rooms. I'd like to get settled in, but I'll see you at breakfast. Seven o'clock. I'll cook."

He blew her off again the next morning. When she came in, he was strapping on his utility belt, getting ready to walk out the door.

He nodded to the baby monitor. "Carmichael is still sleeping. He should be up soon. He slept through the night for the first time since getting here. I have to go."

She propped her hands on her hips. "What about our date?"

His laser green gaze sliced to her, and she cringed

inwardly at her unfortunate word-choice. The word probably added to his irritation at being questioned at all.

"Our *appointment* will have to wait until tomorrow. The Mayor called for a breakfast meeting. Was I supposed to tell him I couldn't make it because I had to feed my son?"

"You say that as if feeding your son isn't important." Walking to the table for the baby monitor, she sent him an aggravated glare. "Did you even suggest an alternative time?"

"No." He shrugged. "We often meet over breakfast. We're busy men, it's easiest to get our session out of the way early."

"And that was fine when you were on your own. Now you have a son who needs your attention."

"He'll get it tomorrow morning." He grabbed his keys and headed for the door. He slid on mirrored shades, which added an extra layer of stern to his tough visage. "Don't attempt to interfere with my work, Ms. Rhodes. You won't like the results."

Nikki fumed as he closed the door on her— figuratively and literally.

She stormed into the kitchen and took her ire out on innocent pots and pans.

"Oh, shoot. Wait!" She went running for the door, to catch Trace before he left, but when she stepped out on the deck it was to watch his SUV disappear down the street.

"Dang." Stubborn man. He'd riled her both last night and this morning, so she'd forgotten to ask about the car seat for Carmichael. She assumed it must be in Trace's vehicle, because she hadn't found it when she went through the house and garage yesterday. There was no stroller, either. Nor playpen or walker. The only baby items were the crib and dressing table and a highchair.

He needed to pick up the necessities from his in-laws' place or buy new ones, because she and Mickey were prisoners without them. Back in the kitchen, she frowned at the cupboards, reminded they were also low on groceries. She began to plot her evening. There was more than one twenty-four-hour superstore in the county.

If she had to call 911 to get his attention, she and Trace would be visiting one before the night ended.

CHAPTER FOUR

NIKKI was ready for Trace when he got home at seven that evening. She sat alone at the dining-room table, her purse in front of her, along with a small cooler of food. The elusive Russ was playing with Mickey in his room down the hall.

She'd covered dinner and a sitter; she didn't want Trace to have any wiggle room to get out of going shopping. Mickey was as sweet as could be, and a good baby, but he expected to be held all the time. Nikki literally couldn't get anything done. And without a car seat or stroller, she remained housebound.

It might be unfair to expect Trace to shop after a twelve-hour day, but expecting her to care for a baby without the proper equipment was equally unreasonable.

He walked in the door and over to the dish to drop in his keys. He glanced around, then looked at her.

"What's up? Are you going someplace? Hey, I'm sorry I'm late." He rubbed a hand over the back of his neck in a weary gesture. "Time just disappears. Is Carmichael sleeping?"

"No. I hired Russ to watch him tonight. Carmichael needs some things. You and I are going shopping."

"Not tonight." Dark brows lowered in a frown. "I'm tired and I'm hungry. We'll go tomorrow."

"We're going tonight," she insisted. "I've only been here two days, and I already know not to trust the promise of tomorrow."

His scowl darkened, but he couldn't deny the allegation. "I thought I made it clear how I feel about being manipulated."

"Then don't force it on me." She patted the cooler and recited the list of items Carmichael required. "I've packed you dinner. Believe me, I wouldn't ask you to go out if I didn't really need these things to care for him properly. I'm tired, too, but we need to go tonight. How did you even get Carmichael home without a car seat?"

He looked pained. "There was one. It was too small, so I took it down to the station to have on hand in case of an emergency." He sighed. "Do I have time for a shower and change of clothes?"

Relieved to have his co-operation, she grinned. "If you hurry."

"Do you want a modular unit for a playpen, or will the portable crib work?" Trace asked as they stood in the baby aisle of the superstore.

"Oh, do they have modular units here?" Nikki

stepped back to view the merchandise better. "Where? Does it list the dimensions?"

"I don't see them here. A friend has one. I can find out where he got it, or order it online, but you'd have to wait."

She took in their two carts, swollen with large boxes. It contained a fortune. "Oh, yeah, we don't have to get everything tonight. I wasn't thinking of the expense."

"Let me worry about the expense." Injured pride added bite to his response. "I'd rather finish it tonight. I can afford whatever is needed for my son."

"Of course. I didn't mean to imply you couldn't." Maybe she could use that pride to motivate him on an emotional level. "Thank you for coming out tonight. I've really been stuck these past couple of days. Carmichael is a good baby but—"

"He wants to be held," Trace finished, and she met his gaze in a moment of shared understanding. "I know."

"Let's go to the toys. He needs to become engaged in activities that hold his attention. Russ brought over some of his niece's blocks. He says Carmichael will play with them for an hour or more."

"Huh?" Trace made a show of turning toward the toys. "Let's get us some blocks."

She laughed, and quickly caught up to him. "When are you going to pick up the rest of his stuff?"

He looked blank. "What do you mean?"

"His stuff. For his room. Toys, stuffed animals, wall hangings. Things with color and form to inspire his mind—that stuff."

"Oh. There wasn't any of that in what my father-in-law brought."

"So M— Carmichael has no stuff? That's kind of sad." Shocked and saddened by the revelation, Nikki spoke without thinking, but regretted her lack of forethought when she saw the humor fade from his face. She tried to save the moment. "But, hey, that means you get to choose his stuff."

"Me?" A shadow passed over his features. "I wouldn't know where to start."

"It's easy," she encouraged him. "What did you have in your room as a kid?"

"Here are the blocks." Pushing into the toy aisle, he made a point of studying the displays. Finally he said, "My room looked pretty much like Carmichael's, except with a bed instead of a crib."

"Oh, Trace," she whispered. "You're breaking my heart."

He glanced at her and his eyes softened. "No need," he assured her. "You don't miss what you never knew."

Caught by his compelling jade gaze, she moved closer. "You have a chance to give him something you never had."

He nodded, and then moved his gaze down to his side. "You're touching me, Ms. Rhodes."

So she was. Both arms were wrapped around his strong arm. Muscles flexed under her fingers as he carefully stepped away.

"Sorry," she said.

"Yeah." Reaching for a box of blocks, he changed the subject. Relieved, she followed his lead. For such a tough character he showed vulnerability at the oddest moments. It was clear to her that he needed Mickey as much as Mickey needed him.

She blinked away weak tears. She'd have to stay strong if she meant to help them find each other.

Back at the house, she checked on Mickey while Trace and Russ unloaded everything from the SUV. After Russ took off, she asked Trace, "How did the other nannies make do without this gear?"

He shrugged. "They weren't around long."

"It was the rules, right? You probably scared them away with all your rules," she teased. But she was serious, too. "I prefer to work in an environment with open communication, more give and take."

"Give and take?" He said the words as if he'd never put them together in the same sentence before.

"Yes. You're the employer and I'm the employee, but we discuss things and come to a consensus of what's best for the baby."

"A consensus?" It wasn't a question but a low voiced challenge.

"Right. You've made it clear you'd prefer to let the baby sleep in the morning while you escape to the sheriff's station. That's your side, and of course we could do that. But then there's my side."

"You have a side?"

"I do. I'm so glad you're getting into the spirit of

things," she said through a smile, her tone carefully soft and easy; it was an attitude she maintained as she continued. "My side is I feel so strongly about your spending time with Carmichael that it's a deal-breaker for me. Either keep to the schedule we agreed on and have breakfast with him in the mornings, or you can find yourself another nanny."

The silence that followed screamed through the living room. Nikki dug her fingernails into the flesh of her palms to keep from squirming under his ferocious stare.

"I don't react well to threats, Ms. Rhodes."

"You know, I'm not really surprised to hear that." No understatement there. She lifted her chin and informed him, "I feel the same way about being blown off."

"Ms. Rhodes—" Ice encrusted her name.

"Mr. Oliver?" She gave chill as good as she got. He needed to know she was serious about this. "Think of it as the terms of my employment. And it's non-negotiable."

"It's a bluff. You said yourself you care about Carmichael."

"Which is why this is so important. I won't stand by and watch him decline further for lack of a steady influence in his life."

"You—"

"Stop." She held up a hand, palm out. "We've already established I won't be here for more than a few months. He needs the person who is going to be here that first day of school, when he learns to drive, and the day he turns eighteen. That, Mr. Oliver, is you."

Unable to dispute the truth, he stood silently glowering.

"Morning sessions with your son are the perfect opportunity to get to know each other better. Show him some attention and he'll love you unconditionally. It's pretty hard to mess that up."

"But what if I do? Mess it up?" he asked, with a concern that revealed a raw vulnerability his gruff attitude had concealed.

Her heart was wrung at the evidence of his fear of failing his son. She could think of no other reason why such a strong willed and private man would open himself to her. More than ever she renewed her vow to help father and son connect.

"I'll help you."

"The first thing you need to do is take off your shirt." Nikki opened a jar of baby food, poured the peaches into a bowl and set it on the table next to where Mickey sat sleepy-eyed in his highchair at the end of the table.

Out of near identical green eyes, Trace sent her a candid stare. "Must we go over the rules again, Ms. Rhodes?"

"Please. You have a one-track mind. I was thinking of your cleaning bill, not your manly form. You can take it off now or change it later. First lesson in feeding your child: babies are not neat."

"Thanks for the warning." Trace stripped off his khaki shirt and draped it over the back of the couch.

"Hey, I'm here to help." Nikki admired the snug fit

of pristine white cotton stretched over wide shoulders when he returned to the dining area. She shook her head silently mourning the T-shirt's pending desecration. Oh, well, neat and tidy was an ongoing battle when you had kids.

"You take that side—" she waved Trace to a seat close to the highchair "—and I'll sit over here." They settled across from each other at the table on either side of Mickey.

"Okay, go ahead and give him a bite. Second lesson is never leave the baby unattended with the food, or you'll be cleaning the whole kitchen."

Trace took the bowl of puréed peaches, dipped the baby spoon in it and held it out to Mickey.

Mickey looked from the spoon to Trace, to her. He did not open his mouth.

"Move it closer," she encouraged Trace. "That's good," she said, when the spoon reached within an inch of Mickey's little mouth. "Sometimes you really have to shovel it in, but I'd rather he came to the food this first time between you."

Instead of going for the bite of peaches, the boy pushed away, leaning his head on the back of the highchair.

Huh? Nikki glanced over at Trace, to find him watching her with a "what now?" expression.

"Maybe he doesn't like peaches?" he offered.

"No. A lot of baby food is orange. Carrots, sweet potatoes, apricots—they make a whole guessing game of it at baby showers. I suppose if he didn't like one of those your mother-in-law may have catered to him and not fed him any orange foods. Did they leave a list of his preferences?"

"No. She wasn't in any shape to put anything like that together, and my father-in-law was too overwhelmed to think beyond dropping the baby off."

"Of course. That's understandable."

"There was nothing but formula and cereal in his diaper bag. There may have been some food in the refrigerator at my in-laws I could have picked up when I got his stuff last weekend, but I didn't think to look."

"She was still feeding him formula?"

"Yeah." He angled his head to the right. "There are several cans in the cupboard."

"If she still had him on formula maybe she hadn't even started him on baby food yet. Basic rule of thumb is formula for the first year, adding baby cereal at three or four months, and moving to baby food and other solids around seven to nine months."

Trace's jaw clenched and his eyebrows lowered in a grim scowl. Anger and shame flashed in his eyes, and she knew he blamed himself at this further evidence of his mother-in-law's smothering influence.

"Listen, those are just parameters. Like my sister says, there are as many theories as there are doctors. Mickey isn't suffering from malnutrition."

To distract him further, she scooted the empty bottle of peaches toward him. "There's baby food in the cupboard. Someone must have tried to feed him something more than cereal."

"That would be nanny number two. I arrived home one night at dinnertime. There was puke-green food all over him, all over her, all over the dining room. He was crying, she was screaming, and trying to force the spoon down his throat. I fired her on the spot."

Nikki chewed her bottom lip as she studied his stern expression. He'd obviously been appalled by the scene he'd walked in on. "That sounds very unpleasant."

"It was out of control."

Ah. The worst of all sins.

"Yes, well. I don't condone force-feeding, but you best prepare yourself. Feeding babies can be a chaotic experience. Most kids are naturally suspicious of any change in their diets. Some will easily try new things, but some need to have the food presented to them several times, and occasionally in different forms, before they take to it."

He frowned, as if it hurt to think about it, then he squared those truly impressive shoulders. "As I don't plan on lowering myself to Carmichael's level, I'm sure we'll manage just fine."

Oh, how the mighty would fall.

"A positive attitude is exactly the ticket," she assured him, figuring some things just needed to be experienced. "A smile helps, too. You know what they say— never let them see you sweat."

Trace lifted one dark brow. "We're talking about a baby here."

"Right." She looked down at her own white blouse and slid back in her chair. "Just remember they sense fear."

Trace grunted a nonverbal reply. Getting a good dollop on the end of the spoon, he presented the bite to Mickey once again. The boy wanted no part of it. He turned his head to the left, and when his father followed with the spoon he whipped his head to the right.

"Ack!" With a squawk of frustration, Mickey pushed Trace's hand away. A splatter of peaches flew through the air to land smack in the middle of Trace's chest. He glumly surveyed his formerly crisp white T-shirt.

"Good thing you took off your uniform shirt," she pointed out, hoping to direct him to the positive view. She got a grunt for her efforts.

His focus on the boy, Trace persevered, and finally got a good portion of the peaches into Mickey's mouth.

A tiny red tongue immediately pushed the food back out, then the baby blew a raspberry, spraying Trace with bright orange polka dots.

Nikki bit back a grin as father and son faced off, with identical frowns of stubborn resolve.

"You're the bigger man here," she reminded Trace, then giggled when they both turned those frowns her way. "You're not going to give up, are you?" she challenged.

"No." He narrowed his eyes at her, but she saw reluctant humor in the green depths before he turned his attention back to Mickey. "Okay, kid, no more spitting. Peaches are good, so open wide."

Before digging in for another bite, Trace licked a smear of peaches from where it had landed on his right thumb.

Mickey's eyes brightened, then he mimicked his

father by licking his fist where he'd wiped the fruit from his mouth.

"Mmm, mmm." Nikki hummed yummy sounds and smiled encouragingly.

"Mmm," the boy repeated, and swiped his tongue over his hand again.

"Look." She grabbed Trace's arm and shook it in excitement. "Mickey's copying you. He likes it. Give him another bite."

Trace glanced up from where her hand rested on his arm. The heated stare he turned on her made her catch her breath. "No touching."

She snatched her hand away. "Seriously? You're in the middle of feeding your son!"

His gaze rolled over her, sensual as a caress, and so intense her skin tingled as if from actual contact.

He turned back to Mickey, feeding him another bite of fruit. "So? You've heard the statistics. The average man thinks about sex every so many seconds. If we aren't actually having sex, we're thinking about it."

Stunned nearly speechless, she leaned back in her chair and crossed her arms over her chest. "You dawg. And yet I'm the one who has to follow all the rules?"

The corner of his mouth twitched, but he came at her from a completely different direction.

"And, Ms. Rhodes? His name is Carmichael." He turned a reproachful stare on her, and she knew she'd slipped up more than once.

She grimaced. "I'm sorry."

She bit her lip, then decided to come clean. Truthfully, deception never came easily to her. Too often her mouth worked before her brain, and honesty just made life simpler.

"I just can't call him Carmichael. I promise it's not meant to be disrespectful, or a control issue. Sure, Carmichael is a fine, distinguished name. But to me it's also cold and hard. And with all the changes in his life Mickey needs warmth and love and acceptance more than anything else. I'd constantly feel like I was scolding him."

Nikki got a first-hand lesson in Trace's interrogation technique as he sat back and ran a laser-sharp gaze over her. His intense regard seemed to see straight to her soul. He assessed, categorized and made conclusions— all without saying a word. Or changing expression. She was ready to spill her deepest, darkest secrets, and she had no idea what he was thinking at all.

He finally broke the connection to focus on mopping up his son's face.

Free to breathe again, she anxiously waited for his response. She hoped they could settle the issue amicably between them, because she really couldn't promise to call the baby Carmichael. In all honesty it probably wasn't harmful to the boy at this stage, but he'd responded to Mickey when he hadn't to the more formal name. That spoke volumes to her.

"Leslie Trace."

"What?" Nikki stared at her employer's stoic profile. Of everything he could have said, that made no sense to her. And when he turned to face her and flashed that dimple-popping grin she completely forgot what they were talking about.

"The name my mom used when I was in trouble." Humor and understanding had replaced the censure. Evidently she'd hit the right mark, tapping into the universal connection of childhood memories.

"Leslie, huh? That had to hurt."

The humor disappeared. "Throw in extra for being a military brat. When my mom had gone, I told my dad I wanted to be Trace. He had no problem with that."

"Rough. How old were you when your mom died?"

"I didn't say she died. But she might as well have. I was ten when she left my dad and me."

"Extra rough. You and your dad must be close?"

"He died before I married Donna. But we weren't really close. Dad wasn't what you'd call demonstrative."

"That must be where you got it." As soon as the words escaped her mouth she knew she'd blown the moment.

Raw emotion flashed in his eyes before he shut down all signs of feeling. He rose to his feet and pushed in his chair in two short, controlled motions.

"Yeah, that's where I get it from." He glanced at Mickey before turning away. "I need to change."

"Trace." She jumped to her feet, but he was already gone. Slowly sinking into the seat, she met Mickey's confused frown. "Yeah, I know. I blew it."

CHAPTER FIVE

TRACE stared at the report on his desk as he waited on hold for the receptionist to make his appointment with the pediatrician. Finding out he didn't know the slightest thing about his son's health had struck Trace hard this morning. He'd depended on Fran to take care of Mickey and actually felt righteous about the decision. Fran and Owen had just lost their only daughter; they needed something—someone—to fill the void in their hearts and lives. Who better than their infant grandson?

How easy to convince himself the couple had been better suited to handle the newborn than an overworked homicide cop, with uncertain hours and no experience with living, breathing kids.

Sure, he'd made the effort to visit and provided monetary support. And, yeah, he'd made the move to Paradise Pines with the intent to take custody. But what it all boiled down to was he'd abandoned his son to a woman sick at heart over the loss of her own child.

He had no doubt Mickey had been loved and coddled. To within an inch of his life.

In retrospect he saw it so clearly. Fran had always had the baby in her arms or seated right next to her. Always insisted on feeding Mickey his bottle because it disturbed him to have anyone else do it.

She'd smothered his son with love to the point she'd stunted his development.

The return of the receptionist pulled his distracted attention from the report and his sorry history as a father. He quickly confirmed the appointment for Thursday at two and disconnected. Right. A microcosm of tension eased from the weight on his shoulders. He couldn't undo the past, but he could make sure they started out fresh, started out right.

He made a note to tell Nikki about the appointment.

Talk about fresh starts.

Trace was in serious trouble there. He didn't know whether he'd made the best decision of his life or a very dangerous mistake. Nikki Rhodes threatened everything he stood for: order, discipline and consistency.

Why, oh, why did she have to be exactly what his son needed most right now?

Trace kicked back in his office chair and stared unseeing out at the reception/dispatch area of the small sheriff's station. Instead of Lydia, his no-nonsense office manager, with a heart as soft as a marshmallow, he envisioned the soft golden beauty of his own personal Attila the Hun.

How had he lost control of his home so fast? His home? Hell, his life. Mornings would never be the same again. Though he admitted to a proud moment when Mickey had taken his first bite of peaches from the spoon. What a sense of accomplishment. They'd grinned at each other, as euphoric as if they'd scored a winning touchdown and then—he cringed to remember this—they'd both turned to Nikki, as if seeking approval of a job well done.

She'd lavished them with praise. *Lord.*

Where was his self-discipline? Where was his pride?

He'd totally lost control. To a five-foot-five bit of fluff in a tight skirt and ruffles.

Okay, she'd thrown him off with her ultimatum, demanding his participation in feeding Mickey; he just needed to regroup and replan, set a new schedule. He admitted he'd been hesitant about spending time with the boy. But this morning's impromptu breakfast session proved he had nothing to fear. He could handle his son.

With a little tuition he'd become quite efficient. Then he'd send the distracting Ms. Rhodes on her way. They'd both be happier when she was teaching again.

For all her lack of structure, the woman had kept her promise to help. What had she said? "The benefit of open communication is you don't have to do everything alone." He had to admit he'd appreciated her assistance at breakfast. Sure he could handle it, but having someone there—it had been nice.

Another one of her precious gems of advice came to

mind. "The good news is once you engage Mickey's affections it'll be almost impossible to lose it. Unconditional love is a powerful thing."

It sounded good. Too good to be true for a man who didn't know the first thing about love.

Nikki sat in one of her least-favorite places in the whole world: the doctor's office. One of the unsung joys of being a military brat was the military health service. Every new visit to the doctor brought a new face, and a new person to poke and prod you.

After the breakfast session the other day, she hadn't been surprised when Trace had insisted on a full checkup for Mickey. The idea that his son might have been suffering in any way drove Trace nuts.

She glanced at the little boy, quietly playing with blocks in his stroller. He was slight, but not noticeably undernourished. He might not have had a varied diet, but he'd had plenty. Still, the checkup couldn't hurt, and if it put Trace's mind at ease it might be worth this interminable torture.

"I'm only here for you." She leaned over Mickey. "And let's get one thing clear up front. I don't do needles—uh-uh, *nada*, no way. If there are shots involved, your daddy is on his own. In fact—" she flipped a block with her finger "—this is the perfect opportunity for father and son to go it alone. Yep, the two of you can bond over tongue depressors."

Mickey picked up the block to hand to her, but

dropped it instead. He gave a small mew and shifted to look over the side of the stroller, then shifted his hopeful gaze to her. He looked so angelic, with his little bow mouth, baby-soft skin and windblown curls.

She handed him the fallen block and earned a smile. She sighed. "Okay, for you I can probably hang tough. But only if your dad asks for help. Otherwise I'm staying put."

"Daddy." He grinned.

"That's right. You and your dad are a team."

He went back to his blocks, and she returned to flipping leisurely through an entertainment magazine. She and three other women sat in navy short backed chairs. The walls and carpeting were beige on beige. An overflowing toy chest in the corner provided the only splash of brightness in the bland room.

The outside door opened and, like every other woman in the room with a sick child, looking for a distraction, Nikki glanced up. And, like every other woman in the room, her heart quickened at the sight of Trace. His broad-shouldered, narrow-hipped frame neatly filled the opening. His air of authority and control—elements he wore as easily as he did the crisp khaki uniform and gun belt—preceded him into the room. And shot up the temperature of every woman within viewing distance.

How unfair was it that the best-looking man in a fifty-mile radius had to be her boss? Not only did that put him both professionally and contractually off-limits, but the man was as disconnected from commitment as it was possible to be.

She sighed, and resigned herself to being his friend. At least he was finally here, and they could get this appointment over with.

The clock over the receptionist's head read two-fifteen exactly. The perky blonde hopped to her feet, her bright smile aimed at Trace. "Sheriff Oliver? The doctor is ready to see Carmichael."

Wasn't that convenient? Nikki met Trace's gaze and slowly stood. The flash of panic, so unlike him, revealed a vulnerability she couldn't ignore. "Do you want me to go in with you?"

"Yes, please." He took control of the stroller and followed the nurse to an examination room.

Trace quickly expressed his concerns to Dr. Wilcox, sparing himself not at all.

An older man, with a ring of graying hair and wire-rimmed glasses, the doctor listened intently, nodding occasionally.

"Well, let's see what the real damage is." Dr. Wilcox smiled at Mickey, who scowled back at the man. With good reason. The doctor asked Nikki to strip the baby, and the poking and prodding began.

For a usually docile child, Mickey certainly made his displeasure known, twisting and turning so Nikki almost lost her grip on the boy.

"Here, let me have him." Trace stepped forward to trade places with her. He easily held the boy in place, but Mickey's distress only increased. He lifted his little arms toward Trace. "Daddy."

Trace's jaw clenched, but he stayed tough.

Thankfully, the doctor soon ended the exam. "Okay, you can dress him." He picked up his chart. "Do you know what inoculations he's had?"

Nikki stepped forward to dress Mickey.

Trace reached in his pocket. "I went by my in-laws' place this morning and found a few things. This is a list of the immunizations he's had. I also called his pediatrician there, and asked for a copy of his file to be sent to you."

"Thanks. That'll be helpful." Dr. Wilcox looked over his glasses to scan the list Trace handed him. "And this looks current." He sat back and folded his arms over a barrel-size chest. "You can calm your concerns. Mickey is in good shape. The muscles in his legs are underdeveloped, which is consistent with your theory that he's been held a lot, but his bones are strong and there are no signs of malnutrition."

Nikki met Trace's gaze, and in that moment felt a sense of connection in their relief and gratitude at the doctor's news. Bouncing Mickey in her arms, she shot Trace a reassuring smile and let the tension drain away.

"Continue feeding him solids, and encourage him to use his muscles. I'll do the blood work and read through his records when they come in, then I'll give you a call. Basically, I don't expect I'll need to see him before his eighteen-month check-up."

"Thanks, Dr. Wilcox, that's good news."

"He's a precious gift, Sheriff," the doctor said seriously. "Treasure him accordingly."

Trace's cool gaze ran over Mickey, once again strapped in his stroller. "Right."

Nikki watched the exchange with little satisfaction. She'd so hoped something good would finally come from a visit to the doctor's office.

After a week of make do trips to the corner mini-market, Nikki finally dragged Trace to the grocery store on Saturday afternoon.

Pushing Mickey in one of the store carts, Nikki rolled over the threshold, and they both sighed at the rush of cold air.

"That's much better, isn't it?" She tweaked the boy's nose.

"Neeki." He grinned and made a grab for her nose, missing by a good eight inches.

She leaned closer and wiggled her nose. "Not going to get me," she challenged, and quickly pulled back when he tried again.

Mickey giggled, but next to her Trace frowned. "You're taunting a one-year-old?"

She simply smiled. "Oh, we've played this game before. He'll get me a couple of times before we're through."

Trace grunted. He looked at the aisles surrounding them, the people wandering nearby. "Let's get this done. I suggest we split up and meet at the register in twenty minutes."

Nikki sized him up. Cool and confident in jeans and

a blue knit shirt, he clearly didn't want to be here. But it was more than the chore that had him off-stride. The man defined the term *loner*. In the week she'd been at the house she hadn't taken a single message for him. She knew he'd kept Mickey's existence to himself. Other than the doctor's appointment, this was his first public appearance with his son in the community.

Well, he needed to suck it up—because, in the way of small towns everywhere, everyone would soon know his business.

"You're out of almost everything, so we won't be out of here in twenty minutes. *And* you ducked out of breakfast yesterday, so you have Mickey-time to make up and this is the perfect opportunity. If we split up, he goes with you."

Trace shrugged. "Fine."

His easy compliance didn't fool Nikki. He was never comfortable handling Mickey alone. No one would know it, watching the two together. Though always gentle, always patient, Trace's need for control kept him from letting his feelings show, or he'd have already earned Mickey's love.

"Okay, then. He's going to want things he can't have, and touch everything within reach, so be firm and keep to the middle of the aisle."

"Really, Ms. Rhodes, I think I can handle a one-year-old in a store."

She lifted a skeptical brow. "That's what you said about feeding him the first time."

He planted his hands on his hips and met her stare for stare. "My point exactly."

Nikki cocked her head and considered him. Peach-stained T-shirt aside, she allowed that he'd persevered until Mickey ate the whole bowl. Since then he'd mastered the art of feeding the child without wearing half the food.

"You're right." But before Nikki stepped back and let him have the cart she needed to issue another warning. "There's one more thing—"

"Ms. Rhodes." He cut her off. "I can take it from here."

"But you should know—"

"We'll be fine." He took the list she held in her hand and tore it in two. "Meet you at the registers in twenty minutes."

Nikki shook her head and walked over to snag a new cart. Oh, well. She'd only meant to warn him that a man alone with a child in a grocery store was a total chick magnet. Actually, that was true anytime, anywhere, but in a grocery store it rose to the level of speed-dating. Or so a single dad had once told her.

But then maybe that was what Trace needed. To meet a few eligible ladies. He'd been a widower for nearly fourteen months. And he had Mickey to think about.

He was a smart man. He probably knew exactly what trolling the store with Mickey would bring.

The two of them deserved some happiness after the past year of hardship. She turned down the juice aisle. So why did the thought of another woman in their lives sting Nikki in the heart?

Five minutes later she saw Trace and Mickey start to roll past her row, but when Trace spied her he made a quick turn. He stopped next to her and without a word transferred the items in her cart to his, before stepping aside and waving her into the driver's seat.

She moved into position in front of Mickey, and assessed Trace out of the corner of her eye.

He crossed his arms over his chest and glared at her. "That was just mean."

"What?" She tried not to laugh at his disgruntled expression.

"Don't play innocent. It doesn't become you."

She grinned. "I did try to warn you."

"Yeah, well, next time I'm likely to be eaten alive by piranhas, make me listen."

She rounded the corner into the meat section. He selected steaks, while she picked up some chicken and pork chops. Moving on to the dairy section, she dared to broach the topic of his love life.

"So you're not interested in finding someone new to spend time with?"

He went still. "No."

She waited for more, but it became clear nothing further would follow. She pushed. "It's too soon? You must have really loved your wife."

He avoided her gaze by reaching for a block of cheddar cheese. "What I felt for my wife doesn't matter now. I need to focus on raising my son."

"Of course. But you shouldn't deny yourself a fulfilling relationship. A partner would be a benefit to Mickey, too."

"And why is it *you're* not married, Ms. Rhodes?" Those amazing green eyes swept the length of her and back up. Heat flooded her cheeks. Those eyes exerted the most astonishing effect on her. As if he saw clear to her soul.

"I've had offers." But none worth giving up her freedom for.

"I'm sure you have," he acknowledged. "Yet you remain single. It's not a bad thing to know your own strengths and failings."

"True." And pretty deep. Had he gotten all that by looking into her eyes? Was her need for independence a strength or a failing?

Disconcerted, she turned down the next aisle and found herself facing an assortment of dog food.

Trace, following on her heels, asked, "Do we now have a pet I don't know about?"

She cleared her throat and continued down the lane. "Don't be silly."

"I don't know," he mused with wry humor, "you've wrought such change in my household anything is possible. I can easily see you thinking Mickey needs a companion, followed by a trip to the pound."

"I'd never do such a thing," she denied, her chin in the air. "Not without discussing it with you first."

He laughed outright. "Thanks for the concession."

"Hey, I'm not the one who'd be walking the dog in the middle of the night."

"I see how it is."

She grinned. "We'll just put the puppy discussion on hold for now."

"Agreed. Mickey takes all my attention."

"Hello! Hello, Sheriff Oliver. It's Mavis Day, from the Historical Society." A tiny woman with a helmet of blue-gray hair in a bright pink shirt rolled up beside them. A white miniature poodle rode in the child's seat in a purple handbag.

"Of course. Mrs. Day," Trace greeted the woman. "How are you?"

"Suffering from the heat, like most of the population. My Pebbles just can't take these high temperatures. Just the thing to spend a bit of time in the cool of the grocery."

"We take our relief where we find it," he assured the woman with a polite smile. "No law against that."

"No law!" Mavis twittered. "Aren't you funny?"

"I make the occasional effort." He turned to introduce Nikki but stopped, and she saw his hesitation. It shouldn't, but that pause hurt.

Because he had his reasons, she smiled and prepared to move on. "Don't worry about me, obviously Mrs. Day has something to talk to you about. I'll be at the baby food."

He frowned.

"Oh, no, dear, you don't have to run off." Mrs. Day waved a wrinkled hand adorned by a truly impressive diamond. "I just wanted to thank you, Sheriff Oliver, for suggesting the pot-luck dinner for the community meeting next Wednesday. Such a thoughtful way of getting people involved in community affairs. But I didn't mean to disturb your time with your new lady-friend and her beautiful daughter."

Oh, my, a double whammy. Nikki sneaked a peak at Trace, noted his narrowed eyes and the hard line of his mouth, but before he could correct the woman, Mrs. Day ran right on.

"I can't wait to tell the ladies at the Historical Society. I will admit I enjoy sharing happy gossip."

Trace turned sideways, so his profile faced the woman, before rolling his eyes. Nikki took that to mean Mrs. Day enjoyed sharing gossip of any kind. The accompanying impatience in his glance revealed his displeasure at being the topic of gossip at all.

"I'll tell you straight, we in the society have been worried about you. Many of us are or have been widows, and we know how hard it is to move on, to rejoin the dating pool. But it's been over a year—"

"Mrs. Day," Trace cut in, his voice a strangled growl.

"It's okay, Sheriff," she prattled on, patting his hand where it rested on the handlebar of the shopping cart. "It's important to accept that life goes on. There comes a time when you have to make a move, or miss your chance at future happiness."

A tickle in Nikki's gut forewarned her this conversation could not end well. Mrs. Day couldn't know the good Sheriff as well as she thought to make *that* pronouncement.

Mrs. Day nodded sagely. "If I hadn't grabbed him up,

the Widow Thompson would have snagged my Mike. He's a good man. He does like those smelly cigars, but he steps out to smoke them. Does his farting out there, too." She turned to Nikki. "As you know, dear, a woman appreciates small considerations like that."

Nikki met Trace's stunned and appalled glance, and knew hers was equally bug-eyed. She bit her lip to keep from laughing out loud. The outrageous statement defied any other reaction.

"Mrs. Day, you have the wrong impression. This is my son, Carmichael, and his nanny, Nikki Rhodes."

Nikki liked the sound of her name on his lips. He continued to be formal with her. Though she called him Trace, and had asked him to call her by her first name, it was always Ms. Rhodes. She suspected he used the formality to foster distance between them.

"Oh." The woman blinked, and then smiled, waving her diamond again. "Your son. Of course. He's a charmer already. These lovely curls fooled me for a moment. And don't worry about the relationship thing. It'll happen. I have a feeling about you two."

This time Nikki didn't dare look at Trace at all. He seemed speechless. To add to the ridiculousness of the moment the poodle now popped up from the purple purse and yipped. Twice.

Mickey jumped, giggled then clapped.

"Shh, Pebbles." Mrs. Day quieted the dog as she glanced worriedly over her shoulder. "Mr. Wilson will hear you." She sent Trace a brazen grin. "I won't keep you any longer. I have to keep moving. Mr. Wilson and Pebbles have a love-hate relationship. She loves the cool air in here, and he hates the fact she's a dog. Oh, there's Millie. Did you hear her mother broke her leg? She was washing windows and fell off a stepladder. Her ma likes to have a cold cocktail on these hot afternoons. I hope she had more sense than to drink before climbing a ladder."

Mrs. Day tucked Pebbles back into her purple habitat and maneuvered her cart around Nikki's.

"I'll just go offer my commiserations."

"Take Pebbles home, Mrs. Day." Trace issued the warning in his official voice. "I wouldn't want to have to run you in because Pebbles and Mr. Wilson got into an altercation."

The woman waved away his advice. "You are so funny."

He watched Mrs. Day trot on to her next victim, then turned to Nikki with a lifted brow. "She thinks I'm joking."

Nope, Mrs. Day didn't know him well at all. Trace didn't joke about the law or keeping order.

"Lighten up, Sheriff," Nikki said. "You don't always have to chase the rules."

CHAPTER SIX

TRACE tossed his keys on the counter and glanced at the clock on the kitchen wall: twelve-thirty in the morning. He headed straight through the house to Nikki's rooms to collect Mickey.

The whole town was buzzing about his business. Asking after his son—or, worse, his daughter. Wanting to know about his nanny service. Offering to set him up with their daughter, sister, niece and, in one unforgettable case, an ex-wife.

He just wanted it to end. Had never wanted it to start. But that had been unrealistic, and the hurt expression on Nikki's face when he'd failed to introduce her to Mrs. Day still haunted him.

He owed her an apology. It wasn't her fault his privacy was being torn to shreds. She deserved better from him.

He knocked once, and then again. After a few minutes Nikki opened the door. Hair mussed, dressed in shorts and tank top, displaying lots of silky soft skin. There'd been a couple of nights when he'd had to pick

Mickey up from here, but this was the latest he'd been. He'd obviously woken her.

"Hey," she said around a yawn, and stepped back. "You're late."

"Yeah. Sorry to ruin your day off."

"Couldn't be helped," she said easily. "Mickey was a big hit at my sister's baby birthing class."

He preferred not to imagine that scene. "I'll bet."

Backlit by the dim room, she looked sleepy, tousled and oh-so-soft. With a fierceness he'd never known, he longed to sweep her up, carry her to the couch and surround himself in her softness. He wanted nothing more than to purge the horrors of the night in the tenderness of her arms.

"Come in." She stepped back, and he moved past her to get Mickey from the playpen beside the couch. After hours of working at an accident, the sweet scent of her skin nearly drove him to his knees.

"The doctor called today. I gave him your cell number."

"Yeah, I talked to him."

"What did he have to say?" She crossed her arms over her chest.

Trace shook his head. It was too dangerous for him to be here. "We'll talk about it tomorrow."

He lifted the slight weight of his son into his arms. Mickey opened his eyes, focused on Trace, smiled and snuggled into his shoulder and went back to sleep.

The trust of the gesture weighed heavy on a night

when he'd witnessed senseless death. How was he supposed to keep his child safe in a world out of control?

"Are you okay?" Nikki ran a light hand from the back of his elbow down his forearm to his wrist. Just as he'd thought, her gentle caress eased some of his despair.

To shatter the illusion he moved away, starting toward the door. "No touching." He tried for lightness and failed miserably.

The concern in Nikki's eyes heightened. She smiled. "This is my place. The rules don't apply here."

"The rules always apply." No rules meant anything went, and he'd have no reason not to taste the lush line of her lips. Soon he'd be looking for a new nanny.

She shook her head. "Not always. Did you eat? Why don't I put on some clothes and come heat up some food for you, and you can tell me what the doctor said?"

"I'm fine." Food sounded good, but more trouble than he wanted to go to this late. "I'm just going to shower and go to bed. Good night." He pulled the door closed and waited until he heard the bolt.

Ten minutes later he had Mickey tucked into bed, and was stepping from the shower when he heard a knock on the back door. It could only be Nikki. He considered ignoring it. Hadn't he faced enough temptation tonight? But he owed her for his previous rudeness.

Sighing, he pulled on a T-shirt and a pair of navy sweatpants and went to answer the summons. He opened the door to a steaming plate of food. Savory aromas floated to him on the night air, making his stomach growl.

Nikki cocked her head and grinned. "It goes against my civic duty to let the Sheriff go to bed hungry."

She'd donned low-riding gray sweatpants, and her pink tank top stopped just above her waist, leaving a band of creamy skin visible. The sight of her made him hungry for more than food.

"Is that macaroni and cheese?"

"It's homemade mac and cheese. Plus smoked sausage and sliced tomatoes."

"Okay, you can come in." He took the plate and left her to follow him. "How did you manage homemade macaroni and cheese with only a coffeemaker and a microwave?"

"It's leftovers from dinner with my sister. It's my mom's recipe. I make it better."

"This is pretty good." He stabbed a piece of sausage. "You'll have to send my compliments to your sister. It must have been rough on the two of you to lose them both together."

"Yeah." She sat down across from him and laid her hands flat on the table. "But they would have wanted it that way. My mother was a good military wife, she went wherever Dad was stationed. They loved each other very much—were the center of each other's lives. My sister and I completed the circle, but they always came first for each other."

"It must be nice to have had such a bedrock foundation."

"There were trade-offs. Mom coped with all the travel by micromanaging what she did have control of—the family."

She reached out, caught herself, and her fingertips stopped just shy of his. How he resented that quarter-inch of space.

"It was bad tonight?" She zeroed in on what was bothering him.

"Two dead at the scene. A man fell asleep at the wheel. Killed himself and his adult daughter. The wife survived, but she'll just wish she were dead."

"Oh, Trace. I'm so sorry. It must be difficult to work accident scenes after losing your wife to a drunk driver."

"I had to leave Homicide. I couldn't make death my business anymore, or deal with it every day. This is better. There's probably the same amount of fatalities, but they're spaced further apart. And it's not the focus of what I do."

"No community meetings when you worked Homicide?"

The corner of his mouth lifted. She had a talent for making him smile. "Hardly. I was just asking myself how I'm supposed to keep Mickey safe in today's world. So much violence. Accidents, disease… Every couple of months there's an accident on the highway. With the casino on the reservation so close we see drunks, sleepy gamblers, tourists coming from the east. Illegal aliens freeze or die from the heat, trying to cross over the mountains. I'm all he has. What happens to him if something happens to me?"

"Trace, you know better. You can't focus on the negative. Make the most of what you have. Build your own bedrock with Mickey. Amanda and I knew we were loved, and that's huge—especially when there are a lot of changes or unknowns in your life."

Great. "And I'm the current unknown in my son's life."

"No, you're the new constant in his life."

"Little Miss Sunshine."

"Please." She rolled her eyes. "I'm more blunt than most people find comfortable. I'm working on my tact," she said with wry humor. "Tomorrow you'll feel better."

"Maybe." But he wouldn't be any less responsible for Mickey, wouldn't be any less alone. He pushed his empty plate away. "Excellent. Your civil servant thanks you."

She grinned, picked up the plate and carried it to the sink. "You know you're not alone." She took a glass from the cupboard, poured some milk and placed it in front of him. "Your in-laws are on the east coast, not dead."

"I think they've done enough damage."

"What about *your* parents? Would they be able to help you out?"

"Ha!" A harsh bark of laughter erupted from his throat. "My parents make Donna's look like parents of the year. At least they erred on the side of caring too much." Maybe the late hour had his defenses down, or maybe he was mellow after the warm meal, but Trace found himself talking to Nikki.

"My mom was the opposite of yours. She didn't want to follow Dad around, but he insisted. He wanted me with him. Don't know why. He wasn't a demonstrative man. Anyway, she'd had enough by the time I was ten, and she left us."

"Trace." Her soft heart overrode the rules and she covered his fingers with hers. "That's so sad—for you and your father. Was he in the military when she met him?"

Her touch warmed him more than her sympathy. Maybe that was why he'd opened up tonight. Because he'd known the tenderness she showed Mickey every day would be his reward.

"Yes. Within a year after leaving us she'd remarried and started a new family."

Her fingers tightened on his. "I hope you know she wasn't a victim. She knew your dad was military when she married him. *She* changed the rules on *him*."

"I learned all I know about emotions from my dad. She said he had no feelings and I was just like him. We weren't enough for her."

"She said you lacked emotion and then she abandoned you?" Nikki's shoulders went up and a fierce glint lit up her eyes, making them gleam like liquid gold. "Stupid woman."

He laughed. Something he wouldn't have thought possible tonight.

God, she made him feel good. Her humor, her compassion, her sheer willingness to go to battle for him turned his melancholy mood into something altogether different.

And altogether more dangerous.

"I like you, Ms. Rhodes." Again his attempt at lightness failed. The words came out husky, a growl of want.

The momentum of her emotions had pushed her forward over the table, so her weight rested on her elbows and their faces were mere inches apart. Eyeing the delicate curve of her mouth, the silky creaminess of her skin, he sought desperately for control.

Smiling sheepishly, she lifted her gaze from his mouth. As their eyes met, hers darkened, and she licked her lips.

"I like you, too, Sheriff Oliver," she whispered.

He watched the words form, her lips shiny with the essence of her, and longed to move the few inches necessary to taste her.

Instead he pushed away from the table, creating vital distance between them.

"You should go."

Nikki let herself in the back door. "Hey, it's just me," she called out, though she doubted Trace heard over the wails coming from down the hall. Still, she continued to speak as she went to investigate. "I need to pick up some laundry."

She stopped in the bathroom doorway. Ah, bathtime. Mickey did not like to be wet. The otherwise sweet and cheerful baby turned into a wild child whenever dipped in water. Throw in a hair-washing, like now, and he was one unhappy, slippery mess.

Trace was kneeling next to the tub on a bathmat, soaked from shoulders to knees. A drop of water fell from his hair to land on his cheek, disappearing into his five-o'clock shadow.

The Sheriff looked good wet. Nikki took new appreciation in why men liked wet T-shirt contests. Transparent cotton clung to his skin, defining hard muscles flexing in motion.

Enjoying the show a little too much, she knocked on the door. "Hey, what's all the ruckus about in here?"

"Save yourself. It's not safe in here." Trace only half looked over his shoulder, but it was enough for her to catch the frown of frustration and concentration furrowing his brow. "And it's a good thing he doesn't talk yet, because the language is pretty ripe."

"Neeki! Neeki!" At the sight of her Mickey renewed his efforts to reach safety, struggling in Trace's grasp and lifting his arms for her to rescue him.

"Stay still, you little eel," Trace said. "We just have to finish your hair and you can get out."

"Hang on." Nikki turned into Mickey's room across the hall.

Carrying a plastic blue puppy back to the bathroom, she could swear she heard him mutter, "Coward."

"I heard that, but lucky for you I'm going to save your hide anyway." She knelt next to Trace, glad she'd worn shorts.

"Oh, I'm lucky," he grumbled, keeping a hold of his slippery son so he didn't fall and crack his head. "Mickey, sit down."

Mickey's frown matched Trace's as he nailed him with a glare and yammered off a string of angry baby talk.

Nikki grinned. "I think it's a good thing we don't know what that means."

"Oh, we've had quite the conversation. I just need him to stay still long enough for me to rinse the shampoo out."

She wiggled her eyebrows at Trace. "Watch how it's done. Hold him steady," she told him, and then, focusing on Mickey, she smiled. "Hey, baby, Daddy just doesn't know the trick, huh?" She brought the blue dog up and wagged it in front of the tearful Mickey. "He doesn't know Puppy gets his hair washed first."

Mickey quieted as Nikki swiped some bubbles up and worked them over the plastic blue head of the toy dog. Distracted, the boy reached for the toy and held it while Nikki made a show of washing the dog's hair. "That's the way," she encouraged Mickey. "We're washing Puppy's hair. And next it's your turn. Smile," she said to Trace, flashing her gaze over him. "That ferocious look probably works wonders with criminals. Not so much frightened little boys."

The frown instantly cleared. A light of humor even touched his green eyes. "Hey, you've got it backward. In case you didn't notice, the kid had the upper hand."

She laughed. "Hand me the small pitcher from the left-hand cupboard," she said quietly to Trace. He placed it in her hand, and she scooped up half a pitcher of water and poured it over Puppy.

Mickey squealed, and dunked Puppy in the water, splashing both Nikki and Trace.

"First dog food, now a puppy in the bath." Trace sent her a sidelong glance. "You're determined for me to get the boy a dog, aren't you?"

"Not guilty," she denied. "I always wanted a dog when I was a kid, but my mom said we weren't settled enough to make a good home for a dog, that it wouldn't be fair. She was right."

"So you're saying we aren't ready for a dog?"

"No." She refused to let him trip her up for his amusement, his own form of distraction. "You said you needed to focus on taking care of Mickey, and I agree with you."

"So no dog?" He grinned, proving she'd caught him in his game.

"Not yet. Good boy," she praised Mickey. "Time to do *your* hair. Close your eyes." She squeezed hers closed for a moment, to show him what she meant. He copied her, and she quickly dumped clear water over his head. He started to whimper. "Hang in there, big boy, only one more time." She made quick work of it, and Trace was right there with a fresh washcloth to dry Mickey's face.

"Nice job." Trace easily lifted Mickey from the water and Nikki wrapped him in a towel. "Thanks for the help."

"No problem." She shrugged easily. "We adults have to stick together."

"I thought you had a birthing class with your sister tonight. What are you doing here?"

"I do, but it's later—not until eight. I came to pick up some things I left hanging in the laundry room."

"In appreciation for the assistance, you're welcome to join us for dinner. It's only hot dogs and beans, but I'm firing up the grill."

"Thanks, but I can't. Amanda is stir-crazy, and since she has permission from her doctor for the classes, she's sneaking dinner in first and calling it all one trip. But it's a tempting offer."

More tempting than it should be. Plain food in the company of the baby she spent all day watching. Like Amanda, Nikki should be thrilled at an outing away from the house. Instead, she felt curiously deflated as she turned away from daddy and son.

"Okay," he said easily. "Thanks for the help."

"Good night." She grabbed her things from the dryer and let herself out the backdoor. Was it her imagination, or had he sounded a little disappointed?

CHAPTER SEVEN

"THE Mayor's office called." Lydia popped her head inside the door to his office. "He's asked the city council to meet at Sampson Hall twenty minutes before the community meeting."

Trace nodded, glanced at the clock on the wall, saw he had over an hour and went back to his report. He'd found it hard to concentrate today, his thoughts constantly traveling back to the scene a couple of nights ago. He'd come close to getting extremely unprofessional with his nanny.

He so couldn't go there.

Mickey needed her. Beyond that she was a complication Trace couldn't afford.

The door to the station opened and in walked the subject of his thoughts. She pushed Mickey in his stroller, with a long, shallow basket perched on the hood over the boy's head.

Everything in Trace came to attention, his body reacting to the long stretch of her legs in skinny black jeans, the teasing pop of a pink tank at the hem and the cleavage under her fitted white shirt even as his mind raced with questions and concern at her appearance.

What was she doing here?

He rose and rounded his desk, watching her chat and laugh with Lydia. Her easy manner eliminated his worry, but not his disquiet.

He shrugged at the tension in his shoulders. He didn't want her here. This place belonged to him—well, and the citizens of Paradise Pines. The point was he needed someplace safe as a retreat from her intoxicating presence. But, no, interfering woman that she was, she had to invade his workspace.

Oh, yeah, he was in serious trouble.

As soon as he stepped out of his office he got hit with the savory scent of fried chicken, which reminded him of the potluck dinner at tonight's community meeting. He had an order of fried chicken himself, to pick up from the diner. The scent grew stronger as he approached the front counter, but he was quickly distracted by the tail-end of Nikki's introductions.

"It's so nice to put a face with a name. It's always good to know when Trace is going to be late. Have you met Trace's son, Mickey?"

Lydia had her elbows on the high counter to help her see down to Mickey's level. The little boy looked up at her with solemn eyes. He switched his gaze to Trace, frowned, and then twisted in his seat, obviously seeking out Nikki's reassuring presence.

She casually moved to the side of the stroller, giving him a clear view of her, and Mickey settled back into his seat. At the same time she moved the cloth-covered basket to the counter.

"Hey," she greeted Trace, her dimple flashing as she smiled.

"Trace, your nanny just introduced me to your son. I never heard you had a child. All this time I've chattered away about my grandkids and you never mentioned you had a little boy." Lydia's teasing reprimand held more than a hint of hurt. "He's so precious."

Damn, moments like this were exactly why he liked to keep his private life separate from his public service. Personal exchanges required too many complex twists of emotional discourse. So what if he suffered occasional bouts of loneliness? He preferred things simple.

"Thanks. He's only been with me a short time. His grandmother has been caring for him while I got settled." Trace hated to explain himself, to expose his personal life, but it was that or subject himself and Mickey to the gossip mill for civic entertainment. That he couldn't tolerate.

"Well and fine. I bet you've missed him every day." Lydia gave a sympathetic nod.

"It's been hard," Trace acknowledged, "but we're together now." He focused his attention on his wayward nanny. "Ms. Rhodes, I wasn't expecting you."

"They called from the diner to say your order was ready." She lifted the red gingham napkin, revealing two dozen pieces of fried chicken. "Mickey and I were looking for something to do, so we decided to save you a trip and pick it up."

It looked as good as it smelled. Her homey touch adding to the presentation. Who knew he even owned a gingham napkin?

"You didn't need to do that," he informed her.

"I know." She glanced at Lydia and shrugged. "He's the perfect boss. He never wants me to go out of my way for him."

"You're a nanny, not a housekeeper." Again with the explanations. How much easier if she'd stayed at home.

Not once had Donna come to visit him at work, and he never remembered his mom dropping in on his dad. Of course if she'd ever shown more interest in what the old man did, got him talking about it, maybe he would have found it easier to express himself at other times. And if his dad had been better at communication maybe his son would be, too.

"Don't worry, there's no extra charge." Nikki waved off his clarification. Instead she grinned and gave an exaggerated look around. "All it's going to cost you is a tour of the place. I've never been in a sheriff's station before. Do you have cells here?"

"We have a couple of holding cells." Now, there was a thought. Maybe one of those could hold her long enough to give him a few minutes' peace. He took control of the stroller and started toward the back hall. "Grab the chicken. We'll begin with my office."

"Don't forget your meeting with the Mayor and the

city council before the community meeting starts," Lydia called after them. He waved an acknowledgment.

For someone who always seemed to move at a slow glide, Nikki easily kept pace. "I really do want a tour, but if you don't have time I understand. I know the meeting starts in an hour. We can do this another time if you like."

What he'd like was her pressed up against his office wall, with the door shut and the blinds closed…

He almost tripped over his own feet as the scene played out in his head.

"Are you okay?" she asked when he came to a dead stop.

"Yeah, fine." Holy heck, where had that come from? "On second thought—" he made a U-turn away from his office "—let's put the chicken in the kitchen."

The illicit vision was wrong on so many levels, yet so vivid he practically tasted her on his lips.

He was the Sheriff, this was his office, she was his employee. And those were only the obvious objections. He had a son to worry about—a son who needed her more than Trace needed his libido ignited.

If none of that existed he *still* wouldn't act on the crazy desire. She was all about love and commitment, and he'd already proved he knew next to nothing about those commodities.

"Have you always wanted to be a cop?" Nikki asked Trace as they neared the end of the impromptu tour. Pride in what he did showed in every word he said as he took her through the small station. She'd been booked, fingerprinted and was about to be processed.

"I was military first. Marine, like my dad. But I decided I liked having more control over my life, so I only did four years. Law enforcement seemed a natural choice from there."

"Structure and discipline on your own terms?"

He watched her out of the corner of his eyes, obviously bothered at being pegged so accurately in a casual observation. Actually, he'd surprised her. She hadn't expected him to be so at ease, so funny. This was where he felt at home.

"As a teacher of twenty to thirty five-year-olds, I'd think *you'd* be a fan of a controlled environment," he challenged her.

She laughed. "What I know, as the teacher of thirty kindergarteners, is that control is an illusion."

"Come on, you give me a schedule for Mickey every day. You have routine down to a science."

"Oh, I'm all about structure and routine," she readily agreed—those were a teacher's biggest tools. But his version and hers were polar opposites. "But in the classroom my day moves from one chaotic moment to the next. When you work with kids you have to be flexible. You never know what's going to happen, so you have to be prepared for anything. I imagine your days are much the same."

He shook his head in disbelief. "You're comparing a kindergarten class with criminals?"

"Of course not," she assured him. "But keeping the peace, monitoring behavior, dealing with cultural differences. It's all part of our day."

"I never really thought of it that way."

"Most people don't, but a classroom is a microcosm of the community. Oh!" She spotted a stack of thick books full of photos. "Are these mugshots? Can I look?"

"Yeah, they're older versions, hard copies. Most mugshots are online now. Technology is great. It helps to narrow down by characteristics—height, weight, coloring, etcetera. But sorry." Trace walked to the counter holding the books and flipped the covers closed. "The pictures are for case purposes only." He shrugged. "Every one gets their privacy protected these days. Even known felons."

"Actually, I can understand that." Nikki fingered the edge of one of the books. "I check the public Web site for sex offenders on a fairly regular basis. And I can tell some people are only there because of indiscretions gone public."

"Let me guess." He stood hands on hips, every inch the hardcore cop. "You think it's unfair for a dumb college prank like mooning someone in a passing car to classify someone as a sex offender?"

"No," she disagreed—surprising him, no doubt. She drew in a calming breath and tried very hard not to think beyond the conversation. "It's a hard line, but if someone is stupid enough to expose themselves in public then it could be a precursor of future deviant acts. When it comes to the safety of kids, I don't think the line can be too hard."

Needing the distraction, and a reminder of all things innocent and good in life, she checked on Mickey. He slept peacefully in his stroller, his thick lashes a dark shadow on baby-soft skin. His sweetness helped settle the ghosts of harsh memories.

When she stood up straight, Trace was too close.

"I'm sorry," he said gently.

"What?"

"You've dealt with a victim of sexual abuse?"

She swallowed hard. Obviously she hadn't been as good at hiding her feelings as she'd hoped. "It was the hardest thing I've ever had to stomach in my life. The helplessness was overwhelming."

"Nikki." He cupped her cheek, his thumb a soft caress as he swept away a tear. "You have to know you helped."

"Too little, too late." For just a moment she rested her head on his shoulder, absorbed his strength and his warmth. "She was so small, so quiet, how could anyone want to hurt her?"

His fingers laced through her hair as he hugged her to him, his touch tender where his body was all hard muscle. And his low voice whispered to her. "There's no sense to be found in these cases. You help where you can and live with what you can't change."

She shook as memories bombarded her. "I've never known such hate. I can't think about it or I lose myself in the rage."

"No," he agreed, "you can't dwell on the bad." He lifted her chin so she looked into his intense green gaze, so close she could see the scars on his soul, and she knew he knew. "You have to focus on the good you did. You can't let the hate win or she won't be the only victim."

"That's what the counselor said. And most of the time I can deal with it. Monitoring the public Web site gives me a sense of being proactive. Being responsible for young kids is huge, and I want to be able to protect them when they're in my care. If I can recognize a predator before he harms a child, it's worth the effort."

"I think you're brilliant. Now, what can we do to put a smile back on your face?" He eased away, but his hand warmed the small of her back, holding her steady. "Do you want to see how my handcuffs work?"

"No," she mumbled, as she took the tissue he handed her. As she mopped her face and his heat retreated, she realized what an emotional mess she'd become. How mortifying. Trace must want to be anywhere but here right now. But as she peeked at him around the tissue he looked anything but terrorized.

"Nikki," he said. Her name. Nothing more. But the softness of it, the intimacy of it, broke down the distance his persistent formality upheld between them.

Even as her mind shouted *bad idea*, Trace stepped close again, lowered his head, and claimed her mouth. On a catch of breath, she opened to him, and he deepened the kiss. A hard arm around her waist swept her closer to him, so they touched from shoulder to thighs, his strength and confidence an intoxicating combination as she melted in his arms.

Ignoring the warnings clamoring through her head, she surrendered to the passion, meeting his tongue with hers in a sliding dance of desire.

It felt so good to be held, to lean—just for a moment—on someone strong and giving.

She drew back at the thought, recognizing despite her passion-drenched senses the fallacy of her conception. She had no right to lean on Trace. This was a moment out of time for her. For him.

She had no doubts he'd be as appalled as she once they regained their equilibrium. Stepping back, she cleared her throat, seeking a less-dangerous distraction.

He'd been wonderful, actually. It had really helped to talk to someone who understood. But time to let him off the hook.

She lowered the tissue and batted her eyes at him. "I don't think I'm ready for handcuffs, but you can let me shoot your gun."

His gaze blazed a molten emerald heat. It took him a moment to move from hot and bothered to cool, calm lawman. Blinking, he cleared his eyes and propped his hands on his gun belt. He narrowed his eyes at her. "You want to shoot my gun?"

"Yes, please."

He shifted his gaze from her to the sleeping baby then back. "Now you're just pushing my buttons. This isn't the time or place for target practice."

"Okay, yeah, a little." She cleared the thickness from her throat and tossed the tissue into a nearby trashcan. "But maybe we could go to the range sometime."

"Guns aren't toys, you know." He looked so torn— all macho cop, but still wanting to distract her from her emotional meltdown. How sweet was that?

"Actually, I do know. My dad was a navy chief. He taught me to shoot. We used to go to the range together."

"Really?" Clearly surprised, he swept his emerald gaze over her with a new level of interest that had her breath catching in the back of her throat.

"Well, then, it's a date."

"He asked you on a date?" Amanda's fierce whisper shouted her amazement. "I knew having a hot boss was going to be trouble. What'd you say?"

"No need to get so agitated." Nikki shushed her sister. "It wasn't really a question. And no definite plans were made. Thank goodness. I told you the agency forbids romantic interaction between nannies and clients. I don't want to lose this job when you have less than a month before you're due."

With a disgusted toss of her head, Amanda settled back in her metal folding chair. "No fair, teasing the pregnant lady."

They were seated on the aisle at the back of Sampson Hall, waiting for the community meeting to start. Mickey still slept in his stroller. After her visit with Trace, and their shared moment together, Nikki had walked across the park, needing the quiet stroll to gather her composure.

The kiss and Trace's mention of a date had thrown her heart into turmoil. These past weeks she'd tried so hard to keep her professionalism wrapped around her, to keep his strength and vulnerability from getting to her.

"Hey, you're supposed to be talking sense to me, not seeking vicarious thrills." Okay, Nikki would *not* be sharing news of the kiss with her sister. She needed Amanda to help bolster her resistance, not encourage her to pursue the enemy. Mickey had already stolen her heart; she couldn't afford to give any of it away to Trace. That way led straight to heartache.

"My husband is gone again, after being away for five months, and I'm the size of an elephant." Amanda patted her swollen belly with love and resignation. "I'll take my thrills where I can find them."

Nikki shot Amanda an aggravated frown. "Not at my expense. You're not even supposed to be here."

"I didn't want to miss the meeting, and I'm just sitting. Come on, just give me a few details. I need something to keep my mind off the ticking clock. I can't believe how much I want this over at the same time as I'm dreading labor and the birth."

Nikki squeezed her sister's hand. "You're going to do fine."

"I'd do better if Dan were here."

Hearing the tears in Amanda's voice, Nikki gave in. Amanda needed distracting, and Nikki needed to talk.

It was also a reminder of how vulnerable Amanda was, how much she needed Nikki to stay close. Which meant no more stolen kisses with the boss.

"Okay, the truth is I asked him out."

"What?" Amanda squealed, causing Mickey to flinch in his sleep. "What about the agency rules? I thought you were determined to keep your distance."

Nikki rubbed Mickey's belly until he settled. "I was. I am. It's just keeping my objectivity is harder than I anticipated."

"Duh. The man is gorgeous."

"He's also intelligent, brave, dedicated and caring, though he tries hard to hide the last one."

A furrow marred Amanda's brows as her concerned gaze met Nikki's. "You're falling for him. Oh, babe, you have to stop."

"Don't be ridiculous."

"I know you and your soft heart. These two are getting to you. Why else would you ask Trace out?"

Nikki waved a dismissive hand. "It wasn't like that. We were in the middle of a heavy moment. I just wanted to distract him."

"By asking him on a date? Are you out of your mind?" Amanda shifted in the uncomfortable chair. "What was the heavy moment about?"

Nikki explained about the tour and the difficult discussion, carefully playing down the part where she'd fallen apart in his arms. "He was trying so hard to make me feel better. I just needed to change the subject."

"So you asked him out?"

"I told him I wanted to shoot his gun."

Amanda just stared at Nikki, slowly shaking her head. "Tell me you're joking."

It was Nikki's turn to shake her head.

"He could interpret that in so many ways!"

"Amanda." Nikki stopped her. "It wasn't like that." Oh, God, it had been exactly like that. "Nothing is going to come of it, so there's no reason to rehash the whole thing."

"I thought you needed me to talk you down from the edge."

"Let's say you scared me straight and call it done. I'm going to get us some food. Stay put and keep an eye on Mickey." Grateful for a chance to escape, Nikki slipped from her seat.

"Mickey wants chocolate cake," Amanda said hopefully.

"Yeah, right. Mickey's playing hooky, and his doctor said he needed to control his weight over the last month." Leaving her sister muttering about mean doctors, Nikki headed to the back of the room toward the buffet table.

A small cluster of women had gathered near the end of the table.

"I'd do it, but I promised several people I'd address the land issue," a slender blond woman said.

"Yeah, I'm supposed to take notes for my neighbor because she had to work late," plump redhead added. "I have her toddler and mine. I was hoping to put both kids in childcare."

"I wish Cindy had let us know sooner she wouldn't be here." The owner of the diner planted her hands on her hips and looked over the crowd.

"We all want to hear about the Anderson endowment. I just know the men are going to want to use the land for another sports park, when this is the perfect opportunity to bring a little culture to Paradise Pines."

"What about your niece, Sarah? Can she come down and babysit?" the blonde asked.

The redhead shook her head. "She's working at the theater in El Cajon this summer."

Nikki stepped forward. "Perhaps I can help. I don't mind watching the kids during the meeting."

As one, the three women turned hopeful gazes toward her.

Trace stood in the corner, his gaze alert on the crowd, talking to a couple of local businessmen. All conversation stopped when Nikki appeared next to his group.

"Gentlemen." She acknowledged the men with one sweeping smile as she handed a plate of food and a cup of punch to Trace. "Carry on," she advised, as she turned on her heels and returned to the buffet.

As preoccupied as she'd been in her hit-and-run delivery of the plate in his hand, there was no way she'd gone unnoticed by the men he'd been talking to.

Sure enough, Trace pulled his glance away from her to find the two men silent, their gazes locked onto Nikki's black-and-white curves.

"Hmm. Why do *you* rate the special treatment?" asked Cord Sullivan, Mayor and owner of the local nursery.

Trace sent his friend a quelling glare.

"So that's the nanny? Nice," said Parker, the local barber, who was loud and coarse by nature. His eyes on Nikki's retreating rear end, the rotund barber was oblivious to Trace's displeasure.

"Get your mind out of the gutter, Parker." Trace sent him a killer stare. "She's my employee."

"Yeah, that's a sweet setup you have going."

Trace invaded the man's space. "What did you say?"

Parker nearly swallowed his tongue to keep another suggestive comment behind his teeth. He blinked and backed up a step. Maybe the man had more sense than Trace had given him credit for. "Hey, I'm just saying she's fine." Parker looked after Nikki again. "If you're not interested, maybe I'll give her a call."

Over Trace's dead body. As if Nikki would give the older man a second glance. She was all sassy honesty, and Parker was brash and oily.

"Don't bother," Trace said, his tone hard, his posture stiff.

"Right." Parker nodded and winked. "Message received."

Trace shook his head, but didn't correct the man. Better that he think Trace and Nikki were involved. That way, the fool would leave her alone.

Not that Trace was jealous.

He had no right to that emotion.

It's a date… The words echoed through his head and he wondered again what he'd been thinking.

And that amazing kiss.

Now, *there* was evidence he'd hadn't been thinking with his mind. He couldn't remember the last time his body had held sway over his head. Maybe being sex-starved and lonely had finally taken its toll, making him delusional.

Nikki had completely absorbed his thoughts during the brief meeting with the city council. Thankfully he'd known what the Mayor was announcing, or he'd have been clueless going into the meeting.

He could not date his nanny. More, he'd be a fool to date Nikki Rhodes. No way he could live up to her emotional standards.

Look what had happened the last time he'd let loneliness direct his actions. He'd ended up with a strained marriage, a son he didn't know and a hot piece of fluff living in his garage.

Okay, that was harsh. But he needed to stay real and he had no business admiring the strength and fortitude hidden under frivolous ruffles and lace. Besides, they were totally incompatible. She liked to chat and he wanted silence. She had big-time control issues and he liked to be in charge. She loved kids and he couldn't even relate to his own son.

Bottom line: he had nothing in common with the loving and dedicated Ms. Rhodes.

Hell, if Donna had lived Trace had no doubt they would have ended up another divorce statistic. Just like his mom and his old man.

Best he forget he'd ever mentioned a date.

Besides, she probably wouldn't even be around to accept an invitation. If a teaching job came along she'd be off and on her way, leaving him and Mickey to pick up the pieces of their lives without her.

No—wait. That had been his mother.

Oh, yeah, serious trouble. In spades. It was not a good thing when he was comparing his nanny to his long-lost mother.

CHAPTER EIGHT

"HEY, little boy, we're home." Nikki parked the stroller on the front deck, unstrapped Mickey and lifted him up. "Are you ready for a snack? I'm ready for a cold drink."

She unlocked the door and stepped inside. As usual she went to set the diaper bag on the sofa, and just stopped herself from dropping it on Trace. He lay stretched out on his back, fast asleep.

"Oops," she whispered. "Daddy's taking a nap."

Trace home in the middle of the day was far from usual.

Still in his uniform, including gun belt, he looked as if he'd come in, sat down and crashed.

"Daddy night-night?"

"Shh, yes—Daddy is sleeping." Not wanting to disturb Trace, she took Mickey to the kitchen and put him in his highchair with some grapes. A glance at the clock on the microwave showed she and Mickey had been away just over an hour. How long had Trace been here? And how long could he stay?

Checking to make sure Mickey was okay, she picked up the phone and called the Sheriff's station. After Lydia answered, Nikki explained the situation.

"I just wanted to make sure he doesn't have any appointments or anything I might need to wake him for," she finished.

"Let me check his schedule." Lydia went away and Garth Brooks sang about the rodeo. "He has a meeting, but I'll call and reschedule for tomorrow. Let him sleep. He's had a couple of late nights."

"Yeah, it was after eleven when he brought Mickey to me last night. I kept the baby for the rest of the night, so I don't know what time he got home."

"It was a bad scene last night. Domestic disturbance. Trace went with the wife and kids to the hospital, then saw them settled in a shelter. Husband will do jail time if she follows through with pressing charges."

"Tough night." How many times had Nikki already said that to Trace? She admired him for his courage and fortitude. His wasn't an easy job, but a necessary one, and he handled it with calm efficiency.

"Tough job." Lydia echoed Nikki's thoughts. "Tell him to forget about coming in unless I call him. I'll get the guys to split his shift. He deserves the rest."

"I'll tell him," Nikki answered dryly. "But I make no promises."

Lydia laughed. "I wouldn't expect you to. The man does have a stubborn streak."

"Do tell. Duty is his life."

"But life doesn't have to be all duty." With that cryptic message Lydia hung up.

Did she mean duty didn't always have to be a heavy load? That the lighter side of responsibility was companionship and caring?

Nikki bet Trace didn't see it that way. Now that father and son were well acquainted—they didn't run the other way when they saw each other coming—it was time they started enjoying each other's company.

"Daddy! Daddy!" Finished with his snack, Mickey banged his empty bowl on the highchair tray and called out for his father.

"Shh." Nikki shushed the boy again, and quickly snagged the bowl away from him. "Daddy is sleeping. And it's time for you to take a nap, too." She wiped his hands and face. "That'll give me time to figure out an activity for the both of you for tonight."

"Night-night?" he said, a scowl forming on his tiny features.

"It's daytime, so just a nap."

"No," he protested, even while a little fist rubbed his eyes.

"Yes, Mickey is a sleepy boy."

"Boo?" He asked after his favorite stuffed animal.

"Yep, it's Boo's naptime, too." Nikki settled Mickey and his stuffed giraffe, Boo, down, and then put in a load of laundry. While she puttered and cleaned, she plotted.

A barbecue might be just the thing. The boys could cook the meat while she put together a salad or dessert. Humming, she took out a couple of steaks to thaw.

Something soft and damp landed on Trace's cheek, then slid toward the corner of his mouth. He opened one eye and found Mickey in his walker, right next to the couch.

"Hey, buddy." Trace yawned. The kid was cute, but the curls had to go. He made a mental note for Nikki to schedule a trip to the barbershop.

Mickey flashed his four-toothed grin and patted Trace's cheek again. "Daddy night-night?"

Trace stretched and glanced at the window. He hadn't slept that late, had he? No, the sun still shone, but the shadows indicated he'd slept longer than he'd intended.

"Nope just a nap." He sat up and scrubbed his hands over his face. "Now Daddy has to go back to work."

"No, no." Mickey jumped up and down in the walker, stood still, and then jumped some more. "No, no."

"Good boy, work those muscles." Some of the anxiety Trace had held on to since the visit to the doctor's office eased. In the past couple of weeks the boy had grown visibly stronger.

Trace glanced at his watch and groaned. "Great. I missed my appointment with the principal."

"No, Lydia rescheduled you for tomorrow," Nikki said from behind him.

Frowning, he turned so he saw her. She stood at the kitchen table. She pulled one of his T-shirts from a laundry basket, folded it, and set the shirt in a pile on a clean towel she had laid out on the table.

"How do you know that?"

"You were dead to the world when we got back. I didn't want to wake you unless you had something scheduled so I called Lydia. She said it had been quiet today and to let you sleep, and that you shouldn't bother coming in unless she called you. She was going to get some of the guys to cover for you."

"Huh, the woman thinks she runs the station. Late nights come with the territory. I can handle it."

"The point is you don't have to. Lydia juggled the schedule." She hit him with a knowing look. "You're just afraid the guys will think you're weak because you came home for a nap."

"I didn't come for a nap. I brought home a file last night to go through before my meeting today and I forgot it this morning."

The corner of her mouth twitched. "Which means you came in, sat down and conked out. I think that says something."

Picking up a couple of plastic blocks from the floor, he placed them on the tray of Mickey's walker. The boy immediately grabbed one in each hand and clapped them together.

When she was right, she was right. Deciding to drop an argument he couldn't win, Trace addressed a new issue. "I told you not to bother doing my laundry."

"I'm not doing your laundry. I'm doing Mickey's

laundry," she said, as she shook out another extra-large T-shirt, crisply folded it and set it on top of two others.

"Either those are my shirts, or you're dating a man named Mickey."

She grinned. "They are your shirts. But I only threw them in because I needed to fill up the load. You wouldn't want me to waste important resources, would you?"

"You always have an answer, don't you?"

Standing, he rubbed a hand over Mickey's downy soft hair. He was now trying to eat the blocks. Trace maneuvered the walker into the middle of the room, giving Mickey space to move around. He immediately pushed himself back three inches. Backward was his main directional pull. He still needed to master forward.

"I am a teacher. I'm supposed to have the answers."

Trace hid a chuckle in a cough. Not wise to encourage the woman. She already challenged his authority at every curve. But she did make him laugh.

"And the towels?" He fingered the stack next to his shirts.

She shrugged. "I love the feel and smell of a warm towel fresh from the dryer. It's a small delight. I didn't think you'd mind."

"Liar."

"Moi?" she asked, all innocence. "Not about this."

"You're spoiling me, Ms. Rhodes." Loose gold tendrils curled over her ears, and he fought the desire to test the sunshine softness. "And I like it too much."

Her eyes flashed. "I think we're past the Ms. Rhodes stage, don't you?"

"I think it's prudent."

"And I think it's too late for that."

"You mean, because of the kiss?" Of course because of the kiss. The taste of her, the feel of her in his arms, still haunted him.

"Yeah." She met his gaze, then looked away, checking on Mickey in the living room. And Little Miss Ostrich surprised him when she asked, "You want to talk about it?"

"Absolutely not. I'm doing my best to forget it ever happened."

That earned him a coy glance from under dark lashes. "How's that working for you?"

"It's not. But it's prudent."

"Hmm." She seemed to consider his diversionary tactics. "I thought you believed in confronting issues head-on."

"Well, Teach, I'm learning new things from you all the time." He grinned when she rolled her eyes.

She continued to tuck and fold, and he sighed. Maybe she'd brought it up for reasons of her own. "Do *you* want to talk about the kiss?"

Her brow furrowed while she thought over his question. The myriad of emotions in her amazing golden eyes matched much of what he felt: confusion, attraction, regret and more.

"Yes," she finally allowed. But she chewed her lip, not saying anything further, obviously struggling for the right words.

Feeling defensive, he assured her, "You don't have to worry. I promise it won't happen again."

Her gaze on his mouth, half wistful, she nodded. "It can't happen again. It's more than just professional ethics, it's written right into my contract. And I have to stay close to Amanda in case she needs me. I can't risk losing this job."

"Of course." The tension in his shoulders eased as he realized she hadn't found his kiss objectionable. It was the situation she stressed over. He shouldn't care, as the kiss wouldn't be repeated, but somehow he did.

"There's Mickey to think of, too," she added, concern evident in her earnest expression. "He may get confused by a change in our relationship. He's making such good progress we don't want to do anything to jeopardize his growth."

"You're probably right."

"It's prudent." With a small smile, she echoed his earlier assurance. "There is something else I'd like to talk to you about. If you're not going back to work, I thought you might grill some steaks and we could eat out on the deck and talk."

"I should go back." He checked his watch, saw there was only an hour left of his scheduled time. He'd put in a lot of extra hours lately, so he could justify the time off. And sitting down to a meal and conversation with

Nikki sounded really good. All the more reason he should get his butt to work.

"Let me check in with Lydia. If it's still quiet, I'll stay and grill."

"Great." She smiled her pleasure. "I'll get these clothes put away and start on a salad." Stacking baby shirts on top of baby pants, she headed toward Mickey's room.

Trace sat on the couch to make his call. He met his son's gaze across the room. "Whatever you do, don't leave us alone tonight."

Every day her attraction for the handsome Sheriff grew stronger. The sooner father and son connected and she could move on the better. For them. And for her. Nikki watched through the kitchen window as the boys "grilled."

Trace had changed into a sky-blue polo shirt that emphasized the width of his shoulders, and a pair of khaki shorts that came to his knees but left his muscular calves on display. He made one fine view.

While he wielded the spatula, he instructed Mickey on the finer points of barbecuing. Mickey listened and chewed on a teething biscuit.

Male bonding at its best. Just as she'd planned. Not scheduled was the joy she took in the family moment.

For a man who held himself aloof, who claimed to have no capacity for emotion, he was amazingly insightful and compassionate. Nikki suspected it wasn't that Trace didn't acknowledge his feelings, it was that he felt things so deeply, and if he allowed himself to feel he couldn't do the work he did without being torn apart inside.

He looked up and met her gaze through the window. He smiled, and butterflies fluttered in her stomach. Not a good sign.

"Steaks are ready," he called.

She waved an acknowledgment, gathered the baked potatoes and salad bowl and joined the boys outside. Under the shade of the umbrella the summer air felt warm against her skin, but the breeze gave the evening a balmy feel.

"This is nice." Trace set the platter of steaks on the table. "Good idea."

Easy conversation followed while they ate. She found out they shared a taste for action movies and biographies, but couldn't be further apart when it came to music and Chinese food. His growing sense of humor delighted her.

They talked briefly about the big announcement made at the community meeting. Nikki had been baby-sitting the kids, but her sister had filled her in on the Anderson endowment, gifting funds and property to Paradise Pines for community development.

"Is it true the men already have plans drawn up for a new sports complex?"

"It's no more aggressive than the women hiring an architect for a museum."

"Please. The cultural significance of a museum over a sports park couldn't be more blatant."

"Kids want to go to the park. They have to be made to go to a museum."

"That doesn't make the need for culture any less important in their development."

"So you're siding with the women?" Even he heard the sarcasm in the question.

She gave him an arch stare. "I am a woman, and I help shape young minds as a living. I can't believe you don't see the value of learning over play."

"Statistics show kids in team sports are more socially adept and less likely to get involved in drugs, alcohol and gangs. I see the value in that."

"Yes, but we already have a sports park. We don't have a museum." Already seeing the argument forming on his lips, she cut herself short. "Never mind. We have to work together. It's best we accept we're on opposite sides of this issue."

"Good idea. Too bad the whole town can't agree to disagree. I see this getting ugly before it's over."

"Keeping the peace." She grinned at him. "That's why you get the big bucks."

"Ha, ha. The big bucks came from my dad's life-insurance policy. And I inherited my wife's trust fund that she got from her maternal grandmother. I didn't want any of it."

Wow. The emotional outburst was so unlike him she stumbled for a response. "It must have helped, though, to allow you to make the move to Paradise Pines and to buy this place."

His fist tightened around his glass. "I can afford to provide a home for my son."

Okay, that hadn't been the right thing at all. Stupid, in fact, with his pride all wrapped up with his loss.

"That's not what I meant. I'm just saying that money isn't intended to replace the people we've lost but to help us adjust to life without them. My mother insisted on life-insurance policies for both her and my dad. Without it neither my sister nor I would have been able to complete college."

"That's different."

"Why? Because we were college-age girls alone in the world instead of a big he-man like you?" She shook her finger at him. "Not only is that sexist, it's disrespectful to the dead. People get peace of mind in life and in passing to know the ones they love will be taken care of when they're gone. I'm sure you've already considered what arrangements you're going to make for Mickey."

He drew a circle on the table in the condensation dripping off his glass of iced tea, conveniently avoiding eye contact. "I already moved his mother's trust fund into his name."

Of course he had. "See? I bet she'd be pleased with the gesture."

"Yeah." Mickey dropped his sippy cup and Trace bent to retrieve it. When he settled back in his seat, tension showed in the tight line of his shoulders. "How is it you can read me so well?"

"I listen," she said lightly, offsetting the near accusation with an airy response. "My mom always said it was a gift. I have a talent for hearing people. She felt it would help me to be a good teacher. And you're not so hard to read." Her bluntness got the better of her. "You're an honorable man, who puts duty above all else."

He gave a sharp nod, as if agreeing with the assessment.

She should stop, she knew it, but something drove her on. She wanted to know more about him, and these odd moments of exposure offered an opening she couldn't resist.

"You want to know what I really see? From little things you've said, I get the feeling your marriage had begun to falter. But it kills you that you weren't able to protect your wife, to somehow keep her safe from the perils of the world that stole her life. Having a child wasn't your idea, and you don't love Mickey, but he's your son, so you'll do right by him and protect him no matter what."

"You can stop now." With an explosion of muscle he pushed to his feet and began to pace. "How can you know all that?" he demanded, his tone cold enough to frost the July night. "Have you been snooping through my things?"

"No. Of course not." Offended, and hurt by the accusation, she recoiled in her seat, crossing her arms over her chest. "You know I'd never invade your privacy in such a way."

"What I know is you're talking about things that are

none of your business." He scrubbed a hand over the back of his neck. "I never talk about my wife. How could you have heard anything to make your deductions?"

She rubbed her arms, unprepared for his fierceness. "You're right. We should stop this."

She glanced at Mickey, to see how he was reacting to the sudden tension. Thankfully he'd fallen asleep, his little head resting on his arm stretched out over the tray. "I should take Mickey in."

"No." Trace reclaimed his seat, scraped the chair closer and propped both elbows on the table. "Answer the question."

This had gone too far. He was upset. She'd wanted to learn more about him, maybe rile him a little, but not to this extent. "Trace, I'm sorry."

"I don't want an apology. I want an answer."

"I really think we should end this."

"Nikki."

"Okay. It's not what you say, but what you don't say. You never talk about your wife except in relation to Mickey. And then you don't call her your wife; it's always 'Mickey's mother' or sometimes her name."

"I'm a private man. I don't talk about myself. That doesn't mean anything."

"No, but people who have lost a loved one generally do talk about them. It's a way to keep them with us even though they're gone. It's okay, you know," she said softly. "You don't have to pretend to feelings you don't have."

He sat back and crossed his arms over his chest.

"Don't tell me what to feel."

"And don't yell at me because you don't like what you're hearing. I'm right, aren't I? Or close enough to count. Otherwise you'd be laughing off my comments as so much fluff."

"I think it's time you left."

"You say you don't do emotions. Wrong. You seethe with emotions. You just don't want to deal with them, so you bury them deep down inside. You didn't love your wife—big deal. It happens. You feel guilty for her death. Not your fault. Get over it."

"Good night, Ms. Rhodes."

Chin up, her heart heavy, she reached for the dishes to carry them inside. "I'll come back for Mickey."

"Leave the dishes. Leave him. Just go."

Oh, she'd go. But not before putting in a fighting shot for Mickey.

"Emotions aren't something you're good at or not. It's just what you feel. How you act on those feelings is what makes the difference. If you can't find a way to open your heart to this sweet boy, he's the one who will suffer."

He made no response, but his eyes had changed from ice crystals to smoldering emerald heat. Good, let him brood.

Fighting off tears, she swept through the French doors to the kitchen, moving quickly toward the back door and the safety of her own rooms.

She stopped midflight, making a sudden decision to escape to the comfort of her sister's company. Let him work for it if he needed her in the middle of the night. Still, she should tell him. She was, as it were, on the clock.

He stood exactly as she'd left him, his stare focused on the dirty dishes littering the table.

She remained on the threshold. "I'm going to spend the night at my sister's. You can reach me there if you need me."

He didn't move, didn't even look at her. "I won't."

Why did the words cut her to the core? "Of course not. You don't need anyone."

Turning on her heels, she left him to his lonely existence.

CHAPTER NINE

TRACE pulled the SUV into his driveway, then reached for the large bag stuffed with sub sandwiches, fruits and salads. He felt foolish, planning a surprise outing, but now he'd moved into the execution phase he settled into action mode. The agenda for the evening flashed through his head.

Pick up food: check.
Fill cooler with ice, sodas and juice: check.
Pack blanket to sit on: check.
Persuade Nikki to accompany him and Mickey to the park: pending.
Apologize for being a jackass: two days overdue.

In those two days Nikki had barely spoken to him. She came after he fed Mickey in the morning, and left as soon as Trace got home in the evening.

He missed her.

Missed her cheerful morning chatter and her pretty

smile as she wished him a good day. Missed her company at the dinner table where she kept Mickey occupied while Trace ate. Missed the way she listened to him talk about his day and how her eyes lit up when they laughed over the crazy things people did.

He hadn't realized how easily she'd slipped past his guard until she wasn't around anymore. He wanted his friend back.

He owed her the apology. Two of the things he admired most about her were her blunt honesty and her insightfulness. How irrational of him to get angry with her when she turned those qualities on him.

She'd been right, and her dead-on accuracy had put him on the defensive. He'd felt exposed, and raw with emotions he couldn't identify. Guilt, fear, inadequacy, anger and more, until his pride had exploded, causing him to send her away.

Time helped him see the discussion more clearly, helped him see she'd been trying to help him.

Using his key, he let himself in the house. A quietness lay over the empty rooms, yet the place smelled great, of chocolate and vanilla, as if she'd baked. Anticipation built. If she were in the mood to bake, his chances had just gone up. He set the bag on the dining table and went in search of his fam—

He cut the renegade thought short. Nikki wasn't family. Yeah, he wanted to kiss her again, touch her, hold her, make her his. But it wouldn't happen, couldn't happen. Mickey liked her, and Trace needed her for Mickey too much to risk messing it up by getting cozy with her. Pending apology case in point.

No, it was best they stay friends.

Now, if his libido got on board, he might just make that work. When he reached the hall, he heard murmurs coming from Mickey's room.

He stepped to the doorway and looked in. Nikki stood over Mickey at the changing table. She'd obviously just changed him, and they were having a deep conversation about him keeping his hands to himself.

"Now, listen, mister, just because I have to lean over you to change your diapers does not mean you get to pull my hair." She poked him in the belly. "You keep your hands to yourself, buster."

Imagining his own hand fisted in her curls, holding her captive for his mouth, made Trace a little jealous of his kid. He didn't blame Mickey for using any opportunity to get his hands on those soft and lustrous tresses.

"Hey," Trace said, not wanting to startle her.

She turned to glance at him over her shoulder. For a moment her features lit up at the sight of him, and then she remembered her irritation and her expression closed up.

"Hello," she responded softly.

Another good sign. A man knew where he stood with Nikki. When she had a mad on she was all cold tones and go-to-hell glances—*after* she'd told you what a dork you were being.

Donna had locked herself away and sulked, and half

the time he hadn't even known why. Was it any wonder he'd given up trying?

"Daddy, Daddy." Mickey's legs twisted and bucked as he tried to sit up, and Nikki fought to finish the changing job.

Trace moved closer, hoping the boy would settle down if he could see him.

"Hold still, you little octopus." She deftly pushed little legs into tiny blue jeans and pulled them up over his butt. "There, all done." She threw up her hands, as if finished tying off a steer.

Mickey rolled into a seated position and grinned at Trace. His little arms popped into the air—a bid for Trace to pick him up. Trace hesitated only a moment before lifting Mickey. The boy immediately wrapped little arms around Trace's neck and laid his head on Trace's shoulder. Trace patted his back.

"Is he sleepy?"

"No. He's just happy to see you."

"Oh. Good." He jiggled the baby, as he'd seen her do. "I was wondering if you had plans tonight?"

She eyed him warily. "I can watch Mickey."

"Actually, we'd like you to join us on an outing to the park."

"You're taking Mickey to the park?" A hopeful note mingled with surprise.

"Yeah." He nodded toward the kitchen. "I have a picnic meal and everything."

"Hmm." She considered him, and then left the room.

He followed her down the hall and to the dining room table, where she peeked into the picnic bag. "Sandwiches, apples and grapes, pasta salad." She turned her head and swept him with a speculative glance. "A nice assortment of goodies, but you're missing dessert."

Moving to the counter next to the stove, she picked up a foil-covered platter. Bringing it to him, she lifted the corner to reveal chocolate-chip cookies. "Perhaps these will work?"

Her playfulness drew him forward. But he stopped short of reaching for her as he wanted to. Instead he bent to smell the cookies.

Looking up at her, he grinned. "Perfect."

Nikki leaned back on her hands and sighed. It didn't get much better than this: a mild summer evening, a soft place on the grass, and a view of father and son feeding ducks at the edge of the pond.

Trace handed Mickey some breadcrumbs and the boy threw them into the water, where five colorful ducks fought over the soggy meal. Mickey giggled and clapped and the whole process repeated.

She had their meal spread over the red gingham table-cloth Trace had included. They could have sat at a picnic table, but Trace wanted the full picnic experience. And Mickey had more freedom to move around on the ground.

"Dinner's ready," she called out.

Trace waved, and a moment later joined her on the makeshift blanket. "This looks great."

"You put it together. I just laid it out."

"Yeah, all my favorites." He settled Mickey between them and put a bib on him.

"Let's give him a few grapes to start out, and I'll feed him after we've eaten."

"Good idea." He took a big bite of ham and turkey sandwich.

She went for the pasta salad and some apple slices and watched him eat. She owed him an apology, and it was going to take more than the chocolate-chip cookies to salvage her conscience.

She didn't know where the conversation had gone so wrong the other night, but she knew it was her fault. Her bluntness landed her in awkward moments. When would she learn the virtue of tact?

Trace deserved his privacy, to grieve in his own way, to make peace with himself, or not, in his own time.

"I'm sorry." The apology came out strong and crisp, the sincerity clearly evident.

But it didn't come from her.

Trace met her gaze over the napkin he used to wipe his mouth. "You were trying to help and I jumped all over you. It was uncalled for, and I hope you can forgive me."

"Only if you forgive me first. I had no right—"

"Stop right there. Never apologize for caring. Not to me, not to anyone." His vehemence startled Mickey, and the boy's chin wobbled until Nikki smiled and tickled his cheek. Mickey grinned and popped a grape in his mouth, happy again.

"Being in the military, in law enforcement, I've seen more situations than you can believe that would have been cured simply if someone had cared." He peered into her eyes until she had to blink to escape the intensity in his. "From the beginning, I've told you things I've never spoken to anyone about. It's because it's there in your beautiful eyes—a genuine sense of caring."

He thought her eyes were beautiful. "Trace, I'm not some rare creature. Lots of people care."

"You're more rare than you think. Look at Mickey." They both focused on the baby, who'd snagged a cookie while they'd been talking and was smeared with chocolate from eyebrows to chin.

Nikki groaned. Now, there was the picture she wanted her boss to see right when he was telling her how attentive she was. Oh, well.

"Kiddo, you're a mess." She leaned over and kissed a clean spot on his cheek. "But you taste good. I might just eat you up." He giggled, and she laughed with him.

Gathering him into her lap, she looked around for the diaper bag. Once she'd located the bag, she found the wipes. "Sorry about that. I'll have him cleaned up in a snap."

Trace took the wet wipe from her and went to work on Mickey's face himself. Mickey giggled and wiggled, trying to dodge his father's efforts. Trace met her gaze over the boy's head. "This is what I'm talking about. A month ago he wouldn't have even touched the cookie, and now look at the fun he's having. He was despondent and sad and now he's happy."

"You have as much to do with Mickey's transformation as I do."

"Not nearly."

"You're wrong. He recognizes he's safe with you. Your steadfastness and the routine you've set give him necessary boundaries. He's thriving in the environment you've created."

"I wish I believed that."

"You can. Before you know it he'll be challenging those boundaries, but that's okay, too. In fact, it's great, because it means he trusts you."

Doubt played over his features as he leaned back on his hands and kicked his long legs out in front himself. "I still say you're the miracle-worker here. Mickey adores you. I'm totally second string."

"Not true." The man needed some strokes. "Mickey isn't the only one that's come a long way in a month. You've made strides, as well." She gently touched his fingers where they lay on the blanket. "He loves you, Trace."

A flash of longing crossed his features before he shut down all emotion. Such a strong, self-assured man. His lack of faith in himself broke her heart.

"I'll prove it," she said, and turned to face him on the blanket. "We'll put Mickey in the middle and let him choose who he goes to."

Lifting Mickey from her lap, setting him at the top of the blanket facing the two of them, she prayed this worked. She believed Mickey loved Trace, but he also cared for her. The truth was he could go either way.

She scooted back a few inches as Trace moved into position opposite her. He rested his hands on his knees and looked at her. "It's all right if he goes to you."

Mickey sat plump and happy at the edge of the cloth. He looked at her. She smiled and subtly nodded toward Trace. Mickey took the hint and turned his green gaze on his dad.

Yes. Relieved and excited, Nikki held her breath. He was going to choose Trace.

But he didn't. Back and forth went his little head. A frown began to pucker. Uh-oh.

"It's okay, baby boy." She softly reassured him.

"Hey." Trace shook a finger at her. "No trying to sway him from the sidelines."

Rolling her eyes, she said, "You are such a guy."

The scrutiny he leveled on her was all male. "Never doubt it."

Fat chance of that, she thought, feeling the potency of him shiver through her. She never forgot he was man to her woman.

At that moment Mickey rolled to his knees. Nikki tensed, urging him with her mind to crawl to his father.

He didn't.

But he didn't come her way, either.

He headed straight down the center, toward the chocolate-chip cookies.

"Oh, no, you don't." Trace swooped Mickey up.

Nikki laughed. "Look at that. He's already a diplomat."

"That's my boy."

Standing in front of Trace, Mickey immediately started in on his new favorite thing, jumping. Pumping and pushing, he squealed in joy. With his new diet he'd put on some weight and become quite the handful, yet Trace handled him easily.

"Well, there's no doubt you're his favorite right now."

"Yeah. It's good to see him thriving." He looked at her over Mickey's head. "Thank you."

"Hey, we're a team."

Trace went statue-still. Even Mickey stopped and looked at her. "I like the sound of that," Trace said.

Mickey put his hand out toward Nikki and she reached for him, but before they connected he suddenly broke away from Trace and took a step toward Nikki.

"Trace, look," she whispered, to keep from spooking the baby. "He's walking." She pulled her hand back a couple of inches, enticing him to take a couple more steps. He rushed those steps and fell into her arms. "Oh, my God, Trace. Did you see that? He walked.

"Oh, aren't you smart? Come here, you." Thrilled with his cleverness, she rained kisses all over his face. He grabbed her hair and hung on, giggling infectiously.

"He's brilliant." Trace clapped his hands, making

Mickey laugh and clap, too. "Let's see if he'll do it again."

"All right." She grinned at Trace, and the pride and wonder on his face made her breath catch. She turned Mickey around and put him on his feet.

"Go to Daddy."

She wondered if he'd try to crawl again, but he didn't even hesitate. Hands flailing to help with his balance, he took off walking. He crossed the two-feet distance between her and Trace in a stumbling rush that almost ended in a fall, but Trace caught him and pulled him close.

"We're in for it now." Trace kissed Mickey on the top of his head and praised him lavishly. "If the way he took to the walker is any indication, we're going to be running to catch up with him from now on out."

Tears burned at the back of her eyes. This was the first time she'd seen Trace display more than casual physical affection for his son. Little pats and an occasional rub of his head were the usual for him. It seemed to be the day for baby steps.

"I'm so glad you were here for his first steps," she said, looking away from the pride in his eyes. Silently she groaned, because she had just realized Mickey might not have fallen, but she had. She was falling hard for Mickey's dad. And she might never recover.

How funny was that? A free spirit falling for a control freak. Not exactly a match made in heaven.

"You're right," she whispered. "Life will never be the same again."

* * *

"Sit down," Trace invited the next evening. He set his plate of spaghetti on the table and pulled out a chair. "You can tell me what you've been wanting to talk to me about."

"Oh." Suddenly nervous about her news, Nikki decided it might be better to catch him later, when he was fresher and not just home from a long day at work. "You're tired. We can talk about it tomorrow."

Her nerves must have shown, because he nailed her with a stare. "We've already put it off several times. You've mellowed me out with spaghetti and meatballs, one of my all-time favorites. The timing doesn't get much better than this."

Uh-oh. She was in real trouble if he started reading her mind.

Summoning a reassuring smile, she jumped into the deep end. "The day after the town meeting the community center received news that their pre-school teacher was quitting. Without notice. They asked me if I'd be interested in the job."

He stabbed a meatball, delivered the bite to his mouth, and chewed, assessing her all the while. Finally he pointed his fork at her. "You have a job."

"Yes, and I explained to them that Mickey would be my first priority. They have no problem with me bringing him to the classes."

Sitting back, he crossed his arms over his wide chest. "One child's not enough for you?"

Okay this was good. He was resistant but willing to

talk. She'd expected less; she'd expected an outright decree to stay home with the baby. Not that he was a chauvinist, but he *was* a control freak. And a bit of a traditionalist. Funny, she actually liked that about him.

"I love Mickey. You know that. And this isn't babysitting; that's separate. These would be actual pre-kindergarten classes, two sessions a day, three days a week. Monday, Wednesday and Friday, nine to eleven and one to three, except there's no afternoon session on Fridays."

"So it's only fifteen hours a week?"

"That's not bad, right? I told them I was looking for something full-time." He scowled at the reminder. "And they said that wasn't a problem, they'd take me for as long as they could have me."

"It sounds like you really want to do this."

"I do." A true grin surfaced. Maybe he wouldn't object after all. "They were desperate, so I agreed to do a test session. I taught the afternoon class today. It reminded me how much I really love teaching."

"You miss it a lot?" He dug into his spaghetti again.

The question made her stop and think. Wow, surprisingly, the answer was she hadn't missed teaching as much as she'd thought she would. She'd enjoyed getting back in the classroom, but taking care of Mickey, sharing time with Trace, brought her a satisfaction that more than equaled what she got from teaching. Unsettled by the revelation, she refocused her attention.

"Yes," she admitted. "These kids were younger than I'm used to, so that presented some challenges, but they're so eager to learn. They absorb knowledge like little sponges."

"So you had fun?" He took a sip of milk.

"I did. If you don't mind, I'd like to take the job. Mickey would be with me most of the time, but now he's started walking, if he gets antsy they said he could go over to the daily care center with other toddlers and play there. It's just across the hall."

"Okay." He nodded. "As long as Mickey's taken care of, I'm fine with it."

Hot after a trip into town running errands, Nikki let herself into the house. Her little refrigerator didn't have a freezer, so she'd stashed some ice cream bars in Trace's.

"Knock, knock," she called, to announce her presence.

No answer. And a pungent smell hung in the air.

She knew they were home; she'd seen his SUV in the drive. On a whim, she grabbed a second bar and went in search of her guys.

She stopped, her heart flinching at the errant thought. Her guys. For now, but not for the long haul. The end of her two months was approaching. Trace no longer avoided his son. She really needed to give thought to saving herself from deeper heartache.

Maybe she'd be better off starting to distance herself from them. It was her day off; she had no real reason to see them.

The infectious sound of Mickey's giggle floated down the hall, stealing her willpower. She followed the sound to his room.

She stepped through the door to his room to find Mickey standing in his crib, throwing toys on the floor.

"If you keep tossing those out, you're not going to have anything to play with," Trace said over his shoulder, his attention on what he was doing. "I'm not coming over there again."

And, oh my, what Trace was doing. Here was the explanation for the smell. Paint. Light blue and bold primary colors, all on the wall facing the crib.

Trace was painting Mickey's room.

The blue was a background for a wall-filling mural of Mickey Mouse and friends. Mickey stood, arms crossed, cocky in a leather jacket, scarf and flying goggles, while his Disney buddies formed a posse behind him, each character wielding sports gear. Donald Duck cocked a bat over his shoulder, Goofy twirled a basketball on one finger, while Minnie simpered over a tennis racket.

"Oh, my God," Nikki breathed, awed by the authentic quality of the drawing. Even half-finished, the colors popped and the characters brought life to the formerly dull room. "This is fabulous."

Trace turned at the sound of her voice. "Hey," he said, his vivid green eyes rolling over her from toenails to hair band, reminding her she'd been in his arms only days before. Then he blinked and stepped back to survey his work. "It's not turning out too bad."

"Not too bad? It wonderful. Did you draw this free-hand? Since this morning?"

"Yeah, I doodle a lot. It passed the time on stakeouts and such over the years."

"This is more than doodling." She walked closer, studying the details. "This is art. You're very talented."

"I've never done anything this big before. So, you like it?"

"I love it. Mickey is going to love it." She handed him the second ice cream cone. "What made you choose Disney?"

Paint-stained fingers tore the paper off the treat. He nodded toward Mickey, who stood in his crib looking down at his toys. "I thought of sports themes, but I didn't want to pigeonhole him so young. This seemed like a good choice."

"It's perfect." She tossed her ice cream stick in the trash. "I'd love to see your sketches sometime."

He threw back his head and laughed. He looked relaxed and happy. Not a look he wore very often. "You did not just say that."

Replaying her words, she flushed, but couldn't regret her come-hither comment. It was the truth—in fact and in suggestive inplication. Even if she did need to keep her hands to herself.

"Probably against the rules, huh?"

"Big-time."

"But I really want to see them."

"Maybe some other time." He tossed his own ice cream stick. "I need to finish this."

"I guess you do." She watched as he went back to brushing color on the wall. Who knew he had this creative side? Proof of a sensitive side she'd long guessed he kept well hidden.

"Whew. The paint fumes are pretty strong in here. Is it safe for Mickey?"

"Yeah. I got the kind that's safe for kids and pregnant women."

"Good." She should have known. He was always careful with the details. She bent to pick up the dropped toys and return them to the crib. "Here you go, baby. Can I help?" she asked Trace.

"It's your day off. You should be out having fun."

"That's later—a barbecue at Amanda's. I can give you an hour."

"I won't turn it down. Can you wield a hammer?"

"With the best of them. My dad was a do-it-yourselfer and I liked to help."

"Great. There's a shelf and a mobile that need to go up."

"I'm your woman."

He sent her an ach glance out of vivid green eyes, but only nodded to the boxes piled on the dressing table. "Thanks."

"It'll be fun." She gathered hammer and nails from the garage and got to work. The mobile went up first, with Mickey watching every move she made.

"Looks good," Trace said. "Your dad taught you well."

"He did. I was a real daddy's girl."

"From what you've told me your family was close?"

"Yeah." She carefully marked her level points. "When you move around a lot you have to count on each other. Dad always found time to spend with us, or allowed us to be with him. He was great."

"You said your mom controlled the family. You two probably crossed swords a lot."

"Not when I was younger and we were traveling around. She was strict, yeah. We weren't allowed to join team sports or spend the night at friends' houses. Amanda and I learned to rely on each other and we grew very close. Mom—" Nikki swallowed around a sudden lump in her throat. She started over. "I realize now she was trying to protect us from being hurt, from making friends and having to leave them behind."

"Good intentions can sometimes have disastrous results," he sympathized.

"She did mean well." Anger, loss, and guilt had Nikki spinning to confront him, her defense of her mom quick and sharp. "Don't make assumptions about something you know nothing about."

He slowly turned, until Mickey's mouse ears framed his head, but it was the compassion in his eyes that she reacted to.

"She was a wonderful mom. Just because your mother abandoned you, don't be making judgments on mine. She did what she did because she loved us!"

"Nikki." He set the paint pallet aside to come to her. He cupped the side of her face, gently running his thumb over her cheek, wiping away a tear. "I'm sorry. Of course she loved you."

His understanding only made her feel worse, because she'd believed the same for the last years of her mom's life.

"No, I'm sorry—so sorry. I should never have said that about your mother. We did fight," she admitted around a strangled breath. "My mother and me. Once I turned eighteen and got to college I found a freedom I'd never known, and suddenly I blamed her for every restriction she ever enforced throughout my childhood."

"Don't be so hard on yourself. It's a normal rite of childhood to rebel at some point."

"But I understand now. I just needed more time with her. But she died instead."

"You said it yourself, Nikki. She loved you, and she knew you loved her, that's all that matters."

"No." She laid her forehead on his shoulder so she didn't have to look at him when she confessed, "The last time I saw her she was trying to give me some advice. I didn't want to hear it. We argued. I left mad." Anguish tightened the constriction in her throat so her voice became a husky rasp. "It was awful. And that's my last memory of her."

"Wrong." His fingers ran through her hair in soft strokes, his touch soothing her. "That's one of many memories you have. No matter how many disagreements you had, your mother loved you, and she knew you loved her. That's what you need to hold on to."

"Right. You're right. I have lots of memories." She lifted her head to meet his perceptive gaze. "Thank you."

He lowered his head and lightly touched his mouth to hers. "You're welcome."

Nikki grabbed the hammer she'd set aside and took out the last of her heightened emotions on the nails supporting the shelf—not least of which was frustration over his kiss. He knew it would redirect her thoughts to him.

She felt better about her mom, but more confused about her feelings for him than ever. So did she bless him or curse him?

CHAPTER TEN

NOT long after he arrived at work Thursday morning, Trace looked up from where he sat at his desk and saw Nikki approaching the glass doors to the Sheriff's station. She had her purse hooked over her shoulder, her phone to her ear, and maneuvered Mickey's stroller one-handed. Her animated expression told him her attention was wholly focused on the conversation.

He hopped to his feet, expecting the heavy glass door to be an obstacle, but it didn't slow her down at all. She simply turned around and pushed her way in with her nicely rounded backside. He arrived in time to hold the door wide while she swung the stroller around.

"I'm dropping Mickey off now," she said into the phone, making his brow rise in question. "Yes, I called the doctor's service again. They said they spoke to him and he'll meet you at the hospital." To Trace, she mouthed the words, "My sister is in labor."

Yeah, being a former detective, he'd figured that out.

Nikki managed to appear both excited and exasperated as she spoke to her sister.

"Do not call a cab. They'd have to come in from the city, and even coming from El Cajon would take fifteen to twenty minutes. Let me talk to Trace, then I'll be there in five minutes."

She smiled and waved when Lydia came to the counter. "Yes, yes. Amanda, I'm hanging up now. Remember to breathe."

Disconnecting the call, Nikki let out a rush of air, and then she grinned big and did a little dance.

"Amanda is in labor. I'm going to be an aunt."

"I gathered."

"I'm her labor coach. I have to go." She bit her lower lip, the excitement replaced by a conciliatory cringe. "I tried Josh, but he's working. And I didn't know who else—"

"Stop." He held up a hand. "Go. Your sister needs you." And Nikki needed to be with her sister. She'd fret terribly otherwise. "I'll take care of Mickey."

"Thank you for understanding. Here's his diaper bag. I couldn't carry everything, so I left his car seat out by your SUV." She wrinkled her nose sheepishly. "Hopefully nobody is foolish enough to steal from the Sheriff."

"Go. Take care of Amanda." Trace took the diaper bag from her and handed over her purse, which she'd given to him instead. "Do you want me to drive you?"

"No. Wow." Her eyes went soft and wide as she thanked him. "You are so sweet, but we'll be fine. I'll feel better if I have my own car, in case I need to run and get anything. Plus, if my brother-in-law, Dan, doesn't get here, I'll need to drive us home. He's in a training class in Florida. He was supposed to be back on Saturday, but he's going to try to get leave to come home early."

"Hopefully that works out. Call me. Let me know how things are going. Or if you need anything."

"I will." Her phone rang. "Oh, my God, I have to go. I'm going to be an aunt!" She gave him a big hug, Mickey a kiss and then ran out the door.

Trace exchanged glances with Lydia. "So, do you think the roads are safe?" she asked.

"I'd have insisted on driving if I didn't think so. She'll be all right once she's on the road." Slightly bemused, he shook his head. "She thought I was being sweet?"

Lydia shrugged. "Most people don't take their jobs as seriously as you do," she explained.

"It's a serious job."

"Yes, it is. And you do it well. The whole town takes comfort in knowing you take the creed 'To Protect and To Serve' seriously."

He nodded, gratified by the acknowledgment.

"But, Trace, just because your job is serious it doesn't mean you always have to be. The girl thinks you were being sweet. Smile and enjoy the perks."

"Perks, hmm?" Trace had never really thought along those lines. He got paid for his job. Perks were neither necessary nor sought after. But what the hell? He couldn't get much done in his office with Mickey here, and it would save him from having to hunt up a babysitter.

"Daddy." Mickey demanded Trace's attention. He looked down to find little arms in the air. "Up."

He hefted the boy into his arms and then stowed the stroller in his office, out of the way. "Radio me if you need me," he told Lydia on his way out the door. "I'm going to take Mickey for a haircut."

"Oh," she lamented, "he'll lose all those lovely curls."

Trace shoved on his sunglasses. "Exactly."

Ten minutes later he stood in the alien universe of What a Woman Wants, the new beauty salon in town. Arms crossed, he leaned against the wall in clear view of Mickey, who sat on a booster seat at one of the stations.

Mickey shrank back from all the women fawning over him, and Trace plainly read the plea for escape his son sent his way. He commiserated, but held tough.

"Sorry, buddy, but those curls are coming off. You'll thank me when you're older."

"Oh, but they're so adorable," a woman in huge curlers cooed. "How can you think of chopping them off?"

Chirps of agreement rained down on him. He shrugged. "He's a boy. Boys don't have curls. Not in my family."

Oh, man. He sounded just like his dad. Instead of the thought bothering him, Trace decided to cut his dad a little slack. Obviously there were times when a father did know best. "I'm tired of people telling me what a cute daughter I have."

A twitter of giggles told him this crowd just didn't understand.

"Okay, that's enough, ladies. Everyone back to their seats so I have room to work here." Dani Wilder, owner of the shop, shooed the women away. The shapely red-head feathered long fingers through Mickey's fine brown hair. "Mickey, you're being such a good boy."

Her gentle way and soft touch eased Mickey. The exact reason Trace had braved the salon rather than take Mickey to the barbershop for his first haircut.

"So, how short do you want to go?" Dani asked Trace.

"I want him to look like a boy."

"Sheriff, you're obviously a man with some nerve, who knows what he wants," Dani said as she went to work on Mickey's hair. "How do you think the An-derson endowment funds should be used?"

Several female heads cocked in his direction, await-ing his response. Maybe the barbershop would have been a better choice after all.

"Well, Ms. Wilder, it's my job to keep the peace, not add to community unrest, so I think I'll keep my opinion for the voters' box."

She stopped her snipping to send him a chiding glance. "Which means you agree with the men."

"Or he doesn't, but won't allow his opinion to be used in the ongoing argument," said Matilda Sullivan, reign-ing town matriarch, from her seat two stations down. "The Sheriff is a smart man, keeps a low profile. Snagged himself a pretty sharp gal as a nanny for this young one."

"Mrs. Sullivan," he acknowledged her. Nikki hadn't mentioned meeting the woman, but as a member of the town board Mrs. Sullivan would have been instrumental in approving Nikki to teach at the community center. "Keep your sights off my nanny."

Delighted, the petite woman laughed. "I'm not sure I can promise that. I only met her for a moment, but I've seen her credentials and her references. And my great-grandson says she's *awesome*."

Her exaggerated mimicking of her great-grandson's compliment made their avid audience chuckle.

"Yes, she's quite a catch," he agreed, and immediately cringed internally as he considered how that sounded.

"Well, well, is that a note of personal interest I detect, Sheriff?"

"No," he answered, a little too quickly.

"Now, don't be embarrassed." The matron smiled knowingly. "It's about time you started dating again. It's hard after a loss, but you have to think of your son. You and Ms. Rhodes would make a delightful couple. Personally, I feel a man in a position of civic authority benefits from the input of a spouse." Her chin rose in haughty disdain. "If our current mayor had a wife and family he might better understand the need for a cultural influence in our town."

Trace ducked his chin to keep from displaying his amusement. "Mrs. Sullivan, our current mayor is your grandson."

She actually sniffed. "Yes, and if Cord had listened to me and settled down to domestic bliss years ago, he'd be better qualified to address the needs of all the citizens of Paradise Pines."

"Ladies, you're making this into a bigger issue than it needs—" He cut off when eight heads in various stages of coiffure snapped his way. Man, the comment about him and Nikki making a good couple must have thrown him off more than he thought, or he would have guarded his words better.

"*We're* making this a bigger issue than necessary?"

Head at a regal tilt, ice dripped from the matriarch's words.

Uh-oh, he'd riled the beast.

"I just meant—"

"You were quite clear. But we're not the ones who already had plans drawn up for a sports complex *before* the announcement of the endowment."

"Yeah," chorused through the room.

"On second thought, Sheriff, I'm glad to hear there's nothing personal between you and Nikki Rhodes. She and my grandson would make a lovely couple. And she may be just what he needs to sway him. A sweet young thing with a master's in Child Development might be just the weapon we need."

And the beast had a vicious bite.

"All done," Dani said, her pronouncement a cheerful trill in the tense room.

Rescued. Before the atmosphere got any more hostile, he grabbed Mickey and made good his escape, wondering all the while if a lovely couple trumped a delightful couple.

Nikki leaned against the wall and stared into the nursery at the beautiful sight of her new nephew. Little Anthony Amare had given his mother a bit of a bad time. But you'd never know it by the peacefulness of his slumber.

Exhausted, emotion overflowing within her, Nikki needed the wall to hold her up. The day had been long, fraught with moments of drama between extended periods of waiting. Amanda had gone through twelve hours of labor, only to be rushed into surgery for an emergency C-Section at the last moment.

It tore at Nikki's heart that she hadn't been able to go into surgery with her sister, but when the decision came they'd had to move too fast for Nikki to suit up.

The baby hadn't been dropping down as he should, and it turned out the cord had been wrapped around his neck. The thought of what could have happened made her heart pound double time.

She was thankful, so thankful, that both baby and Mom had come through okay her knees threatened to buckle from relief. And the arrival of Dan added to the joy of the event.

Knowing mom, dad and baby would soon be together brought tears to Nikki's eyes. Amanda had been in postop until a few minutes ago. Of course Nikki had sent Dan into her. And here she waited, keeping watch over Anthony until they came for him, too. The family deserved their privacy, but after the long, emotional day, it left her feeling a little alone.

She couldn't help but think of Trace, standing alone in front of a nursery window fourteen months ago, shocked by his wife's death and bewildered and overwhelmed by the birth of his son. How did you celebrate the one while mourning the other?

What a nightmare for a man who claimed he didn't do emotion well.

No wonder he'd accepted his in-laws' offer of help. How easy it must have been to let distance grow between him and Mickey. And what a shame when they both needed each other so much.

At least they were finally finding each other.

Inside the nursery, little Anthony scowled and a lump rose in Nikki's throat. Oh, yeah, he was a little Rhodes; he looked just like her dad when he frowned.

She traced his cheek on the glass window, a new wave of emotion making her hand shake. How she wished her parents were here to see their first grandchild.

"You'd be so proud," she whispered. "I never knew, Mom, how big love for a baby could be. Not until Mickey. And now Anthony. I knew love, yeah. You and dad gave us that always. It was a constant in our lives. But this is so huge, so wonderful and scary. I know you're up there, watching over us. And that Trace is right, and you probably don't even remember our last fight. But I do, and I'm sorry."

"Nikki?" A hand cupped the small of her back as a man stopped next to her. "Are you okay?"

Startled, she half turned—and looked into Trace's calm green eyes. Without thought she threw herself into his arms, and sighed as he pulled her close into his warmth.

"I'm so glad you're here," she said into his chest. It only made it more perfect that Mickey slept, crushed between them. Her two guys in her arms. Nothing could be better.

"Hey." Trace lifted her chin on a gentle knuckle. "*Are* you okay?"

"I'm fine. I'm wonderful." She ran a hand over Mickey's new haircut. "Big change."

"It had to be done."

"Looks good." She pointed out Anthony in the nursery, and grinned as he admired the baby. "Mom and baby are both healthy and beautiful. Dan got here twenty minutes ago. Life is good."

"Then why the tears?" His concern, the sincere caring in his gaze, wiped her loneliness out in a single blow.

"No tears." She denied the wetness on her cheeks. "Not today." And, using all her courage, launched herself onto her toes, wrapped her arms around his neck and pulled him into a kiss.

"Nikki," he groaned. Immediately he shifted her into the shelter of his free shoulder, deepened the angle of the kiss and devoured her mouth with his.

As an energizer, passion really packed a kick. Nikki gave as good as she got, tangling tongues, drinking in the taste of him, immersing herself in the embrace. He felt so good she longed to find a flat surface and take the sizzling sensations to the next level.

Finally time and place sank in, and she fell back on her heels, but she didn't break away from him. Instead she snuggled close. The baby was born, Dan was back, finally she could relax her guard.

His hand, warm and soothing, curled into her hair, making her feel cherished.

"What was that for?" Desire deepened his pitch to velvet-covered gravel, rough and sensual.

She licked her lips, tempted to tell him how happy she was to see him, how much she loved that he'd made such an effort to come see her. But it would be a selfish announcement, and it would probably scare the bejeezus out of him. So she simply shrugged and said, "It's a day for miracles."

He raised his brows, but didn't pursue it. Instead, he laid his lips softly on hers again, drawing out the moment before lifting his head. "Congratulations, Aunt Nikki."

Tears clogged her throat. Closing her eyes, she rested against him, savoring the warmth and contentment of being held by the man she loved, stealing these precious moments against a lifetime without him. Now that he and Mickey were bonding, she'd sent out résumés both to schools in San Diego and to a couple of the bordering counties.

"Not that I'm complaining, but why are you here?" she asked him.

"I got your message that you'd be staying over, and I brought you a comfort package."

"Really?" She leaned her head back to look up at him. His cheeks were a ruddy red—but from lingering arousal or embarrassment? Perhaps a bit of both? "You're so sweet."

"You keep saying that, but I'm not sweet at all. I'm practical."

"Uh-huh. It's practical to bring a baby out at eleven o'clock at night to bring me a comfort package?"

The red deepened in his cheeks. "It was only nine when I picked up your message."

"Don't fight it. You're sweet."

"I'd much rather be practical. Or tough. Even cute is better than sweet."

"Well, you are all of those things," she allowed, to make him happy, but she couldn't lie. "And you're sweet, too."

She laughed at his disgruntled grimace. Patting down his pockets, she demanded, "What did you bring me?"

"Hold on." He set her back on her own weight. "It's in a bag here somewhere."

"A bag?" She stepped back to look, and nearly put her foot through the pretty pink package. It stood as high as her knees, and the width spanned a good eight inches. No tissue paper, and the handles were tied together— clear signs he'd done the packaging himself, which only made the gesture more special. A smaller blue bag had toppled on its side. "Oh, my. Trace, what did you get?"

"It's not much. I figured you'd have brought the essentials. These are just a few things to make a long night more comfortable. The smaller gift is for Amanda."

"I love surprise presents." All signs of weariness disappeared as she peeked inside and spied something pale blue and fuzzy. "Let's find somewhere comfortable to sit down. I can't wait to open it."

As she led the way to the lobby, she told him about the delivery, and Dan's late arrival.

"So actually, now Dan's here, I may grab a ride home. I'll check with Amanda, but I'm sure they'd prefer to be alone."

"You can always come back tomorrow," he assured her. "You don't need to worry about Mickey. I've arranged for a sitter."

"You don't mind if I take another day?" In the lobby she sank unto a sofa and patted the spot beside her. Trace laid Mickey down, then sat beside her.

He shrugged her concern away. "You've covered for me plenty. Besides, it's not every day a nanny becomes an aunt."

"No." His easy acceptance of the altered schedule surprised her. This was not the same rigid man she'd met a month and a half ago. Mickey had been as good for his dad as Trace had been for Mickey.

"What did you get me?" She dug into the bag and found a plush fleece blanket, slipper socks and a travel pillow, all in shades of baby blue. "Trace, this is too much. I feel bad, now, that I'm not staying."

"Don't be ridiculous. You always go out of your way to see to our comfort. I wanted to do it. It's not like you can't use these things at home. And, yes, it's okay to lend anything you want to Dan. My feelings won't be hurt."

"Well, thank you." She didn't let the fact the gift came from a sense of obligation upset her. Much. The point was he'd made the effort. "Am I so easy to read?"

"Hardly." An incredulous laugh escaped him. "You constantly keep me guessing. But in some things, like the comfort of those you care about, you are very predictable."

"Uh-huh?" Somewhat appeased, she loaded the items back into the bag. "Oh, here's Dan."

Nikki introduced Trace to her brother-in-law, and then Dan caught them up on Amanda's condition. "They moved her back to her room and brought the baby in, so she's pretty jazzed right now. She wants to see you. You should come, too," he said to Trace.

"Yes," Nikki urged him, "you have to give Amanda your gift. Oh." Disappointment bit sharp when he shifted Mickey in his arms to pick up the blue bag. Hospital rules didn't allow children in the maternity rooms. "I don't think they'll let us bring Mickey."

Trace lifted a dark brow. "I have a badge. There won't be any problem."

CHAPTER ELEVEN

"DIDN'T Amanda look radiant with her son in her arms?" Nikki mused once they were in the SUV on the way home, at a little after one in the morning.

Trace merged onto the freeway, headed east. Amanda had looked unkempt, uncomfortable and exhausted. Exactly as you'd expect after twelve hours of labor and surgery. And, yes, she'd lit up the room with her joy and contentment.

"A mother and her babe are a beautiful thing," Trace agreed.

"You were wonderful tonight." Nikki laid a warm hand on his knee. The heat of her touch blazed straight to his lap. The traffic was light this hour of the morning, so he chanced a glance at her, and then did a double-take.

Her eyes were luminous, shining bright with…love?

For a moment the earth rolled on its axis and his world exploded, becoming bright and perfect. And *right*. As if he'd finally found his life's path. And Nikki walked it with him.

No, he had to be mistaken. Nikki didn't love him. She loved her family. That was it: the love lighting her eyes was for the family she'd just left behind. That explained it.

Which was a relief, right? So why did he suddenly feel deprived and lost?

"Your gift for Amanda was perfect. How did you know to bring her snacks?"

"I did my homework when Donna was expecting. The mother isn't allowed to eat or doesn't feel like eating during labor. After the baby is born she's ready for something to snack on. And I threw in the slipper socks because it can get cold in the hospital."

"Oh, Trace," Nikki breathed. She turned toward him in her seat. "How thoughtful you've been, when this visit must have been very traumatic for you. The memories it must have brought back... Are you okay?"

"I told you I was no good at emotion. My marriage was a perfect example of that. We were compatible; she wanted to get married. I agreed. It was that simple— until it got complicated. She began to complain about my hours. Then she wanted to quit work and have a baby. At first I resisted, but she got pregnant anyway."

"You must have felt trapped. Your sense of honor and duty would have required you to stay with them."

He sat in silence for a moment, remembering his frustration and hurt at having his feelings in such a big decision ignored. It occurred to him that Nikki knew him better after only a month or two of working together than Donna had over three years of marriage.

"At first I was angry. But you're right. Duty and obligation kicked in. I'd vowed for better or worse, and I determined a baby would make things better. Donna wouldn't be so lonely. She'd have her child."

"How did Donna feel about the compromise?"

"We were making the best of it. Donna was excited about the baby, and I was glad to see her happy and occupied."

"You would have made it work," she said, her faith in him obvious, but her tone held an odd edge he couldn't identify.

"I like to think so." He would have tried, *had* tried, but he wondered now if mediocre feelings would have been enough to hold them together through the long haul.

"When she died and Mickey lived it seemed like one big cosmic joke. Kill off the one who wanted the baby and leave him with a messed up dude who knows nothing about childcare and less about providing for someone else's emotional well-being. I was so relieved when Donna's parents said they'd take him. For Mickey's sake more than my own. But it turns out I still messed up."

"You did what was right for everyone concerned at the time. Plus you changed your whole life, your job, your residence, your lifestyle, to make a home for Mickey."

"But I left him with his grandparents longer than I needed to."

"Mostly out of compassion for your mother-in-law."

"But not all. I was no better prepared for a one-year-old than a newborn."

"Yeah, well, a lot of child rearing is on-the-job training."

"You're too soft on me."

"You're too hard on yourself."

He squeezed her hand. "Mickey and I are lucky to have you. You're going to make a wonderful aunt."

Twenty minutes later Trace pulled into his driveway, placed the SUV in Park, and with a tired sigh shut off the engine. He glanced to the right. Nikki sat slumped against the door, a hand curled under her cheek, sound asleep.

He hated to wake her after such a long, emotional day, but she'd be more comfortable in her own bed. Cupping her shoulder, he shook her gently. Nothing. He shook a little harder. She shifted and resettled against the door, clearly out of it.

He decided to take Mickey in first and come back for Nikki. He lifted his son against his shoulder. Such a slight weight. Trace barely remembered him as a newborn. Born early, he'd had to stay in the hospital for a week while his lungs and weight stabilized. Fighting through the shock and grief of losing Donna, Trace had spent days planning a funeral and nights sitting next to an incubator.

It had been the worst time of his life.

He'd been so grateful for his in-laws' offer to take Mickey. Now, as he settled his son in his bed, Trace was thankful to finally have his son in his custody, and he prayed for the strength and fortitude to be a good parent. With Nikki's help, he just might have a chance.

He returned to the SUV for her. Carefully opening her door, he cupped her shoulder to keep her from falling and accepted her weight as she slumped sideways. She mumbled, but didn't awaken.

"Nikki, wake up now," he urged her. "We're home."

"Home," she said, and laid her head on his shoulder.

"Come on, sweetheart, wake up."

"Hmm…" She sighed, and nestled closer.

"Okay, then." He swung her up into his arms, hooked her purse over his elbow, shoved the door shut with his hip and headed inside.

As he climbed the steps to the front deck she roused. "I can walk," she murmured, even as she circled his neck and snuggled against him.

"I've got you," he whispered into her hair. How he longed to carry her straight through to his bed, where he could hold her close during the night and wake up with her in the morning.

He knew in that moment she'd reached depths in him he'd never allowed anyone to touch. Not even with Donna had he ever looked beyond the moment. With Nikki he saw them sitting on the back deck, hands linked, as they watched grandchildren playing in the yard.

He shuddered, recognizing things had gone too far, knowing she deserved better than a ready-made family complete with two dysfunctional males. But wanting, oh, wanting so badly to reach out and grasp love, to know the true meaning of family and commitment.

Inside, he set her on the couch while he went to hunt up the key to her apartment. When he came back, he found her sprawled full-length on the couch.

"Nikki," he called softly, lifting her torso up and sliding into the spot next to her so she couldn't lie back down. "It's time to go to bed."

She opened sleepy amber eyes, blinked at him and smiled.

"Stay here," she said, and then she climbed into his arms, pushing him into the corner in the process, and sprawled next to him. "Home."

She was asleep again before he could protest. Not that he wanted to object. Hugging her close, he shifted his legs up onto the couch to tangle with hers.

Yes, again the world felt right.

He sighed and let his body relax. Surrounded by the sweet scent of apple blossom and woman, savoring the lush feel of Nikki in his arms, he drifted off to sleep.

"Stupid cell service." Nikki clicked the "end" button on her cell phone and tossed it in the passenger seat. The law restricted her from using the phone while driving, but since she hadn't moved more than a quarter mile in twenty-five minutes she figured she was safe. Unfortunately, she had no service, so it didn't matter anyway.

Cars stretched out on the freeway as far as she could see in both directions. Glancing in the rearview mirror, she checked on Mickey. He sat happily in his car seat, eating a teething biscuit.

"I don't know how you can be so calm. Your daddy is going to have my hide if he gets home before we do." She tapped her fingers on the steering wheel. She should have been home thirty minutes ago. "The radio says there's an accident involving a semi near Lake Jennings Road."

The on and off ramps had both been closed, and they were talking about an oil spill. She'd just passed Los Coches, which meant there was no off ramp between her and the accident. Until the road cleared, nobody was going anywhere.

"Daddy?" Mickey called out, and clapped his hands.

"Yeah." Nikki grinned at his response. "He's your favorite person, huh? I'm so happy you two have become good buds."

Trace hadn't been pleased with her decision to drive Amanda into town. With a high wind advisory in effect, and thunderstorms threatening, he'd considered the trip frivolous and unnecessary. Of course that had only made her more determined to go.

Hold back because of the weather? In San Diego County, with its generally mild climate and where the weather forecasters were wrong as often as they were right? Uh-uh.

Rain started to splatter the windshield.

"Oh, wonderful. That's the icing on the cake." Could it get any worse?

"Cake?" Mickey repeated, recognizing one of his favorite treats.

"Sorry, buddy, no cake."

Mickey threw the teething biscuit and demanded, "Cake! Cake! Cake!"

"Mickey, stop."

Now she'd done it. Overdue for his afternoon nap, the usually even-tempered baby went into a cranky fit.

The bland biscuit—she didn't blame Mickey for preferring cake—had been the last of her distractions. Rather than scold him for his behavior, she talked gently to him, giving him her full attention. She explained where they were, and what was happening and promised she'd get him home as soon as she could. He didn't understand the words, but he responded to her reassuring tone and attentive manner and soon settled down. It also helped when she dug Boo out of the diaper bag.

If only Daddy would be so easy to calm down.

All right, so her contrariness had gotten the better of her. But it wasn't all her fault. She treasured her independence, and Trace's suggestions often sounded more like orders. Plus, she'd already promised Amanda a ride into town to meet Dan. It was her sister's first outing since having the baby, and she'd so been looking forward to it. Nikki hadn't had the heart to disappoint her.

But she despised hurting Trace.

She checked her cell again. Nothing. She always lost service through these hills.

In a few minutes he'd be home. He wouldn't know where they were. He'd worry—especially with the weather turning bad.

Hopefully he'd hear about the accident and realize she was stuck.

She'd found such sweet slumber in his arms the other night. How she wished it had turned into more. But, no, he'd let her sleep while he got Mickey up, dressed and fed. Only when Trace was ready to walk out the door had he woken her.

Sleeping in his arms, she had felt cherished and above all else safe. No need to play big sister, nanny, teacher, housekeeper. Not during the hours he guarded her sleep. He'd gone to a lot of trouble, risked some pretty heavy memories for her benefit.

Surely that meant he cared for her beyond what she provided for his son?

A wicked grin formed as she remembered the lingering sizzle in the air ever since. Oh, yeah, he cared. Then she sobered, hoping this stunt—and the anxiety it would bring—didn't ruin everything.

"Trace, call on line three." Lydia's voice floated down the hall, a sure sign she and the new phone system weren't on speaking terms yet.

He picked up the line. "Sheriff Oliver."

"Mr. Oliver?" a brisk voice greeted him. "I'm with the Irvine Central School District. I need to verify employment for Ms. Nikki Rhodes, can you help me?"

Trace dropped his pen on the desk and sat back in his chair, giving his entire attention to the phone call.

"Yes, Ms. Rhodes works for me. What is this in regard to?"

"I'm sorry, I'm not at liberty to say—"

He cut off the privacy mumbo-jumbo. "But you're with the Irvine Central School District? That must mean she's applied for a position there."

"I'm not allowed to discuss the applicant's business." She confirmed his suspicion with her officious disclaimer. "Would you be willing to answer a few questions? How long has Ms. Rhodes been working for you?"

Trace answered the questions on autopilot, while his mind wheeled with the possibility of losing Nikki. Why hadn't she told him she was applying for a job? Was it something he'd done? Something he hadn't done?

Like holding her in his arms all night long and not making sweet love to her. The hardest thing he'd ever done was to leave her sleeping alone the next morning.

And now she would be leaving. A fist twisted in his gut, a cold sense of dread enveloping him.

Of course he knew she'd always intended going back to teaching, but surely she would tell him if she had applied for a position.

Obviously not. And that hurt.

"The résumé indicates she also lives with you. Is that correct?"

"She has an apartment on my property, yes."

"Thank you, sir. Just one last question. Would you consider rehiring Ms. Rhodes in the future?"

Rehire her? Forget that. He didn't want her to go.

Trace drove up to the house as the first raindrops fell, not surprised to see Nikki's car missing from the curb. Numerous unanswered calls to the house since his conversation with the Irvine Central School District had already told him she wasn't home.

A slow-burning anger brewed. She'd gone against his wishes and driven Amanda into town to meet her husband and now she'd got stuck behind the accident blocking Freeway Eight.

Hell, he prayed that was all that had delayed Nikki. If she wanted to risk her neck, he couldn't stop her. But she'd had no right to take Mickey with her.

He tried her cell again, and again it went straight to voice mail.

Lightning lashed the sky as he entered the cool, prematurely darkened house. No lights burned, and there was no sense of the warm welcome he'd become accustomed to since Nikki came to stay.

But she hadn't come to stay; she'd come to work. And now she meant to leave him, to work somewhere else. Thunder boomed, and the rip of lightning outside mimicked what he felt inside: torn apart with anger, loss and pain.

He paced, needing an outlet for his rage.

Where was she? Where was his son?

For so long he'd fought the reality of being a parent, believing any child of his was better off with any family besides him. Yet every day he spent with Mickey made Trace realize how wrong he'd been.

Mickey was a miracle. For better or worse, he loved Trace. And his unconditional trust and affection touched Trace beyond anything he'd ever known.

Trace prayed nothing would happen to Mickey when he'd just found him. God, he loved his son.

Seeking action, Trace called the station, asked Lydia to check on the traffic board and give him current road conditions and accident reports. A few small collisions had popped up—no fatalities, thank the Lord—and they'd cleared a couple of lanes near the semi rollover on eight. Traffic had begun moving through the area.

Relieved to know there'd been no accident-related deaths, he hung up and went to check the window again. Five minutes later Nikki pulled up in front of the house.

He cleared the door and took the steps two at a time to reach her car. She was already out, struggling to release Mickey from his car seat.

"Let me." He moved her aside to reach the sleeping boy. "Where the hell have you been?" he demanded. Not waiting for an answer, he snapped, "Next time you want to kidnap my son, leave your cell phone on."

"I know you're angry." She brushed rain off her cheeks. "But I promise you I exhausted every avenue before taking Mickey with me."

"I'm sure you tried real hard." He grabbed a blanket

from the diaper bag, tucked it around Mickey and then thrust the bag in her hands before heading inside.

"I did try." She followed hard on his heels. "I had Josh lined up, but he got called into work. I only know of three other people you'd allow to watch him. I couldn't reach one and the other two were busy."

"Then you shouldn't have gone." He left her to close the front door, intent on getting Mickey to his bed.

"You say that, but you weren't here." Nikki stopped in the bedroom doorway, heartfelt in her efforts to convince him she was right and he was wrong.

Mickey stirred as Trace changed him. He grinned at Trace, mentioned something about cake, and went back to sleep when Trace settled him in his crib.

"Amanda was so excited about this outing." Nikki continued her explanation. "She was in tears when I suggested not going. Her doctor has told her not to drive for a while, but I knew she would drive herself if I didn't take her. I determined that was the bigger danger."

"Leave your sister out of this. You didn't want to hear a word I said after I mentioned the weather."

"That's because this is San Diego. They're always wrong about the weather."

As if cued, a loud boom echoed overhead, followed by lightning strobing across the sky, backlighting the windows and illuminating Nikki's features in stark relief. He looked for remorse, found none.

With nature on his side, he didn't have to say a word; he simply arched a dark eyebrow.

She propped her hands on her hips. "Anyway, the weather's not why I was late. There was—"

"A rollover accident, blocking the freeway. I know."

Her shoulders slumped in relief. "So you did hear about that? *Good.*"

"Good? How is any of this good?"

"You figured out where I was. I kept trying to call you, but the service was out on my cell."

"I didn't know where you were! I speculated, hoped, prayed, but for all I knew my son could have been under that semi."

Her defiance drained away, along with the color from her face. "That's a terrible thing to say."

"It was a terrible thing to visualize."

"Oh, Trace." She took a tentative step toward him. "You have to know I love Mickey. I'd die before I let anything happen to him."

His anger faded at her words. Any pretense that his overwhelming concern had been for Mickey alone disappeared as he recognized his rage for what it truly was: a poor disguise for the fear he felt at the possibility of losing the people he'd come to love, of losing her.

He bridged the space between them and framed her face in his hands.

"That is not an acceptable alternative," he told her, before claiming her mouth with urgent need.

CHAPTER TWELVE

THE demand of Trace's mouth took over Nikki's senses. Defenses well and truly down, she returned his kisses with eager demands of her own. His arms tightened around her as he lifted and carried her across the hall. She wrapped her arms around him and clung. Sweet relief added the tang of tears to the embrace.

He was right. Nikki hated to be told what to do, and she'd thought she knew better. But she'd been wrong and she knew it.

The thought of Trace waiting here, worried about his son being crushed in a car accident—just like his wife had been—made Nikki sick to her stomach. It had always been about more than the weather, and she should have honored Trace's wishes.

"Hey, no crying." He pulled back to kiss the wetness from the corner of her eyes, to trace the path of despair and erase it with tenderness. He lowered her to the bed, his weight causing the bed to dip as he joined her.

His pace slowed, relaxed, but was no less demanding. Gentle strokes and featherlight touches stoked the flames of desire started by fierce caresses. He delayed only long enough to ask about protection before taking the loving up a notch.

The whistle of the wind and the staccato beat of rain against glass, accompanied by the booming drum of thunder, lent music to the tempest brewing inside the sultry heat of the bedroom. Lightning cracked as they arched in perfect harmony, punctuating Nikki's cry of ecstasy.

Nikki buttered toast, humming a jazzy little tune under her breath. It was a beautiful day. Mickey sat at the table, eating dry fruity loops, waiting for Trace to finish his shower.

Nothing was different from every other morning of the past two months—except everything was different.

"Someone is in a good mood this morning," Trace said as he stepped around her to grab a plate from the counter. "Hey, buddy." He rubbed his hand affectionately over Mickey's head on his way to his customary seat at the table.

Though his tone was more subdued than teasing, she responded with a sassy grin.

"I won't deny it. I'm in a fabulous mood." Picking up two dishes, she carried them to the table, placing a plate of toast in the middle of the table and a bowl of scrambled eggs on Mickey's tray.

She hesitated beside Trace, to see if she'd get a good-morning kiss, but he dug into his food, not looking up.

"I'd think *you'd* be in a better mood," she said, on her way back to the kitchen for her own plate.

His green gaze shot up to meet hers. As enigmatic as always. She failed to read his mood, but got a clue when he asked, "No regrets?"

"I regret making you worry." She slid into the seat to his right. "But spending the night with you? No. What about you?" She tore off a piece of toast, took a tiny bite. "It did get a little out of control last night." She cleared her throat. "Twice."

The thunderstorm had caused some flooding, and he'd been called away not long after they first made love. She'd fallen asleep on the couch, waiting for him to get home, and woken up when he'd picked her up and carried her back to his bed for another round of luscious loving.

"Exactly. I didn't give you a lot of choice."

"Oh, Trace." Nikki reached for his hand. "Is that what's bothering you? Believe me, I was exactly where I wanted to be."

"You're sure?"

"Absolutely. I've wanted to be with you ever since you kissed me at the station."

He glanced at Mickey, as if gauging his reaction.

She sent him a wry grin. "I don't think you need to worry. He's a mite young to understand." She looked down at her plate and the shredded pieces of toast. "It sounds like you're the one with regrets."

"No, of course not." He set his fork down. "Last

night was amazing. You were incredible." His hand turned under hers, his fingers lacing with hers. "I've wanted to be with you, too."

"Really?" Pleased, she flushed.

"Oh, yeah." He lifted her hand to his mouth and kissed her knuckles. "You've taught me there are times when control is highly overrated." Then he released her and stood. "But I have to go."

"Oh. Of course." Flustered by the news he'd been lusting after her, she watched as he took his plate to the counter, then returned to kiss Mickey's head.

"Bye-bye, Daddy!" Mickey called.

Trace rounded the table and stopped next to her chair. He lifted her chin and planted a hard, passionate kiss on her lips. "See you later."

It was a promise that had heat flooding her cheeks while she watched him make his exit. After he was gone, she continued to sit in stunned confusion. From his stilted responses she really had begun to believe he regretted what had happened between them. She understood why, of course.

Honor and duty meant everything to Trace. For him to take advantage of someone in his care and under his protection would be repugnant to him. She liked to think their relationship had progressed beyond employer-employee to friendship long ago, and this was just the next step. But she accepted Trace would be more sensitive to the situation.

Still, the notion he felt shame for what had been

one of the most beautiful nights of her life nearly broke her heart.

She hoped she'd settled any concerns he had.

If his parting kiss meant anything, then she had to believe he'd accepted they were both consenting adults, capable of handling an intimate relationship.

Of course that begged the question: could she handle a relationship with him?

She loved Trace. And Mickey. A glance at the boy showed he'd managed to get as much egg on his tray and himself as he had in his mouth. Rising, she made quick work of cleaning him up, before placing him in his playpen with a few of his favorite toys.

"Have fun, kiddo." Even as she kissed his head and left him to play, her mind roiled with emotions.

She returned to the kitchen to clean up. So much of the time they'd spent together had been right here, in the dining room and kitchen. Had that given her a false sense of family? Of kinship with father and son? Had proximity caused her to manufacture feelings—?

No, that didn't feel right. She loved Trace. He made her feel alive, yet safe. His courage and honor. His seriousness and the fact he believed in what he did. The way he kept saying he was no good at emotions, yet he was infinitely gentle with Mickey and had honestly grown to love his son.

In truth, they worked well together. Their ideas of child-rearing and household scheduling jived so well she rarely felt suffocated by his need for control—

though she'd come to realize that was more her view of him than a reality. His was more a natural confidence, paired with discipline and decisiveness. He didn't have to have his way; when she gave input he listened. He was considerate, always letting her know when he'd be late, and intelligent, and he needed her to make him laugh.

Oh, yeah, she loved him.

And after last night she believed he cared about her, too. But was it enough to make a future together?

"So, are you going to take the job?" Amanda asked, from where she sat feeding Anthony in her small living room.

Nikki put the finishing touches to broccoli salad for their lunch. She'd finally listened to yesterday's cell messages on her way to her sister's, and one had been from Irvine Central School District. When she'd returned the call, they'd offered her a teaching position.

"I don't know," she equivocated, drizzling her special poppyseed dressing over both salads. She set the bowl of dressing on the counter and licked her finger, enjoying the tangy sweetness. One of her mother's recipes. "It's middle school kids."

Amanda took the plate Nikki handed her, then opened her arms so Nikki could take the sleeping baby and place him in his cradle next to the rocker.

"So?" Amanda demanded. "I know you prefer the little guys, but middle school kids need good teachers, too."

"Of course." Nikki waved away the obviousness of that comment. "But—"

She stopped, unable to come up with anything that wasn't a flat-out excuse for the truth. Which was she didn't want to go.

"But?" Amanda prompted.

Nikki just shook her head.

"Oh, Nikki." Amanda rocked forward in the chair to rest a hand on Nikki's arm. "You're not worried about leaving me, are you? Because Irvine is only a few hours away. We'd see each other all the time."

"Not like we do now," Nikki protested. This was one of her main objections. "I'd miss all the important milestones, all Anthony's firsts."

"You love to teach. And you'll be able to afford the condo you've been wanting. I can't believe you're not jumping on this opportunity."

"You don't understand."

"Then make me understand. Do you have another plan? You've always known what you want for your future. This isn't like you."

Nikki set her salad on the coffee table. "It's not my future I'm worried about right now. It's my life."

Amanda narrowed her eyes and scrutinized Nikki. She groaned. "Oh, no."

"I'm in love with Trace," Nikki confessed, reaching for her iced tea to avoid meeting her sister's eyes.

"Nikki, Nikki," Amanda commiserated, and then her eyes went wide. "Oh, my goodness, you *slept* with Trace. I knew it," she crowed, waking Anthony so he cried. "It's okay, baby," Amanda cooed, setting her salad bowl aside to pick up her son. "All is good. Auntie Nikki just got her some last night."

"Amanda!" Nikki said, outraged, looking to where Mickey played on a blanket on the floor. "There are babies present."

"Yeah, right. Mickey is going to run home and tell Daddy we were talking about him. Come on," Amanda coaxed her. "Give up the details. That man is hot."

Nikki fanned herself, agreeing without words, and actually needing the cooling air as memories of the night flashed through her head. Reliving Trace's slow, sure touch, his demanding kisses and driving passion, spiked her temperature despite the air-conditioner blowing full blast.

"That's one word to describe him."

When she left it at that, Amanda pleaded for more. "You can't leave me hanging."

"Let's just say the man is thorough in everything he does."

"So it was wonderful?"

"Oh, yeah."

"I'm so happy for you." Amanda did a little dance with Anthony. "All kidding aside, he's been good for you. I'm so glad you found your way to each other."

"What do you mean, he's been good for me?" Nikki asked, surprised by the comment.

"I've noticed the difference in you these past couple of months. You're more serene, less worried about details and protecting your freedom."

"Really? Huh." Now Amanda mentioned it, Nikki realized she *did* feel more relaxed these days, less pressured to exert her independence—not counting her arrogant episode yesterday. Another indication Trace was the right guy for her.

"Has he asked you to stay?"

"I haven't told him about the offer."

"Nikki!"

"What? I just picked up the message on the way over here."

"So, do you think he'll ask you?"

There was the question of the day.

Before she could answer, her cell rang. Perfect timing. She scrambled for her purse and pulled out her phone. Five minutes later she hung up.

"That didn't sound good," Amanda said.

"No." Nikki swallowed around the lump in her throat. "That was the nanny agency. Trace contacted them today to ask for a new nanny."

Nikki hit the bungalow at full steam. She was surprised to see Trace's official vehicle in the drive. Lucky for him she hadn't had to hunt him down to deliver Mickey into his care, because she had a few words to say to the sniveling coward he probably wouldn't want the world to hear.

The rat hadn't even had the guts to tell her to leave to her face.

Hmm. She tapped her fingers on the steering wheel; maybe she should wait until he left? Then she could pack in peace and find him some place highly public to have her showdown. Why should she care what people thought of him when he didn't care what her agency thought of her?

He deserved it.

But Mickey didn't. She checked on him in the rear-view mirror. He'd fallen asleep on the ride from Amanda's. He'd come so far. Going from a sad little boy, emotionally and physically, to a healthy toddler all giggles and hugs.

She was going to miss him so much.

Better to make the break as fast and as quietly as possible for his sake. With that in mind, she let herself inside.

Trace was in the kitchen, sandwich makings in front of him. Ignoring him, she carried Mickey to his bed-room and put him in his crib. Heart breaking, she ran her hand through his big-boy hair. "I love you, baby," she whispered. "Have a happy life."

When she turned, Trace stood in the doorway. "Hey, I came home hoping we could have lunch."

"Right. Even the condemned get a last meal." She brushed past him.

"What? Hey." He grabbed her hand and drew her to a stop. "You're upset."

"You think?" She twisted her wrist to free her hand. "Let go. You don't get to touch me anymore."

He frowned, but released her. "What is wrong with you?"

She shook her head and walked away. Fast and quiet, she reminded herself. For Mickey.

"Nikki?" For a weak-kneed slug he easily kept pace with her, staying hard on her heels. "Would you stop and talk to me?"

"Now you want to talk? Oh, I forgot. You're real good at talking. To everyone but me."

"Okay—enough." No longer conciliatory, he blocked her way when she headed for the back door leading to her apartment. "You're not going anywhere. Calm down and tell me what changed between this morning and this afternoon."

His supposed obtuseness chafed, making her angrier. "Don't pretend you don't know. You may be a coward, but at least own up to what you did."

"Coward?" he said, low and fierce. "Explain."

She walked away, put the couch between them. She needed distance. More, she needed to pack and get away from here—before she lost any more of herself.

She paced to the fireplace and back. She couldn't do it. She couldn't walk away without some answers.

"You tell me. I was beginning to believe you were going to make the change from broken, unemotional man to a loving man and father. I was wrong."

"I'm not broken," he denied, crossing his arms over his chest, closing himself off. "And I warned you I was no good at emotion."

"Oh, did that sting?" It was wrong to take pleasure in hurting him, but something—rage, or a dim hope she might break through the stone fortress he called a heart so

Mickey didn't suffer the same fate in the future—kept her pushing. "The truth usually does. And when you're so absorbed with dodging the pain of loss and rejection you can't see the good for the bad, then, yeah, you're broken."

"You don't know what you're talking about."

"I know I've heard the bad parts of your past—how your mom abandoned you and your father, how he was an unemotional man. But I've never heard any good memories."

His eyelids flickered, but nothing else moved on his frozen features.

"Before your mother left were there any happy moments? Laughter? Hugs? If not, you were better off without her. And she shouldn't be given any power over your future at all."

"She has no power over me."

"Oh, she does. You're afraid to trust your feelings because you're afraid it won't be enough, like it wasn't enough for her, and you'll be left hurting again. She has power over you, over Mickey, even over me. And it infuriates me."

"You're leaving. Just like she did."

"No, you're pushing me away. I won't stay where I'm not wanted. Life is too short. I'll find someone who will love me back and I'll be happy." Continuing to pace, she wrapped both arms around herself, trying to hold in the pain. "That's one lesson I learned from my mother. I was so worried about finding and protecting my own personal freedom I stayed away from her, for fear she'd steal some of it away from me. Instead I lost precious time with her I'll never get back."

"Nikki." He came around the couch, but she held up a hand to ward him off. He stopped. "How did I push you away? I'm here. I came home for lunch in the middle of the day to see you."

"Please." She didn't bother to keep the disdain from her voice. "If you wanted me to leave why didn't you just talk to me, instead of calling my agency and putting my professional reputation at risk?"

"I didn't…" He hesitated.

Nikki hugged herself, waiting for his explanation, for the big reveal.

The silence ended with Mickey's cries.

She closed her eyes. That was it, then. She'd never know what had driven Trace to push her away. Oh, who was she kidding? She'd just laid out all the reasons.

"You'd better get Mickey," she told Trace. "I need to pack." Walking around him, she let herself out of the house.

Trace watched Nikki walk out of his life. A racking sadness overwhelmed him, rooting him to the spot. His chest felt hollow where his heart should be.

Almost immediately the door opened and she reappeared. Hope soared.

"I can't do this now. I'll come back for my things when you and Mickey aren't here." She moved to the front door, opened it. "Mickey's been at the community center daycare several times. He knows some of the kids. He'll be all right there until the agency can send over someone new." She stared at Trace for a minute, her eyes as sad as he felt. Finally she shook her head. "Goodbye."

And then she was gone. Out of his life. Ready to be a memory. And he let her go, let her think he'd called for a replacement because he didn't have the guts to let an intelligent, beautiful, loving woman into his small little life.

The earth pitched and rolled off kilter, never to be righted again. Cold surrounded him. She'd taken all the warmth with her.

She prized her freedom. The one thing he couldn't give her. And he didn't have anything better to offer. Best for her to go now than after he'd allowed her to become his whole world.

He shook himself, heard Mickey's cries, and thought he was already screwing up.

Mickey's tears dried up when he saw Trace. He jumped up and down and grinned. Trace lifted him, his heart melting when Mickey laid his head on his shoulder.

Nikki had been right. Mickey's love and trust were unconditional, a gift Trace had never expected and vowed to treasure. "It's you and me now, kid."

He carried the baby into the living room and set him down next to the coffee table with a couple of plastic cars.

"Neeki?" Mickey asked, looking around, as if he understood something was wrong.

"Nikki bye-bye," Trace told him.

"Bye-bye work?" The kid wanted specifics.

Trace wouldn't lie to him. "No. Just bye-bye."

"No." Mickey shook his head wildly. "Neeki!" He toddled around the coffee table, grabbed Trace's hand and pulled. "Neeki."

Mickey wanted Trace to go after Nikki, to chase her down and bring her back. "You might actually have a chance with her. She loves you." Trace had no doubt about her feelings for Mickey. "I could probably have parlayed her affection for you into something, but I couldn't settle this time. Not this time."

"Daddy!" Mickey pulled on him. "Neeki."

"This is my fault not yours," Trace told him. "She's going to find someone who will love her…" The words trailed off as he replayed what she'd said in his head and realization dawned. The world slowly righted itself. "'*I'll find someone who will love me back.*' She loves me."

He picked up Mickey, swung him around and planted a big kiss on his mouth. "She loves me. Let's go bring her home."

Nikki brushed the wetness from her cheeks, angry with herself for the tears. She'd started the day with such hope, and now her heart ached, broken because she loved a man too damaged to risk being hurt again.

Well, it was his loss. She'd have given him her love and devotion, traded her independence for a family. She'd have been the best thing that had ever happened to him.

The vehicle in the next lane honked. She glanced over and saw it was Trace. For a moment joy swelled and filled her.

He'd followed her.

Then reality hit. He probably wanted her to honor her contract until a replacement could be found. She took pride in her reputation, but that was an assignment she couldn't accept.

Police lights flashed in her rearview mirror. He was pulling her over. She shook her head and pushed her foot down on the accelerator, defying his authority. He had no legitimate reason to stop her, and her battered heart couldn't take anything more today.

"Pull your vehicle to the side of the road and stop," his disembodied voice demanded.

"I don't think so." She continued to defy him, knowing it would end there. To pursue her any more blatantly would invite public notice and a rejection he wouldn't invite.

"Nikki, pull over now. I only called the agency to free you to accept the teaching job."

She blinked at his reflection in the rearview mirror. Determination stamped his features. He'd known about the offer? She saw heads turning in their direction as she passed the community center. Her hands tightened on the wheel as she turned on to Main.

She was safe. No way he'd expose himself in the middle of town. It would take more than mere affection for him to take such a step.

She deserved a man with the capacity to love as big as she did. Trace had proved he wasn't that man.

The Sheriff's vehicle pulled onto the street behind her, and her heart began to pound faster even as she cautioned herself against reading too much into it.

"Nikki Rhodes, I love you." Not only did he declare himself, he ramped up the volume. "Please stop."

Her throat constricted with emotion, love for him bursting through her in joy and euphoria. He loved her.

Wait. She breathed deep, forcing herself to slow down and to question if he'd really changed and could open himself to a loving relationship. But it was useless.

Trace loved her!

"Nikki." His voice boomed again. "Please pull over so I can ask you to be my wife and Mickey's mother."

"Yes," she whispered, as people turned on both sides of the street to observe their small parade. "Yes, please." Her hands shook as she pulled to the side of the road in front of What a Woman Wants. Women flowed from the shop to see what was going on.

Ignoring the rest of the world, she pushed open her door, ran to the man who held her heart and flung herself into his arms. Trace caught her—as she'd known he would—and swung her around, his head buried against her.

After a moment he lifted his eyes to meet hers. The love she saw shining in the emerald depths made her breath catch.

"You just announced yourself in front of the entire town."

"I love you, and I don't care who knows it." The words reinforced the pledge in his gaze. "I couldn't chance losing you." He set her on her feet and kissed her, his mouth on hers in the sweetest of promises.

"Neeki!" Mickey clapped his hands in the backseat of the SUV.

They looked from the baby to each other. Trace brushed the hair behind her ear. "Marry me. Be the mother of my children. What do you say? Let's give a dog a happy home?"

"Yes," she whispered for him alone, and then, loud enough for the world to hear, she repeated, "Yes!"

Pulling his head down to her, she kissed him, putting all her love into the embrace. Applause exploded around them, the perfect soundtrack for the perfect moment.

NURSE, NANNY...
BRIDE!

BY
ALISON ROBERTS

Alison Roberts lives in Christchurch, New Zealand. She began her working career as a primary school teacher, but now juggles available working hours between writing and active duty as an ambulance officer. Throwing in a large dose of parenting, housework, gardening and pet-minding keeps life busy, and teenage daughter Becky is responsible for an increasing number of days spent on equestrian pursuits. Finding time for everything can be a challenge, but the rewards make the effort more than worthwhile.

CHAPTER ONE

SO THIS was what it felt like to faint.

As if a plug had been pulled out of your brain and all the blood was disappearing in a rush to leave a curious buzzing sensation in its wake.

Alice tried to move her feet but they were lead weights. Just as well she could still move her arm. Catching hold of the metal rail along the side of one of the few empty beds in this emergency department was her best chance of remaining upright.

'Are you okay, Ally?' The voice of the nurse lowering the rail on the other side of the bed seemed to be coming from a very long way away. 'You've gone as white as a sheet.'

'I…' Alice was gripping the rail as if her life depended on it. The black spots interfering with her vision were starting to fade. Any second now and she would be able to take a second look. She must have been mistaken, surely? It couldn't possibly really be Andrew Barrett standing on the other side of this department. He was a world away. In London. A world she'd been only too happy to leave behind in the end.

'Sit!' Strong hands were guiding Alice towards the chair beside the bed. The one the patient's relatives usually sat on. 'Sit down and put your head between your knees.'

Alice resisted the pressure. 'I'm okay, Jo.'

She was. The buzzing was gone. Blood was reaching her brain again almost as fast as it had left, thanks to the increase in her heart rate. 'I'm just a bit...'

Shocked. Slapped by a reminder of a past she had worked very hard to escape from. It probably wasn't even him. Just someone who looked a bit like him from the side. Tall and well built with slightly scruffy dark blond hair and the weathered skin of a man who loved to be outdoors. A figure familiar enough to push a lot of old buttons.

Bright ones like desire.

Much darker ones such as envy.

'Exhausted?' Jo supplied. 'I'm not surprised. What time did you get back home last night?'

'About eleven, I guess.'

'And how long was the drive?'

'More than ten hours. Mostly thanks to the radiator boiling with my old truck trying to pull a horse float over the pass.'

'Oh, no! You poor thing. I'll bet it took an hour or more to offload Ben and get things sorted when you got home, too. You probably haven't had more than a few hours' sleep and that's on top of a week of having to sort your gran's property and everything.' Jo's arm came around Alice in a swift hug. 'Have you even had any breakfast, hon?'

'No.' In fact, it was hard to remember when she'd last

had a proper meal. No wonder she'd nearly fainted. Or was imagining things. The swirl of disturbing emotions was still there. Making her stomach feel a shade queasy.

'Go into the staff room right now and make yourself some toast. And hot chocolate. I'll tidy up in here.'

Again, Alice shook her head. The route to the staff room would mean having to brush past the two men who were peering at one of the wall-mounted X-ray screens on that side of the department. And maybe she hadn't been imagining things. Maybe one of those men was someone she hadn't expected and really didn't want to see. Ever again. It would be too hard going down that particular road again. Negotiating painfully bumpy terrain that led absolutely nowhere.

'I'm fine now, really.' Alice smiled. She was. She could move again. She lowered the rail on the bed and tugged at the sheet that needed changing. 'And it was worth all the hassle. I couldn't have left Ben for more than a week when there was nobody to keep an eye on him and the beach rides more than made up for the stress of having to clean out Gran's place. The last tenants made a hell of a mess. It's no wonder it barely sold for enough to cover the mortgage.'

'At least it's settled.' Jo was moving back to the other side of the bed as Alice rolled up the sheet and stuffed it into the linen bag. 'Having to pay that on top of your rent for the last year's been a killer, hasn't it?'

Alice nodded. There was nothing she could say. It had just been one of those things. It had to be done so she'd done it. The same way she had dealt with all the hard stuff that life had a habit of dumping her in. Head on. Standing tall. Fainting was definitely not an option.

Alice took a deep breath and deliberately shifted her gaze. She was ready to get her bearings.

'Who *is* that?' she asked calmly. 'Talking to Peter?'

Jo glanced over her shoulder. When she turned back to Alice, her eyebrows were a little higher and a smile tugged at one corner of her mouth. 'Andy Barrett. New consultant. Cute, huh?'

Alice couldn't say anything. Hopefully Jo wouldn't interpret her stare as anything more than curiosity.

'He's English. Started work here the day after you left last week. We were all surprised. Turns out that Dave had health issues he didn't want anyone to know about and finding his replacement had been kept well under wraps. Apparently we really scored getting this Dr Barrett. He's been the head honcho at some big London hospital for years. Can't remember which one. Hammersmith, maybe.'

Alice couldn't trust herself to open her mouth. If she did she might tell Jo that it hadn't been Hammersmith. It had been the same hospital she had worked in herself for over a year.

Until she'd been as good as fired.

By one Dr Andrew Barrett.

Jo didn't know any of that story. No one here did and that was exactly the way Alice wanted it to be. No way was she getting pulled back anywhere near that black period of humiliation again. Not now. Apart from the death of her grandmother a year ago and the ten days leave she had just taken to sort out the eventual sale of the isolated cottage the only remaining member of her family had lived in, Alice's life was finally on track again.

She was still staring at the profile of the man who presented a new and very unwelcome threat. Both professional *and* personal.

Why had he come all the way to the opposite side of the earth and picked the one place that was hers? It wasn't as if New Zealand was *that* small. He could have picked one of the larger cities in the north island. Maybe they didn't have as many ski fields or mountains to climb but they had plenty of water. He could have learned to sail. Or surf!

Maybe Pam would know why. Contact with the only friend she had kept from her time in London was well overdue and if what she was seeking was the kind of gossip she deliberately avoided, so be it. Knowledge was power and Alice certainly needed a boost.

Just making the decision to email Pam gave Alice the illusion of regaining some control. About to drag her gaze away from the new member of staff, she only just caught the movement as he raised his left hand to indicate something of interest on the image.

Unaware of the frown on her face, she turned to help Jo smooth and tuck fresh linen onto the bed. The last time she had seen Andy Barrett he had been wearing a wedding ring. A tight band of gold that had successfully suffocated any stupid fantasies she might have nurtured.

He wasn't wearing it now.

The case in Resus 1 was a trauma. A thirty-five-year-old woman who was well known to emergency department staff: one of their 'frequent flyers'. Her boyfriend had gang affiliations and was only too ready to use his fists and his feet when something displeased him, but

Janine had steadfastly refused to lay any complaints against him on earlier visits. Maybe this time would be different, the triage nurse told the consultant. It was the worst punishment they'd ever seen her receive.

Janine lay, oddly quiet, on the bed, her face now so swollen it was obviously painful for her to speak.

'No!' she managed in response to Andrew's careful suggestion. 'No police. I told you. I fell down the stairs.'

Yeah...right. Stairs that had knuckles and heavy boots. The lacerations on her eyebrow and upper lip needed extensive suturing. A cheekbone was probably fractured and Andrew didn't like the ugly purple bruises already appearing on her ribs as a nurse cut away her clothing.

'Can you take a deep breath for me?' Andrew was using both hands to examine her ribs as gently as he could.

'*Ahhh!*' It was the first indication Janine had given of her level of pain.

'Pretty sore, isn't it?' Her breathing was adequate but unsurprisingly shallow. 'What score would you give it on a scale of one to ten, Janine? Ten being the worst.'

'I'm all right.' Janine sounded as if she was holding her breath now. She had her eyes closed and beads of perspiration mingled with the blood on her forehead. She was a long way from being all right.

'Anything else hurting that much?'

A tear escaped puffy eyelids. 'My...arm, I guess.'

The sleeve of a ragged jersey was being peeled away and the deformity of Janine's wrist and lower arm was obvious. Another fracture. Almost open. Andrew could see the bone just under the skin. Checking limb baselines like movement and sensation and perfusion seemed inadvisable until the fracture was secured. Even trying to wriggle her fingers might be enough to break the skin and risk infection. He turned to the nurse and lowered his voice.

'She didn't come in by ambulance, did she?'

Jo shook her head. 'Private car. She was left outside Reception to make her own way inside.'

Andrew's mouth tightened as he shook his head in disgust. He had to bury the anger that might have made him storm out of here if the bastard was hanging around. He had to rid his head of the ugly words he would like to have said to the kind of man who could treat a woman like this.

And, most of all, he had to dismiss the memory of what it felt like to be suspected of being that kind of man. 'Let's get an IV line in and a splint on this arm,' he ordered crisply. 'We'll get some pain relief on board and then do a thorough secondary survey before we start the X-rays.'

Another nurse entered the resuscitation area as Andrew slipped a tourniquet around Janine's arm and tightened it. 'I'm going to put a small needle in your hand,' he warned his patient. 'Then we can give you something for the pain. Okay?'

Janine nodded. The movement made her wince. In his peripheral vision, as he anchored a vein and slipped a cannula into place, Andrew could see the new nurse sliding a well padded cardboard splint under Janine's broken arm and then starting to secure it. Her movements were sure and careful enough not to cause further damage or pain.

He taped the cannula and looked up properly this time, intending to let the nurse know that she'd done a good job. It was just as well he hadn't done this a few seconds ago. He might have missed the vein completely.

Alice Palmer?

He'd known she came from New Zealand. Why had it not even occurred to him that she might be working in a hospital here again? Because the odds of it being the same one he'd been offered a job in by an old acquaintance were so small? Or was it because he'd been so determined to put any thoughts of her and the period of his life she'd been a part of completely behind him?

How ironic that he'd come *this* far to get away from it all. To start again and here it was, staring him in the face. Right beside a case that graphically represented most of what he'd been trying to escape.

He stared back.

How much did Alice know? Not much, presumably, because she'd lost her job before it had started. Unfair dismissal, as it had turned out. And he'd been responsible. He had had every intention of telling her, but when he'd gone to the address the woman in Personnel had given, he'd found an empty house with a 'For Sale' sign outside that had a cheerful 'Sold' sticker planted in the centre. It had been six months after the event, in any case, and someone in Emergency had suggested that Alice had left the country.

He couldn't tell her now. It was ancient history and here she was, working in a senior position so it hadn't affected her career. And if he did tell her, she'd want to know how he knew and that was what had had to be left behind.

For Emmy's sake.

He held her gaze and kept his tone carefully neutral as his brain worked overtime, tossing up whether to acknowledge the fact that they knew each other.

'I'd like some morphine drawn up, please,' he said.

No. He couldn't acknowledge her. That would bring a flurry of interest from others. Questions he didn't want to hear, let alone answer. His next words emerged before he'd had a chance to even think them through. A form of attack as a defensive shield.

'If you have keys to the drug cabinet, that is.'

Heat scorched Alice's cheeks.

She dragged her eyes away from his face. An older-looking face. Thinner and far more distant. Had he changed so much from the man she remembered or was this coolness due to a determination to hide recognition? So this was how it was going to be. They were not going to acknowledge having worked together, let alone knowing what they did know about each other.

A warning shot had been fired. If she said anything about the rumours she'd been hearing before she left London, he would warn her superiors that allowing her access to restricted drugs might be inadvisable.

The unfairness of it added a new element to the emotional turmoil Alice was dealing with. Despite the traitorous reaction of her body earlier, she knew she wasn't in love with the man any more. She'd got over that a very long time ago. About when she'd been standing in front of his desk and he'd said he couldn't trust her enough to let her keep the job she loved.

She'd tried to hate him for that but hadn't succeeded.

Her heart had been incapable of flipping the coin to embrace the dark side of love. Especially when her head, coupled with an innate sense of fairness, had forced her to acknowledge that he'd only been doing what he had to do as head of department. Quite generously, really, when he'd offered her the opportunity to resign instead of launching an official investigation and a paper trail that would have haunted the rest of her working life.

What was really unfair was that she'd never believed the rumours about *him*. Even now, with the dark emotions sparked by seeing the poor battered woman they were treating at the moment and the cool distance he had placed between himself and an old colleague, she knew he was as incapable of hurting someone deliberately as she was of stealing and taking drugs. If Andrew had been interested enough to actually get to know her properly, he would have had—would still have—the same kind of faith in her.

Clearly, he didn't. The implication beneath his request for morphine had been a deliberate reminder of the humiliating rumours she'd been unable to disprove. That he hadn't trusted her. That he'd never really seen who she was. That hurt.

Quite apart from being an intimately personal slight, mud had a habit of sticking. Enough to ruin lives. Alice actually felt sick to her stomach as she pulled an ampoule of morphine from the cabinet and signed the register. She could feel Andrew watching her.

Jo did the drug check with her. The name of the drug. The dose. The expiry date. She watched as Alice snapped the top of the ampoule and slid a needle in to draw it up. Try as she might, Alice couldn't disguise the subtle trembling of her hands.

'You still need toast,' Jo whispered.

Alice needed something a lot more than food. She needed to be a long way away from their new consultant. How could she possibly work with him when he was watching every move she made? Knowing that, despite the best of intentions and for very different reasons, she would have to fight the desire to watch every move he made? Looking for a reminder of the man she remembered. Hoping not to find one, possibly, so she could decide it had been a lucky escape and move on, once and for all.

She could switch departments, she thought wildly. Go into Cardiology. Or Paediatrics. Or Theatre. No. This was where she loved to work. Where she got a taste of everything and the adrenaline rush of helping to deal with major, life-threatening situations. This department was a big part of why her life was on track again.

She drew up the saline to dilute the morphine. She taped the ampoule to the barrel of the syringe to identify its contents and then she walked back to the bed to hand it to Andrew.

Watching Janine relax as the effect of the narcotic took the edge off her pain had a curiously similar effect on Alice. She eyed the bruised and swollen face of the woman again. The marks of brutality on the woman's ribs and the misshapen arm now resting in a splint. The thought of someone enduring a beating like this was horrific. Sickening. Alice raised her gaze, knowing that her reaction would be evident in her eyes.

Deliberately capturing the gaze of Andrew Barrett before that reaction dimmed.

Maybe she hadn't believed any of it but allowing

Andrew to think she might have was possibly the only defence she had.

They both had something they didn't want their colleagues to know. Things they didn't want to lose. Alice was more vulnerable. She had something she didn't want Andrew to know, as well. It was good that he'd chosen not to acknowledge her. Distance was safe and, if it stopped being safe, then she was prepared to fight, if that was what it would take to protect herself.

Andrew's gaze was steady. So was he, it told her.

For the moment at least, this appeared to be a stand-off.

This was a disaster.

Alice clearly knew a lot more than he would have expected. Was she still in touch with old friends in London? People who would be only too happy to gossip about a police investigation involving a consultant emergency physician? That she knew too much was as unfortunate as knowing he was perpetuating a lie by letting her think he still believed the worst of her. But what else could he do?

He'd come this far and had found what appeared to be the perfect place for himself and Emmy. They'd only been here for a little over a week but he'd never seen his daughter so happy. He knew he'd made the right decision despite how hard leaving had been. Running away from it all had gone against the grain so hard it had been painful. An admission of defeat that some would probably interpret as guilt, but he'd done it for his daughter. He wasn't going to let his little girl grow up anywhere within reach of a tainted past.

He couldn't keep running. The world of medicine was surprisingly small and, no matter where you went, someone always knew someone else. Look at the way Dave had contacted him about the possibility of this position when they hadn't seen each other since a short stint in an American hospital together ten years ago.

Andrew was between a rock and a hard place, here. Damned by his conscience whichever way he turned. The unwanted distraction filled his mind as he waited for Janine's X-ray views to appear on the screen in front of him. Should he follow his first instinct and simply talk privately to Alice? Tell the truth and then apologize? Lay his cards on the table and ask for her help?

Why would she want to do that? She'd not only lost her job. When he'd heard that she'd left the country, he'd also heard that the sale of her house had been forced by the bank. That she'd lost everything. He could have talked to her then. Tried to make amends, even, but nobody had seemed to know where she'd gone. And then the real trouble had started and he'd forgotten everything other than trying to survive. To keep Emmy safe.

What could he say now? An excuse that he couldn't have simply taken her word for her innocence and an apology for any inconvenience caused was hardly going to clear the air. It might actually make her jump at the chance for revenge.

The notion was jarring. It didn't fit with the Alice Palmer he remembered from five years ago. The attractive, competent nurse working in his emergency department. A young woman doing her O.E. who'd made friends with his fiancée. Who'd come to their wedding, in fact. She'd been good at her job. Caring. The evi-

dence that she'd been stealing morphine and other restricted drugs had been shocking. Unbelievable, really,
but you never knew with women. Look at how things
with Melissa had turned out.

Oh, *God...* No! Andrew rubbed his temple and then
raked his fingers through his hair. He didn't want to
think about Mel. Or London. Or any of what had been
left behind and that was why working with Alice Palmer
was a complication he didn't know how to resolve.

Images began appearing on the wall-mounted computer screen. It was a relief to focus as he scrolled
through them. The cheekbone probably needed wiring.
The nasty fragmented fracture of the radius and ulna
would require surgery. Orthopaedics were on the way
and someone from plastic surgery should be contacted
to deal with the facial suturing that could be done in
Theatre as well. Andrew turned back to Resus 1. He had
a job to do here. His patient needed care. And protection. A delicate situation when he couldn't know
whether it might make things worse for Janine by encouraging her to lay a complaint about her boyfriend.

Alice would be in Resus 1 as well. Another delicate
situation and Andrew needed more time to try and
figure out what he was going to do about it. Maybe he
could buy time by putting some distance between them.
Adjust his shifts, perhaps, so they spent as little time as
possible in the department together?

No. Why should he have to do that? He was a senior
consultant in this department now and he needed to
start the way he intended to carry on. Alice was a nurse.
A very good nurse, probably, but as far as a balance of
power went, it was weighted firmly on his side. An ad-

vantage that Andrew couldn't afford not to use. He needed to take control and make sure he kept it.

The department was relatively quiet for a long time after Janine had been taken to Theatre. Downright boring, really. Alice was looking after an epileptic man who was sleeping off the post-ictal phase of his seizure, a diabetic patient from a rest home who needed her insulin dose adjusted and another very elderly incontinent woman, Miss Stanbury, who was still suffering the effects of a gastric disturbance and needed rehydrating and frequent changing.

When an ambulance brought in a forty-year-old man with a markedly accelerated heart rate, Alice was more than ready to take on the case.

'This is Roger,' the paramedic told her. 'Narrow complex tachycardia. Rate 196. Oxygen saturation ninety-eight per cent. No cardiac history.'

Roger looked pale and frightened but he wasn't in the kind of danger he would have been in if the spikes on his ECG were wide enough to suggest the ventricles of his heart were in trouble. Alice enjoyed cardiology. She could read a twelve lead ECG better than most junior doctors and she particularly loved this kind of case. One where a dramatic result and relief for the patient could be provided.

'Have you got any chest pain?' she asked Roger.

He shook his head. 'I feel a bit short of breath, that's all. And I can feel my heart.'

'Have you ever felt it going this fast before?'

'No.'

Alice helped the paramedics transfer Roger to the

bed in Resus 2, where they had good telemetry facilities to monitor his heart. She raised the back of the bed so their patient was sitting up, which would help his breathing effort. Jo came in as she was transferring the oxygen tubing from the portable cylinder to the overhead outlet.

'SVT,' Alice told her. 'Is Peter around?'

'No.' Another figure pushed through the curtains as the paramedics took the stretcher out of the small area. 'I've got this case.' Andrew was holding the patient report form the ambulance crew had supplied. A long strip of pink paper recording the cardiac rhythm en route was attached to it and he was looking at the monitor beside the bed as he spoke.

He introduced himself to his patient, who was still looking alarmed.

'Am I having a heart attack?'

'It's one of the possibilities we're going to investigate,' Andrew told him. 'But, so far, we're not seeing any sign of it. Your heart's going a bit too fast to really see what's happening so we're going to try and slow it down for you. Try and relax.'

Roger made a sound like a strangled bark of laughter and Andrew's smile was sympathetic.

'I know. Easy for me to say, standing on this side of the equation, isn't it?' He touched his patient's arm. 'I know this is scary but we're on the case and you're in the best possible place to get things sorted.'

His smile and his touch had a visible effect on Roger, who lay back against the pillow with a sigh and a nod.

They had a hopefully *invisible* effect on Alice.

This was a glimpse of the real Andrew. How many times had she seen the effects of this man's words and smile and touch? She hadn't really been aware of how nobody else quite measured up to the standards Andrew Barrett had set. Or how much she'd missed working with him.

Until now.

Andrew had turned to Jo. 'Got a straw handy?'

'Sure.'

'And grab a technician to come and do a twelve lead, will you, please?'

'I can do that,' Alice said quietly.

'Fine. Go ahead.' Andrew was pulling on gloves. 'I'll get the bloods off.'

Alice could have managed that as well, but maybe the consultants were also finding their day somewhat dull. She pulled the machine she needed from the corner and began attaching all the electrodes needed to get a complete picture of the electrical activity of Roger's heart.

Jo was cutting a short length of plastic straw.

'I want you to take a deep breath,' Andrew instructed Roger. 'Seal your lips around the straw and then blow through it as hard as you can for as long as you can.'

A valsalva manoeuvre was one of the dramatic ways to get this kind of cardiac arrhythmia to revert to normal. They all watched the monitor screen as Roger's face reddened with the effort. There was no change to the rate.

'Get your breath back,' Andrew said. 'And then we'll give it another go.'

The respite gave Alice a chance to get the twelve lead ECG. The electrodes were all in place.

'Try and keep as still as you can,' she asked Roger as she pressed the start button.

But he was too out of breath to comply and the trace was nothing like the clean image Alice had hoped for. Dammit! She screwed up the sheet of paper, hoping that Andrew wasn't watching.

'Let's try that again,' she said calmly. 'If you could manage to hold your breath for just a second or two while the machine captures a picture, that would be great.'

Roger managed but the sheet that emerged was missing several pieces of information that it should have recorded.

'You've lost a leg lead.' Andrew was probably looking at her with the same kind of studied neutrality his tone held. Alice felt her cheeks reddening as she pushed the sticky patch more firmly to the skin of Roger's left ankle.

This was mortifying. Such a simple task that she was more than capable of performing, but she was managing to make herself look completely incompetent. Worst of all, this was more important than it should have been. The old need to attract praise by being the best was so ingrained it was automatic. She still wanted to be noticed. To be *seen*. How pathetic was that?

Andrew was getting Roger to blow through the straw again so he'd be out of breath and she'd have to wait to try getting the recording again. When she did and it worked beautifully, Andrew wasn't even paying attention. Peter had come in and they were discussing the next management step. Because their patient was wide awake, they couldn't use an external electrical charge to the heart to revert the rhythm unless they sedated him heavily. The better option was to try adenosine—a drug that gave the chemical equivalent of a jolt of electricity.

It usually worked a treat and Alice knew exactly what to do. The procedure was tricky because the drug had a very short time of being effective. It had to be injected into the right arm to get to the heart as fast as possible and it had to be chased along with a large bolus of saline. Two people had to work in unison and Alice had been the one to push the flush on many occasions.

A favourite task. A bit of a challenge to get the timing right; a few seconds delay and, sometimes with even the first dose, they would watch the screen and see the heart rate magically decreasing. The adenosine was drawn up. The big fifty mil syringe of saline was drawn up. There was one port of the IV line and both needles would go in at the same time.

Peter was hanging around to watch. The paramedics had come back from tidying their ambulance and they wanted to watch, too. Andrew had the adenosine in one hand, the saline in the other. It took two hands to push that flush as fast as possible so he needed a nurse. One who knew what she was doing.

'Alice is experienced,' Peter said. 'Done this a few times, haven't you, Ally?'

She nodded, aware of a wave of pleasure at the boost to her self-esteem as she moved around the head of the bed to change sides. The perfect twelve lead ECG was sitting on top of the machine she was leaving behind but it had yet to be seen. Alice was more than happy to be given an opportunity to redeem her apparent lack of competence.

But Andrew was looking at the nurse who was already standing by his side. 'Have you done this before, Jo?'

'No.'

'Nothing to it. Hold the barrel of the syringe firmly and put the base of your other thumb on the plunger. I'll inject the adenosine and as soon as you see my plunger hit the bottom, you push in the saline as fast as you can.'

Jo shot a glance at Alice, who had stopped in her tracks and was probably looking as dismayed as she felt.

Alice glanced at Peter but the head of department merely raised an eyebrow. If their new team member wanted to take the time to help staff develop their skills then he could hardly protest.

Neither could Alice, despite feeling even more mortified than she had when she'd messed up getting that ECG trace.

'You're IV qualified, aren't you?' Andrew asked Jo.

'Yes.'

'Then let's do this.'

Jo positioned herself closer to Andrew. Their gloved hands were touching. Side by side. Syringe by syringe. Of course, Jo had no trouble performing her part of the task and then everyone was looking at the monitor.

Alice heard the distinctive sigh from Roger which showed that the drug had reached its target, but she didn't wait to enjoy the potential satisfaction of seeing a successful result. Nobody noticed as she turned and quietly slipped out of the Resus area.

Alice wasn't needed in here. And she certainly wasn't wanted by the consultant in charge.

CHAPTER TWO

Not being able to afford a decent car had its advantages.

You could throw anything into the back of this ancient four-wheel drive. Dogs, saddles, dirty covers—it made no difference. You could also have your foot flat to the floor and not break the speed limit. Even if you were very angry and upset and weren't even thinking about how fast to take the corners, you were safe.

Living this far out of town had its advantages, too. You left the city well behind and could see only the green of paddocks and hills and the deep blue of a late afternoon sky. Autumn colours gilded tall poplar trees and animals grazed peacefully beneath them. Sheep and cattle and fat pet ponies. A goat on a chain was eating the long grass of someone's roadside verge.

Work was left behind along with the city and the further away Alice got, the more she could feel all the upsets of her day receding. Some time out was exactly what she desperately needed. Escape to the place she loved more than any patch of the earth she had ever discovered. Turning off the main road, she drove into a valley. Towards the end of this road was a property

bordered by a river and enclosed by hills like a geo-
graphical hug. Hidden from the world and, for the
moment at least, entirely hers.

The long driveway was lined by oak trees that were
well over a hundred years old. Leaves drifted lazily
from great heights and Alice rolled down her window
to smell the season. A hint of damp moss and rich soil.
A faint whiff of smoke from a bonfire on some neighbouring farm. The chimneys of the enormous old house
weren't giving off any smoke, of course. Why would
they, when the house had been empty for so long?

Finding new owners seemed unlikely in the short
term. Who could afford a rather rundown old mansion
these days when it was a good twenty minutes drive
from the city? The cost of petrol alone would put people
off, never mind the extensive renovations needed and
the effort of keeping up a hilly property of at least fifty
acres. The longer it took, the better as far as Alice was
concerned. She was more than happy to be here as the
only human tenant.

Alice took the fork in the driveway before she got
more than a glimpse of the big house through the trees.
She drove towards the river now. Towards the cottage
that had once housed shearers and had been rented out
a year ago to her friend, Mandy. Seeing the small weath-
erboard dwelling ahead of her, with her dog, Jake,
guarding the front step, Alice could finally let go of everything bad the day had thrown at her.

The shock of being pulled back to a past she had
thought long gone. Having the ashes of a distant one-
sided romance stirred and finding it still showed a
dismaying warmth. Enough of a glow to make the em-

barrassment of being deliberately put in her place as a less important staff member far more intense. Last, but by no means least, was the knowledge that if she wanted to keep the life she'd worked so hard to create for herself, she really would have to fight for it.

Alice climbed out of the truck and crouched to hug her dog, burying her face against his shaggy neck for a moment, feeling his whole body wag pleasure in her return. Alice let out her breath in a long sigh and she was smiling as she stood up.

'I'm home,' she said aloud. 'How good is that?'

Even better, she had a good two hours of daylight left. Time to saddle up Ben and take a gentle trek up the hills, through the forest and back to the river. Her huge black horse was getting on in years now and was probably a bit stiff after the long stint of being shut in the float yesterday. Besides, Alice couldn't think of anything she would rather do to centre herself again. The other things she needed like a good home-cooked meal and a long sleep could wait.

Climbing into soft old jodhpurs and pulling on her short leather boots dispelled any thoughts of uniforms. The smell of well cared for leather as she collected her tack from the stable put anything shiny and clinical on another planet. Best of all was the soft whinny of welcome from Ben when she went out to the paddock behind the cottage with Jake walking close enough to brush her leg.

She was wanted here. Trusted. Loved by her boys. Yeah...life was full of hard bits but it could also be very, very good and this was as good as it got.

A short time later, Alice swung herself up into the

saddle and clicked her tongue. Ben wasn't showing any sign of being stiff. He took the bit and pulled eagerly. Maybe he was thinking of that long empty paddock where the forest track ended. The gentle uphill slope that was the perfect place to stretch out into a good gallop.

Alice grinned.

Yes!

Television was so boring!

Emmeline Barrett was fed up with the squeaky cartoon voices. With a heartfelt sigh, she wriggled around to kneel on the couch backwards, her chin resting on her hands as she gazed out of the window at the green hills and blue skies that were so different from anything she'd ever known it was like being in a fairy tale.

Haylee, her new nanny, was lying on the other couch, flat on her back with cushions under her head and her cellphone against her ear as she continued yet another phone call.

'*No!* Oh, my God! She *didn't*… Oh?' A contemptuous snort followed. 'What*ever*! As if he'd be interested in *her*!'

Haylee had promised to take her for a walk this afternoon. Down to see the river or up to where the trees were thick enough to make that dark and scary patch on the hillside that never failed to give Emmy a lovely tickle inside when she looked at it.

Suddenly, she knelt bolt upright, not even noticing that the interminable phone call was ending on the other couch. Her jaw dropped as she watched a big black horse come out of the forest and start galloping up the hill. A dog was running behind and it had to be a lady riding the horse because Emmy could see long hair streaming out behind the hat she was wearing.

Was it a real fairy tale now? An enchanted forest? Could the lady be a princess? She watched until the magic horse disappeared over the top of the hill and then she climbed off the couch.

'Haylee?'

'Hmm?' The nanny's response sounded remarkably like a yawn.

'Can we go for our walk now? Please?' she added hurriedly as she remembered her manners.

'In a minute, okay?' Haylee's eyes were closed. 'I just need to rest for a bit.'

Emmy scowled. She looked back at her couch that faced the blaring television. She looked at the door which led into the big hallway with the tiny stones that made patterns on the floor. If she went all the way down, there was a really big wooden door that was probably too heavy for her to open, but, if she went the other way, she knew she would find the kitchen and that funny room full of tubs and taps that had a much smaller door. If she went past the clothes line outside that door, she might be able to find the hill.

She might be able to see that magic horse and the princess again.

Emmy looked at Haylee, whose eyes were still firmly shut.

'I'm going to the bathroom,' she announced. 'I need to go to the toilet.'

'Can you manage by yourself?'

'Of course I can.' The indignation was automatic. 'I'm *five*!'

'Cool. Come straight back.'

Emmy got to the door but then turned to watch for a moment longer. She saw the way Haylee's fingers relaxed their grip on the cellphone. Her new nanny didn't even notice when it slipped out of her grasp and bounced onto the floor.

Emmy stopped chewing her bottom lip. With her lips set in a rather determined smile, she went out of the door in search of magic.

Forty-year-old Roger was about to walk out of the door of the emergency department.

'Wait!' Andrew took another glance at the slip of paper in his hand and stepped in front of his patient.

'What for?'

But Roger took a step back towards the bed he'd recently vacated, having rested for a couple of hours after the successful management of his cardiac arrhythmia.

'I've just received the results of the last blood tests we took.'

'You said there was nothing wrong with my blood.'

'There wasn't. The first results came back with completely normal cardiac enzymes.' Andrew tweaked the curtain shut behind him and showed Roger the paper he held. 'This one, however, shows a raised TNT.'

'What does that mean?'

'It means that there's been some damage to heart tissue.'

Roger sat down on the bed. 'You mean, like a heart attack?'

'Yes. The level is low enough to suggest it's minor but we're going to need to admit you and run some more tests.'

'But...I want to go home.'

'I know,' he said sympathetically. 'I'm sorry.'

Roger wasn't the only one who wanted to go home. Andrew's shift had officially finished, but he took the time to explain things to Roger again and then he paged Cardiology and waited for the registrar to arrive so he could transfer care of this patient. Finally, he unhooked his stethoscope from around his neck, put on the pinstriped jacket of his suit and headed for the car park.

Minutes later and he could put his foot down. Just a little, because that was all it needed for a surge of power from his gorgeous new car. The powerful engine purred softly and the miles between work and home evaporated. Andrew sped past the rolling paddocks without seeing the autumn colours of the trees. He barely noticed the goat on the side of the road.

It seemed a very long time since he'd kissed Emmy goodbye this morning and he needed to get back to her. To their new home. To remind himself why they'd journeyed here from the far side of the world. To convince himself it was worth the disturbing prospect of having to work with someone who was such a tangible link to his old life.

He'd won the first round, though, hadn't he? Made it very clear that if they were to work together it would be on his terms. So why wasn't it making him feel any better about the future? Why had he been left with this kind of unpleasant aftertaste as though he was being forced not only to recognise, but to bring out a side of himself that he didn't particularly like?

Andrew slowed just a little as the car bounced over the undulations in the driveway formed by ancient tree roots. He glanced to his left at the fork and caught a metallic glimmer that begged a second look. A horse float was parked under the shelter of some trees. Good. The tenant had returned. Amanda someone, the solicitor had informed him.

Andrew needed to talk to this Amanda. To let her know that, unfortunately, he wouldn't be able to let her renew the lease on the cottage that was due to expire at the end of this month. He needed the cottage as accommodation. The agency had assured him they would be able to find a married couple who would jump at the opportunity of living here and working for him. A housekeeper-nanny and a farm manager. Free accommodation should ensure he got the best available and nothing but the best would do. If the couple had children, it would be a bonus. While he was making arrangements for Emmy to start school in the city, it was too far away to make out-of-school play dates easy. How much better would it be if she had company closer to home?

The sound of the television made Andrew frown as he let himself in through the front door of the magnificent old house. Why on earth was Emmy watching rubbish when she could be outside in the fresh air and enjoying the kind of exercise and surroundings that had been impossible in central London?

Finding the temporary nanny sound asleep on a

couch in the small sitting room that had once been a library was a shock. Andrew snatched up the remote and killed the noise, staring at the young woman in disbelief and then automatically scouring the room for evidence of something worse than being simply asleep. Empty bottles? *Syringes?* Not that it made any difference. History was still repeating itself. He had apparently left his daughter in the care of someone who wasn't competent enough to keep her safe, let alone care for her the way she deserved.

The sudden silence had been enough to wake Haylee.

'Where's Emmy?' Andrew demanded.

'She went to the loo.'

'Oh?' Andrew strode to the door, trying to calm down. 'Emmy?'

He called again but he could feel the emptiness of the house as he stood in the vast hallway. His pace increased as he checked the cloakroom under the sweeping stairway. He took the stairs two at a time to reach the gallery that overlooked the foyer. He checked Emmy's bedroom. His own room. He threw open door after door of rooms that didn't even contain any furniture yet.

'Emmy!'

Downstairs, he found Haylee standing near the kitchen, looking frightened.

'How long were you asleep for?'

'I…I'm not sure. Not long.'

Andrew brushed past her into the kitchen. Empty. Not even any sign of the pantry being raided for snacks. The old laundry was also empty. The back door was open.

'She's gone outside?' Andrew tried to quell a spark of panic. 'By herself?'

'She won't have gone far.'

'How on earth would you know that? You don't even have any idea how long you were asleep.' Anger surfaced with a vengeance. 'And how far do you think she would need to go to get into trouble? There's a *river* out there, for God's sake!'

'I—I'll help you look.' Haylee looked ready to burst into tears.

'No.' Andrew didn't spare the time to look back at the girl. She wasn't to know that he was as angry with himself as he was with her but fear overrode any habit of kindness. 'Get your things and go home, Haylee. I don't want you looking after my daughter. You're fired!'

He scanned the kitchen yard, with its clothes line and pattern of herb gardens surrounded by tall thick hedges that hadn't been trimmed in years. The gateway set under an arch of greenery was overgrown. Almost invisible and only just ajar. Quite enough of a gap for a small girl to have squeezed through, however.

Andrew wrenched the gate open further.

'Emmy!'

Good grief!

There was a small girl standing in Ben's paddock. A very pretty little girl with a mop of blonde curly hair and big blue eyes that were gazing up at her in open admiration. Awe, even.

'Jake!'

The warning was unnecessary. Her large dog had dropped to his haunches well away from the child. He put his nose on his front paws and prepared to wait patiently. Ben also seemed to realise that caution was advisable. He stopped, not even looking at the water trough beside the girl.

'Hello,' Alice said. 'Who are you?'

'Emmy.'

'Hello, Emmy. I'm Alice.'

She swung her leg over Ben's back and slid to the ground, pulling off her helmet and then grabbing the reins before Ben could think of stepping forward. This child was tiny. So fragile-looking close to Ben's fluffy dinner-plate-sized hooves. Especially in that pretty pink dress with her long white socks.

'I saw you,' Emmy said. 'From the window.'

'Oh?' Alice looked around, despite knowing perfectly well there were no windows nearby. This was getting weird.

'Are you all by yourself?'

Emmy nodded. 'Haylee's asleep. She's tired.'

Maybe Alice was too. Suffering from exhaustion. Or low blood sugar or something. Having some kind of delusional experience.

'Are you a princess?'

Definitely delusional. 'No.'

'Is he magic?'

A tiny finger was pointing at Ben. Big blue eyes were looking up. Way up at the head of her horse. Something in the child's expression was very familiar. The kind of longing she remembered from when she was that small. A longing that had become a dream of one day having her own pony.

Alice smiled. 'He's kind of magic,' she said softly.

'Because he makes good things happen. Would you like to pat him?'

Already big eyes widened dramatically and Alice could see the sudden tension in the small body. A flash of fear. She heard the deep breath Emmy sucked in and then saw a determined nod.

'Yes, please.'

Brave kid. Alice held out her hand. 'He wouldn't hurt you. He loves children.'

The diminutive hand went trustingly into hers. 'I'll lift you up,' Alice said, 'so you can reach his neck. That's the best place to pat him.'

Emmy's fingers looked tiny and very pale against Ben's black coat.

'He's big, isn't he? That's why he's called Ben. After Big Ben. That's a clock. In London.'

'I know that.' The child sounded indignant. 'I'm *five*!'

Alice was too startled to smile at the tone. She'd been chatting quietly simply to put Emmy at ease. It was only now that she registered the accent.

'Did you live in London, Emmy?'

'Yes.' Emmy was stretching up to reach Ben's mane.

'Where do you live now?'

'Here.'

She couldn't have walked from a neighbouring farm to get here by herself, surely. That left only one potential home. The big house. It was still quite a walk for a five-year-old to have made by herself. Who was Haylee? A sister? And where were the parents? Did they have no idea of the kind of hazards a property like this could present? What if she hadn't been home or Ben wasn't as gentle as he was? What about the river, for heaven's sake?

Alice would have something to say to Emmy's parents when she saw them.

'What's your last name?' she queried.

Emmy didn't answer. She was busy threading her fingers through a handful of mane.

Alice tried again. 'What's Daddy's name?'

'Daddy.'

Alice smiled. She gave up. Surely someone would come looking for the child soon enough. They were probably busy moving in right now and hadn't noticed her wandering off.

'Would you like to sit on top of Ben?'

'Yes, please.'

'You'll need to wear my hat. It's a special helmet just for people who sit on horses.'

A moment later and there she was. A little princess with blonde curls poking from beneath the helmet, sitting on the huge black horse which made her look like a pea on a pumpkin. A very happy princess. It was the first time Alice had seen the child smile and it was the *best* smile, simply radiating joy, quite contagious enough to have Alice standing there, smiling back.

They could have stayed like that for a very long time. Both totally content, but then Jake raised his head from his paws. The shaggy hair on his neck came up and he emitted a low growling sound.

And then, from some distance behind Alice, came the sound of a man's voice. A very angry man.

'What the *hell* do you think you're *doing* with my daughter?'

* * *

Emmy burst into tears.

Jake's growl reached an ominous level and was re-inforced with a loud bark.

But Alice didn't turn around. She couldn't. Not yet. Not when she'd recognised that furious voice.

By some twist of a malevolent fate, 'Daddy' was Andrew Barrett and he was closer by the moment.

Oh...*God*!

'Don't cry,' she said to Emmy. Or was she talking aloud to herself? 'It's all right.'

'Nooo!' Fat tears rolled down pink cheeks. 'Daddy's cross with me.'

'Actually...' Alice found a smile '...I think he's cross with *me*.'

Emmy's tears stopped. She stared at Alice. 'Why?'

Why, indeed? If anyone was to be blamed for anything right now, it most certainly shouldn't be Alice. She turned and had the satisfaction of seeing Andrew stopped in his tracks. Not only by the menacing form of Jake, who'd positioned himself between his mistress and the threatening man, but by the shock of recognition.

'What are *you* doing here?'

There was dawning horror on the face of her old boss and, for just an instant, Alice had the peculiar notion that he was afraid of her. Totally ridiculous, of course, but it was enough for her to dredge up some confidence.

'I live here. What are *you* doing here?'

'I own this property,' Andrew snapped. 'And you most certainly do *not* live here.'

'Yes, she does, Daddy.' Emmy gave a huge sniff. 'So does Ben.'

'Be quiet, please, Emmeline. I'm talking.'

Good grief! What kind of father was Andrew Barrett? Talking to a five-year-old this sternly made any fantasy of his parental skills evaporate into an unpleasant mist. Alice didn't like what she was seeing. Neither did Emmy, apparently. The small girl stuck out her bottom lip and scowled at her father. Andrew tried to take a step forward and Jake growled again.

'Call it off,' Andrew commanded.

Alice waited for a heartbeat. And then another. 'Jake,' she said softly. Her wonderful dog moved to sit beside her, pressed against her leg.

'And now get my daughter down from that monster.'

That was too much for Emmy. 'He's *not* a monster!' she declared. She leaned forward in the saddle and tried to wrap her arms around Ben's neck. They barely made it to the halfway mark. 'He's lovely,' Emmy said passionately. 'He's my new friend and he's a magic horse. Alice said so.'

Alice was gripping Emmy's leg, unsure of the child's balance. At the same time, she was watching the muscles in Andrew's face move. As though he was trying to digest the mutiny he was faced with and decide how he would deal with it. Or maybe he was trying to understand how this could possibly be happening.

Alice was with him on that one. This was a nightmare! Part of her brain, however, was registering the fact that Andrew wasn't punishing his daughter in any way for the contradiction. Maybe he wasn't as strict and controlling as first impressions had suggested. Or maybe he was just distracted by dealing with *her* for the moment. He didn't look indecisive any longer. He looked furious. His gaze was chilly enough to send a shiver up her spine.

'Where—precisely—do you live?'

'In the cottage.'

Andrew shook his head. 'No. The tenant in the cottage is someone called Amanda.'

Alice nodded. 'Mandy Jones. She signed a twelve-month lease but she decided to go to Italy with her boyfriend. I was already living with her so I took over the lease last October, when it still had six months to run.'

'I wasn't informed of any sub-lease.'

'We saw the solicitor. I signed a contract.'

'We'll have to see about that. Won't we?'

A horrible thought occurred to Alice. What if the contract was somehow illegal? Could Andrew simply kick her out? Where on earth would she go, with a horse and dog? She touched Jake's head with her free hand, seeking reassurance. Trying to stem the awful sinking feeling that, once again, her life was falling apart.

'Alice?'

She turned her face up to Emmy.

'I'd like to get down now, please.'

'Sure. Bring your leg over to this side and I'll help you.' Alice raised her arms and caught Emmy as she slid off the horse. Ben stood like a rock, bless him, but she held the little girl closer for just a moment when her feet touched the ground. Letting her know that she was safe. It was a long time since she'd hugged a child and her arms felt curiously empty when she let go.

Emmy patted Jake on his head and then walked towards her father. 'Come on, Daddy,' she said. 'I'm hungry and I want to go home.' She looked over her shoulder at Alice. 'Can I have another ride, please? Tomorrow?'

'Um…you'll need to talk to your daddy about that.'

A discussion that was unlikely to give Emmy what she wanted, judging by the look Alice was receiving from Andrew right now. If she'd felt unwanted in Resus this afternoon when he'd chosen Jo over her, she felt far less desirable right now. More like something he needed to scrape off his shiny black shoe.

Except his shoes weren't very shiny any more, after storming over the paddock. The ends of his pinstriped trousers looked a little worse for wear, too. No doubt he would blame Alice when he noticed and then she would have to face him again at work in the morning. Not that she had to do anything to gain this man's displeasure. Existing was more than enough.

Alice had to fight the urge to burst into tears the way Emmy had on hearing her father shouting. Just as well she was good at fighting. She'd learned to tap into stronger feelings. Like anger. She raised her chin.

'You might like to let Emmy's mother know it's not a good idea to let her wander around by herself,' she said crisply. 'The river's quite deep in places and it's not fenced off.'

Emmy turned again. She was shaking her head. 'I haven't got a mother,' she told Alice. 'She's dead, isn't she, Daddy?'

'Yes.' The monosyllabic response was giving nothing away.

It certainly wasn't inviting even one of the questions Alice had tumbling in her head. What had happened to Melissa? How long ago? Did Emmy miss her dreadfully? Did Andrew? Was that why he had decided to come to the other side of the world to be a solo parent?

'I've got a nanny instead,' Emmy continued.

'Not any more.' Andrew sounded weary now. 'Haylee's not going to be staying with us any longer.'

'Because she was so tired?'

That got a smile. One that Alice was completely excluded from. The bond between this father and daughter was clearly strong enough for her to have been forgotten as the two of them talked to each other. That impression was deepened as Andrew bent down and Emmy raised her arms to be picked up. And when she was, she wrapped her arms around her father's neck and her legs around his waist and tucked her head against his neck. A fluid series of movements that spoke of a well-rehearsed routine.

'Yes, sweetheart. Because she was too tired to look after you properly. Now say goodbye to Alice. We're going home.'

Emmy peeped over the solid wall of her father's shoulder. Big blue eyes and golden curls, just like her mother had had. The same kind of fragile prettiness that most men had found irresistible, but it had been Andrew that Mel had chosen.

'Goodbye, Alice,' the little girl said.

'Bye, hon.'

She was used to living here alone. It was more than five months since Mandy had gone. She had Ben. And Jake.

So why on earth did watching the retreating figure of Andrew, holding his child in his arms, make her feel not only alone but lonely?

Afraid, even.

CHAPTER THREE

'ARE you sure?'

'I'm sorry, Dr Barrett. This is a witnessed signature and all perfectly legal. The reason I wasn't aware of the sub-lease was because I was overseas at the time it was arranged and my junior partner dealt with it. Unfortunately, the filing of the document was incorrect.'

'So I'm stuck with it.'

'Only for another three weeks or thereabouts.' The solicitor raised an eyebrow. 'You didn't seem concerned about waiting for the lease to expire when you purchased the property.'

'That's because I had no idea who was really living in that cottage.'

'And the tenant is a problem?'

'Yes.' The word was heartfelt.

'In that case…' The solicitor smiled, pulling a blank piece of paper in front of him. 'What is she doing that's unacceptable?'

Andrew frowned. She was just…*there*; wasn't that enough? It was more than enough for him to find it disturbing. Especially when his daughter seemed convinced that Alice Palmer had magic powers of some kind. It was all she could talk about last night and she'd been almost breathless with excitement and talking so fast at times it had been hard to hear everything.

Apparently she had watched her gallop up a big hill with her hair streaming out behind.

'Like a real princess, Daddy. Will my hair grow that long one day?'

His precious daughter had been sitting on that monster of a horse that seemed to have a peculiar name, like Clock.

'Alice would teach me to ride if I asked really, really nicely, wouldn't she? She's a nice lady, isn't she, Daddy?'

The name of Ben had come up more than once in that non-stop stream of chatter that had carried on through dinner and bath time. It had even interrupted the bedtime story.

Andrew's nod was unconscious. 'She may be sharing the cottage,' he informed the solicitor, 'with a man by the name of Ben.'

'Ah…I'll have to check, Dr Barrett, but I'm not sure that would constitute breaking the terms of the lease agreement. Unfair eviction could lead to an appearance in the small claims court if this Ms Palmer was unduly upset by it. Is she—or this male companion—causing any damage to your property?'

'Not that I'm aware of.'

In fact, the neat flower beds and patch of vegetables he'd noticed as he carried Emmy past yesterday had made the area around the cottage look far better maintained than anything else on his vast new property. The general neglect had been something of a shock, to be honest, but that was the downside of making such a purchase via the Internet.

Andrew breathed out in a sigh. He didn't want to 'upset' Alice. Or find himself the bad guy in a minor court case. He would just have to grit his teeth and get through the next three weeks. And hope that Emmy didn't fall any further in love with this 'princess' she'd discovered.

He glanced at his watch. 'Never mind,' he growled. 'I don't have the time for this. I'm late enough for work as it is.'

At least the crisis involving Emmy's care had been temporarily solved. The school had an excellent care facility that was open for extended hours on either side of the school day. Peter had been very understanding about why Andrew would be late in today and he'd also promised to look at the shift roster later so that both the Barretts could get past this hiccup in the settling in process.

And that was all this was. A hiccup. One that might last a little longer than Andrew was happy with, but he could cope. He was still in control, after all.

'This sounds *perfect*!'

'What is it?'

'Five-acre property set up for the horse-lover. Three-bedroomed house, stables. There's a dressage arena and swimming pool and it's only thirty minutes drive to the CBD. Available immediately, it says.'

'How much?'

'Um…six hundred dollars a week.'

Alice almost choked on her coffee. 'Get real, Jo!'

'OK...' Jo scanned the newspaper column. 'How 'bout this? Two-bedroomed cottage on farm. Private and peaceful. Paddock available if required. Two hundred dollars a week.'

'Sounds promising.'

'Oh ...' Jo groaned. 'It's way up in north Canterbury. Probably be a two-hour drive to work.'

A distinctly glum silence fell in the emergency department staff room.

'Do you really think you'll have to move?'

'Yeah...' Alice had no trouble recalling that expression on Andrew's face when he'd seen her on his property. 'And I've only got three weeks until my lease runs out. I might *have* to live in the wilds of north Canterbury.'

'It would certainly be peaceful,' Jo said wryly. 'Seriously, though. Couldn't you just find a paddock for Ben? Look, there's a whole section of grazing for hire. You could move in with me, then, while you're hunting.'

'Are you allowed dogs in your apartment? Large and particularly hairy ones?'

Jo shook her head sadly. 'Not even little bald ones. You wouldn't think of putting Jake in kennels? Just temporarily?'

'No way. He was an abandoned dog when I rescued him. I couldn't let him think it might be happening all over again.'

Jo sighed but smiled at the same time. 'You really love those critters of yours, don't you?'

'They're my family,' Alice said simply. 'No. There's got to be a way round this and I'm going to find it. Later...' She stood up abruptly. 'Come on, Jo. We're short-staffed and we were only supposed to be having a two-minute break, remember?'

'We're not *that* busy.'

'Don't even think like that. You're tempting fate.'

Andrew pushed open the double doors of the emergency department, having left his suit jacket and briefcase in his office, and paused, taking in what appeared to be a scene of bedlam.

The curtains on all three resuscitation areas were pulled shut and the sound of screaming was coming from somewhere behind them. Technicians and nurses were going in all directions. One was pushing a trolley into Resus 1. Another came from Resus 2 with a sealed bag of blood samples and she was heading for the vacuum tube system that would suck them straight to the laboratory. An orderly was trying to manoeuvre a bed past two ambulance stretchers queuing for the attention of the triage nurse. The cubicles all looked occupied.

So early in the day and it was chaos. Controlled, but only just.

Cursing the fact that he was well over an hour late to start his shift, Andrew made a beeline for the triage nurse, trying to ignore the fact that the person doing this important job today was the one person he least wanted to see.

Alice was talking to one of the paramedics standing beside the first stretcher.

'I'm afraid a sprained ankle isn't going to get a high priority at the moment. Can you find a wheelchair and take her through to Reception?' She glanced up and spotted Andrew's approach.

A flicker of something like fear washed across her features, which gave Andrew a pang of something rather like shame. He repressed it firmly. This was good. He was in control and Alice Palmer knew it.

'What's going on?' he queried crisply. 'And where am I needed?'

'We've got major trauma from an MVA in Resus 1 and 2,' Alice told him in exactly the same tone. 'We need someone circulating for the moment.'

Circulating? Looking at minor cases in the cubicles when there was major trauma to deal with? Alice might have the responsibility of assigning priority to patients and deploying the department's resources, but this felt remarkably like her trying to undermine his control.

'Where are all the junior staff?'

'One's gone to CT with an unstable stroke patient. I've got two in the middle of dealing with an arterial laceration and the rest are tied up with the trauma cases. There's a cardiac chest pain in Resus 3 that hasn't been assessed yet.'

'Peter?'

'Resus 1.'

More staff were arriving. Specialists summoned to help deal with the car accident victims. Andrew recognised a cardio-thoracic surgeon and an anaesthetist pushing through the curtains of the first Resus area. In the gap they created, he could see the huge team of departmental staff surrounding the bed in there. They didn't need another consultant.

An alarm sounded from an overhead monitor and Alice glanced up swiftly, touching a button to silence the alarm.

'Resus 3,' she said calmly. 'VPBs.'

Her gaze caught Andrew's and he nodded. The cardiac patient was unstable and his rhythm suggested that he could deteriorate at any time. Even as the thought formulated, the alarm sounded again.

'VF. I'll get the crash cart.' Alice was already moving, turning her head only briefly to look towards the cubicle area. 'Jo? Take over triage, would you, please?'

They arrived in the third Resus area at the same time but it was Alice who took the lead. She had the head of the bed flattened in less time than it took Andrew to step towards the bed. Then she raised her fist and thumped the middle-aged man in the centre of his chest.

A precordial thump. Sometimes, it was enough to jerk the heart into producing a viable rhythm again. Not this time. Andrew tilted the man's head back to open his airway, pulling off the oxygen mask. He found a bag-mask being handed to him. How had Alice managed that at the same time as sticking the gel pads to the man's chest?

'Shock?' she queried succinctly.

'You do it,' Andrew said. 'Where's the airway trolley?'

'Right behind you. Stand clear.' Alice had her finger poised over the button on the defibrillator as the sound of the machine gathering its charge changed to an alarm.

'I'm clear.' Andrew unrolled a sterile cloth that contained everything he would need to intubate the patient if necessary.

'Shocking again at 360,' Alice said. 'Clear.'

'I'm clear.'

A third stacked shock was delivered but there was no

change to the fatal rhythm showing on the monitor. Andrew delivered another lungful of air with the bag mask, noting Alice's perfect hand position as she started chest compressions.

'Where's the rest of the crash crew?'

'Obviously busy.' Alice kept pressing, one hand on top of the other. The sound of agonised groaning was coming from behind the curtain. He could also hear machinery being manoeuvred and orders being barked with the kind of urgency that advertised a struggle to save a life.

'Twenty-five, twenty-six, twenty-seven...' Alice counted aloud.

Andrew picked up the bag-mask again. He would be due to deliver another two breaths when she got to thirty.

'I need someone else in here,' he snapped.

Alice paused to let him deliver the oxygen. 'This is where I work, Andrew.' She might be slightly breathless but the tone was final enough. 'Deal with it.'

It took the blink of an eye for Andrew to realise she'd misunderstood. '*We* need someone else in here,' he said tightly. For goodness' sake, how inappropriate was it to bring personal issues to this kind of scene? 'I need IV access. Some adrenaline drawn up. I'll want some assistance to intubate and I want uninterrupted CPR.'

Alice looked up. Her gaze was determined. Confident. 'If we have to,' she said calmly, 'we'll manage.'

And, somehow, they did.

Extra staff arrived five minutes later but they could only stand and watch. Their patient's airway was secure. IV drugs had been administered and...best of all...a viable rhythm was showing on the monitor.

'Good save,' someone said.

Alice was still on the other side of the unconscious man. She had her fingers on the man's wrist, checking the strength of his radial pulse. Again, she looked up and caught Andrew's gaze and, this time, she held it for a fraction longer.

There was satisfaction in her eyes. Triumph, even. And more. Andrew could see the warm acknowledgement that this had been a team effort. Neither of them could have managed this without the other.

Her face was flushed from the stress and the effort of doing CPR. Some tiny curls had escaped the tight braid her hair was tied back in and one was stuck on her cheek. The dusting of freckles on her nose was like a faint splash of colour coming from the deep auburn of that wayward curl. And her eyes! Was it the triumph of a job well done that made those golden flecks shine against a background of dark hazel? Or were they catching the glow from lips that were lifting into a smile?

'We did it,' Alice said. 'Well done us.'

Andrew could only nod. Returning the smile was too much of an ask when he was grappling with the horrible awareness that he found this woman attractive.

Very attractive.

As if she wasn't causing enough of a problem in his life already, here he was, fighting a ridiculous urge to lean across and brush that curl back into place.

A movement from their patient mercifully doused the disturbing thought.

'He's lightening up.'

'Spontaneous respiration,' Alice noted.

Andrew considered sedation but the rhythm on the screen was steady now. Looking remarkably normal, in fact.

'Let's get that tube out,' he decided. 'And get the cardiologists to come and sort this chap out.'

With a bit of luck, he would be able to sort his own problems concerning Alice Palmer out with equal success. The fact that she was an undeniably attractive woman made no difference.

None at all.

So why did he seem to become increasingly aware of her as the day wore on? He noticed her deftly slipping an IV cannula into a patient's arm as he walked past a cubicle. Saw her patiently supporting a very elderly woman as they moved very slowly towards the toilets. Got caught in the backwash of the smile she sent her friend, Jo, as they passed each other pushing wheelchairs.

It simply wouldn't do.

Fortunately, the department became a lot quieter in the afternoon.

'You needed to get away early, didn't you?' Peter queried. 'To collect your daughter.'

'I should stay on. I still feel bad about being so late in this morning.'

Peter smiled as he shook his head. 'Hardly your fault the place was chaos. You did well managing that arrest on your own.'

'I wasn't entirely on my own.'

'No.' The head of department seemed to be giving him a curiously intent glance. 'Alice is worth her weight in gold, isn't she?'

Gold. Like those flecks in her eyes.

'Indeed.' Andrew's tone was far more level than his state of mind in that instant.

His heart was sinking rapidly on two fronts. Not only had he failed to squash this unwanted awareness of Alice's appearance but his boss seemed to be giving him a subtle warning that she was a valued staff member. Had he picked up vibes that they were finding it difficult to work together?

Had Alice said something to him?

She happened to be behind the triage desk again, only a few steps from where Peter had paused to speak to Andrew and suggest he head home. He could have sworn she sensed his gaze when she looked up and her expression was slightly startled. A flush of colour touched her cheeks—as though she was also aware of his suspicion. As if his suspicion was justified.

Andrew took those few steps towards the desk as soon as his brief conversation with Peter was finished.

Alice threw a swift glance over her shoulder but there was no one within earshot. She raised her chin and met Andrew's gaze squarely.

'You have a problem?'

'I think we might both have a problem,' Andrew said very quietly. 'Don't you?'

'I know I do,' Alice retorted softly. 'Being evicted from my home could certainly be considered a problem.'

'The lease is due to expire. Renewing it is simply not an option.'

The upward quirk of her eyebrows suggested otherwise.

'I need help with my property,' Andrew said evenly,

'and responsible care for my daughter. I don't want staff living in my house and that makes the cottage you're inhabiting essential for other purposes. It's not personal,' he added.

This time the eyebrows were joined by a wry twist of her mouth. 'Sure.'

Andrew sighed. 'Did you really think I was stating a personal preference when I said I needed someone else in that arrest scenario?'

Alice looked away. She focused on one of the telephones on the desk in front of her as though she expected it to ring. Or wanted it to.

'You've made it obvious that you aren't exactly thrilled to be working with me,' she said finally. 'You still believe I took those drugs, don't you?'

'I never said that.' The words came out more fiercely than intended. 'Did I?'

She was silent for a long moment. When she spoke again, her voice was so low that Andrew had to duck his head to catch the words.

'You said you couldn't trust me.'

He had said that. As a departmental head with the responsibilities of many others to consider it was the stance he'd been forced to adopt. He couldn't have afforded to trust her at that point in time, no matter what his heart might have told him.

And maybe he still couldn't. He wanted to, but she had the power to undermine his desperate wish to start again. To build a new life. Something that was too precious to risk.

Alice had looked up again. There was a challenge in her face. And...and *hope*, dammit! This was his chance

to undo the wrong he had done. He could restore a pride
that she had every right to have in herself. All he had to
do was deny his mistrust.

He opened his mouth to do exactly that but there
was a heartbeat's worth of hesitation before any sound
emerged. Just long enough to recognise that yes, the
mistrust was still there, but it was personal and not professional and he could therefore answer her with conviction.

But the damage had been done in that tiny fraction
of time. He saw the way that hope died in her eyes. The
way she turned away, holding up her hand to stop him
saying anything.

'Don't bother,' she snapped. 'I really don't want to
hear it.' Her back straightened noticeably. 'We both
work here and we'll both have to deal with it. Let's keep
it professional, shall we, and leave anything personal in
the past.'

That suited Andrew admirably. 'Sure.'

'If you have any issues with my performance as a
nurse in this department, feel free to discuss them with
me. Or you can refer them directly to Peter.'

'I don't expect to have any issues.'

'Good.' Alice was reaching for the phone that was
now ringing. 'Neither do I.'

Had she really expected him to pat her on the back and
say that of course he didn't believe she had stolen restricted drugs? That he trusted her? Why had she even
entertained such a hope? Because they had worked so
well together on that arrest case? He was good at his job.
So was she. Being able to work as a competent team

should have nothing to do with how they felt about each other on a personal level.

' She was the one who'd been unprofessional and made it personal. Extra staff were certainly called for to deal with a cardiac arrest but she'd misunderstood. Not only that, she'd attacked as a form of defence. Remembering her tone of voice was enough to make Alice cringe even now, when she'd been at home for long enough to exercise and feed her pets and unwind from her day. Had she sealed her own fate by reminding Andrew of the past like that? Especially then?

The scene had not been dissimilar to what had happened just prior to the final straw regarding her employment under Andrew's watch. There'd been a big pile-up on the motorway and Emergency had been stretched to the limits of everyone's abilities. The cardiac arrest had had no chance of being successfully managed when it had been due to such major chest injuries, but she'd been the one working alongside Andrew.

Just how that ampoule of morphine had got into the pocket of her tunic was still a mystery. Or why Andrew had chosen that day to ask her to empty her pockets. On top of the history of drugs going missing on her shifts and the empty ampoules found in her locker, it had spelt the end. Maybe someone else could have planted the empty ampoules, but why would they have put one in Alice's pocket that day? The weight of evidence had been too heavy, despite tearful denial on her part.

Right now, when she was at home and in a place that had always put anything negative into perspective, Alice had the horrible sensation that a ticking clock had replaced her heartbeat for the purpose of reminding her that this refuge was temporary. That any hope of remaining here was in the hands of a man she had just reminded why he couldn't bring himself to trust her.

Positive thinking could only go so far to counteract feeling powerless.

Vulnerable.

It wasn't nearly far enough.

Alice went through her usual routine, but her actions were so mechanical she forgot the little extras like having music on while she cooked the dinner or lighting a scented candle to enjoy while having her bath. She even forgot the cup of tea she always made when she turned on the computer to check her email before going to bed.

The message from her old friend in London was a welcome surprise in her inbox. A bit of moral support from someone who would understand was exactly what she needed. Alice double-clicked to bring the email to full screen size.

'*Good to hear from you at long last,*' Pam had written. And then, after expressing sympathy for the process of finally dealing with her grandmother's estate. '*I'm gobsmacked to hear that Randy Andy has turned up in your neck of the woods!*'

The nickname grated. It always had. Sure, Andrew had had a reputation with women, but it hadn't taken long for Alice to realise that it was the women who did the running and that they never got as far as they wanted with the eligible young doctor. Except for Melissa, of course—the vivacious blonde who'd been assigned to showing Alice the ropes in her new job.

'Forget it,' she'd smiled, after introducing the newcomer to the head of department. 'He's mine.'

'He is,' Pam had confirmed as her friendship with Alice blossomed. 'Or he will be. You just watch.'

Alice *had* watched with disbelief that a man as intelligent as Andrew could have fallen for the campaign. Could he not see that Melissa was more interested in him as a status symbol and guarantee of a secure future? Surely he would see through it. And then he'd see that another woman might be able to offer something a lot more meaningful.

It had been hard to give up the wish that she could be that other woman. Even when Andrew had done absolutely nothing to suggest he would be anything other than faithful to the woman he was in a relationship with. She'd been invited to the wedding six months later, where Melissa's smile had only hinted at triumph and the gorgeous dress made sure that no signs of her pregnancy were showing.

'Mind you,' Pam's email continued, *'I'm not surprised that he went as far away as possible. I was with you on those rumours after Mel kept turning up with those injuries like the broken wrist and the bruises but now I just don't know what to think. It added up to a pretty nasty picture when the file got pulled in for that last admission.'*

So Pam had been there. Alice's lips were parted as she leaned forward a little, reading on swiftly. The gap between her lips grew wider as the unfolding story made her jaw drop.

'She'd fallen down this set of concrete steps,' Pam reported. *'Awful head injuries. She got taken to Theatre but never regained consciousness. She was in ICU on*

a ventilator for weeks and it was all anyone could talk about. The police were involved and what with the evidence in her file right from the start of that marriage there were noises about charges being laid. One of the porters overheard a cop saying that there was a suggestion that Mel had been pushed rather than fallen down those steps.'

Alice's breath came out in a gasp.

No!

She hadn't only watched Melissa in action stalking her intended husband over those months. She'd watched Andrew as well. Had worked with him. Had seen and heard enough to know exactly why Melissa and so many others thought of him as a prize. It wasn't just his looks, though, heaven knew, they were enough. The man was an exceptionally talented doctor without being arrogant about it. He had been generous with his time and knowledge.

And he was gentle. The quality that had captured Alice more than any other. She had seen him use split second initiative, skill and strength to do something like cracking a chest or relocating a dislocated shoulder, but she'd also seen him take the time to do procedures as painlessly as possible. Even if he was over-committed and especially if the patient was a child. She'd seen him reassure a frightened person with words or a touch or...that smile. The one that made the lines deepen around those incredibly blue eyes. That made his face soften and change so you just *knew* how absolutely sincere it was. The smile that had made Alice realise she had—unintentionally—fallen in love with him herself.

She hadn't seen quite that smile since his reappearance in her life but she'd seen that his manner with patients hadn't changed. She'd seen the bond he had with his daughter. There was simply no way she could ever believe he had deliberately pushed his wife down a set of steps. It was...outrageous.

'*I never heard what happened in the end,*' Pam's account continued. '*Andy got suspended as soon as the police investigation got underway and then it just fizzled out. The coroner's report was accidental death and no charges ever got laid but he never came back to work.*'

Why would he? Alice knew better than anyone what it was like to be suspected of something you hadn't done. How impossible it could be to prove innocence and completely clear your name. How the taint of suspicion poisoned everything.

She'd come all the way back to New Zealand to start again, but Andrew's move was braver because he was coming somewhere he'd never been before. As a single father with a young child and no support network of friends and family to help. Alice knew why. He wouldn't want to live with that poison. Imagine if Emmy grew up to hear rumours that her father might have somehow contributed to the death of her mother.

It would be worse than an allegation of stealing drugs, wouldn't it?

Alice sat back, the rest of Pam's chatty email, about the new HoD and who was dating whom, turning into a blur.

Andrew Barrett had more to lose than she did. Someone who knew his history was a threat that could affect his entire life—professional and personal.

A huff of something like laughter escaped her lips. Not only had the poor guy found her working in his new department, he'd come to his new home and found her living on the property.

Unfair.

Ironic.

And, despite the worry about her own situation and the hurt that Andrew's lack of trust still generated, Alice's overriding reaction was to want to reach out to him.

To comfort him.

To tell him that she didn't believe any of it.

She had to try and curb the impulse. Giving him any indication that she cared about him or his daughter to that extent would only make herself more vulnerable. And why should she step out on that limb when Andrew wasn't even prepared to give *her* the benefit of any doubt?

It was impossible to squash her reaction completely, however, and maybe that was a good thing. Alice was too shocked to be able to think clearly right now but surely, if Andrew knew that there was someone on his side—a *friend*—it couldn't hurt, could it? It might even make him reconsider his decision about her lease.

'Things happen for a reason,' she told Jake, as he slumped to the floor beside her bed. Alice flicked off the light and stared up at the ceiling. 'This might sound crazy but there's a remote possibility that all this could turn out to be the best thing that's ever happened to me.'

CHAPTER FOUR

'GOOD morning, Dr Barrett.'

'Ah…good morning, Alice.'

Her cheerful smile had clearly unsettled Andrew. He wasn't expecting her to be happy to see him arrive for work. In fact, the sideways glance he sent her, before checking the pile of notes that had just been delivered to the central desk area, had a distinctly suspicious tinge.

But Alice *was* feeling cheerful. Confident, even. So much better than she'd been feeling yesterday, before receiving that astonishing email from Pam. Being friendly was the safest and easiest course to follow for the moment and it might even work. She knew that Andrew was a good man. He wouldn't set out to make life unbearable for anyone and he would probably do a great deal to help a friend.

'Glorious sunrise this morning, wasn't it?' She'd driven into it on her way to a 7:00 a.m. start. Andrew would have been in a much better position to admire the silhouette of craggy hills against the amazing red glow.

'Mmm.' He'd selected a set of notes. He looked up

at the white board to find the location of the patient he was intending to see.

'April's the best month in Canterbury.' For some reason, Alice couldn't let it go at such a brief, professional kind of exchange. 'Bit of a nip in the mornings but then we get these lovely sunny, still days.'

She was looking at the back of Andrew's head, wondering if he would continue to ignore her. It was quite unfair for a man to have natural streaks of gold that so many women were prepared to pay a fortune to have a hairdresser emulate. He must have been quite blond as a child. Maybe that was where Emmy got the genes from, because, if her memory served her correctly, it hadn't been the shade Melissa had been born with.

'Cold at night, though.' Carrying on this one-sided conversation was a kind of disguise for what she was really thinking about. Alice made it seem even more casual by turning back to her own task of searching for a GP's referral letter that had been faxed through prior to a patient's arrival. 'You must be noticing it in that big house.'

'Not really.' Andrew made it sound a strain to be polite. 'I'm having the chimneys swept today and a load of firewood being delivered.'

'But you've got any amount of firewood for free! There's dozens of dead tree branches all over the place. All you need is a chainsaw.'

'Good point.' Andrew's smile was tight. 'Thanks for the tip. I'll put it on the list of equipment I need.'

He was moving away now, the notes clutched in one hand. Alice couldn't help the sudden vision of a chainsaw hanging there instead. Of Andrew transformed into a good Kiwi bloke, wearing ripped old blue jeans and a black singlet. With the muscles in his shoulders rippling as he pulled the cord to start the motor of the heavy tool.

Her mouth felt curiously dry all of a sudden.

'Pine cones,' she heard herself say in a kind of croak.

Andrew turned his head. 'Sorry?'

'You'll want pine cones.' Her voice sounded more normal now. She could even add a friendly smile. 'Best thing to start fires with. That stand of trees where I park the horse float has heaps of them. Emmy would enjoy collecting them.'

Andrew said nothing. His face suggested that she had no business suggesting what his daughter might enjoy doing. Or giving him advice about power tools or how to start fires. It was just as well he had no idea of the way her stomach had done that peculiar little flip, imagining him with that particular power tool.

Confidence was one thing. Stepping into a space where she was aware of Andrew Barrett's personal attributes was something entirely different.

Don't do it, Alice warned herself sternly. *Don't even think of going there again.*

It would be nothing less than self-sabotage. The notion of a relationship within the safe boundaries of friendship was giving her a way forward. Confidence. Hope that she could keep what she really wanted, which was to keep living exactly where she was. Contemplating making herself vulnerable all over again by going back to finding this man irresistibly attractive was simply not an option.

Peter saved her from having to dwell on such a disturbing option.

'We're short in the observation area, Alice. You wouldn't fancy a stint in there today, would you?'

'Sure.' It wasn't normally her favourite place to work, being well away from the acute management or resuscitation of major cases that came in, but, right now, it was perfect. It would also be well away from their newest consultant.

Except it wasn't.

Eight-year-old Luke had responded well to the management of his asthma when he'd been brought in by ambulance shortly after Alice had started her shift. He'd been resting quietly in one of the cubicles in the observation area ever since but his condition was deteriorating again. Alice could hear the increase in the wheezing sound he was making as she walked past the end of his bed. When she went closer, it was all too easy to see his small ribs protruding with the effort the boy was making to breathe.

'Has Mum gone to get your little sister from kindergarten?'

Luke nodded. His eyes were suspiciously bright and Alice wondered if he'd been more upset than he'd let on at being temporarily abandoned by his mother. Something had certainly triggered his asthma again.

'I'm going to put some more Salbutamol in your nebuliser,' she told him. 'And we'll put this clip back on your finger.' She attached the oxygen saturation monitor. 'And now I'm going to get your doctor to come and check you again.'

The doctor who'd seen Luke early this morning had been off duty for hours. The doctor that came in response to her message to the front desk was Andrew.

'Hey, Luke. How's it going, buddy?' He picked up the chart from the end of Luke's bed.

'Initial attack was moderate to mild,' Alice informed him quietly. 'Pulse ox ninety-four per cent. He responded well to nebulised Salbutamol.'

He wasn't responding well now. Luke's heart and respiration rates were soaring and the oxygen level in his blood was dropping steadily. The little boy was looking tired as well and fatigue could be a major contributing factor to a respiratory arrest which could turn this asthma attack into a life-threatening emergency within minutes.

'Let's add some Ipratropium to that nebuliser,' Andrew said calmly. He perched on the bed with one hip as he picked up Luke's hand. 'You're doing great,' he told the boy. His thumb rubbed over the plaster on the small hand and Andrew raised an eyebrow at Alice. 'IV access?'

'It wasn't used and tissued an hour or so ago. The paediatric registrar said it was okay to remove.'

The tiny frown was a sympathetic flicker and Alice could see the small hand being given a squeeze. 'Luke?' Andrew's tone was gentle. 'I need to pop another wee needle in your arm.'

'No-ooo!' The word was a gasp.

'Sorry, buddy, but we need to give you some more medicine to help your breathing.'

Alice stepped closer, lifting the nebuliser mask to add the requested new drug to the attached chamber. She also squeezed in a new ampoule of Salbutamol and then she eased the mask back over Luke's face and gave his hair a ruffle.

'Dr Barrett is really, really good at this,' she told Luke. 'Better than anybody.'

She gave the boy's shoulder a reassuring squeeze as the tourniquet was snapped into place, noting the way Andrew kept all the other supplies he needed out of sight. All he showed Luke was a small can.

'This stuff is fantastic,' he said. 'It's like spray ice so it stops things hurting too much.' He sprayed the back of Luke's hand.

And then he seemed to forget what he was doing. He stared at one of the bright posters decorating this cubicle that was kept for paediatric cases. 'Look at that poster over there,' he said, sounding astonished. 'Is that elephant really doing what I *think* he's doing?'

The elephant in the picture wasn't doing anything extraordinary, but by the time Luke had looked at the wall and then back again, the cannula was in his vein.

Andrew smiled. 'All done. Wasn't so bad, was it?'

Luke shook his head, too breathless to speak.

Alice felt rather breathless herself. It had been one of *those* smiles. The crinkly-eyed, glowing kind. And it touched a spot on her heart that she had been so sure had healed over completely. It was bad enough being aware of how attractive Andrew was again. It was far, far worse to recognise the kind of connection that only came from being in love with someone.

She held Luke's arm steady to avoid any sudden jerks that might dislodge the cannula, watching as Andrew taped it into place, aware of a growing sense of dismay.

So it was still there. In spades. That awareness of how deft his movements were. How familiar the sight of those hands was because she'd watched them too often in the past. She knew about that tiny scar on his forefinger and how neatly cut his nails always were. She also knew, only too well, what it was like to imagine those fingers touching her own skin. This was no glow from stirred up ashes. Flames were flickering as though they'd never been doused.

'I want some oral Prednisolone,' Andrew was saying as he looked up.

And then he blinked, stopping for just a heartbeat with his lips still parted, and Alice had the truly horrible thought that he could see into her head.

Into her heart.

'Two milligrams per kilogram.' Andrew cleared his throat. 'Get some hydrocortisone drawn up as backup, too, please. Keep up the continuous nebulised Salbutamol and I'd like some IV Salbutamol drawn up as well. I'm going to give Paeds a quick call.'

Alice nodded briskly. This was good. She had plenty to do and a patient to focus on. Andrew would forget about whatever fleeting impression he'd got from her expression and she would make sure he didn't get so much as a sniff of anything less than purely professional interaction from now on.

She knew the worst. She was prepared. If possible, she would avoid any interaction at all. She might even revisit the idea of working in another department for a while. It was probably just the surprise of having this man in her life again that was triggering such an unwelcome reaction. She would get over it. Again.

Luke's asthma attack came under control with satisfying speed but he was admitted to the paediatric ward for close monitoring. For the rest of her shift, Alice put her hand up for every task that took her away from the department. Accompanying patients to specialist test areas, sitting in with social workers making an assessment, even taking on some sluice room duties everyone else was avoiding.

The strategy worked. She didn't even see Andrew again until she was ready to leave at three p.m. She would have avoided him then, too, as she walked down the corridor to the outside doors, but he stepped right into her path.

'Have you got a minute, Alice?'

'Not really. I'm heading home.'

'You're keen to get away, then?'

'You bet. It's a gorgeous day and I want to get home in time to ride Ben before it's dark.'

Andrew had the oddest expression on his face by the time she had finished speaking. He seemed to shrink away from her.

'Ben?'

Alice nodded slowly. 'My horse. You met him, remember? The monster?'

Andrew gave his head a tiny shake, as though trying to clear it. 'Emmy said your horse was called Clock.'

Alice grinned. 'He's Big Ben. Named *after* the clock.'

'Ohh...'

A smile was tugging at the corners of Andrew's mouth but didn't quite succeed. He looked as if he was trying hard not to look pleased. Alice mentally played back the snippet of conversation they'd just had and found herself staring even more intently than she had been. He'd been pleased to discover Ben was a horse.

Why?

The warmth that flickered into life deep inside Alice told her it was because he was feeling some degree of the attraction she was struggling with. If he was, however, it had to be purely a physical reaction. He didn't trust her so it was a no-brainer that it could never be anything more.

Which made it far more dangerous for her because, at the end of the day, if she allowed herself to care again she stood to lose far more than Andrew did.

And that was way too much.

Emmy sat inside the big orange wheelbarrow, gripping each side and bouncing as Andrew propelled it forward over the uneven ground.

'Go faster, Daddy!'

'No. You might fall out.'

'I won't!'

'You might. Besides, we're here already. Look at all these pine cones just waiting for us to pick up.'

'Oooh!' Emmy was climbing out of the wheelbarrow even before it came to a complete halt. 'Are we going to have a fire?'

'We sure are. We bought marshmallows on the way home, remember?'

'I like the pink ones.' Emmy picked up one large pine cone and held it between both hands. She walked importantly back to the barrow and dropped her prize with a flourish.

Andrew hid his grin, swooping to pick up two cones in each hand. This wouldn't take long, despite Emmy's efforts being so laboured, and that was just as well because it was nearly 6:00 p.m. and daylight was fading fast. The chimneys had been swept and the huge mound of split firewood waiting to be stacked was nice and dry. With the help of the cones, he would have a roaring fire going to ward off the chill of the autumn evening before he turned his attention to preparing their dinner.

Dropping another armload of cones into the barrow, Andrew straightened, taking a moment to soak in the sight of Emmy's golden head shining against the dark backdrop of tree trunks. She was squatting and poking at the ground with a stick, clearly absorbed with a new discovery, the task of collecting kindling forgotten. It didn't matter. This kind of time with his daughter and the new adventures waiting for them both were exactly why he'd come here. Emmy was loving it.

Just as Alice had suggested she would.

Thinking about Alice was an unwelcome intrusion but it was hard not to when her horse float was parked not far from where he stood. Turning his head, Andrew could see the cottage. He could see Alice, in fact, hanging some washing on a line strung between two trees.

'Em?'

'I found a bug, Daddy. A big, shiny black one.'

'Can you find some more pine cones? We need to get a move on.'

'Soon.'

'Do it now, sweetheart, or we might not be able to toast marshmallows for supper.'

'Oh. Okay.' Emmy jumped up and ran towards him with a cone. 'Oooh, look, Daddy! There's Alice!'

'So it is.'

'Can I go and ask if I can pat the horse?'

'Not today.'

'When?'

'Alice is busy. See? She's hanging out her washing.'

'You could ask her, Daddy. Ask her when she won't be too busy and when I could have another ride. She said I could if you said I could. Please, Daddy. Please?'

The small face was turned up to his and the desperate desire he could see written all over it was irresistible.

'I'll ask.'

'Now?'

'Not now. We're busy collecting our pine cones.'

'I'll get lots of cones. You go and talk to Alice.' Emmy took a huge breath and held it. *'Please?'*

Andrew sighed. 'Okay. But don't you go anywhere. See how many cones you can find.'

'Sorry to disturb you.'

Oh…God! It was bad enough to have her unwilling landlord turn up in her back garden when she was wearing her dirty jodhpurs and ancient gumboots and a tattered old woollen jersey, but why did he have to pick the precise moment she was pegging out her underwear? At least it was her best pair of knickers—the silky ones that had a nice bit of lace at the top.

He was staring at the small item of clothing and, to his credit, he looked discomfited when he recognised what it was.

'Ah …' Andrew cleared his throat and looked away, but his gaze raked hers on the way and Alice had the impression that he'd been imagining her wearing those knickers.

'I'm almost done.' Alice dived for the last item in her basket. Dammit! It was the bra that matched those knickers. Andrew was looking into the basket as well now. If she just left the bra there, he'd know she was embarrassed and he might guess that the reason for that embarrassment was her awareness of him. Her resolve to keep that awareness totally hidden had to be found and acted on.

Easy, really, if you thought of it the same way as doing something you knew would be embarrassing for a patient. Alice simply had to be matter-of-fact. Brisk and competent. As though she was so used to doing this that it failed to register.

'I know it's a funny time of day to be hanging out washing,' she admitted breezily as she fished for a peg, 'but I leave for work at 6:00 a.m. and it's too dark in the mornings, now.'

'It is quite a drive into town. What made you want to live this far out?'

'You bought this place without setting foot on it, didn't you?'

'I sent an agent to check it out.'

'And that was enough?'

'The pictures were pretty compelling, I have to say.'

'Hmm.' Alice picked up the wooden pole with a deep groove in the top. She put the rope of the clothes line into the groove and then walked forward, straightening the pole and lifting the line high enough to clear the barrier it had made between herself and Andrew. 'That would have been enough to catch the magic,' she agreed. 'I came out to visit Mandy and fell in love.'

Oh, Lord! Why had she used that particular phrase?

Even if she wanted to convey how important it was for her to stay here, the words were inappropriate. Too personal. Possibly too revealing. Alice looked away in a quiet plea for distraction and there it was. She waved at Emmy. Jake left his position beside the tin that held the clothes pegs and moved towards the small figure, his tail waving in a friendly greeting.

'Looks like you're getting a good supply of pine cones.'

'Yes.' Andrew looked back at his daughter and frowned. 'Is that dog safe with children?'

'Absolutely.'

Andrew was still frowning. 'Emmy wanted me to come and talk to you. She's dead set on visiting your horse again.'

'Ben.'

'Yes…Ben.' Andrew wasn't meeting her gaze now and Alice found herself smiling inwardly. Maybe it was his turn to feel embarrassed. But then he did meet her eyes and any intention Alice had of keeping this brisk and impersonal went out the window. She couldn't look away and the contact went on just that bit too long. Long enough for questions to be formed on both sides. Questions she was determined not to ask that needed answers she was certainly not about to supply. She had to find a way of creating a safe distance here.

'You don't want her to.'

'Sorry?' Andrew appeared to have lost the thread of their conversation.

'You don't want Emmy visiting Ben.'

'No, I don't think I do.'

'Because you think he's dangerous? I can assure you he's not. He's the most—'

Andrew was shaking his head. 'That's not the reason.'

'What is?'

He took another quick glance over his shoulder and Alice followed his line of vision. The wheelbarrow was apparently full and Emmy was crouched beside it, her arms around Jake as she hugged the dog. It was dark enough to be harder to see the little girl now except that her hair shone like a halo.

Andrew turned back. 'As you can see, Emmy forms attachments easily. She adores animals and...' he seemed to be scowling at Alice now '...she seems to have taken a fancy to you. She thinks you're a princess in disguise or something.'

Alice smiled. 'She's a cute kid.'

The smile wasn't returned. Andrew looked away. 'The lease on this cottage expires in three weeks and you'll have to leave by then. Preferably sooner. I don't want Emmy upset by your departure and the closer she gets to you and your animals, the more likely that is to happen.'

He knew the names of her pets. It was a deliberate put-down to refer to them as simply 'animals'.

And he wanted her to be gone even before the lease had expired? Would it make any difference if he knew how impossible it was going to be to find somewhere affordable to go, never mind having to pack up her life and shift?

No. He wouldn't care, even if he did understand. Maybe Andrew Barrett came across as caring and gentle and wonderful with his patients, but, on a personal level, Alice had clearly made a big mistake in her opinion of him and, just as clearly, any kind of friendship was not going to be an option. She drew in a careful breath.

This was it. Her salvation. She had another opportunity to flip that coin and learn to hate this man, and if she could succeed this time, then she would have no problem finding the energy and strength she needed to deal with whatever came from any association she had with him. She would escape. Find somewhere else to live and another department to work in. Another *city* to work in, maybe, however painful it would be to up sticks and start all over again.

Some of that pain was already setting in and it made her want to lash out. In defence of her 'animals' if nothing else.

'I need longer than three weeks,' she said. 'It's not easy to find rental property that allows for keeping a horse and a dog.'

'Not my problem, I'm sorry.' Andrew seemed to be finding her gumboots of extraordinary interest. 'I've explained why I need this cottage. It's urgent that I get a suitable childcare arrangement in place. I was late for work yesterday and I can't expect new colleagues to keep picking up any slack.'

He finally looked up and the distance Alice could feel was far greater than when he'd first seen her in the emergency department. He was trying to get as far away as possible and he certainly wasn't going to give an inch as far as her problems were concerned.

This was hopeless. It seemed even more hopeless when Andrew turned his back on her. The conversation was over. Her life, as she currently knew and loved it, also appeared to be over.

'No, I don't suppose you can.' The words came from nowhere, filled with the pain of her own imminent loss. 'I don't suppose you want those new colleagues to know the details of why you've come here, either.'

He turned, very slowly. Even in this half light of dusk, Alice could see the way the colour left Andrew's face.

He didn't have to say a word. The awful allegations he'd had to face hung in the air between them. So did the fact that Alice knew about them. That she could make life very difficult for him if she chose to.

It should have been a triumphant moment, a shift in the balance of power, but instead Alice felt...mortified.

It was a horrible thing to have said. She wanted to pull the words back and she dragged in a new breath to do exactly that. To tell Andrew that she knew how absurd the suspicion had been. That she hadn't believed a single one of those rumours.

That it didn't matter if he evicted her or made work difficult, she would never start a new spread of poisonous gossip. In fact, she would defend him if someone else said anything.

Like she always had.

This was unbelievable.

History was repeating itself.

Blackmail. By a woman. God, did they all think like that? That it was morally acceptable to use whatever means it took to get what they wanted? He should have learned his lesson about trusting women by now.

'I'm pregnant, Andy. You have to marry me.'

'Stay with me or I won't even go near Rehab.'

'Keep quiet or I'll take your daughter away and you'll never see her again.'

Anger came from nowhere. A painfully intense shaft that made him clench a fist and raise it unconsciously as he tried to find the words he needed to tell Alice Palmer exactly what he thought of her and her threat.

He could see her taking in a breath. Opening her mouth to say something. Then he saw the expression on her face change and there was no mistaking the flash of fear.

Oh…*God*! Did she really think he might *hit* her?

His hand unclenched but still moved towards her. He needed to touch her. To apologise and wipe that fear from her eyes. But Alice wasn't looking at him now. Her head had swivelled and she took a step away from him.

'Jake?' she called. 'What's wrong?'

Andrew could hear it now. A volley of barks coming from some distance away. Urgent barking that wasn't stopping.

His own head moved as swiftly as Alice's had. Looking back at the trees and the wheelbarrow to where the dog had last been seen.

To where his daughter had been.

'Oh…*no*!' The word was an agonised growl. 'Where's *Emmy*?'

CHAPTER FIVE

IT WAS hard to run in oversized rubber boots.

Andrew passed her easily but he didn't see the rabbit hole in the dim evening light and he went sprawling, the heartfelt curse following Alice as she kept running towards the sound of her dog raising the alarm. She knew what lay in that direction.

The river.

She could hear it as she got rapidly closer. There was a shallow stretch where it tumbled swiftly over boulders before it hit the curve shaded by willow trees. There was a deep pool in that curve—a swimming hole that Alice had enjoyed using many times over the recent long, hot summer.

Jake appeared to be standing in the choppy swirl of the shallow water. He had stopped barking now and, as Alice got even closer, she could see why. He had his jaws clamped onto a piece of clothing as he held onto a small body that was no longer upright.

Oh, *God*! Alice charged full tilt into the river and promptly slipped on one of the smooth, wet boulders. Heedless of the painful bump to her knee and the icy water now drenching her clothes, she wrenched herself upright and staggered on.

Too late!

The current had been too much for Jake to fight and now he was bounding down river, following the shape that was Emmy, being swept towards the deep pool. Alice went after them, so fast she was already losing her balance as the water got deeper. Deep enough to swim as she fell headlong into it.

Jake was swimming too. If he hadn't been circling at that particular point beneath the willows, Alice would have had no clue where to dive when Emmy's head suddenly vanished.

The water was pitch-black. There were branches of willow, long enough to trail well below the surface and create both an obstacle to finding the child quickly and a dangerous trap that could entangle and drown Emmy in a very short space of time.

Somehow, Alice's hand found something far more solid than leafy twigs. She gripped and pulled and filled her arms with the child before kicking desperately towards the surface of the pool and then downstream to when the water got shallow again. She staggered upright as soon as her feet touched the bottom.

Strong arms came around them both then, guiding them to the side and onto dry ground. For a split second they stopped moving and Alice could feel more than strength in those arms. They created a circle of protection. A place that felt so safe it took her breath away.

Or was she still holding it from that dive into the deep pool? It had all happened so fast. That moment of stillness vanished with the same speed as Andrew pulled Emmy from her arms.

Oh, dear Lord, was the little girl still breathing?

Yes. Not only breathing, Emmy was sobbing now, her arms wrapped around her father's neck so tightly it was a wonder he could still breathe himself.

'It's okay, honey. Shh…you're all right. You're safe.'

The words were a little broken, the overload of relief so obvious it brought tears to Alice's eyes. How many parents would have spoken in anger in the emotional backwash of something being done that shouldn't have been done? Especially when it had led to a life-threatening situation. But these words held no hint of anger. They were pure reassurance. They were a thick cloak of comfort and a promise of protection.

This child meant everything to Andrew, didn't she? He would have risked his own life in a heartbeat to save her. But, if it hadn't been for Jake, this scene could well have been very, very different. Alice began to shake. She was frozen, of course, soaked with icy water, but part of her reaction was knowing how close they had come to tragedy. Jake was a hero! She turned to see her big dog vigorously shaking the water from his shaggy coat and then he looked up at his mistress, his tail waving slowly.

The tears on Alice's face were invisible, thanks to the water still streaming from her hair. She crouched and hugged Jake. Andrew was using one hand to pull open the jacket he was wearing so he could cover Emmy but he was looking down.

'Jake …' His voice cracked and he stopped speaking.

Alice saw the way his eyes squeezed shut and the muscles in his face fought for control. She tried to smile, to tell him that he didn't need to say anything. She understood.

More, she had to take part of the blame for leaving Emmy unsupervised for long enough to get into trouble. She was the one who'd pulled out the verbal trick that had been nasty enough to distract Andrew.

She couldn't smile. Her teeth were chattering so hard she could barely speak.

'Y-you'd…b-be-better g-get Em-my home. D-dry…'

'Come with us,' Andrew said. 'I'll have a fire going in no time. Hot soup.'

'N-no.' Alice shook her head, the movement jerky. She wrapped her arms around herself tightly because she was shivering so violently it felt as if she might actually fall over. 'W-we're g-good.'

And they were. Her pot belly stove had been alight since before she'd begun hanging the washing out and the cottage would be as warm as toast. She had a pile of old towels in the wash house and she could dry Jake off while her bathtub was filling with lovely hot water. They all needed to move now, however, before the chill of a frosty night really set in.

By tacit consent they all started walking. Emmy had stopped crying but her head was buried against Andrew's shoulder and the rest of her was covered by the padded anorak. Her father was talking to her. Reassuring her as his long legs covered the ground at a speed that left Alice and Jake lagging behind.

He didn't seem to notice when she turned towards the cottage. He kept going towards the big house, striding away with his precious burden, totally focused on getting his daughter home and safe.

And that was fine. Perfectly understandable. No doubt he would thank Alice when she saw him at work tomorrow. He might even feel grateful enough to give her a little more time to find a new place to live.

Or not. It was blatantly obvious he needed assistance in caring for his child until she learned the boundaries of what was acceptable behaviour in her new and exciting environment.

Alice was so cold by the time her bath was ready it was hard enough to turn the taps off, let alone peel still-soaked clothes from her body. A curious exhaustion had also set in and the physical effort of tugging free the skin-tight jodhpurs was almost too much. They rolled themselves into a noose around her ankles so she was forced to sit on the bathroom floor. Every time she tried to force the roll of fabric over her heels, either her stiff fingers refused to cooperate or her arms began to ache with the effort.

Jake was lying on the rug in front of the pot belly stove, happily soaking in its warmth as he finished drying. Alice was alone in her tiny bathroom. Isolated in this small cottage. What if she couldn't get the damn jodhpurs off and she was left getting more and more exhausted and hypothermic? If she tried to get up she might fall and hit her head on the side of the old claw foot bath and then she'd have a head injury as well as hypothermia and she might die!

Alone.

How long would it take Andrew to bother coming to the cottage to find out why she'd disappeared? Three weeks, maybe? Until the date she was supposed to have left the premises?

Stupid tears prickled and Alice was so close to simply giving in to them. It took enormous strength to give herself a decent mental shake.

'Don't be so *ridiculous*,' she said aloud.

She put the ball of one foot against the stubborn roll of fabric on the other ankle, braced herself against the wall and pushed. Hard. It worked, on both sides. It was much easier to peel off the soggy woollen socks and the rest of her clothing, apart from an extended struggle with the catch on her bra, but finally she could climb into the deep bath of gently steaming water.

At first, the heat stung her overly cold skin but after a few minutes it began to seep in to warm her flesh. Some time later, after a top-up from the hot tap, it felt as if her bones were thawing at last and her fingers recovered enough to cope with getting the lid open on her shampoo bottle. Alice soaped her hair and then held her breath and submerged herself to rinse the soap clear.

The horror of what had almost happened in the river was receding and she could finally relax and soak in the warm water now scented with the almond essence from her shampoo. She was safe. Emmy was safe, thank God.

More than safe. As the tension was washed away, Alice was taken back to that tiny moment of time when she'd been held, along with the child, in Andrew's fierce embrace. It had given her just a glimpse of what it would be like to be that…*loved*.

And it made her want to cry. Yet again. What on earth was happening to her? Alice Palmer didn't faint in the face of shocking events. She didn't cry, either. She dealt with things. Made the best of whatever life threw at her and moved on. The way she'd learned to from such an early age when her parents had died and she had been sent to live with first her gran and then boarding schools. She'd moved on from relationships and jobs and places to live that hadn't worked out so why was she feeling so unsettled now?

Where had this new poignant ache in her heart sprung from?

Because she'd never been loved the way Andrew loved Emmy?

Yet, she amended firmly. Okay, it hadn't happened so far but surely there was someone out there who could love her like that? One day. Someone who would trust her and care about her and want to protect her and...

...and be there if she got her trousers stuck around her ankles and hit her head on the side of the bath!

Dismayed at the way she seemed intent on pulling herself down, Alice tugged the plug from the bath and climbed out. She dried herself, wrapped her hair in a towel and then put on the warmest pair of pyjamas she could find. The dark blue ones with yellow stars and moons all over them. Ancient flannelette things her gran had given her years ago. A dressing gown was not something Alice had ever bothered acquiring, but Gran's shawl decorated the back of the small couch in her sitting room so she wrapped that around her shoulders to sit in front of the stove and comb conditioner through her hair.

A long and boring chore, given its length, but it was essential if she wanted to keep any kind of control over her curls. And it was relaxing once the worst of the tangles were gone. Alice kept combing, hoping the heat would dry it quickly. Again and again she pulled the wide-toothed comb from her crown to the ends of her hair that reached almost to her waist. The action, combined with the warmth of the stove, was hypnotic. She had no idea how long she sat there. Or when she dropped the comb into her lap. Or how her arms had gone around herself again in an unconscious, tactile reminder of what was filling her mind.

That moment.

The desire to not only be loved by someone that much but to be loved by someone like Andrew.

No. *By* Andrew himself.

Fantasy was another drug. Powerful and compelling. So consuming that when Jake's head rose sharply and he emitted a low warning growl Alice leapt to her feet, allowing no time to remind herself how safe she knew this haven to be. The comb clattered to the wooden floorboards and the shawl slipped from her shoulders as her heart started to pound. The knock on the door a second or two later echoed the thumping behind her ribs.

'It's okay, Jake,' she said reassuringly. 'I know who it is.'

There was only one person it could be at this time of night, on a property that was so far away from any main roads. But why had he come? Was something wrong with Emmy? Was she showing some nasty after-effect from her near drowning? Aspiration pneumonia, perhaps?

Alice pulled open the door, letting in a blast of frosty air and revealing a slightly out-of-breath man.

'What is it?' she questioned. 'What's wrong?'

'Nothing.' Andrew's breath was coming out in white puffs.

'But you've been running!'

'I don't want to leave Em for too long.'

'Is she all right?'

'She's fine. Fast asleep.' Andrew held up what looked like a walkie-talkie radio. 'I'm well within range if she wakes up and calls and it only took me ninety seconds to run here.'

'But...*why*?'

'I had to come.' Andrew was wearing his jacket but his hands were bare. He rubbed them together, obviously cold. The night air was still rushing into the cottage and Alice was suddenly aware of the nip on her bare toes.

She shivered. 'You'd better come in, then.'

Andrew hesitated for a moment. He was staring at her loose, still damp hair. His gaze travelled to her bare feet and must have taken in the pyjamas on the way.

'I'm sorry. It didn't occur to me that you might be getting ready for bed.'

'I'm not.' Alice tried to ignore the heat her cheeks were generating. 'I haven't even had dinner yet. Look, come in. I need to shut this door before we turn my house into a fridge.'

Alice stepped back and Andrew followed. She shut the door. Jake eyed their visitor with deep suspicion.

'I had to come and thank you,' Andrew said solemnly. 'And Jake.'

He looked down at the dog glued to Alice's leg and then, to her astonishment, he crouched so that his face was level with Jake's.

'You saved Emmy,' he told the dog. 'You are the best dog in the entire world.'

Jake looked up, caught the approving curl of Alice's lips and then he eyed Andrew again. His tail waved in a single wag. Andrew held out his hand and Jake stretched his neck to sniff his fingers. The tail moved again and Alice felt the chill as her dog deserted her leg to step closer to Andrew and accept a scratch behind his ears.

Alice stepped closer to the stove. She eyed the shawl puddle on the floor but it was embarrassing enough to be caught wearing old night-sky pyjamas. To don a homemade, multi-coloured creation would be even more bizarre.

'And you.' Andrew straightened with an easy, smooth motion. He walked towards Alice and held out his hand again. '*You* saved my daughter.'

How weird, to be offered a handshake. Except, when Alice accepted, her hand wasn't shaken. Andrew took it in both of his and clasped it firmly.

'There are no words,' he said softly, 'that could tell you how grateful I am.'

He didn't need words. Alice could feel it. Like a miniature version of the circle his arms had created earlier. And she could feel her eyes widening with the wonder of it. The *power*.

She couldn't hold his gaze because it was too much. The longing that stirred deep within her was so sharp it was unbearable. She had to break the contact. To look away and pull her hand free.

'There's no need to say anything,' she managed. 'I...understand.' She dragged in a new breath. 'And I need to apologise. It would never have happened if I hadn't said what I did and—'

'No,' Andrew interrupted. 'I—'

Alice shook her head, overriding the interruption. She had to finish what she was saying.

'And I wouldn't have done it. I was upset but I hate gossip even if it's true. There's no way I would spread rumours that I know have no basis in truth.'

She risked another glance at Andrew to find him looking startled. As though what she'd just said was hard to take in. His steady gaze was penetrating.

'Thank you,' he said slowly. After a long pause, he spoke again. 'And I need to tell you that I never believed you took those drugs. But—'

He seemed to be struggling to find an explanation. Or possibly an apology, but it wasn't necessary. Alice could see how sincere he was and she could feel the weight of mistrust already starting to slide from her shoulders.

'You did what you had to do at the time,' she offered. 'I understand.'

Her acceptance didn't seem to be enough, however. Andrew was frowning now. He opened his mouth but, instead of him making a sound, the radio transmitter in his hand crackled into life. They both heard a tiny muffled cry and then some words, too mumbled to be comprehensible.

'She's just talking in her sleep,' Andrew said.

But that intent look had gone from his face. His attention was diverted.

'Maybe you should go back,' Alice suggested. 'In case she's waking up.'

The single nod confirmed that she had read Andrew's thoughts, but he hesitated as Alice opened her door, in the same way he had before coming in. She thought he was about to say something else, but then he simply gave her another nod and disappeared into the night.

The braid was back again this morning, of course, but Andrew couldn't look at that rope of hair without thinking of how it had looked last night, cascading over Alice's shoulders in a ripple of deep chestnut with copper sparkles from the light. Hopefully, the awareness was mainly due to having to think about hair on his patient.

Seven-year-old Sean had ridden his bike under a low-hanging tree branch and given himself a decent scalp laceration. Andrew was using hair ties rather than sutures to close it. He selected just a few hairs on each side of the cut and tied the first half of the knot to draw the skin together.

'Bit of glue, thanks, Alice.'

She leaned closer to dab a spot of tissue adhesive to the top of the knot. 'You're being very good, keeping still like this, Sean.' Then she caught her bottom lip between her teeth as she glanced up. 'You didn't want gloves?'

Andrew shook his head as he completed the knot. 'There's no bleeding now.' He started the procedure again at the centre of the laceration. 'And it's too hard to pick up tiny bunches of hair with gloves on. I can't feel it properly.'

Explaining his lack of basic personal protection equipment was enough to make him more aware of the feel of the child's hair between his fingers.

Enough to make him wonder whether Alice's hair would feel this silky. Not that he'd want to be holding a piece the size of fishing line, mind you. No. He'd want to bury his fingers in it and crumple it against her head while he positioned it perfectly in order to meet his kiss.

'Will it hurt?'

'Sorry?' What Andrew had flitting through the back of his mind wasn't likely to hurt at all. Quite the opposite!

'When he combs his hair?' Sean's mother was looking anxious.

Andrew finished the last knot. 'He'll need to be careful not to catch the knots with the comb. Don't wash his hair for five days and, when you do, just rub gently over the knots. If they're still there in ten days, you can cut them out.'

'Can I have a bandage?' Sean asked.

'You don't need one,' Alice told him. 'We put special glue on that's going to keep it nice and clean. Like superglue.'

'You superglued my head back together? Cool!'

'You can tell them all about it at school.' Andrew smiled. 'No headache?'

'Nah, I'm good. Can I ride my bike again later?'

'Only if you're wearing your helmet,' his mother said with a sigh. 'Like you're *supposed* to do.'

Sean was still looking up at his doctor. 'What she said.' Andrew nodded. 'You be careful out there, young man. Stop giving your mum frights like that.'

Alice was nodding her agreement. She'd seen how pale Sean's mother had been on arrival, still pressing a blood-stained towel to her son's head. She turned to

Andrew as Sean left the cubicle and the message in her eyes was as clear as if she'd spoken aloud.

Emmy's safe now, it said. Try not to dwell on it.

The message stayed with him as he moved onto his next patient. Yes, Emmy was safe, but he couldn't remember that without remembering what Alice had done without a moment's hesitation—hurling herself into that river to rescue his daughter. She'd read his mind back there in Sean's cubicle, too. His blood still ran cold, imagining what could have happened.

The horrific thoughts had kept him awake for much of last night. Along with the way Alice's apology had made him feel.

Humble.

No. Make that ashamed.

It was a minute or two's walk to get to the woman with abdominal pain who was now in the observation area but needed reassessment, and it gave Andrew a small window of time to think about it yet again. To try and justify his actions.

Okay, he'd told her he'd never believed she'd taken those drugs and that was good but he'd stopped short of telling her he *knew* she hadn't.

He wanted to, but he couldn't.

If there was any way he could prevent it, Andrew was never going to have anyone look at Emmy differently because her mother had been a drug addict. No one. Instinct told him that it would make no difference to Alice but he couldn't guarantee that, could he? He couldn't guarantee that she would never mention it to anyone else and, however small that risk was, it was one he really wasn't prepared to take.

History seemed to be repeating itself in so many ways. Inadequate care for Emmy. A blackmail attempt by a woman. Doing what he had to do at the time. It had been the potential risk to others of being wrong that had made him unable to support Alice's innocence regarding those missing drugs. It was exactly the same as not telling her the entire story now. He was protecting Emmy.

Alice would understand that last one if she ever found out, but why would she? He'd insisted on complete confidentiality from all medical personnel involved with Melissa's treatment and the files were now out of circulation for ever.

The subject need never come up because he was just as prepared as Alice seemed to be to put the past and all its rumours behind them. They had a new bond now, through Emmy.

A bond that seemed destined to become stronger. Mid-afternoon, a trauma case came in that needed full-on attention. Andrew couldn't leave the bedside of the man with a head injury from being knocked off his motorbike. He had to ask Alice to go and get whatever urgent message someone was trying to leave him by phone.

She came back as the staff had stepped away from the centre of the resuscitation area to allow X-rays to be taken of the patient's neck, chest and pelvis.

'It's the after-school care facility,' she informed Andrew. 'Emmy's running a bit of a temperature and has a runny nose. They think she should be taken home.'

Andrew stared through the heavy glass protecting them from an unwanted dose of radioactivity. 'I can't leave right now.' He rubbed the back of his neck. 'It's probably just a cold.'

Alice was nodding but he could see the concern in her face.

'I'll get away as soon as I can but my shift doesn't end till six.' And he was needed again now. The X-ray technicians had finished. His patient needed treatment.

'I'm finished now,' Alice said. 'I could pick Emmy up and take her home if you like.'

The offer was too good to pass up. 'Are you sure?'

'Yes. I'd like to make sure she's all right. After yesterday.'

'Bring her in here if you're at all worried.'

'I will. Otherwise, I'll take her home.'

'Grab my key. They're on the desk in my office. The house key is the big, old one. I'll see you as soon as I can.'

'Don't rush. We'll be fine.' Alice was on her way out of the room.

'Alice?'

She turned back.

'Thank you.'

The fact that Andrew had accepted her offer of help with childcare had been unexpected.

He might not be able to tell her she was worthy of his trust, but actions spoke louder than words and this was a loud shout.

It hadn't been a grudging acceptance because he had no choice, either. He'd thanked her, when it would have been perfectly acceptable to have turned his attention immediately back to his patient. And not only had he thanked her; Alice had been treated to a glimmer of one of *those* smiles.

Directed at herself!

It gave her a warm glow that might have negated the need to build a fire if it hadn't been for poor little Emmy. The girl had red cheeks and overbright eyes and her nose was dripping like a tap. Her chest was clear, however, and her temperature only slightly raised. She wasn't sick enough for it to be any more than a mild viral infection.

'We're going to give you some paracetamol and then a lovely warm bath,' Alice told her charge. 'Have you got pyjamas and slippers and a dressing gown?'

Emmy nodded. 'Are you going to be my nanny now?'

'Just for today, hon. Till Daddy gets home.'

'Coz I'm sick?'

'That's right.' Alice led the way into the kitchen to measure out the liquid paracetamol she'd brought from work. She lifted Emmy to sit on the old scrubbed pine table while she opened drawers to find a spoon.

'I like being sick,' Emmy announced.

'*Do* you?'

'Yes.' Her small face was screwed up in distaste while the anti-inflammatory medicine was swallowed but then Emmy smiled at Alice. 'I think I'm going to be sick for a long time.'

'No, it's just a cold, hon. You'll be as right as rain in a day or two.' Emmy's scowl made her raise her eyebrows. 'You don't *want* to be sick for a long time, do you?'

'Yes, I do.'

'Why?'

'Coz you'll look after me.'

'Ohh.' Alice lifted the child down and then took her hand as they left the kitchen.

Oh, help. Emmy sure knew how to climb right into someone's heart, didn't she? Andrew had made a valid point the other day. Getting attached would make it much harder when she had to leave. For both Emmy and herself.

Maybe this hadn't been such a brilliant idea. Except this was the first time she'd stepped inside this wonderful old house and Alice had to admit she was fascinated.

'Where's the bathroom, hon?'

'Up the stairs. C'mon, I'll show you.'

Alice was being tugged along by one hand. She ran the other up the smooth banister of golden wood, where each rail beneath was intricately carved with vines and flowers. Brass rods held a faded oriental-style carpet in place, which seamlessly extended to run the length of the gallery at the top.

'This is my room.'

There were shelves full of books and toys scattered on the floor. A doll's house in one corner and a blackboard easel where Emmy's name had been beautifully written in different coloured chalks, presumably by her father. Alice turned her head and had to catch her breath.

'You've got a four-poster bed!'

'Daddy told them to leave it in the house. He said it was for me coz I'm his princess.'

Alice touched the drapes of white muslin. 'It's beautiful.'

'I like it...' Emmy nodded '...but I like Daddy's better.'

'Oh?' Alice moved again in response to new tugging. She knew where Emmy was leading her now and had to squash the frisson of guilt that the thought of seeing Andrew's bedroom gave her. She shouldn't be doing this.

Emmy trotted ahead, looking less unwell by the moment, but wiping her nose on her other sleeve. She let go of Alice's hand and climbed onto a much more ordinary-looking bed that had plain, dark wooden ends.

'Why do you like it more than yours?' Alice tried not to look around, but she couldn't help seeing the crumpled shirt in the corner and the handful of coins carelessly dumped on the chest of drawers.

'Coz Daddy's in here.' Emmy sounded as though Alice should have already known that, but she'd been more successful in trying not to think about it than looking around the room, hadn't she?

Trying not to imagine him with his head on those pillows, sprawled across what was a very large space for one person to sleep in. Wearing...what, just pyjama pants and nothing else? She turned away quickly. What if Emmy later told her father how red Alice's face had gone when she'd been in his room?

'Bath time,' she said firmly. 'And then we're going to make a fire and some dinner and you can find all your favourite stories for me to read to you.'

'When's Daddy coming home?'

'When he's finished at work.'

'Before bedtime?'

'I should think so. What time do you have to go to bed?'

Emmy's eyes might be too bright to be healthy but they hadn't lost their determined glint. 'When Daddy tells me to.'

He was a lot later than he'd wanted to be. It had taken time to sort all his patients enough to be happy to transfer their care, and it was after 7:00 p.m. by the time Andrew made it home. He was tired enough to be thinking it was crazy to be living this far from town.

Yesterday's scare with Emmy, a virtually sleepless night and a full-on day with the extra worry of how unwell Emmy might be adding more tension to the last few hours had drained him utterly. His briefcase felt like a lead weight as he dropped it by the hall stand. He pulled off his jacket and snagged it onto a hook and then turned to move towards the kitchen end of the vast hallway.

Something felt very different from the previous times he'd arrived home here. Was it the delicious aroma coming from the kitchen? The warmth he could feel from the slightly ajar doorway that led to the old library? Or was it what he could see in the soft glow of lamplight when he pushed that door open?

Alice sat on one end of a couch, holding a book she was reading from, with her other arm around the lumpy shape that was Emmy all bundled up in a duvet.

Maybe it was because he was exhausted and hungry and worried about his daughter that made this scene seem poignant enough to make his throat constrict painfully. Or maybe it was a combination of this and the warmth and the smell of food. It made him feel as if he'd actually come *home* for the first time he could remember since being a child himself.

Alice stopped reading as he moved further into the room. She smiled but said nothing.

Andrew looked at the still shape beside her. 'Is she okay?'

'Sound asleep,' Alice said softly. 'She had her dinner an hour ago and another dose of paracetamol about thirty minutes ago. I put a hot-water bottle in her bed.'

'I'll take her up.'

He had to bend down to gather Emmy and the duvet into his arms, which put him close enough to feel the warmth of Alice and to imagine what it had been like for Emmy, cuddled against her and listening to her voice reading a story as she drifted to sleep.

It would have felt like home. Like having a real mother for the first time in her short life.

Just as well he had to leave the room and attend to his daughter. Andrew needed time to shake off this odd sensation that he suddenly had regarding Alice Palmer—that he no longer wanted to evict her.

That he wanted... needed to keep her in his life somehow.

He came back downstairs to find her taking a hot meal from the oven for him. A rich-smelling beef casserole and baked potatoes. Homely comfort food.

'Have *you* eaten?'

She nodded. 'I had some with Emmy.'

'Would you like a glass of wine? I think this—' he looked down at the plate of food on the table '—deserves the best red I can find.' He reached into the wine rack beside the old Aga stove and then turned to search a drawer for a corkscrew.

'I...shouldn't. Jake will be wondering where *his* dinner is.'

'Please...stay for a few minutes.' Andrew pulled out a chair. 'I need to thank you properly and I want to ask about how Emmy's been, but if I don't eat I might fall over in a huge heap. Lunch was so long ago I can't even remember whether I ate it.'

Alice sat but it was on the edge of her chair. Andrew put two glasses and the open wine bottle in front of her. 'Could you carry these, please?'

Now she looked really nervous. 'Where to?'

'To enjoy that lovely fire you made.' He picked up his plate. 'Coming?'

'Just for a minute or two.' The agreement sounded deliberate. 'There is something I'd like to talk to you about.'

He didn't find out what that something was until he'd eaten his whole plateful of that delicious food. Until he was warm and full and quite happy with what Alice had been telling him about Emmy's condition. The wine was also contributing to making him feel extraordinarily good.

'What was it,' he enquired, 'that you wanted to talk to me about?'

'Childcare.' Alice got up from the other couch to put another log on the fire.

'Ohh.' The sound was a groan. 'Ringing the agency was on my list for today but I didn't get a spare minute. Thank you again for your help. I don't know how I'd have managed without it.'

'It was no trouble,' Alice said quietly. 'I…enjoyed it. Emmy's a delight.'

'You didn't have to go the extra mile like this.' Andrew set his empty plate on the floor by his feet.

'It was an idea I had,' Alice said slowly. She was still kneeling beside the fireplace. 'I wanted to show you rather than just talk about it.'

Show him? Andrew's head felt a little fuzzy. Had to be the wine because he was looking at her kneeling there with the firelight playing on her hair and face and he thought she was talking about making the fire and dinner and caring for his child. Being a homemaker. A mother to Emmy. A…a *wife*?

And, God help him, but the idea was very, very appealing.

'I could be a nanny,' he heard Alice saying. 'And…a kind of housekeeper. It could work, if I juggled my shifts a bit so I did nights or weekends when you weren't on call.'

'Why would you want to do that? What's in it for you?'

'My home,' Alice said simply. 'I wouldn't want to be paid or anything. I'd just like to keep living in the cottage and you said you needed it for someone who would help with Emmy and things. I can do that. I'd *like* to do it. What…what do you think?'

What did he think? Andrew was aware of a ridiculous wash of disappointment that his tired brain had come up with entirely the wrong scenario. This was a business deal, nothing more.

Except…it could be more. They already had a bond of a past they didn't want to share with others. And a new bond through Emmy. This arrangement could give them a new base. An opportunity for each of them to provide something the other wanted instead of a threat of removing something. A positive spin on a situation they both needed to deal with.

A fresh start, even.

'It might work,' he said slowly. 'But…'

'…But?' Alice's eyes were huge. Fixed on him.

Andrew found himself leaning closer. 'But we'd have to trust each other.' And that was a problem, wasn't it? Hadn't he sworn never to trust another woman after what Melissa had put him through?

'I trust *you*,' Alice said softly. 'Do you think you can trust me?'

She didn't break the eye contact and Andrew was close enough now to see the flecks of gold in her eyes as the flames beside her flickered. He could see the tangle of dark lashes around them and the pale, smooth skin of her face. He could hear the hitch of her breath. Or was that his own?

How come he'd never noticed before that she was such an extraordinarily beautiful woman? A man could fall into eyes like those and not even want to save himself from drowning. It was all he could do not to lean further forward and touch her lips with his own.

'Yes,' he heard himself saying a little raggedly. 'I know I can.'

CHAPTER SIX

IT WAS enough.

That he trusted her and that she could keep the home she loved.

That she didn't have to try and achieve the impossible and make herself hate him.

This was a trial period but, even if Alice hadn't been so determined to make it work, it became rapidly clear that her idea had been brilliant. A bit of juggling was needed in the early days, but their colleagues were willing to help ensure that their shifts didn't clash and that one of them always had their days off on weekends. A routine was established with such astonishing ease it was hard for Alice not to think that this was meant to be happening.

That finally, for the first time in her life, the planets were aligning themselves exactly the way she would have dreamed.

On a day shift, Alice headed to work early and Andrew got Emmy ready for school and dropped her into the care centre on his way to work. Alice would finish at 3:00 p.m. and could get to school to collect

Emmy without her needing after school care. They would shop for groceries if needed on the way home and Alice would help Emmy with her homework, do housework like washing or ironing and then prepare dinner.

Caring for her pets was not an issue. Emmy was only too keen to visit Ben and help groom and feed him and Jake was more than welcome in the house where he would always have hero status.

If Alice had an afternoon shift, she took Emmy to school in the morning and Andrew collected her on his way home. She was more than prepared to put the extra effort into her side of this bargain. Especially when Andrew refused to take any further rent for her cottage or grazing land.

'You have no idea, do you,' he said to silence her protests, 'how much this will be worth to me if it works?'

And it *was* working, even with nights shifts factored in. When Alice had a night shift, she looked after Emmy in the morning and slept while the little girl was at school and when Andrew had to be at the hospital over-night she slept in the big house.

That first morning was a little awkward, certainly, when Andrew arrived home to find her making an early morning cup of tea in the kitchen, still in her pyjamas, but moments of discomfort like that wore off re-markably quickly. Or got dispensed with. Like Alice leaving to go back to the cottage when Andrew arrived home in the evenings to the meal she had prepared.

'Don't be daft,' he told her during the second week. 'You don't need to cook twice. Three times if you count feeding Emmy early. Stay and eat with me.'

If Emmy was still up, they would take their plates of food and eat in front of the fire and sometimes Emmy was allowed to toast marshmallows. If she was asleep, they would eat at the kitchen table. Being alone with each other in front of a fire would have been stepping over an unspoken boundary. This was, after all, an arrangement that happened to suit them both. No more than a second job for Alice. It had nothing to do with a more personal relationship.

Conversation was limited to either Emmy or work. By another tacit agreement, there was a boundary on a timeline. They didn't talk about the time they had worked together previously and they never stepped further back than that to learn anything about families or growing up. It was as if a completely new start was being made and it was either too early or inappropriate to venture into personal space.

And it was enough.

Too much, perhaps.

Given how well things were working, it was inevitable that somewhere along the way in those first weeks hope was born again.

And it blossomed.

Maybe it was the softening Alice saw in Andrew's face as the tension of making this new life work lessened. The smile that accompanied the appreciation he never failed to communicate. Or perhaps it was the day when they both happened to have a Saturday off work and Andrew had knocked at the door of the cottage mid-morning, with Emmy clinging to his hand and beaming triumphantly.

'We were wondering,' Andrew said, 'whether you might be available for a trip into town.'

He was wearing his faded jeans and a warm jersey, his dark blond hair a little more tousled than it ever looked at work, and Alice realised that any downside of this arrangement and the subsequent shift juggling that meant seeing less of him in the emergency department was more than made up for by seeing him like this in his role as a father and on his home ground. Being privileged enough to share a part of his private life.

Quite apart from the smile currently deepening the grooves on his cheeks and making the corners of his eyes crinkle. A smile that could easily persuade Alice she would be available for a trip to the moon if he happened to be asking.

Emmy was bouncing with excitement. 'For shopping,' she informed Alice. 'For *me*.'

'Em's a bit short on clothes and shoes and things,' Andrew added. 'And…um…you're a girl.'

'Like *me*!' Emmy crowed.

'And…as it's been pointed out to me more than once this morning, I'm not.'

'No…you're not…' Alice was caught. Falling into the blue eyes of the man on her doorstep. Eyes that told her she wasn't a girl at all. That she was a woman and that Andrew was a mere male. And that he was as aware of the implications of that as she was.

And Alice knew she was lost. That she would always *be* lost unless—until—Andrew found her.

She was here. She would always be here. When he was ready and if he chose to find her, it would be so easy.

'I'd love to come shopping,' was all she could say.

* * *

It was at moments like this that Andrew had to remind himself very firmly that this was merely a business arrangement. That Alice was doing this because she needed accommodation for herself and her pets.

The problem was, it was working so well that at odd moments, Andrew was inclined to forget. Like now, with Emmy on her booster seat in the back and Alice in the front passenger seat of his car as they made their way into the city for the shopping expedition.

Somehow, over the period of about a month, Alice had become such an integral part of their lives that he couldn't imagine her not being here.

He'd been singing along with both of them to some silly song about caterpillars that was on Emmy's favourite CD but he trailed into silence that nobody seemed to notice. It was a sparkling winter's day with the clearest blue sky he'd ever seen and a breathtaking view of the Southern Alps with a good coating of snow. And his daughter sounded so happy Andrew found himself smiling.

Then he glanced to his left, to where Alice was sitting there in her jeans and a soft-looking jumper in a shade of deep russet...just like the loose braid of hair that fell over her shoulder. She was gamely trying to keep up with a chorus that involved a lot of numbers to do with caterpillar legs and she was using her fingers to try and keep track. Slim, capable, elegant fingers and hands that were a perfect match for the rest of her body.

A body that Andrew was finding increasingly attractive. An attraction Andrew couldn't give in to because he would be risking a status quo that was—almost—perfect.

His smile faded as he found himself wishing away

the past. Wishing that he could be the man he used to be—untainted by a past that had destroyed such a big part of his heart.

Wishing that he'd noticed her properly all those years ago instead of being blinded by Melissa's charms and the flattery of being apparently adored. Before his ability to trust at that level had been damaged beyond repair.

But if he wished all that away, it would mean Emmy wouldn't exist and she was the sun in his universe. His first adult experience of unconditional, reciprocated love. The need to cherish and protect his daughter had flickered into life the moment he'd held his newborn in his arms and the flame only burned more brightly as the years had gone by.

No. He couldn't do anything that would pose a threat to this arrangement that was ensuring Emmy's well-being and happiness. Alice might run a mile if she knew how he was feeling and how hard it was to try and keep his hands off her. He would be abusing a position of power over her as her landlord. Or employer or whatever role she now saw him as having.

Except... Having to concentrate on the traffic as they made their way into the central city gave Andrew an excuse to let his thoughts wander a little further down that track. Sometimes, he had the impression that Alice might feel the same way. The way she smiled, for example, when he came home from work to a house that was feeling more and more like the home he'd always dreamed of. Or when she seemed to be reluctant to head back to the cottage and leave him to tackle the dishes when he insisted on contributing to the housework. Or like that moment outside her cottage today when he'd told her that Emmy wanted female companionship for the shopping trip.

Was it just wishful thinking that made him imagine a crackle of sexual tension?

If so, he was being an idiot. There was no guarantee that any relationship would work, no matter how eager the participants were. He'd learned that painful lesson very thoroughly. And if he started something that turned to custard it would be far worse for both himself and Emmy when Alice made an exit from their lives. The routine they had going now was making it possible for him to settle into his new job and for Emmy to settle into the huge change of starting school.

She'd grown up so much in the last few weeks. His little girl had left babyhood well behind. Her confidence and determination seemed to grow stronger every day. She certainly knew what she wanted when it came to choosing clothes.

'I want jeans,' she announced. 'Like Alice's. And boots.'

'Boots?'

'You know—the ones with the stretchy bits on the sides.'

'Jodhpur boots,' Alice supplied. 'They are quite practical for being outside on a farm.'

'We won't find them in a shoe shop. Maybe another time, Em. We need to get stuff that's useful for school.'

'I want to wear boots to school.'

'No,' Andrew said firmly. 'Shoes for school. Boots for home.'

'So I can get some boots, then?'

Andrew looked helplessly at Alice but she just grinned. 'There's a saddlery shop not that far away. They do boots.'

They did more than boots. Emmy found a rack of child-sized jodhpurs and she turned a look of such pleading towards her father that he shook his head in defeat.

'Why not? You do sit on Ben quite a lot these days.'

The salesgirl was happy to help find sizes to fit. She found a pair of jodhpurs with suede inserts on the back and insides of the legs.

'Sticky bums,' she told Emmy. 'They help you stay in the saddle.'

She held the toggle on the back of the boots as Emmy excitedly stuffed her feet into a shiny brown pair.

'What's your pony's name?' she asked.

'I haven't got a pony,' Emmy said sadly. 'I sit on Ben but he's too big for me to ride.'

The girl looked up at Andrew. 'If you're interested,' she said, 'I happen to know a small pony that would be perfect for a beginner that's looking for a new home.'

'No, thank you,' Andrew said.

'Oh, yes, *please*!' Emmy said at exactly the same moment.

The salesgirl grinned at Alice. 'The advertisement is on the counter. Maybe Mum gets the casting vote.'

The odd stillness that seemed to freeze time was enough to make the salesgirl blush as she realised she'd said something awkward.

Andrew couldn't say anything. He didn't dare look at Alice. But Emmy, bless her, wasn't in the least perturbed.

'I haven't got a mum,' she said. 'She's dead.'

'Oh...' The salesgirl didn't know where to look. 'I'm so sorry.'

Andrew held his breath. It was the kind of sympathetic response everybody offered and, initially, it had been easy to respond to. He'd been grieving as deeply as any widower. Mourning the fact that any possibility of a meaningful marriage was gone. Sad beyond measure that his daughter would grow up motherless.

But he'd been living with that grief ever since Emmy had been born.

Did Alice think it odd that he never mentioned his wife? Or that there were no photographs on display? Did Emmy ever say anything when he wasn't around? Probably not. She'd been only three years old when Melissa had died and she'd only seen her mother before that during the periods that her mother hadn't been resident in rehab clinics. That her mother was dead was a fact she was happy to relate to anyone, as she had just done to the poor salesgirl.

The bond she should have had with her mother had been Andrew's privilege to receive. Past nannies had been loved but hadn't intruded into that bond.

Until now.

Somehow, Alice had crept in and Andrew had no idea what, if anything, he could or should do about it.

Just like he had no idea how to rescue this salesgirl from her obvious, acute embarrassment.

But Emmy had that in hand as well.

'It's all right,' she told the girl kindly. 'I've got Alice now.'

* * *

The embarrassment over her mistaken identity was still there thirty minutes or more later when Andrew steered them all into a fast food restaurant for lunch.

Had it been an attempt to gloss over the incident that had made him agree to all Emmy's desired purchases in the saddlery? Even to the point of taking a copy of the advertisement for the pony and saying he would think about it?

At least it gave them something to talk about over their hamburgers and fries.

'His name is Paddington Bear,' Alice said in answer to Emmy's query.

'Very English,' Andrew noted. 'In fact, he looks remarkably like a Thelwell pony.'

He did. Paddington was a tiny Shetland with long shaggy hair and a very round belly. According to the information on the advertisement, he also had an unblemished record of being a beloved children's pony for the last eighteen years.

'Isn't that extremely old?' Andrew asked.

'Not really. I've known ponies who are still full of go when they're thirty.' Alice smiled at the photograph. 'He's certainly cute and if he's as quiet as this says, he really could be a perfect first pony.'

Andrew shook his head. 'I don't know anything about keeping ponies.'

'But I do,' Alice said softly.

Emmy was apparently entirely focused on dipping fries into the little sachet of tomato sauce and eating them very, very slowly, like a rabbit nibbling on carrots. Maybe she was hoping that if she kept very quiet and wished very hard the adults involved would make a decision in her favour.

She didn't see the way those adults were looking at each other right now.

'What happens,' Andrew asked slowly, holding Alice's gaze, 'when you go somewhere else?'

Alice had to put down her food. Her appetite vanished as her heart skipped a beat. She couldn't look away from Andrew. What was she seeing in that intense gaze? Some kind of plea? An invitation to reveal what was becoming impossible to hide? She had no control over the silent assurance she knew her gaze was sending.

You can trust me. Always.

'Why would I want to go somewhere else?' was what she tried to say aloud. It came out in little more than a whisper.

Andrew made no audible response to that but something changed.

Something huge.

It felt as though time had frozen again. As though the earth had just tilted on its axis. And then she saw a flicker of warmth in Andrew's eyes that had the effect of generating an astonishing heat. Thank goodness she was sitting down, Alice thought hazily, because she was melting here. She couldn't even feel her legs. Couldn't feel anything below the level of that heat low down in her abdomen.

The silence hung there long enough for Emmy's head to jerk up to reveal a small, anxious face.

Alice could feel the drag as Andrew transferred his gaze to his daughter.

'You had enough to eat, pumpkin? Shall I ring the number on that advertisement and see if Paddington Bear is home for visitors?'

The squeal of excitement from Emmy made heads turn all over the crowded restaurant. This time, Alice and Andrew could exchange a glance and share the embarrassment. Dilute it with understanding and amusement.

The way doting parents could.

And it felt…right.

Alice drew in a very deep breath as she emptied their trays of rubbish into the bin near the door. She let it out in a long, almost relieved sigh.

They'd stepped onto a new road. No. An old road for her. One that she'd been stranded on for a very long time. The difference was that Andrew had joined her. And maybe this time it would lead somewhere. It didn't matter how long it took to take the next steps because stepping onto that road at all was the hardest one to take. You couldn't go backwards and it was only a matter of time before forward movement was inevitable.

And it didn't matter how long that was going to take because Alice had been waiting for years. She was more than happy to keep waiting for as long as it took Andrew to catch up. She fully expected that to takes weeks, if not months.

No way was she prepared for it to take only a matter of hours.

She didn't want to go somewhere else.

She wanted to be here.

With him.

For ever?

Despite every argument his mind wanted to produce for the rest of that amazing day, Andrew couldn't get past the notion that he *could* trust Alice.

He wanted to, dammit! He wanted to trust her, heart and soul. Enough to be able to give and thereby receive the kind of love that could last for ever. He'd given away even the possibility of finding that for himself. Until he'd seen something in Alice's gaze back there in the fast food outlet. Something that had touched him in a place he'd believed didn't exist any more.

He knew, on a rational level, that not all women were like Melissa. Self-centred and deceitful and incapable of taking the feelings of others into consideration. And he knew Alice wasn't anything like that.

But he also knew the agony that believing in someone and being proved wrong time and again could cause. He could deal with it himself if he had to, but he couldn't deal with having to try and explain it to his innocent child. Were they already past the point that she could be protected, though? Emmy trusted Alice completely. Loved her.

Andrew could see it in the way his little girl hung onto Alice's hand and looked to *her* for reassurance when she was sitting on top of one small, fat pony, being led around for a trial ride. He saw the look of pure joy they shared when the trial was deemed complete.

For a moment Andrew felt a pang of...not jealousy exactly. A sadness, almost, in acknowledging that Emmy would find people in this world that could share a bond he couldn't share. Others could give her things she needed that he couldn't provide. Was this a part of parenting? A gradual letting go, a tiny piece at a time? Giving Emmy freedom to explore the world and what others had to offer?

And then Alice bent to whisper something in Emmy's ear and she looked up and smiled as Emmy launched herself to hug her father and suddenly he was included in that joy. A part of a totally new adventure. He hugged Emmy but looked over her shoulder at Alice, aware of something warm and tight in his chest as he tried to thank her with a look.

Something elemental was changing today and it was so much to try and get his head around that Andrew was feeling a little dazed. The easiest course of action was to go with the flow, especially when the current was this strong.

All he had to do was produce his chequebook. Do a lot of driving to go home and collect the horse float and then back to collect the new addition to the family, along with enough accessories to fill the back of Alice's truck. Paddington Bear came with everything he could possibly need. A saddle and bridle and warm coats. Brushes and lead ropes and feed buckets.

Emmy was glowing with excitement.

'Look, Daddy! Ben loves him. They're best friends already.'

It looked ridiculous, the giant black horse and the small hairy pony, but, amazingly, they were grazing nose to nose and looking as though they'd known each other for ever.

Andrew had a mental image of Alice on her horse holding the reins with just one hand. With one of those lead ropes in her other hand attached to a miniature version alongside. His stomach did a slow curl. Could he trust Alice to keep Emmy safe?

He had no choice. He could hardly buy a pony for his daughter and then refuse to allow her to learn to ride.

Could he trust Alice further than that?

The real test came later that evening when Emmy, exhausted by the most exciting day of her life, was soundly asleep.

Alice was insisting on being allowed to help clear up after the dinner they'd shared. She had a tea towel in her hands but Andrew grabbed the other end of the cloth.

'I'll do the dishes,' he said. 'You did most of the cooking.'

'It'll only take a minute.' Alice was smiling as she gave a tug.

Andrew tugged back. Harder. Hard enough to pull Alice closer.

So close, she was right there in front of him, looking up, and suddenly the laughter in her face faded. For a long, long moment they stood in absolute stillness and Andrew found himself sinking. He let his eyes make a slow map of her face. The wispy curls of new hair at her temples. The pale skin and delightful dusting of freckles. Those glorious hazel eyes with their golden flecks. A pretty snub nose that he had an urge to kiss the tip of. And then, at last, her lips. So soft-looking. Parted slightly to look...expectant.

Andrew forgot about kissing the tip of her nose. He bent his head so he could touch her lips with his own.

The softness...the sweetness... The electrifying bolt of desire was startling enough to make Andrew jerk back. He saw the same wonder in Alice's eyes but she didn't move. Didn't try and withdraw from him.

He could feel her breath on his face and see the beat of a rapid pulse in her neck. And then the tip of her tongue appeared to touch her lips where his lips had just been and the magnetic pull back was irresistible.

This time he was ready for that shaft of sensation that went through every cell in his body. He could keep control. To explore every delicious part of Alice's lips and mouth. To experiment with different amounts of pressure and let his tongue dance with hers.

He could slide his fingers into her hair and taste that silky skin on the side of her neck. Let his hands drift lower and discover the curve of her breast. He heard her gasp at the same moment he found the hardness of her nipples beneath the soft wool of her jersey.

And then he had to stop and pull back. While he still had some semblance of control. He was breathing hard and so was Alice. They were back to where they'd started. Standing there, staring at each other. But so much had changed.

'I don't want to stop,' Andrew confessed.

'Neither do I,' Alice whispered.

'I…um…haven't got a condom to my name.'

'Neither do I.' Alice licked her lips again and Andrew stifled a low groan of need. 'I…um…I am on the pill.'

'Oh?' *Why*? Was there—or had there recently been—someone else? Okay, this was jealousy. White-hot.

Alice sensed the unspoken demand and gave her head a tiny shake.

'It's not that…' She caught her breath. 'I haven't been in any kind of relationship for a very long time.'

'Neither have I. More than five years, in fact.' Not since Emmy was conceived, just about. How embarrassing was that? 'Beat that,' he said with a wry smile.

'I just about could.' Alice closed her eyes for a heartbeat. Was she also embarrassed admitting to a lack of any love-life?

Andrew swallowed. 'I've never had an STD.'

'Me neither.' Alice opened her eyes again and he could see that she understood what he was suggesting.

He could also see that she thought he was crazy. He *was* crazy. Except…he'd told her he trusted her but he hadn't when it really mattered, had he? He hadn't stood up for her in the face of those allegations about the drugs and she'd ended up losing everything. Her job. Her home. Probably most of her friends.

Going this far in the trust stakes now was like…an apology. A way of putting things right.

Maybe something of what he was thinking was being communicated to Alice because she blinked slowly and when he could see her eyes again he could see that the shock of suggestion was wearing off.

'We did all have to get tested for HIV after that patient bled everywhere in Emergency.'

'I was clear.'

'Me, too.'

So there it was. A desire that seemed equally intense on both sides. A clean bill of health and protection against pregnancy, if what Alice told him was the truth.

It was a question of trust. A huge amount of trust, but Andrew found he didn't need to even think about it any longer. He had an obligation to carry this through.

'I trust you, Alice,' he said slowly. 'Do you trust me?'

'Yes.'

He touched her face, softly trailing a finger from her brow, around her eye, across her cheekbone and finally to brush it across her lips.

'I want you, Alice Palmer.'

She didn't have to say anything. Her answer was in her eyes. In the way she mirrored his action and reached up to touch *his* face. In the way she released her breath in a sigh that held just the edge of a whimper of desire.

Andrew dropped his hand. He laced his fingers through hers and when he moved, she was right beside him. All the way up the stairs.

Into his bedroom.

CHAPTER SEVEN

'So…YOU and Andy Barrett.'

'Mmm.'

Jo eyed her friend with a mixture of respect and envy. 'Lucky you!'

'Mmm.'

'How long has it been going on for?' Jo was setting out the last plastic tray of the sushi she had brought in to share for lunch.

'Oh…a few weeks.'

'And you never said anything!'

'No.' Alice stirred some wasabi into the little pot of soy sauce and then dribbled it over a roll that had a delicious-looking mixture of chicken and avocado. 'I was…it was…'

Too precious to share. Too unbelievably good to be true. Alice had spent the last weeks expecting to wake up and find she was dreaming it all.

Jo was smiling as if she understood. For a moment, the two women ate in silence in the otherwise deserted staff room and then Jo glanced up.

'He's got a little girl, hasn't he?'

'Yes, Emmy. She's five.'

'And that's okay?'

'Better than okay. She's gorgeous.' Alice reached for another roll. 'These are great.'

'Leftovers from dinner last night. My flatmate was celebrating and went a bit overboard on the ordering.'

Alice swallowed her mouthful. 'Emmy's got a pony now. I'm teaching her to ride. She's such a gutsy little kid, she wants to get rid of the lead rein and be galloping over the hills already.'

'Sounds like a match made in heaven.'

'Mmm.' Alice couldn't help the smile that just kept growing.

It would have been enough that she and Andrew were now lovers and that the private times they had together were far more wonderful than any fantasy she had conjured up in the past. What made it breathtaking and had stolen her heart completely had been the way Andrew had trusted her.

She'd told him she was on the pill and protected from the risk of pregnancy and he had *trusted* her. Even when Melissa had probably told him the same thing when she had been deliberately trying to trap him into marriage. With that kind of history he would have been insane to trust her to that degree.

But he had. He still did. By the time either of them had the opportunity to buy condoms, it seemed as if it would be taking back that trust. Negating it.

The bubble of joy that Alice felt encased in these days was all the more astonishing because that level of trust —on both sides—and the fact that neither had suggested any kind of a backward step, made it seem as if they both knew they had found something permanent.

Sane people only had unprotected sex in a relationship where they felt safe. And safe meant commitment, didn't it? An unspoken pact that it was going somewhere important.

They'd both been celibate for so long as well, which implied that casual sex held no attraction for either of them. To take this step was huge.

And the sex was…amazing. Incredible. Andrew made her feel *so* beautiful. So desirable. So—

'Are you going to eat that last roll or just sit there communicating telepathically with it?'

Alice laughed, blushed and reached for the last piece of sushi. 'Sorry.'

'Don't be. It's great to see you so happy and being in love turns anyone's brains to mush. It's a recognised medical condition, you know.' Jo was grinning. 'It's probably just as well that you and Andy don't work the same shifts too often. You gave yourselves away with the static that radiates off both of you when you look at each other. It's a wonder the department still functions properly.'

'Hey, we focus totally on our jobs when we're here.'

Jo gathered the empty containers to dump in the rubbish bin. 'We make people turn off their cellphones so it doesn't interfere with electronic equipment. I reckon people in love should have to be separated. What if you and Andy caught sight of each other on either side of an IV pump? You could have some poor patient being administered a lethal dose of insulin or something.'

Alice was laughing again as she followed Jo back into the department. If anything, the silly conversation was making her even happier. To generate such an obvious aura, the power had to be coming from both sides and that had to mean that Andrew felt the same way she did, even though he hadn't said anything.

It had to mean she wasn't wrong in dreaming of a future with this man. And with the little girl she was coming to love as much as any real mother could.

There was no real reason to drop into the emergency department on his way to pick Emmy up from school. Not on his day off. Well, he *had* left some journals in his office that he would love to catch up on but a text to Alice would have been enough to have her collect them on his behalf.

The house had felt empty all day, that was the problem. Walking over the hills with only Jake for company earlier this afternoon had felt wrong. The weight of that empty feeling in his gut had made him stop at the highest point on the route and gaze down at this amazing property he now owned.

He could see the beautiful old house with smoke curling from two of its chimneys. Funny how quickly he'd got used to living in such a vast space. It was time to start planning restoration work and finding enough furniture to make it all feel homely. The project was exciting but daunting. Hopefully, Alice would have an idea of where to start.

The old shearer's cottage looked tiny in comparison and deserted for the moment with no evidence of a fire and warmth within. Not far from the cottage was the paddock where Ben and Paddington were eating the supply of hay Alice must have fed out before leaving for work before dawn this morning.

The recognition of what that empty feeling inside was all about hit Andrew like a solid object. This place was all about Alice and she wasn't here with him. He needed her here because he was beginning to realise what an integral part Alice was of this whole picture.

Over the last few weeks they had all come to know each other so well. The adults, child and animals. Andrew could touch the top of Jake's head as he stood there, musing, and he loved the way the dog leaned in against his leg, the way he always did with Alice. He was part of Jake's clan now. Worthy of companionship and protection. Part of the family.

It made him catch his breath. Sure, Alice still slipped back to the cottage before Emmy woke in the mornings. They had agreed it was wise to keep up the charade of her occupying her own dwelling and bed but, to all intents and purposes, they were functioning as a family, albeit with two very busy parents who were keeping up full-time employment.

It wasn't a huge stretch of imagination to think of a future that was a little different. One where Alice might want to spend more of her time at home, maybe.

With the children.

He could imagine a toddler, safely strapped into a pushchair and parked in the corner of a paddock with Jake on guard nearby. They would be watching as Alice gave Emmy another one of her astonishingly patient riding lessons. His first born would be wearing the helmet she was so proud of it had to sit on her bedside table at night and her face would be set in those determined lines, like the ones he'd seen yesterday. Paddington had been going round in circles with Alice on the end of the lead rope and Emmy had been bouncing and bumping up and down in the saddle, trying very hard to learn to rise to the trot.

There'd be a high chair at the end of that table in the kitchen and there'd be lots of laughter as a meal was shared.

And then the children would be tucked up in bed and he and Alice would have the rest of the evening to themselves. To talk about their lives and work and children. To dream about the future and, finally, to go to their bed.

They knew each other so well that way now, too. They knew the intricate maps of each other's bodies. The places to touch or kiss or lick that would elicit a sigh of pleasure or a soft sound of escalating need. Andrew knew when to slow down to take Alice to the brink and then make it last until she was desperate for release. For the bone-softening satisfaction that *he* could give her.

He wanted her again, just thinking about it.

He wanted everything she was giving him. Them. And he wanted to erase the nebulous fear that it might not last. Was it too soon to talk about marriage? A commitment for life?

…love?

Yes. Judging by the way his heart rate picked up and his mouth went dry, the prospect was enough to make him afraid. Of what—that she might say no? That he might be wrong and it would be buying into the same kind of heartache he couldn't contemplate enduring again? Especially now, because he knew it would be far worse this time. He'd never felt this way about Melissa. Had never felt this odd emptiness because she wasn't by his side. He'd never once looked at her and imagined her being his wife and the mother of his children the way he had that night when Alice had knelt in front of his fire and offered to be Emmy's nanny.

The decision regarding Melissa's place in his life had been so easy to make. Simply a matter of doing the right thing. Was he hoping at some unconscious level that Alice would make another decision easy and make entertaining any doubts a waste of time and energy? That something would happen to push her more firmly into his arms, like...getting pregnant?

Was that why he'd been insane enough to contemplate having unprotected sex? No. Of course not. He'd never be that irresponsible. On the other hand, if it did happen—eventually—he would be thrilled. The million dollar question was how Alice would feel about it.

Time, Andrew decided on his way down the hill with Jake. He just needed more time to get used to this. To erase those last lingering doubts all by himself. He had to be sure, for Emmy's sake, and there was no rush, was there?

Alice didn't want to go anywhere else.

Something didn't feel right.

Alice couldn't put her finger on quite what it was, but she was feeling almost disconnected from what she was doing. The graph on the chart where she was recording the figures of a blood pressure she had just taken looked oddly fuzzy. And then her stomach rumbled so loudly the young man on the bed grinned broadly.

'Someone needs lunch,' he said.

Alice shook her head. 'I had a huge lunch not that long ago.'

Her stomach growled again and this time Alice felt it turn over and squeeze. She also experienced a very unpleasant wave of sensation that made her skin prickle.

'Excuse me,' she said to her patient.

She needed to go and get some fresh air. Or, better yet, splash a bit of cold water on her face.

She found Jo in the locker room toilets with her hand cupped under the cold tap, scooping water into her mouth.

'Jo! What's wrong? You look awful!'

Jo rinsed her mouth and spat. 'I feel awful. I've just been throwing up. Oh, God, I can't be pregnant.' She raised a very pale face to look at Alice. 'I just *can't* be!'

The mention of throwing up was doing something peculiar to Alice. A wave of nausea so powerful it made spots dance in front of her eyes took hold. She clamped a hand over her mouth and made a dive into one of the cubicles.

A very long minute later, she staggered to the basins to copy Jo's mouth-rinsing technique. Lifting her head with what felt like a supreme effort, she found Jo staring at her in the mirror with a grimace that was a creditable attempt at a smile.

'Hallelujah,' Jo groaned. 'It must have been the sushi!'

Poking his head around the curtain of Cubicle 6, where the busy triage nurse had informed him he would find Alice, the last thing Andrew had expected to find was that she was lying on the bed instead of tending to a patient.

'Good *grief*! What's wrong?' Concern hit him right in the gut. As hard as it might have if he'd found Emmy lying in a hospital bed.

Alice's lips were almost as pale as her face and it seemed to be an effort for her to move them.

'Food…poisoning.'

'Oh, no! Lunch?'

'Mmm.' Alice still hadn't opened her eyes. 'Me and Jo… Chicken…sushi.'

The mention of food appeared to be too much. Alice rolled onto her side with a groan and reached for a vomit container.

Andrew already had it in his hand. He supported her head with his free hand until she was finished and then helped her back onto the pillow. He picked up the damp towel clearly there for wiping her face.

'How long have you been like this?'

Alice managed a faint wry smile. 'Too long.' She tried to take the cloth from his hand but he kept wiping gently and she gave up, her hand flopping back onto the bed. 'I think I'm dying.'

'You'd better not be,' Andrew said mildly, trying to ignore the way her words made him ache to hold and comfort her. Trying even harder not to see the dreadful dark chasm that cracked open in the back of his mind at the thought. 'Emmy hasn't learned to trot properly yet.'

An attempt at laughter only made Alice throw up again.

'Sorry.' But he'd been able to make her laugh even when she was feeling so miserable. Curiously, that made him feel good. 'Poor you,' he added sympathetically. 'I think we'd better get you home, don't you?'

'No.' Alice rolled her head sideways. 'I'll just stay here and die quietly. I'd hate to be sick in your nice car.'

'Where's Jo?'

'Her flatmate came and took her home.'

'And that's exactly where I'm taking you. Home.' He might be taking advantage of the fact that Alice was in no condition to argue, but there was no way he wasn't going to win this round. 'I want you where I can look after you. Don't move, I'm going to go and get a wheel-chair.'

He obtained a pile of vomit containers and their lids as well. And lots of clean towels, which was a good thing because the movement of the car only made things worse. Not that Alice had anything left in her stomach to get rid of. Between bouts of nausea she rested her head back and kept her eyes firmly shut.

Emmy took one look at the closed eyes and pale face through the side window as Andrew led her to the car a short time later and she stopped in her tracks. Her bottom lip trembled.

'What's wrong with Alice?'

'She's feeling a bit sick. She ate some bad food for her lunch.'

His hand was being gripped as hard as a five-year-old was capable of gripping. He could sense the tension in her whole body as she continued staring. Alice still had her eyes closed so she was unaware of the horrified scrutiny.

Emmy's voice had a heartbreaking wobble. 'She's not going to die, is she, Daddy?'

Oh, no! Why hadn't it occurred to him that seeing Alice like this might be traumatic for a child who'd lost her mother?

'No, darling.' Andrew scooped her up. 'She just needs to be looked after for a bit. She'll be feeling much better by tomorrow.'

'But...she *might* die. Like my mummy did.'

'No.' Andrew pressed his lips against Emmy's hair. 'I told her she's not allowed to because you haven't learned to trot on Paddington Bear yet. Come on, we need to get home and then you can help me look after Alice. I'll be the doctor and you can be the nurse, okay?'

'And we'll make her better?'

'We sure will.'

'Are you really, really sure?'

'Yes.' Andrew put Emmy down and moved to open the back door of his car.

'That's good,' Emmy said. 'I don't want Alice to be sick.'

'Neither do I,' Andrew murmured, waiting for Emmy to climb inside so he could do up her seat belt. He took a deep breath, letting his gaze rest for a moment on the back of the auburn head close beside him.

'Neither do I,' he said again, surprising himself with the absolute conviction his words contained.

The worst was over within twenty-four hours but Alice felt about as energetic as a wet dish cloth.

Lying here, propped up on numerous pillows, with her dog beside the bed and a small girl tucked up against her body, Alice thought she might never want to move again.

'Are you *still* here, Em?' Andrew came into the room with a steaming mug on a saucer in his hand. 'You're supposed to be letting Alice rest, remember?'

'I *am*,' Emmy said indignantly. 'I'm just giving her cuddles.'

Alice smiled. 'Very nice cuddles they are, too.'

'Are they helping you get better?'

'Definitely. I haven't been sick for hours and hours now.'

'You'll be dehydrated.' Alice felt the bed dip as Andrew sat down on the edge, reaching to put the mug on the bedside table. 'I thought you might be getting sick of flat lemonade.'

'It *smells* nice,' Alice said cautiously.

'It's tomato.' Andrew smiled. 'I know you're supposed to tempt convalescents with chicken soup, but it's not exactly the flavour of the month around here, is it?'

'No.' For a moment, Alice let herself bask in the knowledge that Andrew had thought of bringing soup at all. That he wanted to care for her. She could feel the firmness of his thigh pressing against hers and the bedclothes might as well have not been there.

Emmy was curled up on her other side and Jake had his head up, sniffing the air and eyeing the slivers of dry toast decorating the saucer that held the mug of soup.

When was the last time Alice had felt nurtured like this? Surrounded by…family.

Not since she was a child and there'd just been herself and her grandmother back then. This felt like a real family. Complete.

She would never find anything else quite like this. No one that she wanted to be with as much as this man and child. It was enough to bring a painful lump to her throat.

'Want to try the soup?' Andrew asked hopefully.

'In a bit.' Alice's voice had a telltale wobble.

Emmy levered herself up instantly. Well practised now in her role as a nurse, she laid a small hand on Alice's forehead. She frowned.

'I think you have a t-tremp—'

'Temperature?' Andrew supplied. He lifted his hand and replaced Emmy's. 'No. It feels just fine to me.'

The touch was soft. He stroked it upwards to smooth unbrushed curls away and the gesture was a caress. One that matched the softness in his eyes as he held Alice's gaze.

Emmy was watching. 'Maybe Alice should go in *your* bed, Daddy.'

'Oh?' Alice could see the way Andrew's pupils dilated a fraction. Desire? Or alarm? 'Why do you say that, sweetheart?'

'Because that's where I go when I feel sick and it always makes me feel better.'

'Oh…' Andrew smiled into Alice's eyes. 'Would it make *you* feel better, do you think, Alice?'

'Um…perhaps not right now.' There was a bubble of laughter growing now. A silent communication that was a shared joy. She was sure she could see a reflection of what she was feeling.

A love so strong it was overwhelming.

'No.' Andrew was nodding gravely. 'Not right now. It's soup time for you. And you, young lady…' He rolled so that he was eye to eye with his daughter over the slope of Alice's hip. 'You need to come with me. We've got one horse and one pony that need some hay.'

The effects of the food poisoning were hard to shake off.

It was several days before Alice felt well enough to

go back to work. That it might take a lot longer to share Andrew's bed again was a disturbing prospect.

'I missed a pill,' she confessed after a long tender kiss as they sat on the couch together late at night. 'Two, in fact.'

'There wouldn't have been much point in taking them when you couldn't keep anything down, anyway.' Andrew's hand traced her ribs and rested on the jut of her hip bone. 'You've lost weight, love. Are you sure you're feeling up to this?'

'I'm fine but…it's too risky.'

'I have a good supply of condoms,' Andrew told her. 'I bought them weeks ago after that first night.'

'You did?' Alice's eyes widened. 'You never mentioned that.'

'Didn't see the need. It's extra protection now, though, if you want the insurance.'

If she wanted it? What was Andrew suggesting—that it wouldn't be a disaster if she got pregnant?

Yes, it would.

Pregnancy had been the way Melissa had trapped Andrew. Blackmailed him into marriage. It was the absolute last thing Alice would want to have happen.

Especially now, when everything seemed to be going in the direction she'd dreamed of. When it seemed more than likely that Andrew would propose to her.

When he was ready. He had to know, as definitively as Alice did, that he wanted them to be together for the rest of their lives. She was quite prepared to wait for as long as that might take.

She didn't have any intention of going anywhere else.

* * *

Jo bounced back from the sushi incident far more quickly than Alice.

'Great way to lose a couple of kilos,' she said a week later.

'Are you kidding? I'd rather hit the gym every day for a month than go through that.'

'You don't look like you're in any state to go near a gym. Are you okay?'

'I've felt better. It's taking a while to feel like eating properly again, that's all.'

The first alarm bells rang the following week when Alice still felt unwell every time she looked at food.

When she realised she was now several days late for her period.

It was easy enough to find a pregnancy test kit in the emergency department and take it into the locker room toilets when she had a quiet moment.

Far harder to try and deal with the shocking result.

She *was* pregnant.

So much for the extra insurance. They'd made love the night before she'd become ill and that had been in the middle of her cycle. The timing couldn't have been worse. Just a few days either side and it wouldn't have mattered that her chemical protection had been disrupted.

Alice sat on the closed lid of the toilet and buried her face in her hands.

She had to face the fact that it had happened.

And that she was now going to have to try and find a way to tell Andrew. To tell him that history was repeating itself. To give him reason to think that she might be no better than Melissa and trying to force him into marriage. *She* had taken responsibility for contraception. *He* had trusted her and she had broken that trust.

It didn't matter how tightly pressed her hands were against her eyes. The tears still seeped through.

CHAPTER EIGHT

DENIAL was a wonderful thing.

Alice knew perfectly well it was only a temporary refuge but it was impossible to resist. Her reasoning was along the kind of lines that had stopped her pushing Andrew to talk about his time with Melissa and what his marriage had been like.

She didn't want to know because, deep down, she was afraid it might tarnish the glow of what they had found in this new life together. And what she had to tell him now would inevitably do the same thing and that meant she would never again get as close as she was at this moment to living her dream. Who could blame her if she wanted to delay the falling of the axe for just a few days?

Enough time to soak in memories to treasure.

The way Andrew smiled at her. That careless touch as he passed sometimes. Just a brush of her hand or touch on her arm or even simply a meaningful glance if they were at work. If she was busy in the kitchen at home, and Emmy wasn't close by, he might lift her hair to drop a kiss on her neck or put his arms around her waist and draw her back so that her rump was nestled in his groin for a second or two.

Even more intimately, there was that look in his eyes just before he kissed her properly. When they lay with their heads on the pillows of Andrew's bed, their faces so close it was hard to focus. That was what Alice was going to miss the most. The feel, more than the look, of being trusted.

Being loved.

For a few days it worked wonderfully well. Increasingly, however, Alice could feel the claws of guilt digging in. She had wanted to win Andrew's trust so much and here she was keeping a secret he had every right to know.

Work was a blessing because it was so much easier to push anything personal so far into the background it could be virtually forgotten. Until she had to deal with a case that hit a little too close to home.

Laura Green was a thirty-two-year-old woman who had presented with sudden onset vaginal bleeding and she was terrified that she was miscarrying. Her husband, John, was with her and, while he was doing a great job of support and reassurance, Alice could see the same fear in his eyes.

'It's okay, babe. Don't cry.'

But Laura was sobbing as she climbed onto the bed and Alice helped her out of her clothes and into a gown. She could empathise with this woman's fear.

Losing her own baby was already unthinkable. It was a part of her. A part of the man she loved. Inside her belly and growing stronger every day.

While the consequences of revealing her secret were

terrifying, there were moments when Alice couldn't help being thrilled. No matter how things worked out between herself and Andrew, she wanted this baby very, very much. She would love it and protect it and care for it.

As a solo mother?

It was unfortunate that the doctor assigned to Laura's case chose that precise moment to enter the cubicle. Even more so that it happened to be Andrew. Thankfully, Alice was busy shoving her patient's personal property into a large paper bag. The rustle of the paper covered her sharp intake of breath and she had a moment, as she bent to push the bag into the basket under the bed, when she could blink really hard and ensure that the threat of tears was banished.

This was one of those chin-raising moments.

If she had to be a solo mother then she would cope. It was a long way from how she would want things to be, but she'd been dealing with that kind of disappointment her whole life, hadn't she? Chasing dreams and then making the best of what was left when the dream evaporated.

And she'd had the feeling all along that what she'd found with Andrew and Emmy was too good to last for ever. She was prepared. Or she would be, very soon.

'How many weeks pregnant are you, Laura?' Andrew was asking.

'Almost ten.'

'And you've had a scan to confirm the pregnancy?'

'Last week.' Laura's voice broke. 'We...we saw the heart beating and...and they said that everything looked...fine.'

'Is this your first pregnancy?'

Laura couldn't answer. She had pressed her face against her husband's chest and he was holding her as her shoulders heaved with silent sobs.

'We've been trying for ages,' John said. 'And…yes, this is the first pregnancy.'

'Any abdominal pain?'

'No.' Laura raised a tear-streaked face. 'Am I going to lose my baby?'

'We'll have an answer to that soon,' Andrew told her gently. 'I'm going to examine you to see whether your cervix is open or closed and, depending on what I find, we'll look at doing an ultrasound test as well. Alice, could you get a blood pressure for me, please?'

'Sure.' It was good to have something to do instead of standing there with her thoughts spinning in ever decreasing circles.

She really hoped that Laura wasn't losing this baby, but the first twelve weeks was when the majority of miscarriages occurred.

How long had Melissa waited to break the news of her pregnancy to Andrew? Had she told him very early before she entered this higher risk period for miscarriage so she could be sure of securing the marriage proposal she desired? Or had she waited out the first trimester to get past a time that many people might consider a termination to be acceptable?

Maybe Alice would be damned either way—too soon or too late.

She wrapped the blood pressure cuff around Laura's upper arm. This was important because, if a miscarriage was underway, Laura's blood pressure could be dropping to dangerously low levels. She picked up the bulb of the sphygmomanometer and started squeezing it.

'This will get tight on your arm for a bit,' she warned.

The pressure inside Alice's head seemed to increase as she watched the mercury level rise. With the stethoscope in her ears, she could hear the rapid pounding of her own heart.

She wasn't anything like Melissa but would Andrew see that?

He still never mentioned his dead wife. Alice had been only too happy to sidestep the issue. To go along with the pretence that Melissa had never existed and therefore didn't matter.

How wrong had she been? Their marriage and the reason for it couldn't matter more now. History repeating itself. It was...huge and dark and very scary.

'Blood pressure's 130 over 85,' she reported.

'Is that good?' John asked anxiously.

'Probably up a little,' Andrew responded calmly. 'Only to be expected given the stress level.' He was pulling on some gloves. 'Tell me about this bleeding.'

'It was so sudden,' Laura said in a horrified kind of whisper. 'I was just standing there and all of a sudden I felt this trickle down my legs and I looked down and saw it was blood and—' Her words trailed into silence.

'She screamed,' John added in a hollow voice. 'I knew something awful had happened. I just picked her up and ran to the car. I didn't even think to call an ambulance or anything.'

'Did the bleeding continue at that rate?'

'No. I had a towel to sit on in the car but there

wasn't much on it by the time we got here. Is…is that good?' Laura sounded more than hopeful now. She sounded desperate.

'Let's have a look.' Andrew made sure the curtains around the cubicle were closed and then drew the sheet back. 'Bend your legs up for me, Laura.'

The examination took only a minute. Andrew's gloves were bloodstained as he pulled them off but his words were as good as could be hoped for.

'Your cervix is still tightly closed,' he told Laura.

'That's good, isn't it?'

'It's not a definitive answer yet but if it was open we'd have to say that yes, you were having a miscarriage.'

'What happens now?' John asked.

'We'll do an ultrasound to check for a foetal heartbeat. If we find one, it will be good news and all we'll need to do is keep Laura under observation for an hour or two to make sure that the bleeding has settled. We'll run some blood tests, too and monitor temperature and things just to rule out any kind of infection being the cause for this.'

Nobody asked about what would happen if they didn't find that heartbeat. The ramifications of that were only too obvious.

It was Andrew who did the ultrasound examination a short time later. John and Laura were holding hands tightly and Alice stood on the other side of the bed. Andrew had a hip on the bed with one hand holding the transducer to position it on Laura's still flat belly. With his other hand, he was pointing to part of the image on the screen which he had angled to allow the young couple to watch.

'That's the bladder,' he said, indicating a darker blob. 'And this is…' he changed the angle of the transducer '…the uterus.'

It felt as if everybody in this space was holding their breath. There were dozens of other patients in this department at the moment and a hive of activity beyond the flimsy fabric of the curtains, but Alice knew she wasn't the only one totally oblivious to anything other than that screen. She watched Andrew press the transducer down a little more firmly. She saw the tiny furrow between his brows.

And then, there it was. A rhythmic movement on the screen. A pulse of life.

Laura gasped and then twisted her face to look up at her husband. The relief and then the hope radiating from both their faces was blinding. Alice had to look away and she found her gaze caught by Andrew.

The look she was receiving was so soft. So warm. He wanted to share the joy of these young parents.

It was too much. The threat of tears so overwhelming that Alice had to look away instantly.

'Excuse me,' she whispered. 'I have to—'

To escape.

She turned and all but ran from the cubicle.

Alice had just bustled past Andrew without looking in his direction.

She was obviously busy, with a sealed bag of blood samples in her hands, but this was the second, or was it the third time, she'd missed the opportunity for eye contact on this shift.

And that was weird.

Almost as if she was avoiding him.

Andrew's frown deepened as he turned back to the X-ray image on the computer in front of him.

'That bad?' Peter stopped to peer over Andrew's shoulder.

'Not at all. Straightforward undisplaced radial fracture. Nothing a short stint in a cast won't make as good as new.'

Peter nodded. 'You must have been thinking about something else, then, to make you look so worried.'

'Was I looking worried?' Andrew tried to sound nonchalant.

'Yep.' The head of department raised an eyebrow. 'You're sure there's nothing I can help with?'

'I'm good,' Andrew said firmly. He smiled to prove it.

'No hassles getting properly settled, then? You're happy you made such a big move?'

'Oh, yes.' From the corner of his eye he could see Alice on her return journey from wherever she'd been taking the blood samples. 'Couldn't be happier.' Andrew felt his smile broadening and couldn't help glancing away from his colleague.

Peter followed his line of sight. 'Ahh…' The murmur was both understanding and approving.

'Hey!' Andrew's call was soft but Alice looked up.

She smiled brightly. Too brightly?

'Everything all right?'

'Of course.' The answer was quick. Alice was looking startled, as if it had been an odd thing for him to ask.

'How's Laura doing?'

'Fine. Bleeding's still minimal so she'll be able to go home very soon.'

Alice had noticed Peter standing behind Andrew now. She looked at the departmental head and then her gaze shifted back to Andrew before sliding away. She *was* avoiding eye contact. Why? Because Peter was there? Surely she realised that everybody knew about their relationship by now so why did she seem...what... nervous?

'I'd better get on with...' The rest of Alice's words were lost, partly because she was muttering but more because she was already moving swiftly away from the two men.

Andrew flicked a glance up at Peter but he was staring after Alice with a rather thoughtful expression. As though he'd noticed something a bit different about her as well.

'I'll leave you to it,' was all he said to Andrew. 'I've got some paperwork I should catch up on while things are quiet. Don't forget that senior staff meeting at shift changeover. The more that can make it the better.'

Andrew's hand curled over the computer mouse, clicking through images to make sure he hadn't missed anything.

He felt as if he was missing something but he knew it had nothing to do with the patient who'd fractured his arm. It had something to do with Alice. With why she'd been distant ever since...

Since they'd worked together earlier to assess Laura with her threatened miscarriage. Since that moment of relief when he'd located the heartbeat on ultrasound and could pretty much guarantee that the young couple weren't going to lose their baby.

Amidst the pleasure of a good outcome for their patient, Andrew had been acutely aware of a much more personal reaction to the scene. An odd flash of longing. He'd spared just a moment to wish that it was Alice on a bed having undergone an ultrasound examination and that he was holding her hand and they were both celebrating the proof that they were expecting a new addition to their family.

Had he somehow communicated something of that longing?

Good grief! If the idea of having a baby of their own was enough to scare Alice off he'd better rethink the whole idea of proposing marriage. Maybe she wasn't ready for that kind of commitment.

Maybe all she'd wanted all along was the guarantee of continuing to live in the place she loved.

No. Andrew actually physically shook his head as he pushed his chair back and stood up, ready to go back to his patient and arrange transfer to the plaster room.

Alice wasn't like that. She'd never use someone to get what she wanted. Deceive them emotionally.

She wasn't anything like Melissa had been.

He couldn't possibly be that wrong about the woman he was in love with. Any doubts he might have had regarding the strength of his feelings towards Alice had been well and truly dispelled during that food poisoning episode. Apart from Emmy, there was no one he cared about this much. Or ever would.

He'd been waiting for Alice to recover completely so that they could enjoy a real celebration. Waiting for the right moment to tell her how he felt and what he was dreaming of for their future.

Clearly, the right moment was not going to be anytime very soon.

Later that afternoon that moment seemed to recede even further.

A skeleton staff had been left in the department for the few minutes when senior doctors and nurses gathered in the staff room. Andrew came in last, having given Laura the all-clear to go home and stop worrying. He scanned the crowded staff room from where he had to stand close to the door, looking for Alice, unsure of whether she was here or not.

He wanted to catch her before she left to collect Emmy from school because he wanted to suggest that he bring takeaway food home for dinner tonight and make things easier for Alice. She still looked a bit peaky even though she should be well over the knock of being so ill for a couple of days.

'I didn't want to send out a general memo,' Peter told the group, 'and I'd appreciate it if what's being said stays in this room, but you're all here because you have keys to the drugs cabinet and I need you all to know there's been some anomalies noted recently in drug tallies.'

There she was—at the back of the room, sitting beside Jo.

It took Andrew a moment to register and then comprehend the strange look Alice was giving him. Her chin was up and she looked defensive. Cold, even.

Oh...Lord! Did she think he'd been seeking her out because of the mention of an issue regarding restricted drugs?

Was it possible that she still believed he had any doubts about her trustworthiness?

Peter was saying something about records needing to be meticulous. About the work he was having to do to try and go through patient notes and match the drugs administered with what had been recorded as being taken from the locked cabinet. Andrew wasn't listening.

He'd left it too long to say something to Alice, hadn't he? With the best of intentions, Andrew had tried to prove his trust in another way, but in that tiny moment of eye contact across the crowded staff room he knew, without a shadow of doubt, that he'd been wrong.

That he was in trouble.

For the first time since they'd got into the routine of this shared care for Emmy, Alice didn't stay to eat the dinner she'd prepared.

'I've got too much to catch up on,' she'd excused herself the moment Andrew came through the door. 'Washing and emails and…you know…domestic stuff.'

And she'd fled, without giving him time to say anything. The way she had after that staff meeting this afternoon. Alice really did need some time to herself. In her little cottage, with Jake for company and a lovely, deep hot bath to soak in.

Time to try and deal with the fact that, after so many blissful weeks, her life was unravelling yet again. Totally. At home and at work, which made this the most difficult crisis she had ever had to face.

Was somebody really stealing drugs in their department? Maybe it would turn out to be a storm in a teacup and someone had just been slack about doing the paperwork. It certainly wasn't her. Ever since her time in London, Alice had been paranoid about the regulations to do with handling restricted drugs. She checked and double-checked absolutely everything and always got someone else to repeat the checks and sign off what she'd done.

She'd still been the first person Andrew had looked at, though, hadn't she?

The mud was still sticking and no amount of soaking in comforting, hot baths was going to wash it out of her life. Just a flicker of suspicion was all it took. Alice was never going to escape the past.

Neither was Andrew, although he didn't realise it yet. He'd know soon enough when Alice confessed and she had to tell him soon because any window of justifying denial was definitely over.

Tomorrow, she decided. She'd tell him tomorrow.

But Alice was working the following day and Andrew had a day off. He took Emmy to a movie in the afternoon and they stayed in town for dinner. Then Alice had an early start and Andrew had a shift that started mid-afternoon and went through till midnight.

She slept in the spare room that night. The one she'd used when they'd first put this plan into action. The bed felt cold and unused. It hadn't been used since she and Andrew had started sharing *his* bed. Alice heard him come in in the early hours of the morning. She heard him call her name very softly from the door.

She pretended to be soundly asleep, hoping that Andrew would come in anyway and get into *her* bed and hold her. Maybe then she could tell him and maybe—just maybe—they could work through it.

Andrew stood there for a long moment. And then she

heard his steps on the wooden floorboards as he made his way to his own room.

The longer she waited, the more nervous Alice became. So nervous that when she and Andrew were working the same shift together a couple of days later, she could barely concentrate on her work.

She dropped things. She bumped into a trolley and sent supplies crashing to the floor. She felt ridiculously close to tears for most of the day. It was no great surprise when Peter quietly asked her to come and see him in his office. Alice knew that Andrew was watching her walk away with the head of department but she couldn't look back. She didn't want to be given sympathy or reassurance she really didn't deserve.

Peter didn't waste any time coming to the point.

'What on earth's wrong today, Alice? You're not yourself at all.'

Alice couldn't deny the accusation. 'I...I'm sorry, Peter.'

'Are you sick?'

She shook her head. 'I've just got...something on my mind.'

'Hmm. I had that impression quite a few days ago. You've been...I don't know...kind of edgy.'

'Sorry. I'll get it sorted.'

'Anything I can do to help?'

Alice shook her head again. 'It's got nothing to do with work.'

'Are you sure?'

Alice blinked. Was he asking her whether this had something to do with her relationship with one of his

consultants? Did everybody know about her and
Andrew now? She couldn't tell him, though. Not before
she'd told Andrew.

'It doesn't have anything to do with the issue we've
got with missing drugs, does it?'

Alice sucked in her breath. 'What do you mean?'

Peter sighed. 'I know about London, Alice. About
why you had to resign from the job you had there.'

Alice gaped at him. 'Who told you about that?'

There was only one possible suspect she could think
of and that was so painful she wanted to curl up and die.
The ultimate betrayal. She didn't want to know but she had
to.

'Was it Andrew Barrett?'

'No.'

It wasn't Peter who answered the question. Alice
jerked her head around to find Andrew standing in the
doorway of the office. He stepped inside. 'I most certainly didn't say anything. In fact, I'm as interested as
you are to find out who did.'

They both looked at Peter who looked away from
Alice to Andrew. 'You replaced Dave when you took on
your position here.'

'That's correct.'

'You worked with him years ago, yes?'

'Also correct. I don't really see what this has to do
with Alice.'

Peter's tone was bland. He was delivering facts here,
not an opinion. 'He made some enquiries from mutual
associates before he approached you. He spoke to quite
a few people and they invariably recommended you
very highly. One doctor told him about the New Zealand

nurse who'd come under suspicion for stealing drugs. Told him how well you'd dealt with a potentially damaging situation in your department. Dave felt obliged to pass the information on to me when he learned that the nurse spoken about was back working here again.'

'You never said anything to me,' Alice said quietly. 'Why not?'

'You've never done anything to make me think there was anything I needed to say.'

'Until now? Until drugs started to go missing?'

'Until now,' Peter agreed. 'When something's obviously upsetting you so much you're unable to do your job with the kind of competency I've come to rely on.'

'Alice had nothing to do with the drugs in London going missing.'

Andrew spoke with such conviction that both Alice and Peter stared at him.

'You sound like you found out who did,' Peter said.

'I did. And it wasn't Alice.'

'Who was it?' The query came from Peter but he was voicing what was filling her mind, along with so much else she couldn't collect the words, let alone say them.

He'd *known*? She'd thought he'd given her the gift of trust but he'd never had a reason to *mis*trust her. It had been an empty gift.

A sham.

Andrew hadn't answered Peter's query because at that same moment, his pager had gone off with a strident alarm that signalled an urgent call. He glanced down to where it was clipped to his belt, turning it enough to read the display.

'Arrest,' he snapped. 'Resus 1.'

Peter was going to accompany him. Both men were moving fast.

'Who was it?' Alice had to ask as they passed. 'Who *did* take those drugs, Andrew?'

He spared her only a graze of eye contact.

'Melissa.'

CHAPTER NINE

SHOCK gave way to anger.

No. Make that cold fury.

All this time, Alice had been so grateful to be given a chance to prove herself. To win Andrew's trust, despite any reason he might have had for doubting her.

And he'd never had that reason. He'd *known* she was innocent. He could have cleared her name years and years ago and saved her the haunting aftermath of that shameful incident. In fact, hadn't she handed him the perfect opportunity to do exactly that?

You still believe I took those drugs, don't you?

He could have told her then. He *should* have told her then. Instead, he'd simply denied ever saying it. And when she'd reminded him that he'd said he couldn't trust her, she could see that the statement still held truth. That was why she had set out to prove herself.

He'd lied to her. By omission maybe, but that didn't make it any more forgivable.

Especially when she had trusted *him* so absolutely, even though she was aware he was keeping an important part of his life a secret. His whole marriage. Emmy's infancy. She'd colluded in sweeping it under the mat but there was no way she would have done that if she'd known how huge that secret was. Or that it directly affected *her*. She'd had a right to that information. As much as Andrew had a right to know she was carrying his baby.

Oh...God! What a mess!

The bottom line was that Andrew hadn't trusted her. For whatever reason—and, whatever it was, it wouldn't be good enough—he'd lied to her.

And she'd really believed that there was a future for them?

Talk about being blinded by love.

Right now, her vision was clouded more by fury and the pain of betrayal.

Having paced Peter's office for goodness knew how long, with her arms wrapped tightly around her body, her head spinning and the pain of grief already closing a vice-like grip around her heart, Alice finally let go of herself, lifted her chin, gritted her teeth and moved.

The cardiac arrest scenario in Resus 1 was obviously not going very well. Through curtains that hadn't been fully closed, Alice could see the flat line running across the monitor where ECG spikes should have been. She could see the crowd of staff around the bed. Jo was doing chest compressions. A registrar stood to one side holding a bag-mask unit and another was drawing up fresh drugs. Andrew, grim-faced, was in the process of intubating what looked to be a fairly young man.

He would be doing everything he possibly could to save that life but Alice didn't have room in her heart to applaud his skill or dedication. If she went down that track she might start trying to understand why he'd betrayed her. To make excuses for him because she so desperately wanted this not to be ending.

But it was. It had to. She couldn't stay with a man she couldn't trust. A man who didn't trust her. She had to deal with it and move on.

Another nurse was recording everything that was happening in the resuscitation effort and yet more staff stood close by. Ready to assist if needed but, for the moment, there was nothing they could do. Peter was one of those extras and he was standing right beside the gap in the curtains. Alice went up to him.

'I'm sorry,' she said quietly. 'I know I haven't been doing my job properly but I'm going to sort it out, I promise.'

'Good.' But Peter was frowning in concern. 'Maybe you should take the rest of today off. I'll get cover arranged.'

'Thank you. I'd appreciate that.' Alice took a shaky inward breath. She could start that sorting out process immediately. 'Could you also please tell Dr Barrett that he'll have to make other arrangements to have his daughter collected from school. I won't be available.'

Peter was still frowning but there was surprise on his face as well. He could see there was more to this than he'd realised. 'Are you all right, Alice? Where are you going to be?'

'I'm fine. Or I will be. I'm going home. I have some urgent business to take care of.' Alice turned away to head for the locker room to collect her things. Urgent was the word for it, all right. How soon could she hope to find somewhere for Ben to go? That had to be the first priority. In a worst case scenario, she and Jake could survive in the truck for a few days but she couldn't abandon her horse.

Could she abandon Emmy?

Andrew?

She *had* to. Before her heart recovered enough to start fighting her head. Before it found a way to make what he'd done somehow acceptable. It wasn't and it never could be. She had to leave as quickly as she could manage and then get as far away as she possibly could.

Was she being a coward?

Yes, but there was only so much pain a person could front up for, wasn't there? Emmy and Andrew had each other. Alice had only herself to look to for protection now.

The resuscitation just went on and on.

Drug therapy produced a shockable rhythm. Defibrillation produced a normal-looking rhythm but, within a minute or two, no matter what they did, it degenerated back to a flat line.

Again and again, they shocked the heart but after nearly an hour they all knew that, even if they could get a rhythm capable of sustaining life, they would be saving someone who would be irreparably brain damaged from too long a period without a normal level of circulating oxygen.

'Time of death,' Andrew finally said in a tone resonant with defeat, 'Fourteen-oh-seven.'

The man had been only forty-four. A health fanatic who'd gone out for a run in his lunch break only to collapse in an isolated park corner where it had taken passers-by too long to see him. He wasn't that much older than Andrew, and that made it even harder to try and explain what had happened to his distraught wife and young children.

Having dealt with that gruelling interview, Andrew found Peter waiting for him with a message from Alice to say that he'd have to collect Emmy himself.

She wasn't available. What the hell did that mean?

'I'd better ring the school,' he said. 'I'll arrange care for her until I finish at six.'

'You could go early,' Peter suggested. 'I'm happy to cover for you.'

'Did Alice say *why* she was leaving so early?'

'She just said she had something urgent she needed to take care of at home.' Peter's gaze was very direct. 'I must say, I've never seen her looking quite that upset.'

Of course she was upset. By telling her that it was Melissa who'd stolen those drugs, Andrew had opened a can of worms he'd wanted so much to keep tightly closed.

What if Alice thought he'd known all along? That he'd been protecting his girlfriend and leaving her to take the blame.

At least he could put her straight on that score.

'I might just take you up on that offer to get away early,' he told Peter.

If he rang the school, he could arrange the care for Emmy anyway and then he could go home alone. He could find Alice and see how much of the damage—if any—he could repair.

Peter was nodding. 'When you see her,' he said, 'please apologise on my behalf for any insinuation I made. Someone came forward after that staff meeting the other day and told me about a messy time on a night shift recently. Multi-victim MVA and they were very short-staffed. I had someone looking into it and they've just told me that a total of seven ampoules of morphine were used that night and the nurse who had the key on that shift totally forgot to go back and sign them off in the cabinet logbook. The matter is closed as far as we're concerned.'

It wouldn't be for Alice, though, would it?

A short time later, with a face that was as grim as when he'd been trying to save the life of that heart attack victim, Andrew left the building.

Fear snapped at his heels. Or wheels. Thank heaven for his car's turn of speed and fabulous road-handling ability.

Putting himself in Alice's place, Andrew wouldn't be surprised to get to his property and find she'd packed up her things and left. He couldn't let that happen. He needed Alice in his life. So did Emmy.

He *loved* her and so did Emmy. He had to fight for both of them. For *all* of them, because they were a family.

Andrew didn't drive to his own house, he took the turn to the cottage and, thank God, her truck was there. Once on foot, it wasn't hard to locate Alice. She was in Ben's paddock, brushing him. Jake sat by the fence but he didn't move to greet Andrew and Alice didn't look up from what she was doing. Fear snapped again and managed to catch hold of his heart.

'Please, Alice. Stop what you're doing and talk to me.'

He got no response. Just a feeling of tension in the air that was a solid barrier. 'At least *look* at me.'

But Alice kept brushing the damn horse. Ben was tied up near the water trough. Almost the exact spot both he and Alice had been that day he'd arrived home to discover that she was his tenant. A saddle hung over the fence behind the trough and Alice was bent over, brushing mud from Ben's legs.

'*Alice.*'

'I can't stop,' she said. 'I've got an awful lot to get done.'

'Oh?' Did she have no idea how important it was for them to talk? Andrew felt as if he was being dismissed. That *they* were being dismissed. She couldn't be doing that so easily. That would make him wrong about so many things and he knew he wasn't that wrong. 'You can't be that busy if you're planning to go riding.'

Alice straightened at that and turned around. Andrew was shocked by the pain he could see in her eyes. It burned into him and he could *feel* it as his own pain.

'I'm riding Ben to his new paddock,' she said tonelessly. 'That way, I've got the horse float free to pack my stuff into.'

'Pack? You're *leaving*?' Even though the possibility had occurred to him, he hadn't really believed it. Or maybe he just hadn't known how hard it would hit him.

'Yes.'

Such a tiny word to have such enormous repercussions. Unacceptable repercussions.

'You can't leave! I won't let you.'

'You can't stop me.'

Andrew opened his mouth but then closed it again. What could he say? He knew Alice was upset. He could understand her being angry but to be walking out on him? On Emmy? He felt as though an enormous chasm was opening beneath his feet. He was in danger of falling and he couldn't think of how to prevent it. Or how to stop Alice. She was right. He couldn't stop her if she was as determined as she sounded. Not physically.

Alice had turned away again. She was reaching up to brush Ben's neck. 'We had a lucky break,' she said. 'When I was driving home I saw this woman out on the road, shifting her goat. I stopped and asked if she knew of anyone who might have some grazing available.'

Andrew heard the wobble in her voice and it felt as if a piece of his heart were being torn away.

Alice was hurting. Badly.

'It's not too far,' Alice continued doggedly. 'We can follow the river and cut across to the farm and...and Jake needs a good run.'

Jake looked as though he was as aware as Andrew of how Alice was feeling. The dog sat beside the trough, watching his mistress intently. Was he waiting for the chance to get close and offer comfort?

Someone had to.

'Alice, please. Let me explain.'

'No need,' she said hurriedly. She was brushing harder on what looked like a perfectly clean area of horse. 'I've put Paddington into the paddock closer to your house. He's got plenty of hay but he'll need some more in the morning.'

She stepped away from Ben, then moved towards the fence where she dropped the brush and reached for the saddle. Andrew moved as well. Close enough to reach out and catch her wrist.

'Listen to me,' he said urgently. 'I know what you're thinking, but I had no idea that Melissa was taking drugs when the trouble started in the department.'

Alice pulled her wrist free. She rubbed it, not looking at Andrew, and that seemed unfair. He knew he hadn't been holding her tightly enough to hurt. He would never deliberately hurt her in any way and that was making this unbearable. Something already tight inside him was stretching further. Getting ready to snap. He watched her pull her saddle off the fence and put it on Ben's back and didn't try to touch her again to stop her.

'When I did find out, I tried to tell you,' he said. 'I went to your address, only to find it empty. With a 'Sold' sign outside. Nobody knew where you'd gone. I was too late and I'm sorry.'

'It took *months* to sell that place,' Alice snapped. 'Months and months where I couldn't get another job or pay my mortgage. It was the bank who put it up for auction and sold it for as much as they needed to cover their debt. I lost everything I'd worked so hard for.'

'I know. I'm sorry, Alice. I can't tell you how sorry I am but I *didn't* know in time, I swear it.'

The huff of expelled breath was disparaging and Andrew's heart sank even further. A dead weight in his chest that was going to pull him into that chasm.

'Would you like to know when I did find out the truth?'

Yes. Of course she wanted to know.

No. She didn't want to hear him say anything more.

Just the sound of his voice was too much. The pain she could hear in it. The sincerity of his apology. Saying sorry couldn't undo the hurt. Or repair the lack of trust.

She kept her head bent, focusing on doing up girth buckles. She made no verbal response but Andrew kept talking anyway, after a pause that had only been long enough for him to draw a breath.

'The day Emmy was born,' he told her. 'When I found I had a baby who was in trouble because of the morphine she'd been exposed to during the pregnancy. When I had to stand back and watch my precious newborn child go through all the agony of drug withdrawal.'

Alice's head jerked up, her eyes wide with shock. It would be a horrific start to life for any baby but this was *Emmy* he was talking about. The little girl she loved dearly. The brave, determined child who was trying so hard to learn to trot on her fat little pony.

'She promised she'd go into rehab. That she would do whatever it took to be a good mother. A good *wife*.' Andrew couldn't help the bitter edge to that last word. 'But you know what she was really good at? Deception. When she wasn't working in the hospital any more she had to find new ways to feed her addictions. And when alcohol wasn't enough she took money I knew nothing about. She found sources for things like cocaine and even heroin in the end. She was so good at covering up her habit that I had to go home more than once and find my child totally neglected to face what was going on.'

The words were tumbling from Andrew in a wash of anger and sadness. Was that why he'd avoided ever talking about it? Because when he took the stopper out there was so much bottled up that he couldn't control it?

'Time after time I sent her off to rehab. Private, discreet clinics. Emmy didn't even recognise her when she came home sometimes. I had to cope with my job and raising my baby and keeping everything a secret and it nearly killed me.'

'Why?' Alice didn't understand. 'Why did it have to be a secret?' Especially now, so long after any danger to Emmy was over. Why did it have to have been a secret from *her*? 'Surely other people knew?'

'Only those involved in her treatment.' Andrew shook his head. 'Mel was an expert in manipulation. She could persuade anyone to fall into line if she was desperate enough. And if charm and sex didn't work, then blackmail was always an option. She threatened to take Emmy away and make sure I never got to see her again. I began to take more and more time off work to make sure she was safe. That they were both safe because I felt responsible. I was Emmy's father. Melissa's husband. There had to be some way I could get the hell that my life had become sorted out.'

Alice closed her eyes for a moment. This was all so horrible but she had to hear it all. 'And the accident?'

'She was loaded up to her eyeballs with prescription drugs that time. Washed down with alcohol. I'd taken Emmy to the park and came home to find Mel in a crumpled heap at the bottom of the stairs. I couldn't prove I hadn't been in the house at the time and I didn't want the details to come out. I was ashamed of myself. The way I'd handled things.'

There was no denying he'd handled things badly. Alice shook her head.

'You've never breathed a word of any of this. It's been like Melissa never existed.'

'It was a past I've been trying to leave behind. For Emmy's sake. You think I want her to know that her mother was a drug addict?'

'And you couldn't tell me because you thought I'd tell *her*?' Alice backed away. 'You really don't trust me, do you? I knew that. You said as much.'

'When? When did I ever say anything like that?'

'That day at work. When we agreed we had a problem. When I gave you the chance to tell me what you should have told me. What I had the right to know—that you knew damned well I'd never touched those drugs.'

'I said—'

'I *know* what you said, Andrew. And when I reminded you that you'd said you couldn't trust me, I saw you weighing it up. Deciding you still couldn't.'

'I wasn't even thinking about London. I was thinking about why I'd left. That I wanted to start again. To give Emmy a life with no shadows from the past.'

'And you thought I'd tell her,' Alice repeated. 'Or someone else. That the rumours would start all over again.'

The reason was there and it didn't help. It was only making things worse.

'You didn't trust me,' she whispered.

It didn't seem to matter what he said; it only seemed to be making things worse. But he couldn't stop. He was fighting for his future here. For his life.

'Of course I trust you. For God's sake, Alice—I

believed you when you told me you were on the pill and it was safe to have sex, didn't I?'

'Well, maybe I can't trust *you*.'

Andrew's jaw dropped. How had she switched the issue like that?

'You never told me the truth and it was *my* truth. *I'm* the one who had to suffer the suspicion. *I* was the one who couldn't get a job and lost my home and all my money. *I'm* the one who's been working here for years, hoping like hell nobody would ever find out why I had to leave my job in London.'

Alice's hands were moving as fast as the words were tumbling from her mouth. She unbuckled the halter on top of Ben's bridle and flipped the reins over his head. Then she was swinging herself up into the saddle.

'Not telling me was as good as lying to me. You don't trust me enough; that's what it boils down to.'

'And you just said you don't trust me,' he countered, still reeling from the attack. How on earth had things degenerated to this point? Accusations of mistrust. Of lying. Both of them hurting. The kind of pain he'd sworn to keep himself safe from, but here he was swimming in it.

Drowning in it.

'And it's true, isn't it? You've had your doubts? What about the day we were talking about your lease? I saw the way you flinched when all I did was clench a fist. I think you believed the rumours that I hit Mel. You looked horrified.'

'I was horrified by what I'd just said. I'm not into blackmail. I'm *not* Melissa.'

'No.' Andrew's breath came out in a huff of anger.

Man, this was pushing those old buttons. 'You'd have to be pregnant and expecting me to marry you to step into those shoes. I can't believe that you would think—'

The look on Alice's face stopped Andrew's words.

She looked…*stricken*.

And something clicked into place. The way she hadn't seemed to recover properly from that food poisoning episode.

Her nervousness.

The way she'd been avoiding him.

Good grief! She *was* pregnant!

Alice had to break that awful stare. The silence.

He had guessed. He *knew*.

She pulled on Ben's reins and kicked.

'No!' Andrew leapt forward and grabbed hold of the reins. 'What on earth do you think you're doing, Alice?'

She was escaping, that was all. Did he think it was dangerous to go riding because she was pregnant or something? She had to get away. She couldn't bear to have any further comparison made between herself and Melissa. She kicked harder and Ben tried to pull forward against Andrew's grip.

'You can't go,' Andrew said. Was that desperation in his voice? 'Please, Alice. I love you. Don't go.'

He *loved* her?

One tiny word, but the power it contained was immeasurable. If there was any way to be found out of this mess, that was where hope lay and it was all Alice needed to halt her bid to escape.

She tugged on the reins. The messages Ben was getting had now confused him completely but he tried to obey. He stopped and swung his head to look around at his mistress.

The movement pulled the reins from Andrew's hands and unbalanced him. And as Ben's head turned in one direction, his huge rump swung in the opposite direction.

Alice watched in horror as Andrew was sent flying. She saw his head hit the side of the concrete water trough.

And then she saw him lying, absolutely still, on the ground.

CHAPTER TEN

ANDREW lay, crumpled on one side. So still that Alice thought he must be dead.

With an anguished cry, she threw her leg over Ben's rump and slid to the ground with a bone-jarring thump. She pushed at her horse.

'*Move*, Ben! Get out of the way. Oh, *God*! What have we done?'

Dropping to her knees, so close to Andrew she was touching his back with her thighs, she bent over him.

Was he breathing?

Yes.

'Andrew? Can you hear me? Can you open your eyes?'

There was no movement on his face that she could discern. Alice placed trembling fingers on the side of his neck to feel for a pulse. She cupped the back of his head with her other hand and she could feel the warm stickiness of blood.

She'd seen him hit his head on the trough and now he was unconscious, with a head injury that could, potentially, be fatal.

The breath Alice had been unaware of holding came out in a sob. As carefully as she could, she examined his head without moving him. To have hit his head hard enough to knock him out meant there was a possibility of a neck injury as well. If she twisted his cervical spine, she could paralyse him for life. Or, worse, kill him. He was breathing and his pulse was steady and strong so there was no urgency to move him.

He was, in fact, lying in an almost perfect textbook recovery position. Alice slid her fingers through his hair, pressing onto his scalp to see if there were any spongy areas that could indicate a skull fracture. All she found, however, was the laceration that was bleeding copiously. She pressed her bare hand to the wound to try and control the bleeding with pressure.

With her other hand, she stroked his face. Touching his forehead and cheek and—very gently—his closed eyelids.

He *loved* her.

As much as this? Enough to feel that her life would be over if he wasn't alive and part of it any more?

He loved her and he trusted her. She *knew* that he trusted her. This whole confrontation had come about because of nothing more than her wounded pride. The fact that he hadn't told her why he believed she had been innocent of the charge of stealing drugs.

What did it matter?

She'd thought she'd been so hard done by, losing her job and that deposit on the apartment. Having to come home and start again, but it was nothing compared to what Andrew had gone through. Discovering the woman he'd married was a drug addict. Watching his helpless newborn suffering through withdrawal symptoms.

It would have torn him apart and, because of what made him the man Alice loved so much, he wouldn't have abandoned his marriage or Melissa. He would have done his utmost to help. To support her through any rehabilitation process. To pick up the pieces and try again. And again.

What was really amazing was that he'd believed in Alice enough to start a new relationship.

He had trusted her *that* much and she had just thrown it back in his face.

'I'm sorry,' Alice whispered. 'I'm so, so sorry.'

He'd come here, with Emmy, to start a whole new life. Of course he hadn't wanted to rake over such a miserable part of his past. They had agreed to leave it behind and she had been a more than willing accomplice.

If he'd told her about Melissa she would have wanted to know it all.

Now she did know it all and all she wanted to do was put it all behind them and start again.

'Please...' she heard herself say out loud.

Please let them have the chance to do exactly that.

'Please, Andrew. You have to be all right. I love you, too. I love you *so* much.'

Blinded by the tears filling her eyes, Alice didn't see the moment when Andrew's eyelids flickered open.

'I love *you*,' he said hoarsely.

'Ohh...' Alice blinked hard. She scrubbed at her face with her hand and tried to take in a deep breath. 'Don't move. You hit your head.'

'I'm okay.' But Andrew was frowning as he focused. 'You...you've got blood on your face.'

'Have I?' Automatically, Alice raised her hand to touch her face and then she realised why the blood was there. 'It's your blood,' she told Andrew. 'You've cut your head.'

His eyes drifted shut. 'You should have gloves on,' he murmured.

Alice's voice wobbled. 'I don't need them.'

She didn't. For the same reason they had known it was safe to have unprotected sex. The trust thing.

And she'd accused him of not trusting her.

She'd said she couldn't trust him because he'd lied to her.

Alice needed to ask Andrew questions to try and assess his condition but, for the moment, her throat was way too tight to allow her to utter a single word.

Andrew opened his eyes again. His voice was stronger this time.

'I love you, Alice Palmer.'

'I love you, too.'

Andrew smiled. 'Kiss me, then, babe.'

Alice bent down and touched his lips. Just a soft, brief press against her own. Andrew made a groaning sound as she lifted her head.

'Oh, God! Did I hurt you?'

'No.'

'What is it, then?'

'I needed a proper kiss.'

Something very close to laughter broke from Alice. 'What you need, my love, is an ambulance. A C collar. Probably an MRI scan of your head.'

'No.' Andrew's head moved in a side to side motion.

'Don't do that!' Alice pleaded. 'Stay still.'

'But I'm all right. I've just had a bump on the head and I'm feeling better all the time. I don't have any pain in my neck. I can wiggle all my fingers and toes, see?'

He demonstrated. 'Now, let me sit up.'

Reluctantly, Alice helped him into a sitting position and then watched him turn his head from one side to the other and then tilt it up and down.

'No pain,' he declared.

'What about your head?'

'That *is* a bit tender.' Andrew felt his scalp. 'Hmm. Good-sized egg, isn't it?'

'It's all my fault,' Alice said. 'I shouldn't have tried to ride away like that.'

'I shouldn't have been stupid enough to try and hang onto your reins. It's just as much my own fault. I'm sorry, Alice.'

'Not as sorry as I am.'

'I'm sorry I didn't try harder to find where you'd gone, back then. I knew it was wrong to leave things like that. I knew I'd only done enough to stop me feeling too guilty. I...was relieved I *didn't* find you.'

'Of course you were. You had more than enough to deal with in your life.'

'I didn't know, then, did I?'

Alice was confused. 'Know what?'

'That I would fall in love with you. Did I tell you that I love you?'

'Several times.' Alice gave him a thoughtful glance. 'Repetitive speech pattern. I think you've got a concussion.'

'I can prove my GCS is just fine. Ask me what day it is.'

Alice complied.

'It's the day I finally said what I should have said ages ago.'

'About Melissa?'

'No. That I love you.' Andrew moved and winced. 'Yes…about Melissa, too. I'll tell you anything you want to know. No more secrets.'

'I don't need to know anything else.'

'Don't you want to know how she did it? How she framed you so convincingly? The way she managed to bump into you that day and drop the ampoules right into your pocket?'

'Maybe later.' Strangely, Alice wasn't even curious at the moment. 'Right now, all I want to do is get you into the emergency department.'

'I'm fine.'

'I'm not going to believe that until someone who hasn't had a bang on the head tells me.'

'Don't call an ambulance.'

'Why not?'

'I don't need one and I certainly don't want one. How are you going to hold my hand if you're following behind in my car?'

'Your car?'

'We'll need to get Emmy. After you've been satisfied that I'm still functioning normally.'

'That's a point. I guess if I drive and you sit very still, it would be okay.' A tiny smile curled her lips. 'You really want me to hold your hand?'

Andrew tried to nod but it was clearly painful. He gripped her hand very tightly instead. 'Always,' he said fiercely. 'Don't let me go.'

'I won't,' she promised.

Alice helped him very slowly to his feet and it took a few minutes to make the careful journey to where he'd left his car.

'I'll go back and take Ben's tack off and put Jake inside,' Alice planned ahead aloud. 'Then I can take you into Emergency for observation and go and collect Emmy.'

'Alice?'

Andrew had stopped moving forward. The arm he had around Alice's shoulders tightened and she turned towards him.

'Are you all right? You're not feeling dizzy or sick or anything, are you?'

'I'm feeling...incredibly lucky.'

'Because you got knocked out? Hardly lucky.'

'Because you didn't ride away and leave me. That maybe I haven't left it too late to tell you I love you.'

'It's not too late, Andrew.'

'I wanted to tell you weeks ago. When you were sick. Before that, even, but...'

'I know.' Alice smiled into his eyes. 'It's huge and some things are too scary to say out loud. I wanted to tell you about the baby before this.'

'But you were scared because you thought I might think you'd planned it. Like Melissa did.'

Alice dropped her gaze as she nodded.

Andrew put a finger under her chin and tilted her face up again. She met his eyes and was instantly captured by the tenderness she could see. And the conviction.

'You're nothing like Mel,' Andrew told her softly. 'You never could be. You're you. So special and so wonderful that I love you more than I can ever hope to tell you. I never expected to find this. I thought Emmy was all I had in the world. All I needed.'

'Emmy is that special.' Alice smiled. 'I can understand that because I love her, too.'

'We're a family. Or we will be. Will you marry me, Alice?'

Alice smiled again and gently urged Andrew to keep walking towards his car.

'Ask me that again when you're not concussed.'

He did exactly that, as soon as the results of the CT scan Peter had insisted on came back showing no evidence of a significant head injury. Well after the wound had been cleaned and stitched.

Andrew waited only until Jo had gone, promising to fast-track his discharge summary.

'I'm not concussed,' he told Alice. 'Or only mildly. Enough to give me a headache for a day or two but not enough to undermine my judgement in any way.'

Alice couldn't resist teasing him a little. Perhaps because she knew what was coming and she wanted to draw this moment out for as long as she could to savour the delicious realisation of her dream.

'You're not supposed to drink alcohol or drive a car.'

'I'm not talking about driving a car.' Andrew caught hold of Alice's hand. 'I'm talking about what's going to drive the rest of my life.'

'Oh…' Alice let herself be drawn closer to where Andrew was sitting right on the edge of the bed. Tugged right between his legs, in fact.

Andrew raised her hand, turning it over so that he

could press a kiss to her palm. His gaze, however, remained locked with Alice's.

'I'm talking about you,' he said softly. 'The first, last and only woman I'm ever going to be in love with like this.'

Alice tried to swallow the lump that appeared like magic in her throat. She knew that conviction of having found 'the One'. She'd known that for her it was Andrew and she'd known that for many years. How unbelievable was it to be standing here, like this? Being touched by this man? Hearing him say the exact words she wanted to say to him?

'You and Emmy and our baby.' Andrew folded her even closer so that Alice's cheek rested against his and they were chest to chest. She could feel his heart beating against her own and she couldn't distinguish which pulse was hers. She didn't want to.

'We're a family, Alice. A perfect family.'

'Mmm.' The sound was a contented sigh.

'So...' Andrew pushed her back, just far enough to see her face properly '...will you marry me, Alice?'

'Yes.'

Such a tiny word but it came with a smile mixed with tears and it was all she needed to say, judging by the exquisite tenderness of the kiss Andrew bestowed on her.

A very brief kiss, because they were mindful of the fact that Jo would come rushing back any second now.

Sure enough, she came in, brandishing a pink slip of paper. She noted how close Alice was to Andrew and her smile broadened. She gave an approving nod as she handed over his clearance as a patient.

'You know what to watch out for,' she said to Alice. 'Any sign that we might have missed something.'

'You haven't,' Andrew assured her. 'I'm good to go.'

But when Jo left them to it, he didn't move.

'Shall we go?' Alice prompted.

'Not yet.'

'What about Emmy?'

'She's fine for a little while. She loves that after school play centre and I want to have another scan.'

'What?' Alice's heart skipped a beat. '*Why?* Is your headache worse? Vision blurry? Can't you—?'

Andrew pressed a finger to her lips. 'Not for me.' He was smiling. 'For you. For *us*.'

He could see she was still worried and his smile faded. 'You haven't forgotten Laura, have you? The threatened miscarriage?'

'Of course not. But…' Alice stopped and held her breath. This was important. As important as everything else Andrew had been saying since the accident.

'When I was giving her that scan to look for a foetal heartbeat, I had this image of it being us.'

Alice stared at him.

'Nothing to do with any complications,' Andrew added hurriedly. 'I was thinking in terms of an ordinary confirmation of pregnancy kind of scan. I wanted to be beside you. Holding your hand and waiting to see that little blip on the screen. I want to see it now. Our baby.'

So that was what that intense look had been about. The one that had been so overwhelming, given the secret she'd been keeping from Andrew.

Alice felt the prickle of unshed tears.

'Did I tell you that I love you?' she whispered.

Andrew feigned an innocent expression. 'I don't think I remember. I do have a mild concussion, you know. Tell me again.'

'Oh, I will, don't worry. You'll get sick of hearing it.'

'Never,' Andrew vowed and bent his head to kiss her again.

EPILOGUE

THE small girl had a very determined expression on
her face.

She stood up tall in her stirrups and then sat down in
the saddle. Up and down, in perfect time with the stride
of her pony, as they went around in a small circle on a
lush green paddock that was bathed by early summer
sunshine.

'Perfect!' Alice called. 'You're posting, Emmy. Good
girl!'

'Great stuff,' Andrew added, a proud grin on his face.

'You can stop now,' Alice told Emmy. 'Your legs
must be getting tired.'

But Emmy kept going. Round and round, her face
glowing with triumph.

Behind the fat, shaggy pony a large dog trotted.
Riding shotgun to protect the child and keep her close
to the rest of the family.

Leaning over the gate to this paddock was a huge
black horse who looked as though he was dozing
happily in the shade of the old tree but his ears flicked

every time Paddington came nearer with his precious burden. He was watching just as closely as everyone else.

Alice stood with her back touching Andrew, who had his arms around her waist.

Or what used to be a waist. Currently, it was an impressive bulge. It was only a matter of weeks now until their son would be born.

'Daddy! Are you watching me? I'm *trotting*!'

'You sure are, darling. I'm very proud of you.'

His gentle hold on Alice tightened a little and the baby seemed to respond, moving beneath those loving hands. What an incredible sensation, being touched by people she loved from the inside and the outside at the same time. Alice let her breath out in a sigh.

'You okay?'

'I don't think I've ever felt this happy.'

'You're not missing being able to ride on such a gorgeous day?'

'Ben's enjoying his holiday and I'm way too busy to ride, anyway. There's still a way to go to get the garden into shape for the wedding.'

'It's too much work for you,' Andrew growled. 'What were we thinking, trying to get the restoration work on the house and garden done before we got married? We should have just skipped off to the nearest register office.'

'You know why.' Alice twisted a little so she could look up at Andrew's face. So that she could bask in the love she knew she would find there.

They'd decided to wait so that Emmy could be involved. Until after the baby was born. Because this wasn't just about a commitment ceremony between a man and a woman who loved each other so deeply.

It was to be a celebration of a new family.

And it would be Christmas time and they'd agreed that this was the most amazing gift anyone could ever give or receive.

A family.

'Look!' Emmy called. 'I can trot. Watch me, Mummy.'

Alice had to pull her gaze from Andrew's to look back at Emmy, but she was still within the circle of his arms.

'I'm watching, sweetheart.'

'So am I,' Andrew added.

They were. They would always watch over and love their children. And each other.

Because that was what families did.

ROMANCING
THE NANNY

BY
CINDY KIRK

Cindy Kirk is a lifelong Nebraska resident who started writing after taking a class at a local college. But her interest in the written word started years before when she was in her teens. At sixteen she wrote in her diary, "I don't know what I would do if I couldn't be a writer."

Not until her daughter was heading off to college did Cindy return to her first love—writing. Cindy wasn't interested in newspaper or magazine articles, short stories or poetry. When she decided to start writing, she jumped feet first into book-length fiction. She loves reading and writing romance, and she believes in the power of love and in happily ever after. An incurable romantic, Cindy loves seeing her characters grow and learn from their mistakes and, in the process, achieve a happy ending.

She and her school sweetheart husband live on an acreage with two cats…one of whom loves to sit next to the computer and supervise her writing. Cindy loves to hear from readers. She invites you to visit her website at www.CindyKirk.com.

To my critique partners Louise Foster,
Renee Halverson and Melissa Green.
Thanks for your insightful comments,
friendship and support.

Chapter One

It was lust, Amy Logan decided as she pressed the dough into the pie crust with extra fervor. Pure and simple lust.

After all, it would be unnatural to live with such a handsome man for three years and not have the occasional urge to see him naked.

Having no sex in years probably didn't help, either, Amy thought, her lips twisting upward in a wry smile. Or the fact that this morning she'd slipped upstairs to get Emma her backpack and caught him just out of the shower.

Oh, he'd been perfectly presentable with a Turkish towel wrapped firmly around his waist. And she'd certainly seen him with his shirt off before.

Every summer he went to the pool at the country club with her and Emma at least a couple of times.

But there was something different about knowing that he'd been naked only moments before. Something about seeing the droplets of water clinging to his broad chest. Something about smelling that delicious mixture of soap, shampoo and clean masculine flesh.

Amy inhaled deeply. Even now if she closed her eyes, she could still—

"Got any coffee left?"

Amy's eyes popped open and she stilled, grateful she faced the wall. Otherwise the object of her desires might think she was having a sensual experience with a pie crust.

Schooling her features into what she hoped was a nonchalant expression, Amy turned.

Dan Major stood in the center of the large modern kitchen wearing her favorite suit. The cut emphasized his broad shoulders and lean hips and the navy color brought out the brilliant blue of his eyes. Still damp from the shower, his short dark hair fell into a careless wave on his forehead.

He was an inch or two over six feet and easily the most handsome man she'd ever known. It only made sense that she'd want to see him naked. What didn't make sense was why that desire had taken so long to surface.

She and the hunky widower had lived side by side for almost three years. Amy had always considered

Dan a good friend. But over the past six months she'd found herself thinking of him in a different way, seeing him not just as her employer and friend but as a desirable man.

"Amy?"

His lips curved upward and she realized with a start that she'd been staring.

Without a word, she reached over and lifted the pot from the warmer. "Can I pour you a cup?"

"I can get my own," he protested as he pulled out a chair and took a seat at the table.

Amy smiled. Dan was the quintessential modern man with one major exception. Despite being only thirty-four and having been raised in a progressive two-income family, Dan rarely helped out around the house.

Unfortunately she had only herself to blame. She'd refused his offers of help so many times, he'd quit asking. The truth was she loved to pamper him and Emma. Keeping his house spotless and clothes laundered filled her with immense satisfaction. She prided herself on the fact that he could always count on a well-balanced, home-cooked meal at the end of the day.

A successful architect at one of Chicago's largest and most prestigious firms, Dan alternated between working in the office or from home.

His schedule was so varied, Amy never knew if he'd be home, at the office, or out meeting with clients. It didn't really affect her. Emma was in first grade this year and gone all day. The only difference was if Dan was home she'd make his lunch and maybe offer a snack in the afternoon.

After all, that's what he was paying her for; that and taking care of his young daughter, Emma. And not only did he pay her, he paid her very well. With the extra money she saved by living-in, she'd been able to get enough cash together to start a small catering business.

Last year when she'd shown Dan her business plan, he'd been surprised, then concerned. He'd asked her point-blank if she was planning to leave. But when she'd reassured him that this was just something extra she wanted to do for herself, he'd been supportive.

Shortly after that he'd had the antiquated kitchen in the large older home remodeled. And best of all, he'd solicited her input and hadn't batted an eye at her request for commercial-grade appliances.

For now she limited her efforts to catering small parties on the weekends and providing specialty desserts to a couple of restaurants. But she held high hopes for the future. One day she'd make enough so she could have her own home—

"I'd be happy to get my own coffee..."

Dan's bemused voice broke through her reverie pulling Amy back to the present. She glanced down at the coffeepot she still held loosely in her hand. Ignoring Dan's teasing comment, Amy quickly poured a cup and set the steaming brew in front of him. No need to ask if he wanted cream or sugar. She had his likes and dislikes memorized.

"Cinnamon roll?" she asked, appealing to his sweet tooth. "I made them this morning. Or I could whip up some bacon and eggs? It would only take a second—"

"I'm afraid this will have to do." Dan glanced at the clock on the wall, took a hasty sip of coffee and pushed back his chair. "I have a meeting at the office at nine and I should've been gone by now."

At the first scrape of the chair legs against the hardwood floor, Amy sprang into action. Grabbing the travel mug from the cupboard, she filled it with the rich Columbian blend that was his favorite.

By the time she was done he was already in the doorway. He turned. "I should be home early, around five-thirty."

Amy let her gaze sweep over him, like it did over Emma every morning, making sure everything was in place. She frowned.

"Wait." She popped the lid on the travel mug and quickly crossed the room. But instead of handing him the coffee, she placed it on the counter and stepped close. "Your tie needs some help."

Grabbing the silk fabric, she loosened the off-center knot and with well-practiced ease, quickly retied it. But instead of taking a step back, she let her fingers linger.

Dan was in a hurry. He'd made that perfectly clear. Her head told her to step back, hand him the travel mug and send him on his way. But her feet wouldn't move. The air surrounding them grew thick. It was as if an invisible web encased them. Time, which had been ticking onward with rhythmic precision, came to an abrupt halt.

The subtle scent of his cologne teased her nostrils. Heat emanating from his body washed over her.

She wanted to pull him close and press her lips to his, relieve this tension that had built up inside her. Instead she dropped her hands, placed them on her rounded hips and gave him a once-over. "Now you look presentable."

Amy had learned long ago the perils of being foolish. And thinking that Dan—handsome, successful Dan, who could have any woman he wanted in the entire city of Chicago—was attracted to her would be the height of folly. He liked her, admired her, appreciated her. But any electricity she felt was definitely one-sided.

"Thanks." The dimple in his left cheek flashed. He reached down and picked up the mug she'd placed on the counter. "And I appreciate the coffee."

Somehow Amy managed an easy smile. "Anytime."

She stood at the door and watched him get in the car. As he drove off, she lifted her hand and waved goodbye, then took a few steps and collapsed in a nearby chair. What in the world had she been thinking?

Dan wasn't interested in *her*. And even if there was a tiny spark of something between them, there was no way she could compete with Tess Major's memory and come out ahead. Other women had tried and they'd all failed. And that's what Amy needed to remember before she did something she'd live to regret.

The smell of warm peach pie filled the large kitchen and Amy smiled as she wiped down the counters. Some women needed fancy clothes or trips to exotic ports, but all it took for her to be happy was a neat, orderly kitchen…

"Something smells good in here."

Amy whirled. Dan stood in the doorway to the dining room, a lazy smile on his lips.

"You're home early." The minute the words left her mouth Amy wished she could pull them back. She'd made it sound as if he was unwelcome when nothing could be further from the truth.

It was just that she always liked to have everything ready and in its place when he came home. But it was only four-thirty and she hadn't expected him for at least an hour. The table wasn't set and Emma was still down the block playing at a friend's house.

"Now that's a warm welcome." Dan smiled and that familiar dimple in his left cheek appeared. "If I didn't know better, I'd think you didn't want me."

His gaze settled on her and she forced herself not to glance away. But it was hard. The intense look in his blue eyes sent a shiver up her spine. "Tell me something, Amy. Do you ever think of me when I'm not here?"

That same electricity charged the air and Amy moistened her dry lips. She shifted from one foot to the other, not knowing how to answer. This morning he'd looked at her as if he was seeing her for the first time.

This was another first. In all the years she'd worked for Dan, he'd never spoken to her like this before. There had always been a professional boundary that had never been crossed.

"Of course I think of you," she finally managed to stammer.

He smiled and paused as if he expected her to elaborate.

But what else could she say? She certainly wasn't about to bare her soul and confess her desire for some skin-to-skin action. Not to mention that her heart had lodged itself in her throat, making speech impossible.

Thankfully Dan didn't press her for more. Instead he crossed the room, flung his suit jacket over a chair and loosened his tie.

Amy could feel her cheeks warm. She turned back to the counter and scrubbed a nonexistent spot with her sponge.

He stopped directly behind her, so close she could smell the spicy scent of his cologne and feel the heat from his body.

She turned and he was right *there.* Just like this morning it struck her how big he was, how tall. How overwhelmingly male in every way.

Her heart picked up speed.

His gaze lazily appraised her and his eyes darkened. "You're so beautiful."

The compliment rolled from his lips like warm honey. It wasn't true, of course. The sprinkle of freckles across her nose and the extra twenty pounds she constantly fought made her wholesome, rather than beautiful. But suddenly, under his admiring gaze, for the first time in her twenty-eight years, Amy felt beautiful.

"Thank you."

His lips quirked. "You're very welcome."

Could she be any worse at this flirting stuff? It didn't seem possible.

She started to ask if his meeting had gotten canceled when he took another step forward and his body brushed hers. In that instant Amy forgot how to breathe, much less talk.

With the gentlest of touches, Dan slid his fingers into the warm silky mass at her nape, letting his thumbs graze the soft skin beneath her jaw.

Waves of chills and heat raced through Amy until she was nearly dizzy. He was going to kiss her; she could see it in his eyes. She tossed the sponge to the counter without shifting her gaze from him.

His lips lowered and she let her eyelids drift shut, anticipation coursing through her...

The front door slammed shut.

Amy jumped as if she'd been shot. Panic raced through her. Emma couldn't find the two of them together. She raised a hand to push Dan away and found only air.

Her gaze darted around the room and after a long second it finally sank in…she was alone. There'd been no Dan and no almost-kiss. Heat rose up her neck. She'd had vivid dreams before, but never with Dan as the star player.

"Amy, I'm home." Emma's childish voice rang out from the foyer.

"In the kitchen," Amy called back. She rubbed her mouth with the back of her hand. Though it had been only a dream, her lips still tingled.

"Is it 'bout time for dinner?" The petite six-year-old bounded into the kitchen, a streak of dirt on her cheek and a grass stain on one knee. "I'm hungry."

Amy couldn't help but smile. Dan often joked that the little girl's stomach was a bottomless pit. Emma could eat and five minutes later be hungry. "Once your father gets home, we'll have dinner. He shouldn't be too late."

Amy opened her arms and the girl ran to her. When Amy had been Emma's age, hugs had been in short supply. She'd vowed when she had children, she'd make sure they knew they were loved.

Amy couldn't imagine anything better than having a family of her own—a husband to love, a child to cherish.

Her arms tightened around Emma. One day she'd be a mother. But for now, she had Emma to love.

Emma laid her head against Amy's chest. "I love you."

Tears sprang to Amy's eyes at the child's sincerity. "I love you, too, pumpkin."

Yes, for now this would most definitely do.

Chapter Two

Out of the corner of his eye, Dan Major saw a
stylish young woman across the bar and realized he
knew her. He smiled and she waved.

"Another Dan fan?" Jake Stanley's lips curved
upward. "How in the world do you do it?"

"Stuff it, Jake." Dan grabbed some peanuts from
the basket in the center of the table and popped them
in his mouth.

Seeing old girlfriends only reinforced why Dan
found it hard to date. He liked the companionship but
women always seemed to want more. Bree was a
perfect example. Though she'd professed to being
devoted to a singles' lifestyle, after a couple of
months, she'd changed her tune.

Dan sighed and glanced around the bar. Although it was only Thursday night, the place was crowded with women from nearby businesses. He suspected that was why Jake had insisted on coming to this bar.

Looking for love in all the wrong places...

For some reason the words to the vintage song popped into Dan's head. But the lyrics didn't fit his life. The last thing Dan was looking for tonight, or any other night, was love.

Jake shot Dan a speculative gaze. "Speaking of Dan fans, how's it going with Miranda?"

"Her name is Melinda." Dan kept his tone deliberately offhand. "And we're not seeing each other anymore."

"Let me guess." Jake lifted a finger to his lips and pretended to think. "*You* broke up with *her.*"

Dan grabbed another handful of peanuts, strangely irritated by the knowing look in his friend's eyes. "What does it matter who decided to end it? The point is it wasn't working."

"It wasn't working because she wanted more than sex," Jake said conversationally, resting his arms on the table. "Things heat up, you back off."

"You don't know squat." Dan's tone was sharper than he'd intended but it had been hard losing Melinda. Just like Bree, she was a nice woman and he'd enjoyed her company. But he refused to promise more than he could deliver.

Jake placed his drink on the table and lifted his

hands. "Whoa, buddy. I wasn't saying there was anything wrong with playing the field—"

Dan ignored the envious look in his friend's eye. The truth was Dan didn't like being on the dating merry-go-round. But the longer he was with a woman, the more they seemed to want, the more they seemed to need. He'd yet to find a woman who was content to keep it casual. "I made it clear from the very beginning that I didn't want to get married again. Why is that so hard for women to understand?"

"Because regardless of what they say, they want that ring on their finger." Jake lifted a hand and motioned for the waiter to bring him another drink. "I know you've got this thing against marriage but I think you should reconsider."

Dan took a sip of beer. Jake had it all wrong. He didn't have anything against marriage. He'd loved being married to Tess. From the time he'd first laid eyes on the perky blonde, he'd known she was the one. When they'd said "I do" he'd happily planned on spending the rest of his life with her. His heart twisted.

"You'd have someone to warm your bed and that little girl of yours would have a mother," Jake continued.

Dan shoved aside his memories and smiled at the thought of his daughter. Of all the things he valued most in his life, his six-year-old topped the list. "Emma is coping with the loss of her mother. Amy takes good care of her."

Amy had been his daughter's nanny for three

years and Dan knew she loved Emma as if she were her own. She'd made the house a home for both of them.

"Which is all well and good," Jake said. "Until 'nanny' finds a man and decides to get married and leave you."

Amy wouldn't leave me.

Dan bit back the words, shocked at the strength of emotion the thought evoked. He started to say Amy didn't even date, but stopped himself again. There *had* been one guy recently…

He'd been surprised—stunned would actually be closer to the truth—when Amy had casually mentioned she was going to the movies with someone she'd met at her cooking club. In all the years she'd lived under his roof, Dan couldn't remember her dating before. Amy just never seemed like the dating type.

Not that she was ugly or anything. Far from it. With her brown hair, green eyes and a smattering of freckles across her nose, Amy had that natural, all-American look that any man would find attractive. And she was smart. While she always had an opinion on the latest current events, she also liked to listen. Any man would be lucky to have her for a girlfriend or wife.

A tightness filled his chest. Jake was right. If she left, he'd be stuck. He'd never find another nanny like Amy. He might even have to do what Jake suggested and remarry. A chill traveled up Dan's spine.

Since he'd been fifteen, Tess had been the only woman Dan had ever wanted in his life. His wife had been beautiful, smart and a rising star in the fashion world with her innovative clothing designs. For the first five years of their marriage, life had been wonderful. Their careers had flourished and the old house they'd purchased in Lincoln Park was perfect for a growing family.

But after Emma was born, Tess had decided there would be no more children. She loved her daughter but her pregnancy had been difficult and Emma was a fussy baby. And when her new line took off like a skyrocket, her career began demanding more of her time and energy.

Dan had reluctantly put away his dream of a large family, but he hadn't given up completely. When Emma was two he'd convinced Tess to have one more, promising her a full-time nanny. That's when Amy had come to live with them. But the second baby he'd wanted so much had died along with Tess.

Guilt washed over him, mixed with an overwhelming sense of loss. He'd give anything to be able to go back and tell Tess he didn't care about having another child or a playmate for Emma, he only cared about having *her* in his life.

"Mark my words, it's going to happen." Jake, appearing to revel in his role as a prophet of doom, pulled Dan back to the present. "It's just a matter of time."

"Amy isn't going to get married." Even if he didn't fully believe them, saying the words out loud made Dan feel better.

She couldn't leave. He depended on her to keep

his household running smoothly. And he really liked having her around. Over the past couple of years they'd become good friends. He couldn't imagine what it would be like if she wasn't there.

"She'll get married." Jake nodded his head to punctuate the point. "She's hot, in a plump sort of way. If she lost some pounds, I might be interested in dating her myself."

Despite knowing Jake's penchant for women who were model-slim, the comment set Dan's teeth on edge. Maybe it was because he knew how Amy struggled with her weight and how self-conscious she was about the few extra pounds that made her more curvy than pencil-thin.

"Amy doesn't need to lose an ounce," Dan said. "And even if you wanted to date her, I know you too well to let that happen."

Jake just laughed.

"Can I interest you two in some wings?" The waiter leaned across the table and slid Jake's second drink in front of him.

Dan's stomach growled and he realized with a start that lunch had been hours ago. He glanced at his watch and swore. Reaching into his pocket, Dan brought out a couple of bills and tossed them on the table.

"I'll take a plate of the barbecued ones," Jake said to the waiter before shifting his gaze to Dan. He lifted a brow. "You're leaving?"

"I'm late." Dan grabbed his briefcase and rose to his feet. "Amy will have dinner on the table."

"I forgot." Jake sat back in his chair, an inscrutable look on his face. "Superwoman does it all—cleans your house, cares for your kid *and* makes your meals. If you could just get her naked, you'd have it made."

Dan ignored the crude comment—and the hint of envy in his friend's tone—and simply smiled.

It was true. Amy had breakfast waiting for him every morning and dinner ready every night. The house was always spotless and, when he entertained, she worked behind the scenes making sure every little detail was covered. Best of all, she cared for Emma as if the child were her own.

No, as long as Amy was in his house, all was well in Dan's world.

"Dinner was fabulous, Amy." Dan wiped the corners of his mouth with the linen napkin and heaved a contented sigh. "And that dessert—"

"It was good, wasn't it, Daddy?" Emma's blue eyes sparkled the way they always did when her father was in the room.

"It certainly was, princess." Dan's fond smile lingered on his daughter. "Amy is a great cook."

Amy pushed back her chair and rose, unable to stop the warm flush of pleasure at the compliment. There was nothing she enjoyed more than trying new recipes. She hadn't been sure how Emma and Dan would react to the citrus-glazed salmon, but she'd been fairly certain they'd love the sour cream peach pie with homemade ice cream.

She hadn't allowed herself even the tiniest of bites. A Moment On The Lips, Forever On The Hips had become her new mantra.

"Can I get either of you anything else before I clear the table?" Amy's gaze shifted from Dan to Emma.

"No, thank you," Emma said.

Amy shot the little girl a smile of approval. She'd been working with Emma the last couple of months on her manners and it was obviously paying off.

"And how about you?" Amy's gaze settled on Dan. She'd lived in his house for over three years and firmly believed she knew him better than he knew himself. Like now, she couldn't help but notice the lines of fatigue edging his eyes. Lately he'd been working too hard…and socializing too much.

Last Friday night, she'd lain awake until 1:00 a.m. waiting for him to come home before she'd finally fallen asleep. She wasn't sure what time he'd come in but the next morning he'd been at the table at eight, ready to take Emma to the zoo as promised. Saturday night he'd stayed in. They'd all gone to the park and had a picnic, then came home and played board games on the porch until it was time to go to bed.

Being home on a Saturday night had been just one of the signs that another of Dan's relationships had come to an end. It hadn't surprised her. Melinda had been calling a lot and trying to cozy up to Emma. Amy could have told her such behavior was the kiss of death. If a woman wanted to keep Dan Major's interest, she had to act like she didn't care. That's why Amy had kept a tight lid on her burgeoning desire for him. As far as he knew, she didn't feel anything more for him than simple friendship. She was his housekeeper, his daughter's caregiver and his friend.

Occasionally he'd confide in her, knowing what he said wouldn't go any further. She savored those times and the closeness she...

"Earth to Amy." Dan's voice broke through her reverie.

She looked up with a start to find Dan and Emma staring at her.

Emma giggled. "You were spacing out."

Amy blinked and warmth crept up her neck.

"What were you thinking about?" Dan asked, a curious glint in his eye. "You had the most interesting smile on your face."

I was thinking about you.

The words rose unbidden to her tongue and when Emma giggled again, for a second Amy feared she'd said them aloud. She searched for a plausible explanation. "I was thinking about Steven."

"Steven?" Dan frowned. "Who's that?"

"He's her boyfriend," Emma said. "Amy and Steven sittin' in a tree, K-I-S-S-I-N-G. First comes love—"

"You were kissing a man?" The shocked look on Dan's face would have been funny at any other time. "In front of Emma?"

"Of course I wasn't, I didn't," Amy said quickly, embarrassed warmth coloring her cheeks. She shifted her gaze to Emma. "And Steven is my friend, not my boyfriend."

"You talked to him for a long time on the phone today," Emma said. "And you were smiling when you hung up."

"He's my *friend*," Amy repeated. She glanced at Dan. "I've told you about him. He's the guy from my cooking club. We were exchanging lasagna recipes."

Dan's dimple flashed. "Lasagna recipes?"

"That's right." Amy lifted a brow. "You find that amusing?"

"Not at all," Dan said smoothly. "I think it's nice that you two have so much in common."

Amy pulled her brows together, not sure if he was being serious or insulting.

"We both like to cook," she said finally.

Dan's finger traced the raised pattern on the lace tablecloth and when he spoke his tone was decidedly offhand. "You two have been going out for what—a couple of months now?"

"Something like that," Amy said. She still didn't think of Steven as a boyfriend since, until recently, most of the "dates" had revolved around cooking group events.

Something flickered in the back of Dan's eyes but he remained silent.

Unexpectedly Emma lifted her gaze to Amy. "Do you love him like my daddy loved my mommy?"

The girl's question took Amy by surprise and she answered honestly. "No, I don't."

"Do you think you *could* love him?" Dan asked.

"I don't know," Amy said when she realized Dan expected an answer. "I guess anything is possible."

Dan tucked Emma into bed and reveled at this perfect child he and Tess had created. He loved her with an intensity that took his breath away and his heart ached at the thought of all the pain she'd had to endure in her short life. All because of his selfish desire to give her a brother or sister.

"Good night, princess." He brushed a kiss across her cheek. She was his priority and nothing mattered more to him than ensuring her happiness. "I love you."

"I love you, too, Daddy."

"Amy will be up in a minute to say good-night." His stomach tightened into a knot. Usually he and Amy tucked Emma in together. But tonight, *Steven* had called and Amy had said to go on without her.

A tear trailed down Emma's cheek and her brows pulled together. With her big blue eyes and honey-blond hair, she looked more and more like her mother every day.

Dan's heart tightened. "What's the matter, sweetie?"

The little girl's bottom lip trembled and a few more tears fell. Though Dan wanted to make better whatever was bothering her, he forced himself to wait. He'd learned you couldn't rush Emma. When she was ready, she'd tell him what was bothering her. *Then* he'd make it all better.

"Is Amy going to marry Steven?"

The words hit him like a punch to the chest. Dan didn't like the idea of Amy marrying Steven, either, but somehow he managed to keep a smile on his lips. "She said he was just her friend. Remember?"

"But sometimes friends get married." Emma pushed herself up to her elbows. "When Grandma Ann married Grandpa Hal she said he was her good friend."

Dan's mother had been widowed for many years when she and her old friend Hal had decided to tie the knot. Theirs wasn't the romantic love she and his father had shared but they were content together. Even if Dan could explain it adequately, he wasn't sure a six-year-old could understand.

"Daddy." Emma's voice trembled. "Amy's not going to marry him and leave us, is she?"

Dan's jaw clenched at the thought of his daughter enduring one more loss. But Dan knew it wasn't just Emma who'd suffer. If Amy left it would leave a hole in both their lives.

"She's not going to leave." He pulled Emma close and planted a kiss against her hair. "Not if I have anything to say about it."

The resolve in Dan's heart resounded in his voice. He didn't care what the cost. He'd do whatever it took to keep Amy in his household…and Emma happy.

Chapter Three

After leaving Emma, Dan took the back stairs to the kitchen. He rummaged through the refrigerator for several minutes before he realized he wasn't hungry or thirsty.

He grabbed the paper and headed to the porch. Perhaps reading about people with real troubles would help him forget his own.

Amy wasn't going to leave, he told himself. He paid her well and she loved taking care of Emma. As far as that guy Steven was concerned, if he was truly interested in Amy he wouldn't be talking about *recipes* with her.

Reassured by his logic, Dan opened the paper and

turned to the financial section. He'd barely started reading when he heard footsteps.

Amy pushed the screen door open with her shoulder. "Thought you might like a snack."

Dan jumped to his feet and took the tray from her. The faint scent of lilacs teased his nostrils. It was an old-fashioned scent but one that suited her. He glanced down.

A thin slice of lemon topped each glass of lemonade and the assorted cookies perfectly arranged on the decorative plate looked like they could have come from a gourmet bakery.

"These look fabulous," he said.

Amy blushed a becoming shade of pink and took a seat in a wicker chair.

Dan placed the tray on the tiny table in between the two chairs, handed her a glass and took the other for himself.

Though he still wasn't particularly thirsty, she'd gone to a lot of work and Dan wasn't about to disappoint her. He lifted a glass to his lips and took a long sip. "Perfect."

Satisfaction filled Amy's gaze. "It's always better when the lemons are freshly squeezed."

"You squeezed these?"

She laughed—a pleasant laugh that reminded Dan of the tinkle of bells. "With my own two hands."

Dan didn't need to ask if she'd made the cookies. They were too perfect *not* to be hers.

"Snickerdoodle." He filched one from the center of the plate. "My favorite."

"I think I knew that," Amy said with a teasing smile.

Dan returned her smile and decided he'd been foolish to worry. Amy was happy in his household. She wasn't going anywhere.

She glanced at the paper. "Are you looking at the classifieds?"

Dan handed her the section and returned his attention to the stock quotes. They drank lemonade, ate cookies and read in comfortable silence. Dan never felt pressured to make small talk with Amy. If there was something to discuss, it was brought up. Otherwise, it was okay to just relax.

Dan wasn't sure when he first became aware that Amy was doing more than just reading the Want ads. Maybe it was when he noticed the pen. Every so often she'd make a quick mark on the page.

What was she doing?

He could ask but he already felt like he'd gone over the line at dinner and didn't want to overstep again. Amy was a private person and Dan had always subscribed to the notion that if she wanted him to know something, she'd tell him.

"Jake and I stopped for a drink after work." Dan hoped if he started talking, so would she. "You'll never guess who I saw."

Amy lowered the paper to her lap. "Who?"

"Bree Northcott." Dan wasn't sure why he'd brought the woman up, other than she'd been one of the few women he'd dated Amy had seemed to genuinely like. "She was the blonde who—"

"I remember Bree," Amy said. "And Kellycat and Todd."

Dan paused. "Who?"

Amy giggled. "Her cats. A Scottish Fold and an Abyssinian."

The words meant nothing to him. He only remembered one was furry and the other short-haired.

"Those Scottish Folds are so beautiful." An almost dreamy lilt filled Amy's voice and her lips curved upward. "But so hard to find."

"I don't know anything about cats."

Amy's smile vanished. "That's because you don't like them."

"You're right," Dan admitted. When he'd been small, his neighbor's Siamese had gone ballistic when he'd tried to pick it up. Ever since that day, Dan had given all felines a wide berth. "I don't like them. And I'd certainly never want one, let alone two, in my house. Thankfully Tess and I agreed on that."

Amy's expression didn't waver but her gaze shifted back to the paper.

He had the feeling he'd missed something. A sudden thought struck him.

"Emma hasn't mentioned wanting a kitten, has she?" Though Dan would give his daughter the sun and moon if he could, he drew the line at a cat.

"Not to me." Amy's gaze remained fixed on the paper.

Dan heaved a sigh of relief. "Good."

"She'd never ask because she knows how you feel about them," Amy added.

Though she'd made the comment matter-of-factly, Dan could have sworn he heard an underlying hint of reproach. He frowned. "Are you saying Emma is afraid to talk to me?"

"Not afraid," Amy said. "But—"

A loud boom of thunder split the air and Amy jumped. The newspaper on her lap went flying and the napkins on the tray flew off in a gust of wind.

Dan met Amy's gaze and the concern in her eyes mirrored his own. "Emma."

His daughter was deathly afraid of storms and the thunder had been loud enough to wake the dead, let alone a light sleeper.

"You go," Amy said. "I'll stay and pick up."

The wind began to blow in earnest, ruffling the newspapers he held in his hands and threatening to topple the empty lemonade glasses.

"No," Dan said. "She'll want you, not me."

Though it pained him to say so, in this instance it was the truth. During thunderstorms, it was always Amy who Emma clung to, not him.

Amy nodded and touched his arm. "Thanks."

Another loud clap of thunder rent the air and Amy hurried off before he could ask why she was thanking him. After the door slammed shut, a few drops of rain plopped on the sidewalk and Dan didn't have time to think. He'd lived in the Midwest long enough to know he needed to hurry. He rounded up the paper, grabbed the plate of cookies and empty glasses and headed inside.

He'd barely made it through the door when the rain began in earnest, the wind spraying droplets of water across the floor of the porch.

By the time Dan reached the kitchen, sheets of rain pelted the windows. He placed the cookies and glasses on the counter and dropped the wad of papers onto the table. The classifieds that Amy had been reading somehow ended up on top.

Though Dan told himself it was none of his business, he found his gaze drawn to the circled items.

An icy chill traveled up his spine. Real estate in the suburbs? The price range seemed a little out of her league, but it might be manageable, depending on the size of the down payment or if there were two incomes. *Steven.*

Had she lied when she'd said the two of them were just friends? In his heart he didn't think so. But she'd mentioned more than once how much she longed for a house of her own.

His fingers tightened around the paper. He couldn't imagine this home without Amy. If she left, Emma would be devastated. But Amy wouldn't leave, he reminded himself, because he was committed to doing whatever it took to make her stay. He'd learned long ago that most things could be had, for a price. He just had to find out what it would take to keep Amy in his household.

* * *

Amy leaned back in the rocker and sighed with contentment. Though she knew many would say Emma was too big or too old to be rocked, Amy enjoyed being close to the little girl.

Emma had run into her arms when she'd entered the bedroom. Amy had learned long ago she couldn't talk Emma out of her fear; what reassured and calmed her most was to be held. So, she'd taken a seat in the wooden rocker and Emma had crawled onto her lap. For a long moment Amy had just held her close. Once Emma's tears had stopped, Amy had started to sing. Her voice hadn't been good enough to make Swing Choir in high school but Emma didn't complain. These songs from past and present Broadway musicals were Emma's lullabies.

Now Emma slept, her cheeks still showing remnants of the tears that had flowed so freely only minutes before. Amy stroked the little girl's hair and wondered if Tess had ever rocked Emma to sleep and marveled at this perfect child she'd created. Amy liked to think so. She let her mind drift back to the time she'd first met Tess.

She remembered her vividly—the wispy blond hair, the pretty elfin features and the immense blue eyes. Tess had been a petite dynamo who could charm the socks off a complete stranger and bring her handsome husband to his knees with a single smile.

Tess had been three months from delivering her second baby when Amy had first come to live in the

Major household. Even pregnant Tess had been cute and trendy, a fashionista on the cutting edge of the latest styles.

Emma had been almost three, a shy, sensitive child who reminded Amy more of herself than of her gregarious parents. Shortly after Amy had arrived Tess had confided that she found it hard to understand how a child of hers could have so many fears.

Perhaps because she'd been plagued with those same insecurities, Amy had felt a kinship with Emma. They'd bonded immediately, which was good considering Tess hadn't been around much.

Tess had been launching a new line and all her time and attention had been focused on work. When Amy had casually asked Dan if Tess planned to keep up this pace after the baby was born, he'd just laughed and said Tess wasn't happy unless she was going ninety miles an hour.

Amy wasn't sure if Dan was kidding or not. Surely Tess planned to slow down and spend some time with Emma once the baby was born. But in the end, Tess never got that chance. The placenta had unexpectedly separated from the uterine wall and, despite a valiant effort by emergency personnel, she and the baby had died.

Even after three years the memory of that night still made Amy's heart ache. It had been such a horrible time in all their lives…

"Is everything okay?" Dan's voice sounded from the doorway.

Ducking her head, Amy shoved the memories aside. Though she knew Tess was never far from Dan's thoughts, he never talked about that period and she never brought it up.

She leaned her cheek against the top of Emma's head and gained her composure. "Emma was a little frightened, but she calmed right down."

Amy sensed, rather than saw, Dan move across into the room. He squatted by the rocker and touched her arm. The feel of his hand against her skin took her by surprise and reminded her of her earlier daydream. Her heart flip-flopped in her chest.

"I was asking about you," he said.

"Me?" Her voice came out as a high-pitched squeak and Amy nearly groaned aloud wondering what had happened to her normally unflappable composure.

"You haven't been yourself lately," he said softly. "Is there anything you want to tell me?"

Amy met his gaze and her breath caught.

Something flickered in his eyes and she wondered if he felt the electricity, too. But when she looked again, only simple concern reflected back at her.

"I'm just fine." Amy forced a bright smile. "Everything is great."

"Is there anything you want?" Once again his gaze searched hers. "Anything at all?"

Dear God, it was like her fantasy had come to life. The spicy scent of his cologne wafted about her and something quivered deep in Amy's belly. Perspiration dotted her brow.

His gaze locked with hers and Amy could feel herself being pulled into the blue depths.

"What is it you want, Amy?" he asked again. "Tell me and I'll give it to you."

Amy searched his face, looking for what she wasn't sure.

I want you. The words hovered on the edges of her lips. *Take me in your arms and kiss me.*

But as much as she longed to say the words, Amy had learned the hard way what happens when you're needy and demanding.

"It doesn't take much to make me happy," Amy said finally, not really answering his question.

His brows drew together and he appeared to consider her words. After a moment he rose to his feet.

"Let me take her," he said. "The storm has passed. She should sleep all night now."

With well practiced ease, Dan scooped Emma into his arms and lifted her to his chest.

Amy's breath caught at the look of love on his face. She'd been scarcely older than Emma when her beloved father had been killed in a car accident. She'd never experienced such unconditional love since.

Emma might not have Tess, but she wasn't alone.

Unexpected tears filled Amy's eyes but thankfully Dan was too busy tucking Emma into bed to notice.

"I'll see you downstairs." Amy rose from the

rocker and moved quickly across the glossy hardwood to the door. Dan believed she was a strong, practical woman and she didn't want him to think differently.

Dan brushed a kiss across Emma's cheek and turned to find Amy hurrying toward the door. "Hey, wait for me."

He rose and followed her with his lengthy stride but she didn't slow down. If anything, she increased her pace.

Then, like a scene from a slapstick comedy where someone slips on a banana peel, Amy's feet flew out from under her. A startled cry sprang from her lips.

Dan responded instinctively. With his heart in his throat, he lunged forward and grabbed her from behind. There was no time to think. No time to consider where to place his hands.

Amy wore a bra, but the moment his hand gripped the soft mound of flesh, the contact might as well have been skin-to-skin.

Amy gasped and turned, her cheeks two bright spots of pink. He immediately dropped his arms to his sides and took a step back. Heat rose up his neck.

While Amy's face gave nothing away, her hand trembled as she carefully straightened her shirt.

Guilt coursed through Dan. He captured her gaze, willing her to see by the look in his eyes that he was sincerely sorry. "Amy, I—"

"Daddy?" Emma's sleepy voice sounded from across the room.

Dan whirled. But he'd barely taken a step when Emma snuggled into her pillow and her eyelids drifted shut. "Love you, Daddy. Love you, Amy."

"Love you, princess," Dan called softly, but the girl was already asleep.

Dan took a deep breath and turned back to Amy.

"Thanks for catching me," she said, not giving him a chance to continue his apology. "I'm usually not so clumsy."

"I'm usually not so rough." Dan shoved his hands into his pockets. "I didn't even realize where I was—"

"I was thinking of making some hot cocoa," Amy said.

Hot cocoa? It was seventy degrees outside.

But the desperation in her smile told him all he needed to know. She preferred to pretend nothing had happened.

Dan returned her smile, relieved they wouldn't have to have an awkward discussion.

Amy lifted her gaze, her tongue nervously moistening her lips, her eyes wide and very green. "Want some?"

It was a simple question but Dan's body put its own spin on the words. Heat flowed through his veins like molten lava and he suddenly felt like a hormone-ravaged teenager. The intense feelings took him by surprise. But feeling crazy was one thing. Acting crazy something else entirely.

This was Amy, after all.

"Dan?" she prompted, her voice sounding oddly breathless. "Hot cocoa?"

He shook his head. "I'm not in the mood."

Not for hot cocoa, anyway.

Amy met his gaze and her cheeks darkened to a deep rose. For a second he had the sinking feeling she could read his thoughts.

"Suit yourself," she said with a slight smile. "I'll be in the kitchen if you change your mind."

After she left, Dan checked Emma one last time before heading for the stairs. This morning, he hadn't a care in the world. Now, he was lusting after his daughter's nanny and he had nothing but worries.

As he approached the kitchen, he could hear Amy humming. The Broadway show tune sung a trifle off-key told him more than words that he hadn't completely screwed up. At least not yet.

The last remnants of tension eased from his shoulders and Dan decided that maybe he was in the mood for that cup of hot cocoa after all.

Chapter Four

"I understand you're upset about your neighbor dying in that car accident," Dan said in a soothing tone, his fingers tightening around the receiver. He'd been sympathetic for the first twenty minutes of his mother-in-law's call, but his patience was wearing thin. For the last half hour she'd talked nonstop about George, her neighbor, and how he wouldn't have died if he'd heeded her advice and not ridden his bike after dark.

It didn't help that Dan had had a particularly crummy weekend. Amy had gone out with Steven on Friday night and Emma had been cranky.

Today he'd thought they'd all go in-line skating down by the lake after breakfast and maybe catch some lunch at Navy Pier, but once again Amy had plans with Steven. Dan couldn't help but wonder if she was deliberately avoiding him...

"—Emma's welfare."

Dan realized with a start that while his thoughts had been wandering, Gwen had continued to ramble.

"What did you say about Emma?" He relaxed his hold on the phone. There was nothing he liked better than talking about Emma with her doting grandparents. In fact, he'd tried to steer the conversation around to Emma several times in the last thirty minutes but Gwen had been too focused on her neighbor.

"I said you need to make sure that your will names us as Emma's guardians if anything happens to you."

"Nothing is going to happen to me." Dan forced a halfhearted laugh.

"We all think that," Gwen said. "But George didn't plan to die and neither did my daughter."

Though Gwen had never come right out and said it, Dan knew she blamed him for Tess's death. Tess wouldn't have gotten pregnant a second time if he hadn't been so adamant about wanting another child.

"I've already made provisions for Emma," Dan said.

A moment of stunned silence filled the phone line.

"I'm surprised your mother would agree," Gwen said. "What with having a new husband and all."

"Actually my mother didn't think she'd have the stamina for a young child." Dan had been disappointed but he'd appreciated his mom's candor. "A friend here in Chicago has agreed to raise Emma if something happens to me."

After his mother had said no, Dan had approached Amy and she'd seemed touched by the offer.

"A friend?" Gwen's voice rose. "Who is this person? Have I met him?"

Dan hesitated. Gwen had been wealthy her entire life and in her mind a nanny was a servant and as such would never be considered an appropriate guardian for her only grandchild.

"Emma belongs with family," Gwen continued when Dan didn't respond. It wasn't so much what she said as how she said it that reminded him of Tess. Spunky Tess, who used to lift her chin and show him her stubborn face when they disagreed.

Some of his irritation dissolved in the remembrance. Gwen and Phil had loved their daughter and they loved Emma. Unfortunately they could be harsh and unyielding in their views and he had no doubt, given time and opportunity, they'd end up crushing Emma's gentle spirit.

Even now, he had to monitor their interactions with his daughter. They compared Emma to Tess at every opportunity and Emma always came up lacking.

"My mind is made up," Dan said. "I'm not going to change it."

"Well, if anything happens, this friend of yours will have a fight on his hands." His mother-in-law's voice turned frosty. "We will not let our granddaughter be taken from us. And I happen to know that family is always given extra weight in custody issues."

Dan's knuckles turned white at her obvious disregard for his wishes.

C'mon, Dan. I know she can be difficult, but be nice to them. Please. For me.

The memory of Tess's familiar plea stopped his sharp retort. Instead Dan forced a conciliatory tone.

"Gwen, it's been great talking to you but I need to go." He ignored her murmur of protest. "Be sure and tell Phil hello."

Dan clicked off before she could get another word out. Though he had a thousand and one things to do, he didn't move a muscle. He sat staring at the phone, cursing his mother-in-law's high-handedness and wondering what in the world he was going to do now.

Dan sat at the kitchen table and tried to read the paper, but his gaze kept straying to Amy. She'd returned from her afternoon with Steven in a lighthearted mood. Her skin was rosy from the sun and her green eyes sparkled like emeralds. She looked, he thought, uncommonly pretty today.

When she leaned over to put the casserole in the oven, he found himself staring at her smooth thighs and the rounded curves of her breasts.

Dan inhaled a deep, steady breath. This had to stop. He really hated that his gaze lingered on those long, supple legs. And he didn't like noticing the way her shirt clung to every curve or just how nice those curves were.

This was all Jake's fault, he thought irritably. If he hadn't mentioned Amy dating, Dan wouldn't have looked at her in that way at all. For three years she'd been his daughter's nanny. Now, all of a sudden, he'd realized she was a woman, too.

Oblivious to the turmoil her shapeliness was causing, Amy closed the lower oven door and turned. "Have I told you how much I love this double oven?"

Her cotton top accentuated her full, generous breasts, and for a fleeting moment Dan found himself wondering what she'd look like naked. His mouth went dry and it took everything he had to return her smile and concentrate on the question. "Only about a million times."

She laughed. "I think you're exaggerating just a bit."

The sound of her laughter made him smile. Maybe he was exaggerating, but Dan had no doubt the reason she'd been so content in his household had a lot to do with the kitchen. Last year he'd had the entire area redone and Amy had supervised the construction. Since she used it the most, it had only made sense she should have input into the final product.

She'd been so thrilled with the results that when the last contractor had walked out the door, in a moment of pure joy she'd thrown her arms around

Dan's neck and given him a hug. He hadn't given it a second thought. Afterward she'd been embarrassed, but he'd understood. She'd just been given her dream kitchen on a silver platter.

But it wasn't really her kitchen, was it?

Maybe that was why Amy continued to date Steven. Amy was practical. The Lasagna Man might not make her heart beat faster—not yet anyway—but he could give her companionship and a permanent home of her own.

But so could I…

The thought surprised him. He shoved it aside but it immediately boomeranged back. This time he considered the idea. He and Amy shared many common interests and most importantly, they both loved Emma. In a way, he and Amy hooking up made its own kind of sense.

Dan glanced at his watch and headed to the back porch. When Amy got home, he'd be waiting.

Amy shifted her gaze out the window of Steven Mitchell's lakeshore condo. The lights of Chicago blinked back at her. All evening she'd found herself mesmerized by the view.

Her lips curved up in a smile. It had been a wonderful evening, thanks to her very gracious host. She turned back to tell him that but before the words could leave her lips, Steven reached across his dining room table and took her hand.

She wasn't surprised he'd gotten caught up in the

mood. Though that's not how it had been intended, the evening had taken a decidedly romantic turn. Crystal glittered in the candlelight and classical music in the background added to the ambience.

"Dinner was fabulous." In the dim light, Steven's eyes looked more black than gray. "You really outdid yourself."

Amy resisted the urge to gently remove her hand from his grasp. It wasn't that she minded holding hands with Steven, she just didn't want him to get the wrong idea. After all, she'd meant it when she'd told Dan that she and Steven were merely cooking buddies. Though it was beginning to look like Steven might want more…

"Simply fabulous." Steven breathed the words, his gaze riveted to her.

Amy forced herself to chew and swallow. She wasn't sure why Steven was laying it on so thick but she couldn't help but be flattered. Still she forced a nonchalant air as if having a handsome man flirt with her was an everyday occurrence.

"Beef tenderloin can be so boring." Amy lifted the wineglass to her mouth with her free hand. "The secret is the parsley sauce with cornichons and capers."

"You have just the right touch." Steven's thumb caressed her palm and Amy almost inhaled her Merlot.

What was happening? The stars definitely had to be in some kind of funky alignment. First, she'd found herself practically salivating over Dan and

now Steven—who'd always respected the boundaries she'd set—seemed determined to push into new
territory tonight.

Amy had the feeling she was partially to blame.
Two weeks ago, when Steven had taken her to a
fancy French restaurant, she'd happened to mention
how tired she was of cooking the same boring meals
that were Dan and Emma's favorites. She longed to
cut loose and try some fun, fancy recipes for a
change.

Steven had immediately jumped on the idea. He'd
suggested that every week they take turns making each
other a meal of their own choosing. Last week Steven
had treated her to a fabulous evening of Indian cuisine.

Tonight had been her turn to shine. But when she'd
agreed to the plan, she hadn't considered *where* she
would prepare a meal when it was *her* turn. After all,
she could hardly use Dan's kitchen to entertain Steven.

When she'd said as much to Steven, he'd merely
smiled and offered her the use of his place. Unfortunately the only night this week that worked for
him was Sunday, a day usually reserved for Dan and
Emma. But Steven was going out of town on
business for two weeks and he'd insisted he couldn't
wait that long to see what treat she had in store for
him.

"Amy." Steven's husky, deep voice broke through
her reverie. "Have I told you how beautiful you look
this evening?"

Amy lifted her eyes to find his gaze focused on

the cleavage displayed by the silky black cocktail dress. Her face heated beneath his admiring gaze and she shifted uncomfortably in her chair. Dressing up for the evening had been Steven's idea. She'd been a bit hesitant, but had decided to go along with the suggestion.

It certainly had helped set the elegant, romantic mood. Of course, the fact that Steven's condo overlooked the lakefront didn't hurt, either. The first time he'd brought her up here, she'd been stunned. In class, dressed in blue jeans, he'd seemed like just another food devotee. Sure, she'd known he was an attorney, she just hadn't realized he was so wealthy. Or so…attractive.

The tuxedo he wore emphasized his lean, muscular build. Like Dan, his hair was dark and cut short, but instead of being blue, Steven's eyes were a piercing gray. She could see why he was so successful in the courtroom. Those eyes missed little.

"I'm flattered," she said.

"You don't believe my compliment." His brows pulled together in puzzlement. "Why is that?"

This time Amy gave in to the urge and slipped her hand from his, nervously brushing back a stray strand of hair from her face.

She wondered if he'd be as impressed if he knew that the black cocktail dress she wore had been purchased at a consignment boutique. But even she had to admit the cut flattered her full, firm breasts while minimizing her curvy hips. She'd pulled her hair back in a loose, French knot and taken extra care with her makeup. At the last minute she'd impulsively added the pair of diamond earrings Dan and Emma had given her last Christmas.

"Amy."

She blinked, realizing his question hadn't been simply rhetorical.

"Beautiful?" Amy forced a laugh. "C'mon, Steven. Even you have to admit extra pounds and freckles place me squarely in the nice-looking but definitely-not-beautiful range."

She made the observation without the slightest hint of guile. She wasn't fishing for compliments. She was, quite simply, stating the facts.

Still, she half expected Steven to argue. Instead he laughed, the tiny lines around his eyes crinkling. "No wonder I like you so much."

There it was again, a shift into the personal realm. And the smoldering look in his eyes told her if she didn't shut it down now, things could get uncomfortable.

"Did I tell you Chez Gladines at Navy Pier has contracted with me to provide French pastries on a trial basis?" Amy couldn't keep the note of pride from her voice. "Apparently their chef had been a real prima donna and an expensive one to boot. When she up and quit on them, they decided to give me a chance."

While the restaurant manager hadn't given Amy

a long-term commitment, at least she had a foot in the door.

"Congratulations." A smile split Steven's face. "I wish I'd known earlier, I'd have taken you out to celebrate."

Amy had waited to mention the news for that specific reason. She didn't want to give him the chance to act like a boyfriend. He was doing enough of that already. Last time they'd eaten out, he'd refused to let her pay her share. If he *were* her boyfriend, she'd be all about letting him treat her. But they were simply good friends and that's how she wanted to keep it.

She let her gaze linger on his handsome face. Steven was a great guy with all the qualities she was looking for in a man. Why couldn't she like him as more than a friend? Why couldn't she love him? What was holding her back?

Amy smiled and held out her glass for more wine.

After filling her glass, Steven leaned back in his chair and shot her a speculative gaze. "What did King Dan have to say?"

Amy rolled her eyes. Steven had never met Dan but he'd taken in a few of her comments and decided he didn't like the guy. Like when she'd mentioned once in passing how much Dan liked to be waited on, she'd never expected Steven to take the funny, little incident and make a big deal out of it.

"Was he happy for you?" Steven pressed.

Amy shrugged and took a sip of wine. "I haven't mentioned it to him yet."

"Why not?" Steven lifted a sardonic brow. "Too busy making his coffee?"

"Making the coffee pays the bills." Amy kept her tone deliberately light and offhand, refusing to get sucked into rehashing something that had already been discussed. Still, it seemed no matter how many times she tried to tell Steven taking care of Dan and Emma was her job, he always tried to push her to think of herself, too.

"I know why you haven't told him. You're afr—"

"The opportunity hasn't come up." Amy spoke slowly and distinctly so there would be no misunderstanding. "But when I *do* tell him—and I do plan to tell him—I know he'll be happy for me."

"Don't kid yourself." Genuine concern filled Steven's gaze. "If he had it his way, you'd never leave. Never go on to bigger and better things. You deserve your own dreams, too, Amy."

The unexpected vehemence in Steven's tone took her by surprise. But she just smiled because she knew he really meant well. He was wrong about Dan, though…and about her.

Chapter Five

Amy shut off the car's ignition and leaned back against the seat, too tired to get out. The clock on the dashboard read eleven forty-five and exhaustion oozed from every pore. Her normal bedtime was ten-thirty and when she'd started to yawn while discussing the merits of using liqueurs, she'd known it was time to head home.

As she'd started toward the door, Steven had pulled her to him. Then he'd asked if she'd consider spending the night. The crazy thing was, for a second she'd been tempted. It had been so long…

But in the end she'd said no, frightened by the serious look in his eyes and her own ambivalent feelings. Besides, there was only one man she wanted in that way and he was waiting for her at home.

The garage door slid smoothly downward and, heaving a resigned sigh, Amy stepped out of the car and headed for the side door. Unlike Steven's condo with its underground parking, Dan's house had been built in the early 1900s when detached carriage houses were de rigueur.

But Amy didn't mind the short walk to the house. The temperature had dropped slightly and the autumn coolness was a welcome break from the warmth of the car. She could feel herself begin to wake up.

How she loved the lush yard with its large trees and beautiful arbors and the way the fragrant smell of flowers mixed with the scent of freshly-cut grass. During the day squirrels chattered a mile a minute and birds chirped happily. But now all was quiet. She stopped just short of the house and inhaled, taking in the beauty around her.

Amy vowed that when she bought a house it would have a nice yard. She remembered all too well the tiny apartment she'd shared with her aunt after her mother had dropped her off and never came back. She'd had to play outside on the concrete…

Shoving the memory aside, she decided it was too nice a night to ruin with thoughts of the past. She should go straight to bed but the idea of sitting for a few minutes in one of the large Adirondack chairs on the back screened-in porch pulled at her.

It would be so peaceful, so—

"How was your evening?"

The familiar deep voice stopped her cold. Dan sat in one of the chairs on the porch. She could count on one hand the number of times he'd stayed up past ten-thirty on a work night. Concern rippled up her spine. She moved forward quickly, her heart picking up speed with each step. "Where's Emma? Is everything okay?"

"She's fine." Dan rose and held the porch door open. "Went to bed for me without any problem."

Amy exhaled the breath she'd been holding. "So nothing is wrong?"

"Why would you think something is wrong?"

"You're up," Amy said. "You're always in bed by now."

"You're dressed up." His gaze traveled the length of her body. Amy could hear the surprise in his tone and though she wasn't a bit cold, she shivered.

He'd known she was going out with Steven. But he'd been upstairs when she'd left and he'd obviously assumed this had been a jeans and T-shirt evening.

"I made dinner for Steven at his place."

"He made you cook?" Dan's brows pulled together and she could hear the censure in his tone. "When you were dressed like that?"

Amy heaved an exasperated sigh and dropped into a chair. What was it with these men?

"He didn't *make* me do anything." Amy kicked off

her heels. "We're taking turns cooking each other dinner. Steven likes to dress up. Do things nice. He thinks it adds to the ambience."

Even in the dim light, Amy could see the surprise in Dan's eyes. He opened his mouth, then shut it.

She paused, waiting for him to disagree. After all, that seemed to be the pattern between the two men.

"I agree," Dan said.

"You do?" Amy's voice rose despite her best efforts to control it.

"Of course," Dan said, his tone conversational and pleasant.

Amy let her shoulders drop and the last of the tension exited her body. Finally, here on this quiet porch, she was back on familiar footing and could relax.

Tonight had not been the evening she'd anticipated. Instead of being the kind, supportive friend, Steven had tried to play the boyfriend card. She'd hated to shut him down but she didn't see that she had much choice. Not when her feelings for Dan were growing stronger. She slanted a sideways glance.

Dan had leaned back in his chair, lacing his fingers behind his head in a relaxed pose. "Does Steven live close?"

"Not far." Though it might not be very Emily Post, Amy brought her foot up and massaged her instep. The stiletto heels might look great but they were a killer. "He lives in one of the condos by the Pier."

The words had barely left her lips when Dan scooted his chair to face hers. "Give me those."

Amy widened her eyes. "Pardon?"

"Your feet," he said. "Those kind of shoes take their toll. I used to give Tess a foot rub all the time. Put them here."

Amy hesitated. While he wasn't suggesting they get naked and jump into bed, what he was suggesting somehow seemed just as intimate. Before she had a chance to respond, he reached down and rested both her feet on top of his muscular thighs.

"Ah—" He began to gently massage her foot from the toes to the ankle and any words of protest died on a sigh.

"You are incredible," she breathed.

The dimple in his left cheek flashed. "Well, thank you, ma'am. I aim to please."

He shifted his focus to the sole of her foot, his fingers moving in circular motions from the base of her toes to the heel, the pressure of the circles steady and even.

Amy closed her eyes and let the waves of pleasure wash over her.

"I don't believe you've ever told me what Steven does for a living."

The question seemed to come from a great distance. Amy's eyelids fluttered as he turned his attention to her toes.

"He's an attorney." Utterly relaxed, Amy leaned her head back against the chair. "I guess he's handled some high-profile cases but I've never heard of them."

Steven had told her more than once about his practice but she must not have been paying very close attention because right now, with Dan's thumbs pressing into the arch of her foot, she couldn't remember any details.

"What's his last name?" Dan asked in a low, soft voice.

"Mitchell." Amy moaned. "Oh, Dan, if I'd have known I was coming home to this, I'd have never stayed out so late."

"That's okay," Dan said in a hypnotic tone. "Next time just remember…there's no place like home."

A loud buzzing sounded in Amy's ear and she brushed at the irritation, her hand connecting with something hard and plastic.

It took only a second for her to realize she wasn't on a far-off beach making love to Dan in the sand. She was in her bedroom with her new clock radio buzzing angrily up at her from the floor. Reaching down, she hiked it up by its cord, bringing the time into focus.

She gasped. It should have gone off an hour ago. The bus would be coming for Emma in twenty minutes and Dan, well, right now he was on his own.

Amy jumped out of bed, but stopped almost instantly, swaying slightly as her hand rose to her pounding head. She had only two or three glasses of wine with Steven, but after Dan had finished her foot massage, he'd brought out a bottle of Kendall Jackson and she'd had a couple more glasses.

Unlike her mother, Amy took responsibility for her own actions. She'd pay the price today. She'd never make Emma and Dan suffer.

Ignoring her aching head, she hurried to the bathroom. After splashing cold water on her face, she ran a brush through her hair and pulled the long strands back into a ponytail. A second later her pajamas hit the floor. Grabbing a pair of gym shorts and a pullover cotton shirt, she dressed as she headed toward the door, snagging a pair of flip-flops on the way. She slid her feet into the shoes and took the stairs down two at a time.

Emma stood in the kitchen on a chair, a box of cereal clasped tightly against her chest. When she caught sight of Amy she smiled and held out the Cheerios.

"Look what I got." Emma thrust the box outward, unbalancing herself.

Her heart in her throat, Amy crossed the room in three quick strides and scooped Emma into her arms. While she knew she should probably scold the child for climbing on the chair, Emma looked so pleased with herself, Amy didn't have the heart.

"Cereal sounds good to me, too." Amy swung the girl to the floor. "How about you get the place mats from the drawer and I'll get the milk and juice."

"Is there room at the table for one more?"

Amy shifted her gaze and her heart skipped a beat. Dan stood in the doorway, dressed casually in khakis and a polo shirt. His appearance answered one of her questions. Obviously today was going to be a work-from-home day.

"There's lots of room." Emma spoke before Amy could answer. "And we got a whole box of Cheerios."

"Or I could make French toast? Or eggs and bacon?" Amy asked. Unlike his daughter, Dan had never been a big cereal fan.

"Cheerios sounds good to me."

"Emma, grab an extra place mat for your father." She shifted her gaze to Dan. "Coffee this morning?"

"Extra strong." A teasing glint filled his blue eyes. "Someone kept me up way too late last night."

Amy's heart skipped a beat. For a second she let herself believe that Dan was flirting with her. But, by the time the rich aroma of the breakfast blend filled the air, she'd gotten her emotions—not to mention her foolish thoughts—under control.

"Can I put the bowls on the table?" Emma offered Amy an imploring glance.

"*May* I put the bowls on the table?" Amy corrected, taking the dishes from the cupboard and handing them to Emma along with three spoons. "And, yes, you may."

It wasn't long until cereal and juice were on the table along with steaming cups of coffee for her and Dan.

Emma had barely finished spooning the last soggy

"o" into her mouth when the school bus honked. Taking one quick sip of orange juice, she pushed back her chair. "May I be excused?"

Amy cast a quick glance over Emma.

Hair brushed and pulled back with two clips.

Jumper and turtleneck on right side out.

Navy-blue knee-highs and shoes.

Amy smiled and nodded her approval.

"Goodbye, Daddy." Emma gave her father a quick hug. "Bye, Amy."

Another honk sounded and Emma's eyes widened with alarm. She grabbed her backpack and raced through the house. Only a few steps behind, Amy moved to the large parlor window. She watched Emma get on the bus before she returned to the kitchen.

Amy paused in the doorway, surprised to find Dan still sitting at the table, reading the paper. Normally, when Dan worked from home, he headed upstairs to his office once Emma left for school. He looked up briefly when she entered the room, giving her a distracted smile. Amy stuck the cereal bowls and juice glasses in the dishwasher before topping off Dan's coffee and resuming her seat.

Lifting her cup to her lips, she gazed across the table. "I take it you're working from home today."

"Actually, I've decided to take the day off." He raised his gaze from the newspaper. "Want to play hooky with me?"

Amy's shock must have shown on her face because he chuckled. "I've got some time I need to burn before the end of the year. I thought we could go to Long Grove. Check out the antiques. Maybe grab some lunch?"

Amy placed her cup back on the saucer, surprised by the steadiness of her hand. Was she hallucinating or had Dan just asked her out? Her eyes searched his. While she wasn't sure what she'd expected to see, disappointment coursed through her at the simple friendliness reflected there.

"Amy?"

The day Amy had planned flashed before her—a little light housecleaning, replace the zipper on one of Emma's dresses, then try out a new recipe or two. Chez Gladines was closed on Mondays so Amy didn't need to worry about making pastries. There was nothing on her agenda even half as appealing as a day in Long Grove.

She loved the small community with its quaint atmosphere and plethora of antique shops. The few times she'd been there hadn't been nearly long enough.

But to go with Dan?

A thrill of pleasure raced up her spine at the thought of being his date. No, she firmly reminded herself, if she went it'd be as a *friend,* nothing more.

Amy took one last sip of coffee. "Just give me a few minutes to freshen up and do something with this hair."

"You look fine." Dan tilted his head, his gaze slowly surveying her. "Actually, way more than fine."

Her skin warmed beneath the heat of his gaze, but Amy held no illusions. While Tess may have been beautiful enough to hop out of bed and hit the ground running, Amy didn't have that luxury. She shoved back her chair and stood.

"Give me twenty minutes," she called over her shoulder on her way to the stairs.

Dan didn't argue. Instead he cupped his hands around the mug, leaned back in his chair and stared into the dark Columbian brew.

It had been almost midnight before Amy had pulled in the driveway last night. Dinner with someone who was only a cooking "buddy" would never have lasted so long. He'd been wrong to think the Lasagna Man was no threat. He still couldn't believe Steven Mitchell was Amy's "friend." The attorney was well-known in the Chicago area and had a reputation for getting what he wanted, whether that was an acquittal for a client or some young socialite dazzled by his charm.

Dan had been at a couple of large parties where Steven was in attendance. While they'd never been introduced, Dan had noticed the guy never lacked for feminine attention. It would be so easy for someone like Amy to be taken in by a guy like that. A man who knew all the right things to say to get a woman in his bed.

Maybe he already has…

Dan pressed his lips together and his fingers tightened around the coffee cup until his knuckles turned white.

As offensive as it was, Dan let the idea percolate.

Could it be that Amy and Steven were already lovers? While it was *possible,* after a moment of serious contemplation Dan concluded that the relationship between the two hadn't reached that point…yet.

But why would Steven drag his heels? Unless…he'd fallen for Amy. After all, Amy was the kind of woman a man married, not just dated. Maybe, Dan thought, he should be concerned that Steven and Amy hadn't had sex. Still, just the thought of Steven *kissing* Amy set Dan's teeth on edge. Dan couldn't delay any longer. He had to convince Amy that the only place she belonged was here, with him and Emma.

To convince her, he'd have to go the hearts-and-flowers route. It was the only way to reach her. Because, though she'd deny it to her death, Dan knew the truth. Amy Logan was a closet romantic. The books she read always had a happy ending. Her favorite movies were romantic comedies where you walked out of the theater holding hands and feeling good. Such a woman would never be wooed by pure logic.

"I'm ready."

Amy stood in the doorway wearing a skirt, form-fitting sweater and a tentative smile. Her freshly washed hair glistened and she must have applied some makeup because the freckles he liked so much were barely noticeable.

Dan rose and offered her the smile that had been winning him hearts since grade school. But when he spoke it was straight from the heart. "You look absolutely lovely."

A becoming shade of coral colored her cheeks. "I wasn't sure what to wear. I didn't want to dress up too much, but you did mention we'd be going to lunch so I didn't want to be too casual."

His heart warmed. She was chattering the way she always did when she was nervous.

"You look perfect." Dan stepped forward and took her hand. "And we're going to have a great day. I guarantee it."

Chapter Six

Atrio of tiny bells welcomed Amy and Dan into the small antique shop in Long Grove. Amy paused in the doorway and let memories from her childhood wash over her. Lace curtains at the windows. Shiny hardwood. The smell of cinnamon in the air. All reminiscent of the turn-of-the-century home that had been in her father's family for generations.

After her parents divorced, she'd lived in the old Victorian with him. Those had been the happiest years of her young life.

Impulsively Amy turned. She slipped her hand through Dan's arm and gave it a squeeze.

"Thanks for bringing me here. I adore this place." Her gaze darted around the well-kept cottage which, despite its extensive inventory, somehow managed to give the appearance of being homey, rather than cluttered. An old Victrola played a once-popular dance tune in the background. "My aunt Verna would love it, too."

"Is that the aunt in Minnesota?" Dan asked. "The one you lived with after your father died?"

Amy nodded, her gaze lingering on a sterling silver brush and comb set. "She always said if she had a big old house, it'd be filled with antiques."

But there had been no rambling two story for her aunt. No house at all. Only a one-bedroom apartment with a fold-out sofa that doubled as a bed. Verna had worked as a secretary in the Mankato school system and her salary had been barely enough for *her* to live on. When her sister's young daughter had been added to the mix...

"How is Verna doing?" Dan asked in a conversational tone. "I haven't heard you speak of her recently."

"She's good." Amy picked up a Rookwood pottery vase, promptly putting it down when she saw the price. "She retired in May and spent the summer traveling across the country visiting friends. Now she's working on deciding what she wants to do with the rest of her life."

"You think she'll stay in Mankato?"

Amy picked up a Strawberry Shortcake lunch box. She'd had one just like it. Her father had given it to her for her seventh birthday, just weeks before the accident.

"Amy?"

She shifted her attention from the lunch box back to the conversation. "I'm sorry. Did you ask me something?"

Dan smiled. "Is your aunt staying in Minnesota?"

"She's not sure." Actually Verna had talked about moving to Chicago so she could be close to Amy. Amy had been checking out real estate in the area and while she'd love to have her aunt in the same town, she wasn't sure it was going to happen. "She took her retirement in a lump sum so it gives her some options."

A petite gray-haired woman who reminded Amy of a wren with her bright, shiny eyes and quick movements appeared from behind a large bureau. "May I help you?"

The woman's gaze lowered to Amy's hand and Amy realized she still held the lunch box. She quickly placed it back on the shelf. "We're just browsing."

The moment the words left Amy's lips she realized she'd answered for both of them. While Dan hadn't mentioned looking for anything specific he *had* chosen Long Grove with its abundance of antique stores for their excursion.

She turned and lifted her face to him. "Unless you have—"

"Nothing specific in mind." Dan slipped his arm around Amy's shoulders and returned the woman's smile. "We'll let you know if we have questions."

Amy's breath caught in her throat. Thankfully Dan seemed willing to carry the conversation because the minute he'd pulled her close, she'd lost the ability to form a coherent sentence. She told herself the gesture was simply a casual one between friends. The trouble was her body hadn't gotten the message.

But as much as Amy longed to give in to the warm, tingling that went all the way to her toes, she held tight to her common sense, slipping from the light embrace as if she'd seen something she absolutely couldn't resist. Scanning the aisle, she found what she was looking for in a black and white kitten curled up on a shelf.

Amy shifted her gaze back to the woman. "You have a cat."

The woman beamed like a proud parent. "Her name is Oreo. She'll be six months old on Saturday."

"May I hold her?"

The woman nodded. "She spends most days here in the shop so she's used to strangers."

Amy moved down the aisle, barely aware of the woman and Dan following her. The animal reminded Amy of Mittens, the cat she'd had when she lived with her father. But as she drew closer the differences between the two became more apparent. Mittens had been pure black with four white feet, while Oreo had white on his chest as well.

"You are so pretty." Her voice rose and she found herself speaking in that high-pitched tone usually reserved for babies and animals.

The kitten stirred and stretched.

Amy bent down and gingerly scooped up the sleeping cat, holding it against her chest.

Dan's brows pulled together in puzzlement. "I never knew you were such a cat lover."

Amy gently stroked the soft fur. "I had one like this when I was only a little older than Emma."

"Is Emma your daughter?" the woman asked.

Dan smiled, the way he always did when Emma's name was mentioned. "She's six."

"That's such a sweet age." The shopkeeper's gaze turned sharp and assessing. "Do you two have other children?"

It only took a second for Amy to realize that the woman had assumed she and Dan were married. She opened her mouth to clarify but Dan spoke first.

"She's our only one," he said.

"You're young," the woman said. "There's plenty of time for more."

Dan gave a noncommittal smile and changed the subject.

The woman stayed with them the entire time they walked around the store, but the minute they exited the shop, there was only one question on Amy's lips. "Why did you let her think we were married? That Emma was *our* child?"

Although it was late September, the sun shone bright overhead. Unfortunately Dan had already slipped on his sunglasses, hiding his eyes.

"What did you want me to say?" he asked, his tone as expressionless as his face. "That you were Emma's *nanny?*"

"I *am* Emma's nanny."

He took off his glasses, his gaze direct, his eyes an intense blue. "You're much more than that."

A warm flush of pleasure stole its way up her neck. All the way home, Amy found herself pondering the words, sternly admonishing herself every time she was tempted to read too much into them.

By the time they reached the city, she'd decided that what he'd obviously been trying to say was that she was his friend, a part of the family, not just an employee.

They were about ten minutes from home when her cell phone rang. Amy was going to let it go to voice mail but Dan turned down the volume on the radio. Reluctantly she dug the phone out of her purse. Even if Steven hadn't promised to call her before he left town, the ring tone told Amy it was him.

"Hello, beautiful." Steven's deep voice resounded in her ear. "Have you had a good day?"

"I've had a *very* good day." Just thinking about the past few hours brought a smile to her lips. After visiting most of the stores in town, Dan had treated her to lunch at a quaint little café. Then they'd topped the day off with a triple-decker cone at an old-fashioned ice cream parlor.

Amy had promised herself she'd stay away from sweets, but ice cream was really more of a dairy product than a dessert, wasn't it?

"I wish you were coming with me," Steven said. "Boston is beautiful this time of year."

Amy had always wanted to see Boston but she

knew if she'd gone that Steven would expect more than just a sightseeing partner.

"I'm sure it is," Amy said. "Tell me again how long you'll be gone?"

"Hopefully not more than two weeks," Steven said. A teasing note sounded in his voice. "Are you going to miss me?"

Amy hesitated. She cast a sideways glance at Dan. His gaze was focused straight ahead on the road. He didn't appear to be listening but...

"Um, hmm." Amy decided to leave it at that.

"Is he there?" Suspicion filled Steven's tone. "Is that why you can't talk?"

Amy forced a casual laugh. "Dan and I are just getting back from Long Grove."

"Listen, Amy," Steven said. "My plane is boarding so I'll keep this short. You're his employee. That's all you are. That's all you'll ever be. Getting more involved with him would be a mistake."

For a second Amy sat there stunned. Sure, she'd spoken of Dan more often than she probably should but she'd never suggested there was anything between them. Or even that she *wished* there could be more. So why was Steven concerned? Unless she wasn't as good at hiding her emotions as she thought...

Amy could hear the overhead announcing final boarding. "I better let you go."

"A mistake, Amy," Steven said, sounding genuinely concerned. "Don't be fooled. Promise you'll be careful."

"I promise," Amy said, her voice as tight as the fingers gripping the phone. While she found his concern touching, she was horrified at the thought of Dan seeing through her as easily as Steven.

"Good." Though relief flowed through Steven's voice, she could still hear the worry.

But Steven didn't give her enough credit.

She knew better than to get involved with Dan.

No matter how much she was tempted.

Dan had never been the type of guy to eavesdrop, but in the small cab of the Land Rover it was impossible *not* to listen.

It didn't take a genius to realize Amy was talking to Steven. As far as Dan was concerned it was a bad sign that the guy had called. Steven had seen her the past three days and yet he still felt the need to touch base today?

Amy slipped the cell phone into her purse. "That was Steven."

"Do you two have plans tonight?" Dan did his best to keep his tone offhand. After all, he couldn't risk appearing disapproving. The last thing he wanted was to push her into Steven's apparently all-too-eager arms.

Amy shook her head. "He's headed to Boston."

"Really?" Dan relaxed against the seat. A thousand miles away was the perfect place for the guy. "What's he going to be doing there?"

"Some case," Amy said. "He didn't go into much detail."

"I'm surprised he didn't ask you to go with him," Dan said, the lightness in his tone at odds with the tightness still gripping his chest.

"He asked," Amy said. "I told him I had obligations here."

Dan didn't know what disturbed him more—that Steven had obviously felt comfortable enough to ask or that Amy had referred to him and Emma as "obligations." "How long will he be gone?"

"Two weeks," Amy said with a sigh. "It might even be longer."

Dear God, she actually sounded like she was going to miss the guy. The relationship must be moving faster than he thought.

Emma's face flashed before him and Dan remembered the promise he'd made her. A promise he fully intended to keep. Though he'd never been impulsive or one to move forward without careful thought, he realized suddenly that his little girl's happiness might depend on his quick action.

Two weeks. More than enough time to make Amy fall in love with me.

It was a crazy thought, but once it flitted through his consciousness, it took hold and wouldn't let go.

Fourteen days.

To become her friend.

To become her lover.

To become her husband.

Chapter Seven

Amy leaned over Emma, brushed a kiss against the sleeping girl's forehead then tiptoed out of the bedroom.

After dinner the three of them had gone for a long walk. By the time they'd gotten back it had been time for Emma's bath. Amy swore the child was asleep before she'd finished toweling her dry.

"Amy." Dan's voice resonated from the intercom in the hallway. "Could you come down here, please? There's something I'd like to discuss with you."

"Of course." Amy pulled Emma's bedroom door shut, wondering what could be so important that it couldn't wait until morning.

Household concerns were normally discussed

after Emma left for school in the morning, never at night. But then, Amy reminded herself, this day had not been "normal" in any sense of the word.

Having workaholic Dan take time off to go shopping had been only the beginning. He'd let the woman in the antique store think they were married, and his reason hadn't made a bit of sense. At dinner he'd been distracted, yet afterward when they'd gone for a walk, he'd been jovial, entertaining her and Emma with funny stories from his boyhood. When they'd stopped at the park, Emma had headed straight for the slide. Amy had started to sit on a nearby bench but Dan had insisted they check out the swings.

She'd laughed. He'd teased. And each time his hands had settled on her waist, Amy's heart had soared higher than the swing.

No. The day had *definitely* not been normal.

Amy hurried down the stairs, eager to find out what could be so important.

Dan smiled when he saw her.

"Come in." He stood outside the parlor and waved her through the doorway.

Although the day had been more Indian summer-like than fallish, a cheery fire burned brightly in the hearth. The room, which Tess had turned ultramodern shortly before her death had been returned to its original decor two summers ago.

Amy had never been sure if the change had been made because Dan hated black and silver as much as she did or if the room had reminded him too much of Tess. His wife had been as chic and stylish as the room and Amy could only surmise that every time Dan had walked through the door he'd been reminded of what he'd lost.

Dan gestured to a chintz-covered Windsor. "Please sit down."

Amy took a seat, while Dan continued to stand. After a few moments he moved to a spot just in front of the fireplace. He stared into the flames and a flicker of unease inched its way up Amy's spine. Whatever was on his mind was obviously serious.

Amy tilted her head. "Is something wrong?"

Dan turned and raked a hand through his hair. He crossed the room and dropped into the chair beside Amy. "I've got something to say and I'm not sure how you're going to respond."

Shifting uneasily in her chair, Amy could feel a chill travel up her spine. This *must* be serious if supremely confident Dan, a man who always knew where he wanted to go and how to get there, was nervous and unsure.

But why? What could he possibly have to say that would cause him such distress?

There was only one thing that made sense. Today had been a gift, one last pleasant day with him and Emma, just like the day her mother had taken her out for ice cream, then dropped her off and never came back.

"You're letting me go." The words slipped past her lips despite her determination to let him speak first.

"No. No. No." Dan leaned forward and took her cold hand, clasping it firmly in his. "That is— No. I'm definitely not letting you go anywhere."

The breath Amy had been holding came out in a whoosh and relief flooded her body. "Then, what…?"

"Actually *this* is what I need to discuss with you." Dan cast a pointed glance at their joined hands.

Horrified, Amy realized her fingers now interlocked with his. She tried to pull away but he held on tight, his lips curving upward.

"I'm as bad at this as I thought I'd be." Dan leaned forward, resting his elbows on his knees, his hand still gripping hers. "I like you, Amy. And I think…I hope…that you like me, too."

Amy pulled her brows together in a puzzled frown, trying to understand what he was saying and coming up blank.

"Of course I like you," she said finally.

"I'm talking as more than a friend." Dan spoke quickly as if afraid she'd interrupt. "I want us to get to know each other better, see where it might lead."

Amy's heart slammed against her ribs. More than a friend? For a second she wondered if she was dreaming. She closed her eyes then opened them. Nothing had changed. She swallowed hard and somehow managed a light tone. "You want us to…date?"

He lifted a brow. "You sound shocked."

Amy forced a laugh and glanced around the

room. "Where are the cameras? This has to be some kind of joke."

For a second Dan looked startled, then he grinned. "No wonder I like you so much."

"You don't—" Amy said. "Not in that way."

Dan's smile faded. His gaze turned serious. "Lately there's been this…connection between us. You have to have felt it, too."

Amy could feel the heat rise up her neck. It wasn't really a question and for a second she hoped she wouldn't have to answer. But the watchful look in his eyes told her he expected a response. She paused then slowly nodded, hoping she wouldn't regret the admission.

A look of relief crossed Dan's face. "You agree."

"I agree that sometimes there is this 'energy' between us." Amy carefully chose her words. "But I'm not convinced acting on it is in either of our best interests."

"Why do you say that?" Dan asked, his eyes as expressionless as his face.

Amy heaved an exasperated sigh. "How about for starters that I'm your employee?"

"So?"

"So if you get tired of me like you did Bree and Melinda, I'm still around. Taking care of your child. Maintaining your house." She jerked her hand from his. "You have to admit that having an ex-girlfriend living in your home could be awkward."

Amy rose and moved to the fireplace but even the

warmth of the flames couldn't drive the chill from her body. She had to be practical. They both had to be practical.

"Anything more than just a simple friendship between us would be a mistake," she continued. "A big mistake."

"I disagree," Dan said, not even taking a second to give the matter some thought. "I'm not going to get tired of having you around. We won't have to worry about—"

"We *do* have to worry." Amy whirled around. "Or at least *I* do. I like working for you, Dan. And I like taking care of Emma. I don't want to do anything to screw that up."

"I don't see how us going out—"

Amy threw up her hands. The guy wasn't stupid. How could he be so clueless? "Because the odds are it's going to be a mistake. Just like your relationship with Bree. Just like Melinda. You—"

"Those women were different." He stood and an odd desperation filled his tone. "You can't compare my relationship with them to you and me."

"Why not?" Amy lifted her chin. "There was probably much more chance of those relationships succeeding than one between us."

"How can you say that?"

"Easy. They're from your social circle." Amy almost added "and they're both beautiful" but decided that made it sound as if she thought he was superficial, which she didn't. "You have similar interests—"

"Hold it right there." Dan's eyes flashed blue fire and he crossed the room in several long strides to stand beside her. "If anyone can get along, it's you and me. Think about it. We've lived together for three years in harmony. How many couples can say that?"

But they weren't a couple. She was his employee. And though he didn't seem to want to grasp the subtleties of the differences, they were huge. For one, how did a woman go about dating a man whose laundry she folded?

Besides, Amy knew what would happen if they went out. She'd fall in love with him. She was practically in love with him now or certainly infatuated. It wouldn't be long before she'd get scared, then needy and he'd send her away. Just like her mother had…

"Amy?"

She lifted her gaze and found Dan's eyes filled with a gentleness usually reserved for Emma.

"I know you're scared," he said softly. "Heck, I'm scared, too. I believe there could be something special between us. But we'll never know for sure if we don't give it a shot."

His nearness made it difficult to think, to be objective.

"I need some space. Some time to consider what you're suggesting." She offered Dan a tentative smile. "I'm flattered. I just—"

Before she knew what was happening Dan had tugged her to him. "Tell me this isn't what you want…"

His lips closed over hers. She told herself to push him away but the raw hunger she'd been keeping in check surged. And when she raised her hands, instead of increasing the distance between them, she pulled him close, drinking him in, discovering quickly that reality easily outshone even the most wonderful of daydreams.

Dan changed the angle of the kiss and deepened it, shifting one hand to cup the back of her head, holding her still for the hot, sweet hunger of his mouth on hers.

Amy welcomed the moist heat and the penetrating slide of his tongue and met it with her own. He stroked long and slow, hot and deep, and she kissed him back the same way, eagerly and instinctively.

A shivering…sliding…feeling ran down her spine and when he pulled her so tight she could feel his arousal against her belly, the world exploded in a blistering wave of heat and passion.

He scattered kisses along her jawline, down her neck and then…lower still.

Her breasts strained against the bodice of her dress and when his tongue dipped into her cleavage she heard herself groan, a low sound of want and need that astonished her with its intensity. Dazed and breathing hard, Amy pulled back.

There was shock in Dan's eyes. "Amy, I…"

"It's late," she said, her breath coming in ragged puffs. "Let's talk tomorrow."

Without giving him the chance to change her mind, Amy headed for the hall. She moved quickly, not stopping until she'd reached her room and locked the door behind her.

Utterly confused, Amy sank down on the bed. Her fingers rose to her swollen lips. Though she'd often wondered what it would be like to kiss Dan, her fantasies hadn't come close to the real thing.

This was what had been missing when she'd kissed Steven. It was this tingle, this thrill. But that still didn't mean it would be wise to get involved with Dan. Amy struggled to pull her thoughts together. This was a major decision. One not to be made lightly.

But did she really have a choice? Now that they'd kissed, could they really ever go back to how they were before?

The clock struck one. Amy sighed and plumped up her pillow. She knew it wouldn't make a difference. Even the endless parade of imaginary sheep she'd spent the last hour visualizing hadn't helped. Try as she might, Amy couldn't make herself fall asleep.

She'd told Dan they'd talk tomorrow but she still didn't have a clue what she was going to say.

If only he hadn't kissed me…

Being in his arms, feeling his mouth on hers had been incredible. When he'd acknowledged feeling something more than friendship it had been alternately a dream come true and her worst nightmare. Dan had so many good qualities. He was kind and gentle and totally devoted to those he loved. She'd seen the way he was with his wife, the way he was with Emma.

On the other hand, she remembered what happened to Bree and Melinda. The minute they'd started to care, to hope for something more permanent, to demand more than they were getting, they'd found themselves alone.

Of course, the two hadn't realized what Amy had always known—Dan was still in love with Tess, would probably always be in love with Tess.

Amy understood what it was like to love someone who didn't love you. She'd been abandoned by her mother and left for Aunt Verna to raise.

Amy understood what it was like to want permanence. All she wanted was a home, a family and a cat. It wasn't much but at the moment her dream had never seemed more out of reach.

Amy understood that when you cause trouble, when you become demanding, you only push people away. That's why during her growing up years, she'd never given Verna one reason to get rid of her.

But Verna had relatively low expectations.

Amy wasn't sure the same could be said of Dan. After all, Bree and Melinda and the countless women before them hadn't been able to keep him happy. What made her think she could?

Perhaps Steven was right. Maybe it would be foolish to become involved with Dan.

Still, she was tempted. Despite his flaws, she was

attracted to Dan. She'd been daydreaming about him, hoping he'd see her as more than just his daughter's nanny. Now that he had, could she really just walk away because she was scared?

Amy tightened her jaw. She'd never been a coward or a quitter. She was strong and smart and talented. If things didn't work out she'd survive.

It was time she took charge of her life.

It was time she fought for what she wanted.

It was time she gave Dan a chance.

Chapter Eight

"Something smells good."

Amy looked up from the griddle at her employer. "Hotcakes. With blueberries."

Emma looked up from her plate. "An' Amy even made the syrup hot."

"Wow." Dan grinned and Amy's heart skipped a beat. "I feel like I died and went to heaven."

"I don't want you to go there." Emma's smile faded and her fork dropped to the table with a clatter. "I want you to stay here with me."

Amy's heart went out to the little girl. She reached over and ruffled Emma's hair. "Your daddy isn't going anywhere, sweetheart. It's just his way of saying he likes my hotcakes."

"Amy's right, princess." Dan dropped a kiss on Emma's head and shot Amy a grateful look before taking a seat at the table.

Amy placed a cup of steaming coffee in front of Dan but he continued to talk to Emma and didn't even look up. Even as she turned back to the stove, Amy could hear Dan's low, reassuring tone. Her heart warmed at the sight of the two heads together. By the time her own hotcakes were done and she joined them at the table, Emma was giggling.

Amy had barely taken her first sip of coffee when the school bus horn sounded. In a matter of minutes, Emma was out of her seat, racing toward the big yellow vehicle, a spring in her step and a bright smile on her face.

After making sure Emma was safely on the bus, Amy returned to the kitchen. She wasn't surprised to find Dan still at the table. His measuring look told her he'd deliberately stayed to talk. And she knew just what he wanted to discuss.

She pretended not to notice and took her time pouring the syrup. "Big plans today?"

"I'll be in the city." He gestured with one hand as if brushing away a troublesome mosquito.

Amy forked a bit of hotcake. "It's supposed to be unseasonably warm today."

A look of exasperation crossed his face. "I don't want to talk about the weather. Not when there are more important things we need to discuss."

The impatience was so typically Dan that she had to smile.

"Oh, all right," she said in her most lofty tone, "I guess I'll give you a chance."

Surprise skittered across his face. "You will?"

Amy heard the disbelief in his voice and her heart fluttered. After swallowing a piece of hotcake that seemed to have grown to the size of a baseball, Amy forced a casual, offhand tone. "Unless you didn't mean what you said. I mean if you were only joking…"

"Of course it wasn't a joke," he said, seeming upset that she would even think such a thing. "I'm just surprised. I guess I was convinced you were going to turn me down."

Amy frowned.

"But I'm happy you said yes," he added hastily.

"So." With one finger Amy traced an imaginary pattern on the tabletop. "Where do we go from here?"

Dan took a sip of coffee and leaned back in his seat. "How about my company party at the Palmer House Friday night?"

Amy lifted her head and met his gaze. The party, she knew, was always an elegant affair. It would either be a fabulous beginning for the two of them or a train wreck. But she wasn't going to let fear hold her back any longer.

She smiled. "It's a date."

The chandeliers in the ballroom of the Palmer House Hotel in downtown Chicago glittered brightly and the scent of fresh flowers filled the air.

The clink of crystal mingled with the sound of laughter and conversation. As Amy stood in the entrance to the large room and gazed out over the multitude of men in tuxedos and women in sparkly dresses, her heart lodged in her throat. What had she been thinking?

The place teemed with important people—men and women who Dan interacted with on a daily basis. Some of whom she'd met…as his nanny. She knew what they'd think when they saw her at his side. Either they'd think that Dan had lost his mind…or they'd think he was banging the nanny and she'd made him bring her.

Amy was seconds away from bolting when Dan took her hand. Her heart fluttered and she lifted her gaze.

He smiled. "I'm so happy you came with me."

"You are? Why?"

He laughed and the lines around his eyes crinkled. "Because I always have a good time when I'm with you."

The tension and anxiety, which had held Amy in a stranglehold, eased and she relaxed for the first time since they'd left the house. Dan was right. They always had fun together. Tonight would be no exception.

"Can I get you a glass of wine?" Dan stepped close, shielding her from an unsteady drunk with a loud voice and a drink in each hand.

Even after the man moved past, Dan remained close. Amy's heart fluttered and she looked away, not wanting him to see the desire in her eyes. She smoothed the skirt of her black cocktail dress. It was the same one she'd worn when making Steven dinner, but if Dan had noticed, he'd been too polite to say a word.

Once she'd gained control of her emotions, Amy lifted her gaze. "I'd love some wine. Preferably red."

Dan's gaze lingered on the tall white pillar behind Amy's back as if anchoring her place in the crowded ballroom.

"Don't move." He slanted a quick kiss across her lips. "I'll be right back."

Then, he was gone.

Amy touched a finger to her mouth and wondered if he had any idea the effect he had on her. How he made—

"Amy?" A feminine voice pulled her from her reverie. "I almost didn't recognize you. What are you doing here?"

Turning, Amy pulled her thoughts together and flashed Bree Northcott a welcoming smile. "I came with Dan."

Impulsively Amy gave the pretty blonde a hug. Bree looked fabulous as always in an emerald-green dress that showed off her lithe, model-like figure to full advantage.

A tiny frown momentarily marred Bree's brow. "I thought I heard Dan was coming stag."

"He changed his mind," Amy said in a light tone. "Who are you here with?"

According to Dan, the party was for the architectural firm and their clients. Bree worked as an attorney for a tax firm, or at least she had the last time Amy had spoken with her.

"I came with Jake," Bree said.

Amy tried hard not to show her shock. As one of Dan's closest friends, Jake had often been at the house and Amy knew him quite well. Or at least as well as she *wanted* to know him. She'd never liked the way the man looked at her—as if he was imagining her naked—or the suggestive comments he made when Dan wasn't in the room.

"He's kind of slimy." Bree lifted a shoulder in a slight shrug. "But I wanted to come to this party and he was my ticket in."

"I didn't say there was anything wrong with him," Amy said quickly.

"You didn't need to." Bree laughed. "I could see it in your eyes."

Amy nearly groaned out loud. She'd thought she'd mastered the art of keeping a poker face, but lately she'd been falling short. Way short.

"I like Jake—"

"Stop." Bree touched Amy's arm. "The guy has sex on the brain and the only thing he cares about is scoring. Please don't feel like you have to defend him to me."

"He *is* kind of slimy," Amy admitted.

"Very," Bree said with extra emphasis.

The two women laughed.

"Why did you want to come to this party so badly?" Amy asked. "I mean it's nice and all but…"

As far as Amy was concerned, a woman would have to be beyond desperate to come with Jake.

This time it was Bree's turn to shrug. "There was someone I was hoping to see here tonight. But…it's pretty hopeless. He's always had eyes for someone else. It's a shame I like her."

"My, my, two beautiful ladies." Jake sidled up to Bree and leered at Amy. "Don't you look de-lec-table."

Amy offered the man a polite smile. "Haven't seen you in a while."

"Been busy," Jake said. "Unlike Dan, I don't have someone waiting on me hand and foot when I come home at night."

Amy wasn't sure how relevant the answer was to her comment but Jake was obviously making a point. If his goal was to remind her of her place in the social hierarchy, he'd accomplished his mission.

Amy felt a tap on her shoulder and she turned. Dan moved to her side and made a great show of handing her a glass of wine. "Tonight, my dear, it's my turn to wait on you."

Bree heaved a resigned sigh.

Though Dan's tone was light and his lips turned up in an easy smile, the tightness in his jaw told her that Dan had not found Jake's comments amusing.

She took a sip of wine and when she lifted her

gaze, she found Jake blatantly staring at her cleavage and Bree staring at Dan.

Amy ignored them both and turned to Dan. "Would you like to dance?"

She didn't particularly want to show off her lack of coordination but right now she'd rather be out on the hardwood floor than standing around being ogled by Mr. Slimy.

"I'd love to." Dan placed his glass on a nearby table and held out his hand.

Amy placed her glass next to his and took his hand, smiling a goodbye to Bree. She still didn't know who Bree had come to the party to see but she had a suspicion. Yet Dan had chosen her.

The dance floor was crowded, so thankfully Amy didn't feel conspicuous. Instead of everyone staring and pointing out her decided lack of rhythm, she and Dan were just one couple swaying to the band's beat.

"I thought you told me you didn't dance." Dan's tone was teasing and his eyes warm.

"I didn't. I mean, I don't." Amy tried to follow Dan's lead and pretend she knew what she was doing. It wasn't easy. Not only because her feet had a tendency to trip over each other but because his nearness was wreaking havoc with her self-control. Was there anything more attractive than a gorgeous man in a tuxedo? The contrast of a crisp white shirt with the dark fabric of his tuxedo coupled with his handsome face sent her heart racing.

And the way he smelled... Just breathing in the

spicy scent of Dan's cologne made her heart beat faster. The feel of his strong arms around her brought back memories of the last time he'd held her close. Like he was doing now.

She rested her cheek against his chest. "I lied."

This time it was Dan's turn to stumble. "What about?"

"I *have* danced before." Her heart tightened with the memory. "With my dad. He'd turn on the stereo, lift me off the floor and we'd dip and sway to the music."

"I do that with Emma sometimes," he said.

Though she didn't lift her head and she couldn't see his face, Amy could hear the smile in his voice.

"You're a good father," Amy said.

"I don't know about that," Dan said. "I didn't do so well after Tess died."

She heard the emotion in his voice and her heart went out to him.

"It was tough," he said with a sigh. "Emma reminded me so much of Tess. She still reminds me of Tess. Of what I lost."

Amy didn't even need to close her eyes to remember that time. Dan had been beside himself with shock and grief. Emma had been confused and frightened. The fact that Amy had lost a parent at a young age had helped her relate to the little girl...and to her distraught father.

"It was a difficult time for everyone," Amy said.

"I couldn't have done it without you."

"Yes, you could," she said firmly. Dan was good and strong and faced his challenges head-on.

Her own father had been such a man. After her parents had split, Amy's dad had found himself with sole custody. His love had been constant and all she'd needed. "You remind me so much of my father."

"Your father?" The look on Dan's face would have been laughable at any other time.

"Stop." Amy tugged him back to her and began dancing even as heat rose up her neck. "I just meant you're a great father. Just like my dad."

"Whew." Dan pretended to swipe some sweat from his brow. "That's a relief."

"He was a good guy." It was all Amy could think to say.

"Tell me about him," Dan said, his tone low and enticing. "I know you said he died when you were Emma's age, but I don't know much more than that."

Amy hesitated. She'd spent so many years *not* talking about him that it was difficult to know where to start.

"He was wonderful," Amy said. "My mother hated him. My aunt didn't know him but she told me to forget about the past and focus on the future."

"I can't imagine how hard it would be on Emma if anything happened to me," Dan said, almost to himself.

"Nothing is going to happen to you," Amy said quickly. "But if anything does, I promise I'll do everything in my power to give Emma a happy life. You know what she means to me."

"A person doesn't have to be family to raise and love a child." A strange undercurrent wove its way through Dan's words.

"You're right," Amy said. "In fact, looking back, I'd take a stranger over my mother any day."

Chapter Nine

Dan pulled Amy close and let the music wash over him. She'd done it again. Without even knowing it, she had managed to reassure him that he'd chosen the right course of action.

Tess's parents were nice people but with their strong personalities and domineering ways they wouldn't be the right ones to raise his sensitive daughter. Despite what his mother-in-law believed, family *wasn't* always the best choice. Of course when he married Amy she would be family, part of *his* family. His arms tightened protectively around her. He'd make it good for her, too. She would never want for anything.

What about love?

Dan shoved the question aside. He could name a dozen couples who'd married for "love" and were now divorced. Besides, there were all sorts of love and levels of caring. While he would never lie to Amy and say he loved her when he didn't, he'd show her in every way possible he cared. Because he did care. Very much.

The band's lead singer launched into a romantic ballad and Amy snuggled close, the clean fresh scent of her hair teasing his nostrils. When she'd come down the stairs tonight, the sight of her had taken his breath away. He'd immediately noticed that she'd chosen the black dress from the other night…the one he liked so much.

For a moment he'd almost mentioned how happy he was to see it again. But just in time he'd remembered Tess's opinion on wearing the same party dress twice and had kept his mouth shut. The last thing he wanted was to hurt Amy's feelings. He couldn't imagine a dress being more perfect and he'd been proud to walk into the party with her at his side.

"Thanks again for coming with me," Dan whispered against her hair, his hand caressing her bare back.

"Thank you for the invitation." She lifted her head and smiled. "I'm enjoying myself."

"You sound surprised."

"I've never been to an event like this. I wasn't sure what to expect." Amy glanced around the room. "I have to admit I was a bit nervous."

Dan had thought as much. He'd felt the uncertainty in the hand that had clutched his arm when they'd walked into the ballroom. That's why he'd stayed close. Other than getting her a glass of wine, he hadn't ventured from her side.

When he'd come to parties with Tess, networking had been the name of the game. She'd go off in one direction and he in another. At the end of the evening they'd reconnect and maybe share a dance or two before heading home. That way of operating had become second nature and it had been the same with the women he'd dated after Tess's death. He'd never considered doing it any other way. Spend an entire evening with a woman who had nothing on her agenda except him? Dan found himself enjoying the change.

He liked being with Amy and it felt good knowing she was content just being with him.

"Ready for a trade?"

Dan turned to find Jake standing in the middle of the dance floor, Bree at his side. But for all the attention he gave her, the statuesque blonde might as well have been a stranger. Jake had eyes only for Amy. Or rather…Amy's breasts.

Dan tightened his lips. He hadn't liked the way his friend's gaze had settled on Amy's cleavage earlier and he didn't like it now. She tensed in his arms and Dan could feel her heart beating wildly. It was obvious she didn't want to dance with Jake but Dan sensed she wouldn't make a scene if he agreed.

It was equally obvious Bree didn't share Amy's

reluctance. She stepped forward, in anticipation of the trade.

"Sorry." Dan tightened his hold on Amy. "Tonight I'm a one-woman man."

Without another word Dan whirled Amy away and they danced off across the hardwood, leaving Bree and Jake openmouthed and staring.

Dan could feel Amy relax in his arms. The tense look that had blanketed her features eased.

"One-woman man?" A giggle punctuated Amy's words. "I can't believe you said that. It sounds like a title to a country-and-western song."

Dan grinned. The relief in her eyes told him he'd made the right decision.

"I meant every word," he said. "Tonight I'm all yours. And you're all mine."

You're all mine.

The possessive note to Dan's voice sent a thrill up Amy's spine. She'd never wanted to "belong" to any man, but tonight she found herself enjoying the feeling of being cherished and protected.

When Jake had wanted to change partners Amy had frozen, like a deer trapped in a headlight's glow. The last thing she'd wanted was to be within ten feet of Jake—much less in his arms—but how could she voice that sentiment knowing Jake and Dan were friends? Especially with Jake standing right there.

But she needn't have worried. Dan had taken control and Amy seriously doubted Jake would ask again. She heaved a contented sigh. This evening was quickly falling into the category of events that she would remember forever. Amy didn't have many such memories, which made tonight even more special.

"You know what I'd like to do?" Amy abruptly lifted her head and gazed into Dan's eyes.

He wiggled his eyebrows. "Dance with Jake?"

"Um, no." Amy tried to keep her expression serious but his lighthearted teasing made that impossible. "I'd like a picture."

Dan's company had hired several photographers to provide guests with mementos of the evening's festivities. They'd set up a couple of stations in the ballroom and had been busy snapping pictures all night.

The backdrop of fresh flowers they were using reminded Amy of something you'd see in prom pictures. Not that she had firsthand knowledge. When Amy had been in high school, she'd never gone to any of the dances. There hadn't been money in her aunt's house for fancy party dresses. Instead Amy had worked those nights, waiting tables, serving her fellow classmates.

Still, it wasn't as if she looked back on that time with regret. Except…she'd secretly longed for a picture of herself all dressed up with a handsome male at her side.

"Pictures?" Dan's gaze shifted to the nearest photographer who was just finishing up with a gray-haired couple.

The doubt in his eyes told her he wasn't keen on

the idea. Feeling gauche and unsophisticated, Amy quickly rallied, offering up a little laugh, pretending she'd only been joking. "I just thought it might be fun to show Emma. But you're right. It's a crazy idea."

Crazy or not, Amy couldn't keep her gaze from glancing in the direction of the camera one last time. She expected Dan to take the out she'd offered, but when she turned back to him he hesitated, his gaze lingering on her face.

"I don't think it sounds crazy at all. I think it sounds like…fun," he said, his eyes clear and very, very blue. A slight smile lifted his lips. "Kind of déjà vuish…like high school."

Amy's heart gave an excited leap, but she forced a nonchalant tone. "That's kind of what I was thinking."

The rest of the evening raced by. Amy got her picture taken with Dan—despite some ribbing from Jake, which Dan squelched with a single glance— then danced some more.

Amy's intuition had been right. Jake didn't ask to exchange partners again. Amy kept an eye on Bree and discovered the woman's gaze seemed to be permanently fixed on Dan, a sad look in her eyes. Amy now knew exactly who Bree had come to see.

By the time they were ready to leave, it was after midnight. Amy stood off to the side, while Dan retrieved her shawl. Though normally she'd be in bed by now, Amy wasn't the least bit tired.

She glanced at the pictures in her hand. The

photographer had instructed her to face Dan and place her hands flat against his chest. After she'd done as he'd asked, he'd positioned Dan's hands on her waist. Amy had been drowning in the deep blue of Dan's eyes when the photographer had snapped the picture…

"Are you ready?"

Amy's head jerked up. Dan stood in front of her, holding out her shawl. He was looking at her, not with the blatant invitation she often saw in men's eyes, but with a combination of unmistakable interest mixed with a hint of uncertainty.

Amy shoved the photo back into the decorative folder and let him wrap the silky fabric around her. She glanced down at her watch. If she could believe her former classmates, a milestone evening was considered a failure if you went home before dawn. It was barely past midnight. "You know don't you that if this *was* prom night, we'd never be going home this early."

Like Cinderella faced with turning back into a scullery maid, Amy hated the thought of the evening ending so soon. They could at least grab a bite to eat and talk over a cup of coffee. "Want to stop somewhere on our way home?"

"Sounds good to me." Dan's eyes darkened. "I'm definitely in the mood."

His comment didn't make much sense until they were in the car and Dan started talking about the make-out point in his town.

"It was on a hill." His lips curved upward in remembrance. "Overlooked a lake. The view couldn't be beat. Not that we spent much time gazing at the moon."

Amy's smile froze. Dan wasn't planning to stop for a burger. No, thanks to her ambiguous question, they were going to park.

Her body turned hot then cold at the thought of locking lips with Dan in the warm intimacy of the car.

"How about you?" Dan asked. "Where did *you* go?"

Amy took a steadying breath and wondered what he would say if she admitted that the only place she'd gone on prom night was back to her aunt's apartment after a grueling shift at the restaurant.

She had her pride. She couldn't let him know she'd been such a nerd. Her mind raced. Other than renting rooms at the hotel where the dance had been held, she couldn't recall any of her classmates mentioning a specific place they'd gone to park. "Mostly back roads. No place specific."

Dan turned off the highway onto a residential street. "A deserted road it is."

Amy's heart skipped a beat. She glanced out the window. The night was dark with only a sliver of moon. Large trees lined both sides of the road, their large, leafy branches arching overhead, creating an air of intimacy in the vehicle passing below.

It wasn't long until the row of houses gave way to farmland and pavement turned to gravel. Still Dan continued to drive.

"How far are we going?" Amy asked.

"Not much farther." Dan shot her a sideways glance. "Just enough so we won't be disturbed. Of course, I seem to recall it was that fear of discovery that made the experience so exciting."

His wicked smile fired her blood and for a second she forgot to breathe.

Dan wheeled the car to a stop at the side of the road, flipped off the ignition and the lights.

"This was a good suggestion." Dan's voice was soft and low in the stillness. "I was hoping we could go somewhere after the dance."

"You were?" Though Amy tried to keep her voice casual and offhand, it came out breathless and a whole octave higher than normal.

Dan nodded. "Once we got home I knew there'd be no privacy."

Amy knew he was right. Emma was a light sleeper. Odds were the little girl would be up and down the stairs before the baby-sitter was out the door. But they weren't in Dan's house. They were in the car. Alone. Just the two of them.

Feeling like a nervous schoolgirl, Amy shifted in the seat and faced him. A curious thrumming filled her body.

"I'm not sure my aunt would approve of me being here alone with you." She shot him a saucy smile. If she'd been seventeen, Amy had no doubt she might have said something very similar.

"I've got an idea." Dan tugged her wrap from

her shoulders and flung it into the back seat. "Let's not tell her."

Though the temperature inside the car was comfortably warm, Amy's skin turned to gooseflesh. She'd meant the teasing words as a joke and had been unprepared to have him play along.

Heat pooled low in Amy's belly and she decided if Dan was interested in being seventeen for the night, she would go along.

"I'm not sure I can trust you." Amy crossed her arms over her chest and stuck out her bottom lip. "I've been warned about boys like you. You only want one thing."

"That's not true." Dan's voice remained sensuously soft and low. He trailed a finger up her arm leaving a flash of heat in its wake. "I don't want just *one* thing…I want lots of things."

His crooked smile was endearing but there was something in his tone, in the underlying seriousness lurking behind the playfulness that set up a fluttering in her stomach. He studied her for several seconds and she found herself holding her breath.

"I'd like to kiss you," he said finally. "Is that okay?"

Amy chewed on her lip and tilted her head, pretending to ponder the question. "I suppose…as long as you don't try any of that fancy French stuff."

"You don't like to French kiss?"

The shock in his voice made Amy smile. She wasn't sure if it was the teenage Dan or the adult who was most distressed.

"I've never tried it." Amy clasped her hands primly in her lap like a virginal teen. "Aunt Verna says that kind of kissing is bad."

Amy had never discussed such a topic with her guardian, but she couldn't imagine Verna thinking anything else.

"Hmm." Dan slipped an arm around Amy's shoulder and nudged her to him. "I don't want to contradict the woman but French kissing is very good. Don't take my word for it. Give it a try. Then decide for yourself."

His arms closed around her. "I want you to know that I would never do anything to hurt you."

Amy's body was now pressed so tight against Dan that she could feel the heat radiating from his body. She drew a calming breath only to find herself immersed in the rich, spicy scent of his cologne. With her heart pounding, Amy moistened her lips with the tip of her tongue. "I know—"

The words had barely left her lips when his mouth closed over hers. Slow and sweet the kiss teased and tantalized and the desire Amy had held in check broke forth and surged through her veins like a raging river.

She slid her fingers into his soft hair, pulling him closer, the uncontrollable fire burning inside her demanding more than slow and sweet. But Dan's hands remained respectfully at her waist and his kisses, while intoxicatingly sensual, remained close-mouthed and chaste.

When his lips left hers to scatter kisses along her jawline and neck, Amy groaned with frustration. He was doing as she asked, but couldn't he tell she'd changed her mind? Dear God, did she have to spell it out to him?

His lips reached the curve of her neckline then moved back up.

Amy decided she'd had enough. A woman could only endure so much frustration. "I changed my mind."

His mouth paused on her neck. He lifted his head. "You want me to stop?"

"Yes." But when he pulled back, Amy realized with sudden horror what she'd just said. "No. I mean I want you to move on."

Amy knew she wasn't making much sense. But could she really be expected to think rationally with his warm breath caressing her neck?

"Move on?" He lifted a brow. "I don't understand."

"I want you to kiss me. *Really* kiss me."

The puzzled look in his eyes told Amy she still wasn't making herself clear.

"Ooh-la-la," Amy said, her French accent worthy of a kindergartener. *"Comprenez-vous?"*

The dimple in his cheek flashed. "But your aunt—"

"Screw my aunt."

Dan's lips quirked upward but he wisely withheld comment. "Anything else you'd like me to do?"

"Maybe," she murmured, glancing up at him through lowered lashes.

"You want it." Pure male satisfaction filled his tone. A high school boy couldn't have sounded more proud.

No need to define what *it* was. She'd experienced *it* on more than one occasion and though the experiences had hardly been memorable, having sex wasn't something a woman forgot.

"Nice girls don't go all the way," Amy said, sticking to her virgin persona. "I just want to kiss...maybe fool around a little."

Even in the darkness, Amy saw Dan smile.

"So everything but." Dan pretended to mull over the idea. Finally he nodded. "That still gives us a lot of territory to cover."

"Depends," Amy said, being deliberately vague, keeping her options open. "I might decide to stop with French kissing."

"I don't think so."

The arrogant undertone raised her ire. She sniffed. "Don't be so sure."

His gaze dropped. "What about these?"

Unexpectedly Dan reached forward and brushed the silky fabric of her bodice with the back of his knuckles. Her nipples instantly hardened beneath his touch. Amy gasped.

"Think how much fun it would be—" his voice turned deep and seductive "—if this dress wasn't in the way."

Amy didn't even have to close her eyes to visualize the erotic scene. With her dress out of the way, he would be free to use his mouth and hands to the fullest.

Her breasts strained against the silky fabric and an ache filled the juncture of her thighs. She craved and wanted this man in a way that defied logic. Still, being half-naked in a car with a randy male was something a teenager might do, not a responsible adult. And yet, she couldn't quite bring herself to refuse. As if Dan could sense her wavering, his lips closed over hers.

"Please." He spoke softly against her mouth. "It's prom night. We're not children. We can do what we want."

Amy had never been much of a rebel. The wildest thing she'd ever done was to dance in a conga line at a local bar on a friend's twenty-first birthday.

We can do what we want.

It was prom night. Or as close to prom night as she was ever going to get.

He deepened the kiss and Amy welcomed the moist heat and slow, penetrating slide of his tongue. A purr of passion rumbled in her throat. Dan was an irresistible temptation and the kiss made her hungry and restless for more of him.

She wouldn't sleep with him…that would be just plain foolish. But *everything but* did hold a certain decadent appeal. Amy turned in her seat and offered him the back of her dress. "Unzip me, please."

Chapter Ten

Unzip her?

The moment the words left Amy's lips, part of her wanted to laugh and pretend she'd only been joking. But the other part, the part that wanted, no, *needed* to feel his hands on her body kept silent, waiting for Dan to make the next move.

For half a heartbeat Dan hesitated as if he, too, realized the enormity of the step they were taking. But then his hand moved to the zipper and the back of her dress eased open.

Amy's skin turned to gooseflesh and anticipation skittered up her spine. While she didn't expect Dan to go caveman on her, she did expect things to start moving. But Dan didn't seem in any hurry.

After what seemed an eternity he placed a lingering, openmouthed kiss on the back of her neck. The
mere touch of his smooth, moist lips sent blood
surging through her body. Amy closed her eyes and
exhaled a ragged breath. This was definitely a good
start.

Now, if only the dress was off…

Despite knowing it would only take the slightest
of shrugs to drop the silky garment to her waist, Amy
waited. As eager as she was for some skin-to-skin
action, she was a traditionalist. Old-fashioned to the
core, Amy liked the man to take the lead. But when
Dan placed his hand against her back, Amy jerked
upright and stiffened, her reaction more like a high
school sophomore who'd never been touched than a
mature woman.

"Relax," he said in a low soothing voice, rubbing
his palm lightly over her skin.

Amy's face burned with embarrassment and she
opened her mouth. But once his hand settled on her
back, she found it difficult to breathe, much less talk.

His fingers were strong, yet gentle and her entire
body tingled at his touch. Warm shivers of sheer
pleasure coursed through her veins.

"Mmm," she sighed. Had she died and gone to
heaven? It seemed entirely possible.

"Want me to continue?" His deep voice held a
teasing lilt.

"Mmm-hmm," was all Amy could manage.

Thankfully Dan understood what she wanted.

While scattering kisses across her shoulders and up her neck he continued to gently move his hand over her lower back. With each slow stroke, each unhurried touch, her desire grew. When he slid his hand upward, she moaned softly and arched her spine against him.

He played her like a fine violin, drawing her out, making her respond as she'd never responded before. The darkness and solitude inside the car lent a dreamlike air and Amy wasn't sure what part of this wonderful experience was fantasy and what was reality. But whichever it was, one thing was certain—she didn't want it to end.

"That feels incredible," she said, exhaling a long breath. She desperately wanted Dan to keep touching her. Her breasts ached to be touched and lower, between her thighs, she felt a heavy warmth and a dull throb.

His hand slipped deeper inside the dress and curved around her waist. Slowly and ever so sensuously, his hands slid upward until his fingertips were no more than an inch from the underside of her breast.

Breath held, eyes closed, Amy quivered with anticipation. She felt him lean close, felt the warmth of his breath on her shoulder, felt him gently turn her in the seat so she faced him. Her eyes fluttered open and excitement coursed through her when she saw the gleam in his eyes. There was a promise there, one that said there was more, much more to come.

"You are so beautiful." His voice was soft and gentle as a caress.

Though she knew he was only being kind, Amy loved the way the words sounded on his lips. She wished she were beautiful. For herself. For him.

Dan saw the wistful longing in Amy's eyes and he vowed that by the end of the evening she'd believe his words. He'd make her *feel* beautiful.

A warm rush of emotion filled him. Amy was such a good person. So kind. So sweet. So incredibly sexy.

He raised a hand and cupped her face. Lowering his head, he pressed his mouth against hers. He ran his tongue over the fullness of her lower lip, coaxing her to open to him, sweeping inside when she did. She tasted of wine and breath mint, a ridiculous combination that was wildly erotic.

She curled her fingers into the fabric of his shirt and leaned into the kiss, her tongue fencing with his. The slow, delicious thrust and slide brought his body to high alert.

Her skin was like warm silk beneath his fingers and Dan fought the urge to slide his palm upward and feel the firm weight of her breast in his hand. He reminded himself there was no reason to rush. They had all the time in the—

A light flashed and a sharp rap sounded on the window.

"Sheriff's deputy," a deep voice announced. "Everything okay in there?"

Amy jerked back, her eyes, which had been heavy-lidded with passion, suddenly wide-open. "Police."

Dan whirled in his seat and stifled a curse. Despite the outside darkness and his vehicle's tinted windows, he could still see the uniformed officer and the flashing lights.

"I need you to step out of the car," the man ordered.

"I'll take care of this." Dan flashed Amy what he hoped was a reassuring smile, pushed open the door and stepped out into the cruiser's spotlight. "What seems to be the problem, Officer…Wayne?"

Though it had been almost five years since he'd seen Wayne Bojanski, Dan recognized him immediately. Wayne had been his buddy in grade school, a casual friend in junior high and a football teammate at Barrington High.

"Dan Major?" A grin of recognition split Wayne's ruddy face. "I never thought I'd find you and Tess gettin' frisky on a country road."

Dan's smile faded as the realization hit. Wayne didn't know about Tess. He'd last seen Wayne at their ten-year high school reunion and back then Tess had been very much alive.

Dan didn't even need to close his eyes to remember the evening. That night had been classic Tess. She'd been laughing, dancing up a storm and charming everyone in sight. But it all seemed so long ago and Dan was surprised to find that the memories of Tess didn't hurt as they had before.

"Tess died three years ago," Dan said finally as the silence lengthened.

Wayne's eyes widened. His mouth dropped open. "You're kidding."

Yeah, Dan wanted to say, I'm kidding, she's really alive. But he understood Wayne's comment was just an expression of his shock and disbelief.

"It was sudden," Dan said. "A medical problem."

Wayne pulled his mouth shut and cleared his throat. "So then, who's in the car?"

Dan blinked, the blunt question catching him off guard. "A friend." Normally cool and collected in any circumstance, Dan found himself stammering. "We had some things to discuss and wanted some privacy."

"Friend? Discussion?" The deputy's lips twitched. "C'mon, Dan. This is ole Wayne you're talking to…"

Dan couldn't help but smile. Okay, so maybe his explanation was pretty lame. He probably should just admit he and Amy had been parking. After all, Wayne and his wife, Tami, had spent more than their fair share of time locking lips—and doing God knows what else—in the back of Wayne's old Buick.

But the words wouldn't come. Something in Dan wouldn't let him joke about it with Wayne. He couldn't shrug off the feeling that by doing so, he'd cheapen what he and Amy had shared.

"It's quiet out here," Dan repeated, lifting his chin and meeting Wayne's gaze head-on. "Not many distractions."

"Good for discussions," Wayne added, barely able to keep a straight face.

"Is this going to take much longer?" Amy's voice came from inside the Land Rover.

Wayne's face broke into a grin and a devilish gleam lit his eyes.

"You can go now. I'm sure you and your friend have a lot to *discuss.*" Wayne placed an arm companionably around Dan's shoulder and lowered his voice. "You just have to do it somewhere else."

Dan couldn't speak for Amy, but for him dirt roads no longer held any appeal.

"Don't worry," Dan said. "You won't see me around here again."

Wayne glanced at the car then back at Dan. "One more thing—"

Dan wished he could just jump in the Land Rover and speed away. He remembered that tone. Wayne had always considered himself to be an expert on women. He loved to offer his own kinky brand of relationship advice. Dan braced himself.

"I'm sorry to hear about Tess." Wayne kicked the gravel with the tip of his boot. "I liked her. She was spunky."

Dan's heart stuttered, the unexpected sentiment taking him by surprise. He silently accepted the condolence. Dan appreciated Wayne's words. But he didn't want to talk about Tess tonight or even think about her. This evening was about the future, not the past.

The deputy wasn't even in his cruiser when Dan pulled away from the side of the road and cast a sideways glance at Amy. "Thanks for getting things moving back there. Wayne will talk forever if you let him."

Amy's lips quirked upward. "I guessed as much."

"I'm sorry about that." Dan gestured toward the darkness. "I didn't plan on the cops showing up."

Though his gaze was on the road, Dan sensed Amy's scrutiny.

"You knew him," she said simply.

"Wayne and I go way back…to kindergarten. We played football together in high school." Dan kept his tone deliberately light. "The guy always did have bad timing."

"It was probably for the best," Amy said in a matter-of-fact tone. "I have the feeling things would have gotten out of hand."

"And that would have been a…bad thing?"

Amy chuckled and Dan felt the tension ease from his shoulders. At least he could still make her laugh.

"I'll definitely remember tonight." Her lips twitched. "A girl always remembers her first time."

Startled, Dan's brows shot up.

"The first time—" Amy's smile widened "—I was ever busted by the cops."

When she began to laugh, he laughed along with her. Her eyes shone like the finest emeralds and the enticing scent of her perfume wafted around him. All he wanted to do was pull over and take up where they'd left off. But Dan wasn't seventeen. He was an adult and wise enough to realize they'd been lucky. Five or ten minutes later and Wayne would have gotten an eyeful.

No, a car was *not* the place for a romantic interlude with Amy. But there were plenty of other options they could explore.

"Tonight was definitely an evening to remember," Dan said. "Care to go out again and make some more memories?"

Amy lifted a finger to her lips and thought for a moment. "As long as the memory doesn't involve law enforcement or dirt roads."

Though he agreed wholeheartedly, Dan couldn't resist a little teasing. "Where's your spirit of adventure?"

"Oh, I can be very adventurous." Amy shot him a sultry look from beneath lowered lashes and Dan's mouth went dry. "It's just that when I'm kissing someone, I don't want to worry about being interrupted…especially not by the police."

Impulsively Dan reached over, grabbed her hand and brought it to his lips.

"Next time there won't be any interruptions," he said. "I guarantee it."

No interruptions.

Amy stared up at the ceiling of her bedroom. When she and Dan had walked through the front door, their time alone had come to an abrupt end.

Dan had done his best. He'd kept his voice low and hurriedly paid the sitter. But Emma must have had her "Daddy radar" on because Dan had barely ushered the baby-sitter out the front door when Emma had come running down the stairs.

The child's appearance had brought reality back with a vengeance. Amy was once again the nanny and Dan was, well, Emma's daddy and her employer. While Amy understood—and completely agreed with—the need for discretion around Emma, she still felt like a child whose favorite toy had been snatched from her hands.

Amy's fingers rose to her mouth as the disappointment resurfaced. She hadn't even gotten a good-night kiss. Unless you counted the ones in the car, that is. A smile touched her lips. She never realized parking could be so much…fun.

Dan certainly knew how to kiss. When he held her in his arms and his lips closed over hers it was as if nothing else in the world existed. It was—

A familiar melody rang out from the cell phone on her nightstand and Amy jerked upright. She glanced at the clock and frowned: 2:00 a.m. Why would Steven be calling at this hour?

Amy considered letting the call go to voice mail but curiosity got the better of her. She grabbed the phone and flipped it open. "Hello."

"Amy." Even across the airwaves she could hear the surprise in his voice. "I didn't expect you to answer. I was just going to leave a message."

While Amy wasn't used to getting calls at this hour, she welcomed the distraction. Maybe talking to Steven would take her mind off Dan and help her relax. "I usually shut off the ringer but I guess I forgot."

"I'm sorry I woke you."

His distress was palpable and Amy hastened to reassure him. "You didn't. I was lying here looking up at the ceiling, trying to decide if I should count sheep or get up and read when you called."

"I've had trouble sleeping, too," Steven said in a low, husky timbre. "I wanted to hear your voice, even if it was just a recording."

Warning bells sounded in Amy's head. She liked Steven but the truth was, she hadn't given him much thought since he'd been gone. Of course if it had been Dan who'd been out of town...

"—fly here."

Amy's fingers tightened around the phone. She realized with sudden horror that while her mind had been wandering, Steven had continued to talk. The question was, about what?

"Fly to Boston?" Amy asked, slowly, cautiously.

"I want you with me," Steven said in that take-charge way that was as much a part of him as his hand-tailored suits. "My days are booked, but you could shop or sightsee. We'd have evenings together."

Amy couldn't help but be flattered that he'd want to spend his free moments with her. Steven was a handsome man, a successful attorney...not to mention a fabulous cook. He had a lot to offer a woman.

But even if she was interested, there was no way she could go.

"You forget I have a job." She deliberately gentled her tone wanting him to understand she appreciated the offer even if she couldn't accept. "It's impossible for me to get away."

"A-my." She could almost see Steven shaking his head. "Dan Major can find someone else to watch his daughter and clean up after him for a week."

"I'm sure he could," Amy said, feeling a pang of distress at the thought. "But I was actually referring to the Chez Gladines business."

Getting this chance to show off her talents was a major accomplishment for an untried chef. Amy wasn't about to let the opportunity slip away before she'd proven herself.

"I have this job on a trial basis," Amy explained. "Keeping it is very important to me."

"I understand." Admiration filled Steven's voice. And something else. Something that sounded like relief. "That job is your first step toward true independence."

Amy pulled her brows together. "I've been on my own since I was eighteen."

Silence filled the phone line for several seconds.

"Don't take this wrong, but you really *haven't* been independent. Not in the truest sense of the word." Once Steven got started he seemed to warm to the topic. "You went from your aunt's home to your first nanny job and from there to your current position."

Amy's heart picked up speed and irritation warmed her face.

"You make it sound like I've been mooching off these people," she said. "I work hard for the salary I receive. Just because free room and board is part of my fringe benefits, that doesn't mean I'm not independent."

Steven had definitely hit a nerve. From the time Amy had been small she'd been determined to be self-sufficient. She was not going to end up like her mother, depending on a man to "take care" of her.

"You have so many talents, Amy," Steven said. "I just want to make sure you take the chance to develop them."

Amy's anger fled, replaced by curiosity. "Why do you care?"

"Because I like you."

It was a logical answer but there was something in his voice, some element of restraint that told Amy this went beyond a pat answer. "There's more to it than that."

After a moment of silence, Steven spoke. "My mother worked for years as an administrative assistant for a wealthy Chicago industrialist. She was a smart woman with a lot of talent but he refused to promote her. Having her around met *his* needs."

Amy leaned back. "What happened?"

"He decided it was in his best interest to move to France last year." Steven's voice tightened. "Now she's in her late fifties and back pounding the pavement."

Amy could appreciate Steven being protective of his mother but it sounded as if she'd made a choice to stay in the job. Just like Amy had. "But she could have gotten another job at any point. Couldn't she?"

"Of course," Steven said. "But he constantly told her how important she was to him, how they were a team…until he no longer needed her. He used her, Amy. I don't want to see that happen to you."

The degree of bitterness in Steven's voice startled her.

"Still—"

"Think about it," Steven said, his voice low and tight. "If Dan remarries, the new wife might decide she wants you gone and just like that you're history."

"I don't think Dan—"

"He doesn't even have to remarry," Steven continued. "What happens when Emma gets older? Goes off to college? All I'm asking is that you don't make the same mistake my mother did. Make yourself and *your* dreams a priority while you're still young and capable."

Amy sank deeper into her pillow, a sense of emptiness creeping over her. She could see why Steven was effective in the courtroom. He was passionate and very persuasive.

"Amy? Are you still there?"

"I'm here." She forced the words past a sudden tightness in her throat. When she'd graduated from high school, there had been no money for further schooling. Being a nanny had started as a temporary solution, a way to support herself while she attended cooking school at night.

She'd completed her courses shortly before Tess died. She couldn't have left Dan and Emma then. But did that mean she had to spend the next ten or fifteen years standing off to the side watching Dan and Emma live their lives but never *really* being a part of their world? Even after tonight, what if their relationship didn't move forward? What if Dan married someone else?

She thought she'd stayed with the Majors out of love for Emma, but was that simply an excuse? Had she stayed out of fear instead? Or for Dan?

"Are you angry?" Concern filled Steven's voice.

Amy took a deep, steadying breath. Her inner turmoil was *her* problem, not his. "No. I'm sure you only want the best for me."

"I do." His voice took on urgency. "I care—"

"Listen, Steven, I'd love to talk more but I need to get to sleep." Amy had enough on her mind. She couldn't deal with what she feared could be a declaration from Steven.

"May I call you tomorrow?"

"Of course."

"One last suggestion." Steven spoke quickly as if he sensed her finger hovered over the End button on her phone. "Don't get personally involved with Dan. It'll just make leaving his household that much harder when the time comes."

When, not if.

Amy's heart twisted. The warning had come a little too late. "I'll keep that in mind. Good night, Steven."

"Sweet dreams."

Amy clicked off the phone. Sweet dreams? Was he kidding? She had so much to think about she'd be lucky if she slept at all.

Chapter Eleven

Amy rose the next morning, pulled on her clothes and headed to the kitchen. She told herself she'd been foolish to spend half the night worrying over her budding relationship with Dan. She was different than Bree and Melinda and her situation was nothing like that of Steven's mother. Steven had his own agenda and it obviously included coming between her and Dan. Well, Amy wasn't going to let that happen.

The sound of talk radio came from the kitchen. Amy paused in the doorway and all her doubts slipped away. Dan sat at the table reading the paper.

He looked up when she entered the room. Even with his hair still mussed from sleep and a slight shadow darkening his cheeks, he still made her heart skip a beat. "Hey."

"Hey, yourself." Amy returned his smile and, instead of moving to the coffeemaker, she pulled out a chair and took a seat at the table. "You're up early."

Dan lowered the paper to the table. "Couldn't sleep," he said, closing his hand over hers. "Someone was on my mind."

Amy willed herself not to blush. Still her cheeks warmed. "Yeah, right."

"I'm serious." Dan's eyes twinkled. He looked more devilish than serious. "You didn't even give me a good-night kiss."

A warm flush of pleasure washed over Amy. So she wasn't the only one who'd felt cheated.

"Emma was there," Amy said in a light tone. "We could hardly kiss in front of her."

Dan looked around the room, his movements exaggerated. "I don't see her now."

Amy's gaze never left his. "I checked on her before I came down. She was fast asleep."

"We saw last night how quickly that can change." Still holding Amy's hand, Dan pushed back his chair and stood.

Amy followed his lead. "Are you saying there's no time to waste?"

Even as Amy said the words, he pulled her to him. "Oh, yeah."

A brush fire of heat sizzled through her as he lowered his head.

His lips brushed softly over hers, once, twice with a teasing gentleness. Parting her lips, Amy touched her tongue to his bottom lip. In a heartbeat the kiss changed.

With a low groan, Dan wrapped his arms more firmly around her. His mouth covered hers. She was completely surrounded by him, by the delicious feel of his body against hers. Warmth emanated from his skin. His large hands combed through her hair then slowly skimmed down her back. She reciprocated but went a step further, tugging his shirt from the waistband, slipping her hands inside.

Desire, hot and insistent, gushed through her. She ran her palms up his back, reveling in the contrast of smooth, firm skin over hard muscle. Everything faded except the need to feel more of him. Taste more of him. Touch more of him.

Logic told her to slow down but unfortunately logic wasn't in charge. Besides, he was having none of it and she wasn't about to argue.

He lowered his head and ran kisses down her neck. She arched back. A low groan escaped her as his lips dipped lower.

"A-my." The childish voice coming from the top of the stairs broke through the fog of arousal engulfing her. "I can't find my pink shirt. Do you know where it is?"

Apparently equally startled, Dan froze, lifting his head.

Amy cleared her throat. She knew exactly where

to find the garment, but she didn't want Emma down-stairs any sooner than necessary. "I'll be up in a minute to help you look."

Pulling in a much-needed deep breath, Amy returned her attention to Dan and found him studying her with enough simmering heat to melt a polar ice cap.

"That was some good-night kiss," he said finally.

She swallowed. "It was okay."

"Okay?" The dimple in his cheek flashed. "Only okay means we'll have to keep practicing."

A wealth of emotion rose inside Amy, surprising her with its intensity. No longer could she lie and tell herself she thought of Dan as merely a friend. He turned her on by just being in the same room. His kisses had more kick than, well, than anything she could think of. But it was Dan, who he was, what he stood for, his wit, his charm, that drew her to him.

She'd tried to keep her heart safe but every look, every smile, pushed her a little closer to the edge. She only wished she could be certain that if she went over that edge…he'd be there to catch her.

Dan pushed open the front door and headed down the steps. Once he reached the sidewalk he turned left. Bagels and Jam was only three blocks away. Hot, fresh blueberry bagels had been his getaway excuse. He'd felt the need to put some distance between him and this unsettling woman who had all but turned him into one big, pulsating hormone. His reaction to her bordered on embarrassing.

God knew he'd been ready to devour her in the kitchen. When she'd first walked into the room with her shiny hair tumbling around her shoulders in a tangle of curls, every one of his nerve endings had jumped to attention. She obviously hadn't taken the time to apply any makeup because a spray of delightful freckles marched across her nose. She looked fresh, clean and good enough to eat.

If Emma hadn't gotten up when she had, Dan didn't doubt for a second that things in the kitchen would have quickly burned out of control. While Amy seemed willing, he didn't want to rush her into something she might regret.

Last night and this morning had told him the attraction was there. While he would never love her like he loved Tess, at least lack of passion wouldn't be an issue.

Dan found himself distracted as he pushed open the door to the shop. The place was surprisingly busy. He stood at the end of the line behind an attractive woman with salt-and-pepper hair who looked vaguely familiar. He must have caught her eye when he came in because she turned, a spark of recognition lighting her gaze.

"Aren't you Dan Major?" she asked.

"I am." Dan's mind raced. He tried to place her but no name was forthcoming. He was just about to admit that fact when she stuck out her hand.

"Angela Bartgate," she said. "My late husband Tom and I used to live two doors down from you on Deming."

"Of course." Dan's hand closed over hers. Now he understood why he hadn't remembered her. They'd only met once or twice. She and her husband had left the neighborhood shortly after Dan and Tess had moved in. "You moved to...Wisconsin?"

Angela nodded. "Our daughter lives in Madison. We wanted to be closer to her." A shadow passed over the woman's face. "Tom was getting ready to retire. But he never got the chance. He was killed by a drunk driver six months ago." Her voice thickened. She blinked rapidly for several seconds.

Dan's heart went out to her. Though he'd only met her husband once, Dan knew firsthand what it was like to lose a spouse.

"I can understand what you're going through," he said. "My wife, Tess, died three years ago."

The woman's eyes widened with shock and sympathy filled her gaze. "Oh, my goodness, no. What happened?"

"Are you two ready to order?"

The bored voice seemed to come out of nowhere and Dan realized with a start that they'd reached the counter. They ordered and made light conversation while they waited. When their drinks and food were ready Dan reached for his wallet. "These will be together."

Angela glanced up at him. "You don't have to do that."

"I know." Dan handed the man behind the counter a twenty. "I want to do it."

"Would you like to sit and have a cup of coffee with me?" Though Angela's voice remained calm and composed, the hopefulness in her eyes spoke of desperation. "I'm visiting friends down the street and they both like to sleep late. Tom and I were both early risers. Mornings are still hard for me."

Dan thought for a moment. Amy and Emma would have plenty to do until he got back.

"Sure," Dan said. "I'd love the company."

It wasn't true, of course. He'd walked down here specifically for the solitude. To reflect on what had happened last night and again this morning. But Angela's pain was almost palpable and Dan remembered how lonely he'd been when Tess had first died. He couldn't begin to imagine how much worse it would have been if not for Amy.

"Looks like there's a table by the window," Angela said.

Dan was determined to keep the conversation light, but the minute they sat down, the woman leaned forward and rested her hand on his forearm.

"I'm so sorry to hear about your wife," she said. "What happened?"

Dan shifted uncomfortably in his seat. While thoughts of Tess no longer sent waves of pain crashing over him, he still didn't like talking about that time. But short of being rude, he didn't see that he had any other choice.

"Tess was pregnant with our second child." Opening a packet of raw sugar, Dan dumped the granules into his cup. "There were complications. She and the baby died."

"How heartbreaking." Tears filled Angela's eyes. "I still remember the first time we met. It was a glorious fall day. Tom and I were working in the yard. You and Tess were pushing your daughter around the block."

Dan remembered that day, too. Emma had been fussy. He'd put her in the stroller, planning to give Tess a break so she could work on a new design that was giving her trouble. But at the last minute Tess had insisted on coming with them.

"You two were so much in love." Angela's eyes grew misty. "Just like Tom and I."

Dan took a sip of coffee, not really tasting it. "It seems like such a long time ago."

"I assume you still live in the same house?"

It was a logical assumption. After all, she'd run into him just down the street from where she'd once lived. "Still there."

Angela broke off a piece of scone but made no attempt to eat it. A curious glint lit her eyes. "Have you remarried?"

"No," Dan said. "It's hard to think of being married to anyone but Tess…"

Dan let his voice trail off as he added another packet of sugar to his coffee. He took a sip and grimaced at the sweetness.

"My friends tell me I'm too young to spend the rest of my life alone." Angela stared down into her latte for a moment before lifting her gaze. "But Tom was my soul mate. I'm never going to find anyone I'll love like that again."

The image of Tess flashed before him. Spiky blond hair. Big blue eyes. An enchanting smile. She'd been his first love, and from the time he'd been a boy, his only love.

But then another image intruded. One of caramel-colored hair, bright green eyes and a sprinkling of freckles.

Tess had been wonderful, a real gem. But as time went on Dan was finding it impossible to think of Amy as second best to anyone.

He wrapped his fingers around the coffee cup, the warmth a vivid contrast to his suddenly cold hands. "I've considered marrying again. Emma needs a mother and I...well, it'd be nice to have a companion."

Companion?

The minute the word left his mouth, Dan knew it was all wrong. Companion conjured up images of a buddy, not an emerald-eyed temptress who made his day brighter by simply being in the same room.

"Still, I'm not sure it's fair to marry if you're not in love," he added before he could stop himself.

Normally Dan wouldn't consider discussing an issue of a personal nature with a stranger. But then, Angela wasn't a part of his daily life and he couldn't—wouldn't—air this concern with anyone he might see again.

Certainly not with his mother who'd tell him he needed to be honest with Amy. Or with Jake who'd tell him flat out to do what was best for *Dan* and not worry about the nanny.

Dan wasn't sure what he wanted from Angela, unless maybe it was for her to validate that marrying him would be a good thing for Amy. *Even if romantic love wasn't part of the equation.*

Angela took a bite of scone and chewed thoughtfully. "I think we'd both be surprised at how many people marry for reasons that have little to do with love."

"I can see where it could happen," Dan said. "Take my situation for example. I have a child that could really use a mother and I can't imagine spending the next fifty years of my life alone. Still, is settling the right thing to do?"

But…was marrying Amy really settling? He preferred to think of it as—

"I can understand not wanting to be alone." Angela stirred her latte and her brows furrowed.

"It could be a win-win situation. Marriage could be a good thing for her, too," Dan inserted before she could continue, feeling like a lawyer presenting a case, desperate to get all the evidence in before a verdict is rendered. "I could give her the life she's always wanted."

"That might work," Angela said, but the doubt in her voice sent unease creeping up Dan's spine. "As long as—"

Dan kept his face expressionless, hoping she couldn't hear the pounding of his heart. He lifted a brow.

"As long as the life she's always wanted never included a man who loves her."

Dan leaned back in his desk chair and stared unseeingly at the computer monitor. He'd come back from the bagel place, edgy and out of sorts. While he'd been able to keep his emotions under control, it had still been a relief when Amy had left to take Emma to dance class.

Angela had given him a lot to think about. Dan grimaced. He'd never thought he'd be in this predicament. He'd never thought his wife would die young. He'd never thought he'd have to worry about what would happen to his daughter should a similar fate befall him.

"Dan?"

He turned in his chair.

Amy stood in the doorway, a glass tumbler filled with iced tea in one hand. "I thought you might be thirsty."

Dan glanced at the clock, surprised to discover so much time had passed. He hadn't even heard her return. "How was the dance class?"

Amy smiled. "They're practicing for the *Nutcracker*. Emma is so excited. She's just a Snow Angel but you'd think she had the lead."

Although the finer points of ballet escaped him,

Dan liked watching his daughter jump and spin. He smiled and, obviously taking the gesture as a sign of real interest, Amy went into more detail about the lesson. But when she started throwing around technical ballet terms she lost him.

If this was important to Emma, then it should be important to Dan. He knew he should be focusing on the tale she was weaving, but Amy's red lips made it impossible for him to concentrate. The freshly applied color made her lips look plump and juicy, like the most delectable of strawberries. And recent experience had taught him that those lips *tasted* as good as they *looked.*

Dan's gaze dropped to take in the sight of her distracting curves and long legs. There was a lump in his throat, a mixture of lust and fear and something else he couldn't identify. Dear God, what was happening to him? The woman stops in to offer him some tea and talk about his child and all he can think about is jumping her?

Or was focusing on the physical attraction that simmered between them a way to keep from thinking about other, deeper issues?

"Dan?"

He blinked and realized she'd quit talking.

"Is something wrong?"

"No." He shook his head. "Fifth place and pivots. Fascinating stuff."

A tiny smile hovered on the edges of her lips. "It's fifth *position* and *pirouettes,*" she corrected. "And I can tell something is on your mind."

Without waiting for an invitation she crossed the room, placed the tea on a coaster at the edge of the desktop and took a seat. "What's going on? Spill."

What's going on is that I want to marry you because I need a mother for my daughter and a companion for myself but now I'm not sure that'd be fair to you.

A look of distress filled her gaze and for a second Dan worried he'd spoken his thoughts aloud. But then he realized it was his silence she was reacting to, not to any words. His mind quickly searched for a plausible excuse for his inattention. "Actually, I was wondering about Thanksgiving."

An expression he couldn't decipher flickered in her eyes. "I hadn't thought much about it."

Dan couldn't hide his surprise. Although Amy had holidays off, they'd always spent them together. And she'd always gotten into the holiday spirit way before the actual day, planning menus and what they could do to make the day special for Emma. Of course that was before Steven.

"I'm hoping you'll spend the day with us," Dan said. "Unless you have plans with someone else?"

A startled look crossed her face before her eyes grew shuttered.

"I sort of thought I'd stick around here." Her gaze lowered to the desktop and her finger traced an imaginary pattern on the glass.

Relief flowed through Dan. He couldn't imagine spending the day with anyone else. She'd been a big part of his Thanksgiving for the past three years. The first year she'd single-handedly prepared a meal for him and Tess and a houseful of guests. The next year Tess was gone and Dan had no interest in entertaining. Though he'd told her not to bother, Amy had made dinner and insisted he sit down and eat. Every year she'd outdone herself.

Impulsively Dan rose, rounded the desk and took a seat in the chair next to her. Taking her hand, he gently caressed her palm with his thumb.

"I can't imagine spending Thanksgiving with anyone but you." His gaze remained riveted to hers. "You're the one I want with me. Understand?"

Amy entwined her fingers with his. The deep blue of his eyes drew her in and she found herself slipping from the firm shore of what she'd always known to a place where she could be over her head in an instant.

But she wanted him and when he tugged her to him she went willingly, eagerly. While he hadn't said he loved her, he'd come close. For now that was good enough.

Dan raked his fingers through his hair, grateful for Emma's nonstop chatter beside him as they walked to the park.

You're the one I want with me.

Even to his ears the words sounded like a declaration.

After his talk with Angela, Dan had vowed that he would not mislead Amy about his feelings. If she committed to him it would be based on the friendship and trust that existed between them—not because he implied he was in love with her.

Because he wasn't in love with her. Tess had been his soul mate and everyone knew you only got one of those.

"Amy's making a booberry pie for Thanksgiving," Emma said. "I don't think I've ever had that kind. Have you, Daddy? Is it good?"

Dan pulled his thoughts to the present and to his little girl. He smiled down at her and love welled up inside him. "I have and it's very good. Especially with ice cream."

"I can't wait for Thanksgiving." Emma did a little dance on the sidewalk. "Amy makes everything good."

Dan wasn't sure if his daughter was talking about merely the food or the atmosphere. Either way, he had to agree.

He cast aside any lingering doubts and solidified his decision to marry her. She'd be a good wife. A wonderful mother. A passionate lover. He'd do everything in his power to make her happy.

Now all he had to do was get her to say yes.

Chapter Twelve

Amy glanced at the clock on her dashboard and pressed harder on the accelerator. Dan had taken Emma for a walk while she'd finished her French pastries. But dropping them off at Chez Gladines had taken longer than she'd planned. Now she was late. After so many years in the school system, Aunt Verna didn't tolerate tardiness well.

Amy had been looking forward to puttering around the house, finishing a few projects and most of all just spending the day with Dan and Emma. But Verna was in town and wanted to see her. How could she say no?

She'd thought she was meeting her aunt at a restaurant for coffee. But the address Verna gave her led her to a brick home in Lincolnshire. If Aunt Verna's Saturn hadn't been in the driveway, she'd have thought she was at the wrong place.

Amy glanced at the piece of paper on the seat next to her, then back at the numbers on the mailbox. That was the address she'd been given. And that *was* her aunt's car. So, this must be the place.

In less than a minute, Amy stood on the front stoop, listening to the ring of the doorbell echoing through the house. The door opened and relief flowed through Amy at the sight of her aunt. Verna stood in the doorway, ramrod stiff, her lips pursed together. "You're late."

The bluntness was typical Verna. Her aunt had never been a subtle woman. Sugarcoating was something only done to cookies. Still, over the years Amy and her aunt had bonded and she'd come to love the taciturn woman.

"Well, are you going to stand there staring, or are you going to give me a hug?" The words shot from Verna's lips like a bullet.

Amy laughed and wrapped her arms around Verna's stiff shoulders. "I've missed you."

But the hug only lasted a second before Verna pulled away, her voice brusque. "Now that we've given the neighbors plenty to talk about, come inside and I'll show you the place."

Amy followed her aunt into a large living room with a fireplace across the far wall. Other than Verna's sofa and love seat, there wasn't much else in the way of furniture. Several cardboard boxes sat in the middle of the floor. The place had a definite just-moved-in feel to it.

She turned to her aunt. "Is this yours?"

Verna's lips curved slightly upward. "Mine and the mortgage company's."

"I didn't know you were that serious about moving." Amy tried to keep the hurt from her voice. She couldn't believe her aunt had bought a house and moved without telling her.

"It dropped in my lap," Verna said. "My friend decided to participate in a teacher exchange program with a school in Germany. Her kids are grown and she plans to buy a town house when she returns."

"I never thought you'd leave Mankato." Amy remembered how active Verna had been in the small Minnesota community. "You knew practically everyone in town."

"I've got friends here," Verna said, ushering Amy into the kitchen.

Amy's smile faded.

"And family," Verna added hastily.

Amy resisted the urge to sigh. While deep in her heart she knew her aunt loved her, she'd always felt more like an obligation. That was part of the reason she was so determined to marry for love. She wanted the man she married to be as crazy about her as she was about him. For once, she wanted to come first in someone's life.

"Have a seat," Verna ordered, gesturing toward an

oak pedestal table already set for tea. "We'll have tea and cookies before I show you around."

Amy sat down and, with typical Verna efficiency, the tea was soon in her cup and several cookies on her plate.

"Tell me what you've been up to." Verna nibbled on a shortbread cookie, a curious glint lighting her eyes. "Are you dating anyone?"

"I've gone out a few times with a guy I met in my cooking club," Amy said. "He's nice."

Nice. Not special. Not like Dan.

If she and her aunt were confidants, Amy would have mentioned Dan, maybe even sought her aunt's advice. But Verna had never really made an attempt to get to know Dan, despite Amy's repeated tries.

Verna lifted a perfectly tweezed brow. "Are you spending Thanksgiving with him?"

"Steven hasn't asked," Amy said. "But if he did I'd have to say no. I'm cooking dinner for Dan and Emma."

"Working on Thanksgiving?" Verna's mouth drew together in disapproval. "Surely that man can spare you for one day."

Amy's spine stiffened and she dropped her cookie back to the plate. Aunt Verna and Steven always made it sound like Dan was some sort of ogre when nothing could be further from the truth. Emma and Dan were like family. She *wanted* to celebrate the holidays with them.

"Of course he'd give me the day off if I asked him," Amy said, unable to keep the indignation from her voice. "But I love to cook and holidays are a big deal for Emma—"

Verna's eyes flashed. "It's also a time for you to be with your family."

Amy suddenly realized this wasn't about Dan. This was about Verna. For the last five or six years her aunt had spent Thanksgiving in Texas with a close friend and her family. But buying the house must have put her in a bind and now she was facing a holiday alone.

Reaching across the table Amy covered her aunt's hand with her own. "Come and spend Thanksgiving with us. I know Dan would love to see you again."

"You talk like it's your house," Verna said in a no-nonsense tone. "He's your *employer,* Amy, not your husband."

Amy's cheeks burned as if she'd been slapped. "I think I know who he is, Aunt Verna."

Her words were as measured and clipped as her aunt's had been.

"I didn't mean to make you angry." Verna's eyes were clear and direct. "But I'm worried about you."

Amy gave a little laugh. "Worried? Why?"

Verna's gaze never wavered. "You're twenty-eight years old. It's time you had a family of your own."

"But—"

"Hear me out." Verna raised a hand. "I know you enjoy being that child's nanny, but you're not getting any younger. It's time you started thinking of yourself. Started thinking what it is you want out of life."

I want Dan.

Amy kept her mouth closed. She already knew what her aunt would say if she mentioned her daydreams about Dan, about how she hoped they could one day be a family. Verna would tell her she needed to be realistic, to see life as it was, not how she wished it would be.

"I love Emma," Amy said instead. "She and Dan are like family."

"You've been there too long," Verna said. "You're too attached."

Of course she was attached. For the past three years Dan and Emma had been her family. The three of them had spent every holiday together. And not just holidays. She'd been there to celebrate Emma's birthday...and Dan's. And they'd celebrated hers.

Amy took a sip of tea, met her aunt's gaze and took the plunge. "Lately Dan has been making noises like he'd like to date me. Maybe see where things could go between us."

Verna closed her eyes and visibly shuddered. "A recipe for disaster."

"Maybe not," Amy said. "We've always gotten along so well."

"Because you're his employee," Verna said. "You wait on that man hand and foot."

"I do—" Amy started to protest then stopped herself. Her lips curved up in a rueful smile. "Okay, I'll admit it. I like to pamper Dan."

Verna didn't even crack a smile.

"That's precisely why you get along so well." Verna stabbed the air with one finger for extra emphasis. "He says jump, you ask how high."

"You forget taking care of him and Emma is my job," Amy protested.

"And what about those other women he's dated?" Verna asked. "I seem to recall you telling me that everything was fine until they started making demands."

"Yes, but that was different."

"How?" Verna pressed. "Has he mentioned love?"

Amy rubbed the bridge of her nose between her thumb and forefingers, feeling a headache coming on. "It's just different."

Verna leaned forward and took Amy's hands in hers. This time there was only kindness and caring in her gaze. "Forget the fantasy. Make a life for yourself. Find someone who truly cares about you…and what you want. Before it's too late."

Amy drove home from Verna's, feeling irritable and out of sorts. While she told herself that her aunt didn't know what she was talking about, Verna's comments played on her deepest fears.

Was she crazy to think that Dan could really love her when she'd witnessed firsthand his love for Tess? Had her own desire blinded her to the reality of the situation?

The problem was she couldn't deny that Steven and her aunt had an advantage she didn't. They could step back and make a judgment based on fact, not emotion.

By the time Amy pulled into the garage, she'd convinced herself she'd been foolish to think Dan could ever care for her in a 'til-death-do-us-part kind of way. Hadn't she seen how it had gone with Bree and Melinda? He was in between women and he found her attractive. Period. End of story.

She shut off the ignition, not sure whether to be sad or happy to see Dan's Land Rover in the garage. She needed to end their short-lived relationship. If things went any further, it would be impossible for her to stay.

And she did want to stay. On this subject Verna was wrong. There was no reason she couldn't continue to build her catering business while taking care of Emma and Dan. And regardless of what anyone else thought, Amy could not just walk out of Emma's life. Amy knew what it was like to lose someone you loved. She knew what it was like to feel abandoned. She knew what it was like to feel alone in the world.

But Emma isn't alone. Emma has Dan.

Amy shoved the thought aside. Maybe she *was* staying for herself but there was absolutely no reason she couldn't have a full and complete life of her own *and* care for Emma. But first she had to set some limits on her relationship with Dan.

She walked into the house fully prepared to do just that only to discover he wasn't home. A note on the kitchen told her Emma was spending the weekend with a friend but said nothing of Dan's whereabouts. Amy only knew that with his car in the garage, he had to be close.

Tension knotted her shoulders and the headache that had hovered on the edge of her consciousness at her aunt's house began to pound in her temples. Swallowing a couple of Tylenol, Amy headed upstairs to relax for a few minutes.

After locking the door to her suite of rooms, she stripped off her clothes and padded into the bathroom, the soothing jets of the whirlpool tub calling to her. She wasn't sure how long she relaxed in the scented water, listening to music, but by the time she got out her headache was barely noticeable.

She considered getting dressed and doing a little housework but quickly discarded that notion. After all, this was her day off. So instead, Amy picked up a book to read. Almost randomly, she chose a popular romance and the magic of the book propelled her to her bed, where she spent the next hour propped up against her pillows reading.

She was halfway through the book when the ringing phone jarred her from the pages. After waiting several rings to see if Dan was back and would pick up, Amy grabbed the receiver. "Majors' residence. This is Amy."

"Amy, this is Philippe from Chez Gladines." The confident masculine voice held the faintest hint of a French accent. "How are you this evening?"

"I'm fine." Amy managed to get out the words without stammering. Other than her initial job interview, she hadn't had a lot of contact with Philippe.

"Your pastries are *très magnifique,*" Philippe said. "Very popular with the customers."

Amy relaxed her death grip on the phone. "You called to—"

"I called to offer you a full-time job," Philippe said. "I'd like you to take over all the desserts and pastries at the restaurant."

"But I still have two months left of my trial period," Amy said.

"You have already proven yourself." Philippe's decisive tone brought home the reality of the offer. "Come in on Monday and we'll discuss salary and benefits. If you're interested, that is."

"I am interested." Amy's head spun. Being a full-time chef at a place like Chez Gladines had been a pie-in-the-sky dream. Now the position was being handed to her on a silver platter. The only problem was this job wouldn't work with her nanny position. "I do have another full-time job but I will most certainly consider your offer. I could be there around one on Monday?"

"I'll see you then," Philippe said. "And, Amy—"

"Yes, Philippe?"

"I really hope you take it."

Amy clicked off the phone and sat there, stunned. Several of the waiters had mentioned how well her desserts had been selling, but she'd never thought it would lead to a permanent position.

But what about Dan and Emma? Her heart twisted. Dan paid her to take care of Emma and the house. How could she possibly do both jobs at once? Lots of women do, a tiny voice in her head whispered. Tess had a demanding career and a family. But Tess, Amy reminded herself, was Dan's wife, not an employee.

Amy pressed her fingers against suddenly throbbing temples. Dear God, why did her life have to be so complicated?

She gave herself a sudden shake. This was ridiculous. Tonight was her night off. She refused to ruin the evening by obsessing over the negative. She'd get a bottle of wine, have a couple of glasses to celebrate the offer and finish the book she'd been reading. She'd think about all the implications tomorrow.

Grabbing the chenille robe from the foot of the bed, Amy pulled it on over the boxer shorts and tank top and cinched the belt tight around her. She dropped the book into the pocket. After sliding her feet in a pair of tiger-striped mules, she headed down the stairs.

By the time she reached the main floor, the throbbing at her temples had reached bongo drum proportions. She stopped in the kitchen and found some Advil in the bottom of her purse. Swallowing a couple, she glanced at the clock. She'd give the pills a half hour. If two didn't help, she'd up the dosage to prescription strength.

She pulled a bottle of wine from the rack, hoping

a little Merlot might be just what the doctor ordered. By the time she'd poured herself a glass, the long flight of stairs to her room held little appeal. She decided to stay on the main level and relax in the parlor.

The renovated parlor had terrific ambiance not to mention a chaise lounge and a fireplace. Though the robe Amy had on was thick and fluffy, the air in the house held a definite chill. The thought of basking in the warmth of a gas log suddenly seemed irresistible.

In a matter of minutes she sat on the chaise, a fire burning brightly in the hearth. She had a wineglass in one hand, her book in the other. But Amy found it difficult to concentrate.

Despite her determination, her thoughts drifted to the decisions she faced and she couldn't focus.

Her heart tightened and a few tears slipped down her cheeks. How could she leave Emma? She couldn't love the little girl any more if she was her own daughter. And Dan—how could she tell *him* goodbye?

Darn it, this wasn't fair. To realize one dream, she had to give up another? Or did she? Tess had been a career woman. Would Dan support her?

The pounding in her head increased and despite knowing it would only make things worse, Amy couldn't help herself. She began to cry.

Chapter Thirteen

After walking Emma to her friend's house, Dan stayed to have a beer and admire their recent renovation work. When the football game came on the big screen, it seemed rude *not* to stay and have a beer. But as the sun started to set he realized it was time to head home. Ted invited him to stay for supper but Dan had other plans for the evening.

When he got close to home, a light in the parlor window beckoned and he quickened his pace. He wondered if Amy would be interested in going out tonight. Maybe they could take in a movie. With Steven still gone, she shouldn't have other plans.

His jaw clenched at the thought of the arrogant lawyer but he reminded himself that he was taking care of that situation. By the time Steven returned, Amy would be his fiancée.

Dan pushed open the back door, expecting to find Amy in the kitchen. But that room was empty as was the dining room. He was in the hallway when he heard her. His heart stilled in his chest at the plaintive sound.

He hurried to the parlor. She looked up when he entered the room, hastily brushing aside her tears. Though Dan told himself that if something bad had happened, she'd have called him on his cell phone, fear still gripped him in a stranglehold.

"Is it Emma?" Dan could barely get the words out. How something could happen in the short time it had taken him to walk home, he didn't know. All Dan knew was he'd never seen Amy this shaken. "Did Ted or Abigail call?"

"No." Amy drew a shaky breath and forced a smile. "They didn't."

Relief flowed through him, but then he realized something still had upset Amy. And if it didn't involve his daughter…

Dan's heart softened at the look of distress furrowing her brow. He found himself wanting to kiss and make whatever was bothering her all better. But even after what they'd shared, pulling her into his arms seemed too familiar a gesture. He settled for moving across the room and taking a seat next to her on the chaise. "Tell me what's wrong."

"It's nothing." She smiled. "I just have a lot on my mind."

If not for the fact that she rarely cried, he might have believed her. His mind raced as he tried to figure out what might have upset her. She'd been in good spirits when she'd left the house this morning. His gaze narrowed. "You went to see your aunt."

She looked down at her hands for a moment before lifting her gaze.

"She only wants what's best for me." Amy pressed her fingers against her temple. "Everyone only wants what's best for me."

Dan forced a light tone. "And what is that?"

"It doesn't matter." She closed her eyes briefly and exhaled a ragged breath, then rose to her feet. "My head really hurts. I'm going to bed."

Now that she mentioned it, he could see the lines of strain around her eyes.

Dan stood, put an arm around Amy's shoulder and steered her out in the hall toward the stairs. "Get into bed and I'll bring you some warm milk."

Amy scrunched up her nose.

"You don't like warm milk?"

She shook her head then winced at the movement. "Not so much."

"Come to think of it, neither do I." Dan smiled ruefully. Hot milk had been his mother's "cure for all that ails you." It had been the first thing that had popped into his head. But he decided it was more appropriate for insomnia than for a headache. "How about some aspirin? Extra-strength Tylenol?"

"There's some Advil on the kitchen counter," Amy said, glancing down the long hall. "I could take a couple more."

"I'll bring them up."

Amy turned to him and laid her hand flat against his cheek, her eyes soft and luminous. "Thank you for being so nice to me."

His skin tingled beneath her touch and he was tempted to capture her hand and kiss her palm. But this, he reminded himself, wasn't about *his* wants and needs, it was about making Amy feel better.

"Don't worry about a thing," he said. "That headache is as good as gone."

Amy climbed the stairs, her feet as heavy as lead weights. Crying had brought her headache back with a vengeance. When she reached her room, Amy headed straight for the feather bed. She threw off her robe and slid beneath the covers. But even as she told herself to relax, her mind returned to her dilemma.

She wanted the job but she wanted Dan and Emma, too. She already knew what Aunt Verna and Steven would say. But they didn't understand. Dan wasn't simply her employer, he was her friend. He cared about her. And she cared about him…

"Here you go."

Amy looked up to find Dan standing next to the bed, tray in hand. Instead of just a pill bottle and water, there were two cups of tea and a plate of cheese and crackers.

Placing the tray on a side table, Dan handed her the pills and water.

Amy sat up, popped two tiny tablets into her mouth and washed them down. Although she'd been careful not to move too quickly, the pounding in her head exploded. She winced and brought her fingers to her temples.

"Here." Dan took a seat on the edge of the bed. "Let me do that."

He sat so close Amy could feel the heat from his body. "That's okay. I'm—"

"Stubborn," he interjected, his teasing smile taking the sting from the word. His fingers brushed hers aside and he slowly began to massage her temples.

"Humor me," he said in a low, soothing tone. "I want to help. And I've been told I'm quite good at this sort of thing."

After several minutes, the pounding in her head eased. Some of the relief was due to the pills and the wine. But some was definitely due to Dan's magic fingers. She sighed. "That feels good."

"You're so tense." Dan's brows furrowed. "Let me see if I can get rid of some of this tightness."

His hands moved to her shoulders. Kneading the muscles between his strong fingers, he worked on the knots until she sighed with relief.

When his fingers slid beneath the spaghetti straps of her top to focus on her shoulders, it hit Amy that she was *naked* beneath the shirt.

She shivered.

"Why don't you lie down?" he said. "You can cover up and get warm and I'll massage your neck."

"You don't have to."

Dan placed a finger over her lips, stilling her words. "If you say that one more time—I'm going to have to—"

Kiss you. Amy silently filled in the blank before abruptly turning on her stomach. She found herself oddly disappointed when he pulled the sheet up past her waist.

"Do you have any lotion?" he asked.

"On the dresser."

He was back in a second and, after rubbing the lotion between his palms to warm it, his fingers went to work on her shoulders.

No massage Amy had ever experienced before had affected her in this way. The others had been ad-ministered by strangers, licensed professionals. Not by Dan who made her heart beat faster by just walking into a room.

"If you want, you can rub my back, too," Amy said.

His hands momentarily stilled on her neck and she wasn't sure which of them was more surprised by her boldness.

"Unless you don't want to," she said hurriedly.

"No, that's fine," he said in a casual tone. "Do you want me to do it over the sheet? Or…?"

Amy chewed on her lip. Dare she voice her true preference? Oh, what the heck.

"If you're going to use lotion, it'll have to be skin." Amy kept her tone nonchalant as if they were discussing the night's dinner menu instead of him putting his hands inside her shirt.

"Skin it is." Dan pulled the sheet back to her waist and his hands slid beneath her shirt.

Amy swallowed a gasp.

His hands moved against her skin, slid up her arms, across her shoulders, then down her back. It was the softest, most tantalizing sensation, made more so by the knowledge that it was Dan touching her with such care, such firm strength.

Her nipples tingled and an ache of wanting made her squirm. Each time his fingers traveled down the side of her body, Amy found herself hoping he'd take a detour to the front. But he was a perfect gentleman.

After several minutes Amy was ready to scream with frustration.

He was being kind.

He was being solicitous.

He was driving her crazy.

Amy wanted more, but she wasn't sure if asking for more was wise. After all, there were so many good reasons to remain lying on her stomach pretending this was simply a back rub.

But when he leaned close and pressed a kiss against the back of her neck, she'd had enough. Without giving herself a chance to think twice, Amy flipped over. "I think I need a total body massage in order to completely relax."

It was as bold a statement as she'd ever dared to make but to her relief her cheeks remained cool. Dan's gaze met hers. She could see surprise in his eyes, but there was something else there as well. A spark of hot desire that told her she wasn't the only one who wanted more.

The knowledge made her bolder still. She forced a teasing tone. "Unless you're too tired? Or maybe you have a headache?"

He shot her a wink. "I think I have enough stamina to go the distance."

The distance. Amy's mouth went dry.

"What about *your* headache?"

"Headache?" Amy blinked and realized the throb had disappeared. "All gone."

"Great." Dan leaned close and brushed her lips with his.

The shadows had deepened and the bedside lamp bathed them in a golden glow, creating a private little world, a tiny island of glowing beauty with just the two of them in it.

Dan's lips moved down and he was soon exploring the soft skin behind her ears and down her neck, his mouth open against her, as his hands massaged her shoulders, her arms.

"Does that feel good?" he murmured.

"Oh, yes." She exhaled the words. "But now instead of being cold, I'm hot."

His eyes darkened. "I want you to be comfortable."

Dan hooked the spaghetti strap of her T with one finger. "Less clothes might help."

"How about you?" Amy swallowed past suddenly dry lips. "Aren't you hot?"

Dan didn't answer. Instead he sat up, quickly unbuttoned his shirt and shrugged it off then shot her an expectant gaze.

Without taking her gaze off his muscular chest, Amy yanked her tank top over her head and sent it sailing across the room.

For a long moment Dan simply stared. "You're so beautiful," he said. "I could look at you forever."

"More," she said, although if pressed she couldn't have said whether she wanted him to touch her or say more pretty things.

Every part of her longed for his touch, his caress. Just when she thought she was going to faint with anticipation, he cupped her breasts in his hands, gliding his thumbs over her aroused nipples.

She moaned low and deep, and grasping his hair in her fists, she tugged his head down. He appeared to know instinctively what she wanted, burying his face between the soft fullness of her breasts. His teeth scraped over one perfect swell followed by a slow, wet, luxurious lap of his tongue.

Amy gasped in delight, her fingers biting into the muscles of his upper arms as she arched her back, silently begging him for more.

Opening his mouth wide, he suckled her hard and deep and laved her nipple with the flat of his tongue.

She closed her eyes and gave into the sensations racking her body. Yes, oh yes, this was what she'd longed for. This was what she'd dreamed about.

She couldn't keep still. Her hips lifted, she laced her fingers through his hair, encouraging him as he continued. The world seemed distant, dissolved, and Amy was aware of only the two of them as he gave her the intimacy her body and soul craved.

His fingers closed around the top of her silky boxers, which were on the floor in a matter of seconds.

Amy lifted her gaze, her pulse skittering at the blue fire in his eyes. No man had ever looked at her with such hunger, such desire. But no matter how much he wanted her, it couldn't come close to how much she wanted *him*. She hooked her fingers around his waistband.

"Off," she demanded.

She didn't have to ask twice. His pants and boxers landed in a heap somewhere behind him, and he stood before her, in all his naked glory.

Her eyes widened. Her tongue moistened suddenly dry lips. She knew she was staring but she couldn't help herself. He was so big. Broad shoulders. Large hands. Huge…

"Amy." The single, husky-voiced word sounded faintly like a question.

She wanted to reply, to say his name but she could only open her arms to him. He came to her then, leaning her back against the pillows, the breadth of his shoulders spreading her legs wider. When he pressed his open mouth against the sensitive skin of her inner thigh, Amy nearly jumped off the bed. The sight of his dark head between her legs, the brush of his tongue dampening her flesh brought a deep groan to her throat.

"You smell so good," he whispered, his warm breath caressing her. "Like flowers."

He blazed kisses all the way up her leg, across her belly, then moved away, leaving her quivering with need while he grabbed a tiny foil packet from the wallet in his pants' pocket and readied himself for her.

Amy stilled at the brush of his erection against her. For the first time she felt fear nip at the shimmering edge of arousal. It had been so long. And he was so…magnificent.

He must have sensed her hesitation because he stopped. "If you're not sure…"

She could see his need, his desire, on his stunning face, in his brilliant eyes.

This was Dan, she reminded herself shoving aside any doubts, and she trusted him. She wound her arms tightly around his shoulders and wrapped her legs over his.

"I want you." Amy lifted herself up, moving her hips against his in a sensual rhythm as old as time.

Desire swamped caution as need, raw and wild, returned to consume them both. The urgency built, higher, hotter, then broke fiercely inside her, his name on her lips when she clawed his back and shattered. His hands on her hips, he held her tightly, his thrusts deep and hard, fast. On a groan, he shuddered violently, again and again.

When he stilled, she slid her arms around his neck and drew him close. The weight of his body pressed her into the mattress. Smiling, Amy sank into the softness and brought him with her.

"I'm crushing you," Dan said when he could think again, when he could breathe. His heart was still thundering in his head, his lungs burning.

"No." Amy tightened her hold on him. "Don't move."

Dan couldn't have moved if his life depended on it. No experience had ever left him this spent, this weak. It took all he had to lift his head and gaze down at her.

Her face was flushed, her lashes a damp tangle on her cheeks. As he watched, a single tear slipped free, tracing a silvery path across her temple before disappearing into the caramel-colored softness of her hair.

His heart contracted. "Amy?"

Her lashes lifted slowly.

"Are you okay?" he asked quietly. "Did I hurt you?"

"Yes. No. I—" She lifted an unsteady hand to touch his face. "Thank you."

He grabbed her hand and pressed it against his mouth. "The pleasure was all mine."

"It was incredible," Amy said, still looking dazed.

"If you ever need another back rub…" Dan let his voice trail off and shot her a wicked grin.

Her laughter created all sorts of interesting sensations, none of them having anything to do with humor. Dan groaned, swallowing her gasp as he began to harden inside her.

"Again," he whispered.

Shivering, her hands clinging to his shoulders, Amy gave him what they both wanted.

Chapter Fourteen

Amy woke before dawn, not certain she could move, let alone get out of bed.

The pillow under her head was crooked, half-stuffed under the headboard. The bed was a mess, covers pulled loose and twisted, her plush down comforter on the floor. She had the vague memory of Dan pulling the top sheet over both of them but it now lay pooled at her feet.

Still, she wasn't cold.

Her gaze slid to the man sleeping soundly beside her. He lay sprawled on his stomach, one arm thrown across her body, his hand resting just below her bare breast, fingers open and relaxed.

Dan had been an amazing lover. Tender and gentle

one moment, then lusty and demanding the next. Amy had only been with two other men and with both of them she'd been a passive participant.

But not last night. Her gaze lingered on the thin red lines on his shoulder blades from her fingernails.

Such loss of control wasn't like her. She was quiet. Reserved. And according to her last boyfriend, undersexed. She wasn't the type of woman who left marks of passion on a man's back. Not the sort of woman who ever had moments of passion, for that matter.

Her gaze lingered on Dan's sleeping face. He looked younger in sleep, some indefinable tension gone. She still couldn't believe Dan was here with her. The man she cared for, the man she felt achingly close to, the man she loved…

Amy stilled as the reality washed over her. Despite her best efforts to keep her heart safe, she'd given it to Dan. While Amy desperately wanted to believe he felt as she did, she knew better than to confuse the physical act of making love with the emotional feeling of love.

Yes, it would be very foolish indeed to read too much into what happened last night. For now, just being close would have to be enough.

Amy cuddled up next to Dan and let her eyelids drift shut.

Dan stared at Amy's sleeping form. Last night had blown him away. Though it'd be easy to put what had happened between them down to just great sex, he knew what they'd shared went beyond the mere physical.

There had been a connection between him and Amy. When they'd touched, the trust they had in each other allowed for no reservations, no awkwardness. As the caresses had become more hurried, more desperate, a wealth of unexpected emotion had risen up in him.

Just looking at her now, so innocent, so vulnerable, made him want to pull her close and protect her. No one could take care of her the way he could. No one would be as good to her as he would. No one.

Amy stirred, murmuring something he couldn't understand before snuggling into the pillow. A strand of hair lay curled against her cheek. Dan's fingers itched to tuck it behind her ear. But he knew it wouldn't stop there.

He'd already kept her up half the night and if he stayed in bed much longer, he'd end up waking her so they could make love again. He'd never experienced anyone like Amy before. And he wanted to experience her again. And again. But she looked so peaceful that he didn't have the heart to disturb her. Casting one last regretful glance at his sleeping beauty, Dan retrieved his clothes from the floor and crept out of the room.

Dan normally kept his showers short, but this morning he found himself standing under the warm spray, trying to make sense of his tangled emotions.

He lifted his chin and let the water beat against his face. He could no longer deny it. His feelings for Amy went beyond friendship. While he didn't want to call what he was feeling love, he knew he cared deeply for her. Their lovemaking had made him realize just how empty and hollow his life would be without her in it.

It was time. Time to move forward. To make Amy a permanent part of his life. To formally ask her to marry him.

She wants your love, a tiny voice deep inside niggled. Amy deserves to be with a man who loves her.

Dan shoved the voice aside. Amy deserved to be with the man *she loved.* And all the signs last night said that was him.

His mind returned to the task at hand. Before he could propose he needed a ring. Dan thought for a moment.

Grandmother's engagement ring.

His initial impulse was to discard the notion. But it lingered. Dan had never been quite sure why Gram had left the ring to him. At the time, Tess already had a square-cut diamond solitaire set in glittery platinum, a ring as hip and modern as Tess herself. His grandmother's ring, with its ornate old-world charm and intricate scrollwork, would have been totally wrong for her.

But not for Amy.

Amy was a traditionalist whose jewelry and clothing reflected a kinder, gentler time. Dan's lips curved upward. The diamond had been locked in the parlor safe for almost six years. It was time it saw the light of day.

Sunlight streamed through the windows, warming Amy's face. She rolled over, her outstretched arms finding only an empty bed. Her eyes popped open.

Surely I didn't imagine...

Amy sat up and the covers fell away. The cool air turned her bare skin to gooseflesh. She shivered and pulled the sheet up to her chin, a wry smile tipping her lips. No, last night hadn't been no dream.

She had a sudden memory of looking into the mirror and seeing Dan's naked back, muscles rippling as he moved over her. No, the kisses, the caresses, the unquenchable heat had been very real.

The evening had been a revelation. She'd always respected Dan. She'd always liked Dan. Last night she'd realized she *loved* Dan. Though it sounded goofy— and she'd never say it aloud—when they'd come together, Amy had felt as if she was finally whole.

"Amy?"

She lifted her gaze. The object of her affection stood in the doorway, his face freshly shaven with hair still slightly damp from the shower. He was also...fully clothed.

Disappointment coursed through Amy. It might be broad daylight. They may have just made love only a few hours earlier. But God help her, she wanted him naked and back in her bed.

"I wondered where you'd gone." Her casual tone was at odds with her racing heart.

"There was something I needed to do," he said with a slight smile. His gaze dropped to the sheet now wrapped tightly across her chest.

Amy's nipples hardened. As his gaze lingered, every nerve ending inside her began to buzz. She was tempted to let the sheet drop and see if she could entice him out of those clothes. Somehow, without her quite realizing how it had happened, she'd somehow made the leap from shy prude to wanton woman.

"Mind if I sit down?" he asked in a sexy voice that slid through her like fine wine.

"Not at all." Amy scooted over, letting the sheet drop ever so slightly.

His gaze didn't leave her face.

Get a grip, she scolded herself. Last night was fun and games. Today, it's business as usual.

"Have you thought about what you want for lunch?" Amy tucked the sheet firmly around her. "I've got leftover roast beef and some Swiss—"

Dan closed her lips with his finger. "We can deal with food later."

His gaze grew thoughtful. "I've been thinking about last night. You just didn't seem like yourself."

Amy's blood went cold. If this was about all her loud moans she was going to pull the pillow over her

head and never come up for air. She'd never been
vocal during sex before. But she hadn't been able to
help herself. Not when Dan possessed an uncanny
knack for finding the most sensitive spots on her
body.

"You seemed…distracted," he added.

Distracted? Hardly. From the instant his hand had
settled on her skin, he'd had her full attention. Her
face must have reflected her surprise because Dan
smiled.

"Before the back rub," he clarified. "You'd been
crying."

Amy didn't want to remember what had been on
her mind before she'd lost herself in his touch. But
it all came rushing back. Aunt Verna's blunt comments. And the phone call.

She'd been excited, yet at the same time, worried.
Worried Dan wouldn't be flexible and that she'd be
forced to make a choice she didn't want to make.

While Dan had been supportive of Tess and her
career, Tess had been his *wife*. She was just his
employee. That's why her neck had been tied in
knots. And even now just thinking about the decision
she faced brought the weight back to her shoulders.

"Philippe from Chez Gladines had called," she
said, then stopped. How much should she tell Dan?
And was now really the best time? After all, she
hadn't had a chance to consider the offer and decide
what it was *she* wanted to do.

Obviously misunderstanding the uncertainty in

her eyes, Dan leaned forward and took her hand. "Bad news?"

"Unexpected." Amy sighed. "Confusing."

"They were foolish to let you go." His fingers closed around hers. "I'm not going to make the same mistake."

"I don't think you understand." Amy began, "They didn't—"

"Because I know what a gem you are," Dan continued as if Amy hadn't spoken. "You're a wonderful woman. Smart. Fun. Not to mention incredibly sexy."

His eyes darkened. When he trailed a finger across the top of the sheet she forgot all about Philippe. When he cupped her chin and covered her mouth with his, she forgot everything but him. It was a gentle kiss, a sweet kiss, but Amy was in the mood for naughty, not nice. She grabbed Dan's head and deepened the kiss.

He responded immediately and she reveled in the moist heat and slow, penetrating slide of his tongue. He stroked long and slow, hot and deep, and she kissed him back the same way. Intense and uninhibited.

Just like last night, the room dipped and swayed.

A purr of pleasure rumbled in her throat.

"I can't get enough of you," he whispered against her hair when she pulled away.

Amy caressed her palm along his cheek, skimmed her thumb along his full bottom lip, her gaze riveted to his. "I feel the same way."

"You have to know how much I care for you."

Dan's voice grew husky. "There isn't anything I wouldn't do for you."

Amy's heart pounded. When she spoke, her voice seemed to come from far away. "What are you saying, Dan?"

"Last night gave me hope," he said. "Hope that you cared for me as more than just a friend."

Amy noticed he'd said *care,* not *love.* But then, this was unchartered territory for both of them.

"I do care for you, Dan. Very much." Amy tried not to read too much into his words but she couldn't help but wonder if maybe…just maybe…her dream of happily-ever-after was sitting on the bed with her. "Surely you know I'm not the type of woman to sleep with a guy unless I…care for him."

A look of relief crossed his face. "I was hoping that was the case."

He shifted and reached into his pocket. When he pulled out a tiny velvet box and flipped it open, Amy gasped.

Without missing a beat, Dan slipped off the bed and dropped to one knee. "Amy Logan, would you do me the honor of becoming my wife?"

The room spun wildly. For a second Amy wondered if this was just another one of her vivid daydreams.

She blinked once.

Dan was still there.

She blinked again.

He hadn't moved.

Her heart stuttered at the hope mixed with a healthy dose of uncertainty in his eyes.

Amy hesitated for a moment, wondering what had brought about this unexpected proposal. Unless…their recent closeness had made him realize what her heart had known for so long.

She shifted her gaze to the antique diamond. Love welled up from deep in her heart and spilled past her lips. "Yes, oh, yes, I'll marry you."

Dan smiled broadly and slipped the ring on her finger.

It fit perfectly.

Like it had been made for me.

It was a sign, Amy decided, a sign that she and Dan were meant to be together forever.

She couldn't take her eyes off the ring, *her* ring. She loved the way it sparkled in the light, loved the heavy filigreed work reminiscent of a bygone era. But most of all, she loved the man who'd given it to her.

"It was my grandmother's," he said hurriedly as if disturbed by her intense scrutiny. "If you don't like it—"

"I love it." Amy's fingers curved inward, protecting the ring. "I'll love it forever."

I'll love you forever.

His gaze searched hers. "You really mean that."

Amy's gaze dropped again to the stone then back to his face. Familiar. Known. Increasingly beloved. "Absolutely."

"It looks beautiful on you," he said. "*You* look beautiful."

Amy resisted the urge to laugh out loud. She couldn't remember the last time she'd been so happy. "This is a wonderful day."

"You're right." Dan's hand closed over hers. "I can't wait to tell Emma the news."

Amy giggled from sheer joy. "She'll be an adorable flower girl."

A look of surprise crossed Dan's face. "You want a big wedding?"

Amy hesitated. Like most women, from the time she'd been a little girl, she'd just assumed she'd have a wedding with all the trimmings. But she'd picked up on the reservation in Dan's tone and she wanted him to feel free to voice his preferences.

"I'm not sure," Amy said. "I guess I never thought much about it."

"Big or small, it's up to you." Dan brought her hand to his lips and nibbled on her fingers. "As long as it doesn't take too long to plan. I can't wait for you to be my wife."

An overwhelming feeling of love washed over Amy. "I can't wait for you to be my husband."

Dan smiled. "Want to go out and celebrate?"

"I'd love to celebrate," Amy said. "But we don't need to go out."

Her fingers reached for the buttons on his shirt. "We can do that just fine right here."

Chapter Fifteen

Amy took a sip of wine and stared at her hand. The light in the Italian restaurant might not be the best but the stone still glittered nicely. She lifted her gaze to find Dan staring with an indulgent smile.

"You have the most beautiful eyes," he said. "They sparkle when you look at the ring."

Heat rose up Amy's neck and she wasn't sure how to respond. He probably thought she was being ridiculous, going all gaga over a diamond. But it wasn't only the ring, it was the sentiment behind it that made her all soft and mushy inside.

"I didn't mean to embarrass you." Dan reached across the table and took her hand. "I'm happy you're so excited. I'm excited, too. We're going to have a great marriage."

The bustle of the popular eatery faded and Amy found herself drowning in the deep blue of Dan's eyes. Of course they would have a great marriage. With love as its foundation...

Her thoughts stilled. When they'd made love, when he'd proposed, when they'd hopped into bed again to celebrate, not one "I love you" had crossed his lips. Amy knew that for a fact since she'd been waiting for him to seal their union with the words. Still, how could they have connected so profoundly in bed if *love* wasn't at the foundation of their relationship?

"Penny for your thoughts." His thumb caressed the top of her hand.

Guilt coursed through her. This was supposed to be a celebration and here she was ruining it by worrying about who was going to say those three little words first.

"Tell me," Dan said.

Amy wasn't about to demand he declare his feelings. But there *was* still some unfinished business to discuss.

"I was just thinking about my conversation with Philippe."

When Amy had spoken with Philippe, she'd feared she'd have to choose between the job and her life with Dan and Emma. Now, she thought happily, she could have it all.

Dan released her hand and took a sip of wine. "Don't give him a second thought. It's his loss."

"You don't understand." Amy couldn't keep the note of pride from her voice. "Philippe offered me a full-time position. My desserts have been a big hit and he asked me to be in charge of all desserts."

"Wow." Dan raked a hand through his hair and sat back, appearing more stunned than pleased by the news. "I don't know what to say."

"How about 'congratulations'?" Disappointment at his lack of enthusiasm made her voice sharper than she'd intended. "Philippe could have offered this position to a dozen other chefs."

"I'm sorry. Congratulations." His tone was sincere and apologetic and her anger eased. "I'm not surprised they want you. You're a great chef."

Amy's heart warmed at the praise and she felt her irritation melt away. "Thank you, Dan."

He forked a piece of ravioli and brought it to his mouth. "What did he say when you told him you couldn't do it?"

Amy nearly choked on her orzo. She took a sip of water and straightened in her seat, taking a moment to compose herself before responding.

"You don't want me to take it?" Disappointment ran thick and heavy through her voice. Right or wrong, not having him share in the joy took some of the luster off the offer.

"Are you really considering it?"

She ignored the shock and disbelief in his voice and nodded.

Dan's eyes grew shuttered. "You need to do what's best for you."

"No." Amy leaned forward and rested her forearms on the table. "This isn't just about me anymore. When you get married, the other person's happiness should be as important as your own. You assumed I wouldn't take the job. I need to know what your reservations are."

Dan wiped the corners of his mouth with the tip of his linen napkin, his expression still guarded. "Call me selfish but I like having you around. Since Emma is in school all day, I know you've had more free time. But after we're married, I was hoping we could start working on giving Emma a couple of brothers or sisters—"

He stopped and Amy realized she must look as startled as she felt. "Unless you don't want children. We've never discussed it but I know how much you like kids. I just assumed you'd want a baby or two..."

Amy's breath caught in her throat. Dan wanted her to have his baby. Her hand moved to her flat belly. What would it be like, Amy wondered, to have Dan's baby? Of course last night he'd taken precautions to ensure that wouldn't happen, but she couldn't imagine anything more wonderful than to have a child grow out of the love they shared.

He really *did* love her. A lump rose in Amy's throat. Tears filled her eyes.

"Hey." He grabbed her hand. "If you don't want—"

"I'd love to have a baby." Her voice trembled with emotion. "Actually, I want lots of babies. A whole houseful."

"Good," he said and she could hear the relief in his voice. "That's settled."

In her happy fog, it took a second for Amy to realize that not only had she agreed to have a baby, somehow she'd agreed to give up her career. A momentary pang hit her. Even if she got pregnant right away, it'd be almost a year until a baby came. During that time she could get some great experience at Chez Gladines. Not to mention contacts that could be invaluable if she chose to continue with her own catering business.

"Want to go home and make a baby tonight?" Dan's deep voice broke through her fog.

Startled, she glanced up. The heat of his gaze burned her skin and set a fire smoldering deep inside.

"We're not married yet," Amy said. Getting pregnant would be another, even bigger commitment. Though at the moment, hopping into bed and making a baby was just what she wanted to do.

"Not a problem," Dan said. "We can pick up our license tomorrow and get married the next. Unless," he added, almost as an afterthought, "you want a big wedding?"

The way he said the words made it clear that wouldn't be his preference. While part of her wanted a big wedding with the long white dress, the sensible side said she was being foolish. Other than Aunt Verna she had no family and only a handful of friends.

"Not big," Amy said. "But I do want to get married in a church and have a small reception."

"We can get the license this week," he said. "And be married by the weekend."

Amy's head spun, barely able to fathom the thought that by this time next week she could be Dan's *wife*.

"Would you two care for dessert?" The waiter stood tableside, pad in hand and pencil poised.

Amy glanced at Dan. "I don't care for any."

"None for me, either," Dan said. "I'll wait until we get home."

Amy waited until the waiter left before casting a curious glance at Dan. "The chocolate cake is all gone. You ate the last of it yesterday."

"That wasn't the dessert I was thinking of," Dan said. His gaze dropped to her lips, then downward to linger on her breasts before returning to her eyes.

The rush of hunger that surged through Amy surprised her with its intensity. They'd made love several times during the night and again this morning. But instead of being satiated, her desire for him only seemed to grow.

"I'm hungry, too," Amy said. "Mind if I join you?"

Dan's smile widened and a devilish glint filled his eyes. "I wouldn't have it any other way."

* * *

The next morning, they made love one more time knowing it would be the last time until after the wedding. Once Emma returned from her friend's house, Dan would stay in his room and Amy would stay in hers.

After they dressed, Amy started toward the door, already planning what she was going to make for lunch, when Dan grabbed her hand.

"Not so fast," he said with a smile. "How about we walk down to Bagels and Jam? You can get one of those chocolate chip scones you like so much and I can sit and admire your beauty under the fluorescent lights."

Amy laughed at the absurd compliment, but she didn't refute the words because when she was with Dan she *felt* beautiful.

"It'll be like a date," she said lightly.

His hand cupped her cheek and his lips met hers for a warm, sweet kiss. "A date with my almost-wife."

Amy flushed with pleasure. He threw that word around as if he loved the sound of it as much as she did. Today, they'd start letting people know. She'd call Aunt Verna. Dan would call his mother and Tess's parents. Then it would be official.

As they left the house and strolled down the leaf-strewn sidewalk, contentment wrapped itself around Amy like a favorite coat. The temperature hovered in the mid-forties and the sun shone warm against her face. Even the breeze held some warmth.

Walking down the street with her hand nestled in Dan's, happiness welled inside her. Amy wanted to whistle. If she'd been a better singer she might have burst into song.

My cup runneth over.

She'd never truly understood those words before now. Impulsively Amy stopped and pulled Dan to her. She wrapped her arms around him and pressed a long, lingering kiss against his lips.

"Wow," he said, a broad grin splitting his face. "What was that for?"

"I'm so happy," Amy said.

Dan trailed a finger down her cheek. "I feel the same way."

He took her hand and they continued down the street.

"You know what's crazy?" Amy said, after they'd gone another block. She didn't wait for an answer since the question was strictly rhetorical. "When people used to talk about finding their soul mate, I thought it was corny. Now I understand. That's exactly how I feel about you."

Dan's fingers tightened around hers but he didn't have a chance to speak because the bagel shop loomed and he gallantly stepped forward to open the door for a woman in front of them.

The woman, a statuesque brunette with sprinkles of gray in her hair, looked back. Instead of moving through the doorway, she paused. Her lips curved up into a broad smile.

"Why, Dan Major, what a surprise." The woman shot him an exaggerated wink. "We're going to have to stop meeting like this."

Beside her, Amy felt Dan stiffen but his smile was warm. "How nice to see you again."

Amy had met most of Dan's friends but this woman wasn't the least bit familiar. She stood beside Dan, patiently waiting for an introduction. While Dan normally had excellent manners, he made no attempt to introduce her. It suddenly hit Amy that he must have forgotten the woman's name.

"Hello," Amy said pleasantly, holding out her hand. "I'm Amy Logan."

"I'm sorry." Dan quickly recovered. "Amy, this is Angela Bartgate. She used to be a neighbor."

"Pleased to meet you, Amy." Angela took Amy's outstretched hand and shook it, her smile open and friendly.

A gust of wind blew Amy's hair into her face. When Amy reached up with her free hand to push the wayward strands back, Angela gasped.

"What a stunning ring," the woman said.

Amy proudly held out her hand. The stone shot sparks of color in the sunlight. "It originally belonged to Dan's grandmother."

"It's lovely." Angela's gaze shifted from Amy to Dan before returning to Amy. "I must say this is quite a surprise. Dan and I ran into each other yesterday morning and he didn't say a word about being engaged."

Amy laughed. "That's because he hadn't popped the question yet."

"Soon you'll be newlyweds." Angela's eyes softened. "I remember when my husband and I were first married…"

Angela began to reminisce and somehow—Amy wasn't quite sure how—she and Dan found themselves sitting with Angela.

Normally quite social, Dan seemed unusually quiet. Or maybe it was because Angela kept asking questions and Amy kept answering. By the time Amy finished her scone, she figured Angela probably knew as much about her as her closest friends.

Every so often Dan would throw out a comment, some anecdote about something they'd shared and Amy had to resist the urge to pinch herself to make sure this was real.

Dan glanced at his watch. "We're going to have to get going. I told Ted we'd pick up Emma."

He'd barely finished speaking when his phone rang. Dan pulled it from his pocket and glanced at the readout.

"I need to take this." He rose to his feet. "If you'll excuse me…"

Dan moved to the far end of the shop where there were more empty tables and less chatter. Amy's eyes weren't the only ones that followed him. She caught several women staring. Women always noticed Dan.

Yet, he chose me.

Amy still couldn't believe it. He could have had almost any woman.

"You love him."

Amy pulled her thoughts back and looked up to find Angela's gaze on her. She thought about denying it, but decided she was being ridiculous. Dan was her fiancé. Love was supposed to be part of the equation.

"I do love him," Amy said. "It took me a while to realize it but I think I've loved him for a long time."

A thoughtful look crossed Angela's face. "He loves you, too."

"What makes you so sure?" Amy's lighthearted tone was at odds with her rapidly beating heart. Somehow she even managed to throw in a little laugh. "Other than this ring on my finger, of course."

"The way he looks at you," Angela said. "My husband, Tom, used to look at me that same way."

A warm rush of pleasure washed over Amy, quieting her fears.

Angela shook her head. "I can't believe how much that man had me fooled."

"Your husband?"

"No, your fiancé," Angela said. "Yesterday when we talked Dan had me actually believing his next marriage would be based on practicality, not love. And now, here he shows up madly in love and engaged."

Amy swallowed hard past the sudden lump in her throat. *Practicality?* Had Dan just been playing a part for Angela? Or was that how he truly felt?

Angela took both of Amy's hands in hers. "I'm so very, very happy for you both."

Amy's only response was a wan smile.

Very, very happy?

That's the way she should feel. Instead, Amy had never felt worse.

Chapter Sixteen

When Dan had returned from his phone call and told Amy Jake was coming over, she turned quiet and solemn. As they walked home, she scarcely spoke. He wondered if she was upset that he hadn't talked much around Angela. The truth of the matter was he felt awkward after his previous conversation with the woman. Not to mention he didn't want to give Angela a chance to bring up what they'd discussed.

Or she could be upset because he'd left her to talk to Jake. She'd seemed in good spirits up to that point.

He took her hand, surprised to find her fingers ice cold. "I didn't mean for us to get stuck spending all that time with Angela."

"That's okay," Amy said, not looking at him. "She's a nice woman."

A sense of unease crept up Dan's spine. Something wasn't right but he couldn't put his finger on what.

"Jake won't stay long," Dan said. He'd tried to tell his friend today wasn't good, but as usual Jake didn't listen. "He has a problem with a project he's working on that supposedly needs immediate resolution."

"I've been thinking," Amy said slowly, keeping her gaze focused straight ahead. "It might be better if we didn't tell any more people about the engagement. Not just yet."

"Why would we want to do that?" he asked slowly. Now that Amy had agreed to marry him, he didn't want her to change her mind.

Amy lifted a shoulder in a shrug. "Everything has moved along pretty fast," Amy said, sounding incredibly weary. "It might be good to slow things down a bit."

Red flags popped up in Dan's head. He didn't want to read too much into what she was saying. But between her body language and her words, he had the definite impression she was getting cold feet.

"Is it—" he took a deep breath and plunged ahead "—that you're not sure you want to marry me?"

He cast a sideways glance, surprised to discover Amy wasn't at his side. He spun on his heel and found her standing in the middle of the sidewalk.

"This isn't about me." Amy's voice was so low he could barely hear her. "It's about you."

"Me?" Dan's heart beat like a hammer in his chest. "What about me?"

"Angela said when you two talked before she'd gotten the impression if you did marry again it would be because of practicality, not love." Even though the day was warm, Amy crossed her arms over her chest as if she were cold. "Is that why you're marrying me, Dan? Because I'm quick and convenient?"

Ah, now he understood.

Amy did a good job keeping the pain from her voice but Dan knew her too well to be fooled. Angela's words had hurt her. Dan clenched his jaw. Next time he saw the woman he'd let her know what he thought of her meddling.

"For your information Angela brought up the topic of marrying for companionship, not love," Dan said. "I already *have* friends and companions. I don't need to marry to have that."

Amy's gaze searched his. Whatever she saw there must have satisfied her because she smiled and didn't object when he took her hand.

But as they walked home Dan couldn't help but wonder if she'd noticed he hadn't fully answered her question.

He still hadn't said he loved her.

Amy listened to Emma's chatter in the car with half an ear. When Jake had arrived, Amy had volunteered to pick up Emma. She'd planned to walk to the Martins's house knowing that would give her even more time alone, more time to think. But the wind had picked up and the air had taken on a decided chill.

When Amy had pulled into the Martins's driveway she'd taken off the ring before getting out of the car. While Dan's comments on their walk home had partially allayed her fears, she hadn't wanted to get the girl's hopes up. Not until she was absolutely sure Dan was marrying her out of love, not practicality.

She loved Emma too much to cause her pain.

But Dan loves Emma, too.

Not to mention, he wants us to start a family. A man wouldn't do that with someone he didn't love, someone he considered only a companion.

"Are you going to read to me tonight, Amy?" Emma asked.

Amy blinked and shifted her gaze to Emma. "Of course I am. How far did you get last night?"

The *Santa Paws* books were above Emma's reading level but perfect for reading to her. On Thursday night they'd finished the first book in the series and Emma had taken the second, *Santa Paws Returns*, with her to her friend's house.

A look of disappointment crossed Emma's face. "Nina's mother didn't have time."

It didn't surprise Amy. Abigail Martin had been one of Tess's closest friends. She was a career woman. Very nice, just not very child oriented.

"Well, I must say that's good news," Amy said.

Emma looked quizzical.

Amy shot her a wink. "I won't need to catch up on what I missed."

The giggle that escaped from Emma's lips made Amy smile. Her heart swelled with love. If she and Dan did marry, she'd not only be Dan's wife, she'd be Emma's mother. Stepmother, she corrected herself. But she didn't feel like a step-anything. She couldn't love Emma more if the little girl was her own.

For a second Amy was tempted to open her purse, pull out the ring and put it on...

"Amy." Emma squirmed in her seat. "Can you unlock the door? Rehn is on her porch and I want to say hi."

Amy looked up with a start and realized they were in front of their house. Rehn, the little girl who lived next door, was outside helping her mother put up holiday decorations. Pulling to a stop into the driveway, Amy unlocked the car door.

"Put up your hood." Amy's tone brooked no argument. "And I want you in the house in five minutes. That'll give you plenty of time to say hello. Understand?"

Emma nodded, opened the car door and slid out.

Amy waved to Rehn and her mother before pulling into the garage. Rehn's mother, Margaret, had a life Amy envied. A rewarding career. Three beautiful children. *And* a loving husband.

Yes, Margaret had it all. Just like Amy would have if she married Dan.

Amy pulled the ring from her purse and put it on.

She'd been foolish to doubt Dan. Her life was on the upswing and the way she looked at it, it could only get better.

Dan glanced at the clock on the wall and wondered when Jake was going to leave. Amy and Emma should be back any minute and he wanted his friend gone.

But instead of getting up to leave, Jake leaned back in his chair as if he had all the time in the world. "So how *is* our favorite nanny? Are we going to be hearing wedding bells soon?"

Dan didn't really want to discuss his engagement with Jake but he certainly didn't want him hearing it from someone else and jumping to all the wrong conclusions.

"As a matter of fact, yes," Dan said after a long pause. "I asked Amy to marry me last night."

Amy paused in the hallway just outside the dining room. She'd seen Jake's car in the driveway and planned to slip up the backstairs but when she heard her name, she couldn't help herself from eavesdropping. She'd always had a curious streak and she couldn't wait to hear what Dan would say. Would he tell Jake he loved her?

Amy held her breath.

"Did she accept?" Jake asked.

"She did."

Amy smiled at the satisfaction in Dan's voice.

"Way to go, buddy," Jake said. "I didn't think you'd pull it off."

Amy pulled her brows together. Pull what off?

"When you said you were going to make her fall in love with you, I wasn't sure you could do it," Jake continued. "But you were determined."

"Jake—" Dan began.

"'Course you had a lot riding on this," Jake said. "Those in-laws of yours won't have a snowball's chance in hell of getting Emma now if anything happens to you. Especially if you have Amy adopt her."

Amy's heart pounded. Her knees went weak. She placed a hand against the wall to steady herself. The proposal had all been part of a plan? A scheme?

"It's not about that—" Dan said.

"'Course not," Jake interrupted with a sardonic laugh. "Like I told you before, for the price of a ring and marriage license you get a nanny, a housekeeper and someone to warm your bed. I'm just happy you finally listened. Say, what's she like in the sack? Any good?"

Dan murmured something Amy couldn't hear. But it didn't matter. She'd heard enough. Amy choked back a sob, remembering Angela's words about Dan's motives for marriage. The woman had been right the first time.

Dan's proposal didn't have a thing to do with love.

Making it through the rest of the day took every ounce of Amy's strength. If this just involved her and

Dan, she'd have packed her bags, thrown the ring in his face and walked out without looking back. But because of Emma, Amy pretended she hadn't overheard Dan's conversation with Jake.

She plastered a smile on her face, made dinner and ignored Dan's teasing comments and flirtatious looks. When it came time for Emma's bedtime, she asked Dan if she could put Emma to bed herself. By the pleased look in his eye, she knew he thought she was planning to discuss their engagement with the little girl. Amy saw no reason to correct him.

Emma begged her to read an extra chapter and instead of just one, Amy read three. She savored every moment knowing this was the last time she and Emma would share such closeness.

As she read, Amy's eyes filled with tears. When Emma noticed, Amy blamed it on the story. Finally Amy closed the book. She could no longer delay the inevitable. She shut her eyes for a moment and prayed for the right words. Words that would convey to Emma how much she was loved. Words that would help the child to understand that none of this was her fault.

"Emma." Amy cleared her throat and clutched her hands together to still their trembling. She did her best to inject some excitement into her voice. "I got some fabulous news today."

Emma tilted her head. Despite the late hour her eyes were bright and inquisitive. "You did?"

"Mmm-hmm." Amy forced a smile to her face. "The restaurant offered me a full-time position."

"That's good," Emma said. "Right?"

"Very good." The tightness in Amy's chest made it difficult to speak. She leaned forward, brushing Emma's silky hair back from her sweet face. "Unfortunately it's going to take a lot of my time."

"I'll help," Emma said. "I'm a good helper."

Amy's heart clenched. "Yes, you are."

Damn Dan and his misguided attempt to protect his little girl.

Amy drew a ragged breath. This wasn't going at all the way she hoped. She tried a different tactic. "You remember my aunt Verna?"

Emma nodded. "She gave me your stinky."

Startled, Amy sat back. "Stinky?"

"It goes down the steps."

"Oh, you mean *Slinky*." Her aunt had won the girl over with that gift. "Anyway." Amy took a deep breath. "Aunt Verna has a new house and she wants me to live with her."

Emma's tiny brow furrowed. "But you live here."

At that moment, Amy would have given anything to go back to the way it used to be—when Dan was only her employer and not her lover, when life was simple and uncomplicated. How had she let her own desire blind her to what was really important?

"I know. But my aunt needs me." Amy took Emma's hand. "But I'll be around so much you won't even have a chance to miss me."

Tears welled up in Emma's blue eyes. "I don't want you to leave."

Amy swallowed past the lump in her throat. "We'll see each other all the time. I promise."

"I love you." Emma's voice trembled.

"I love you, too, princess." Amy brushed her tears away with the back of her hand. "That will never change."

"Promise?"

Amy wanted to sob at the trust in the little girl's eyes.

"I promise. I'll always be in your heart," Amy said. "And you'll always be in mine."

She bent over and kissed the little girl's forehead, her own tears mingling with Emma's. She sat at the bedside for the longest time, stroking the child's hair and murmuring words of reassurance until Emma drifted off to sleep.

If there was a way she could stay and retain her dignity, Amy would do it for the sake of Emma. But Emma deserved a better role model than a woman who'd let a man use her.

Amy deserved better, too. That's why, after she told Dan just what she thought of him and his deception, she was walking out the door.

Dan leaned back in his favorite chair, his fingers laced behind his head. He hoped he'd read all the signs correctly and that Amy was upstairs now telling Emma about the engagement.

While he'd thought they'd tell Emma together, when Amy said she wanted to tuck in Emma alone, he didn't protest. Amy had always been very sen-

sitive to Emma's feelings, and if *she* felt broach-
ing the subject one-on-one was best, he'd defer to
her judgment.

He'd never have been able to do that with Tess.
Children to her were mysterious creatures. She'd
loved Emma to death but she'd never understood
Emma's sensitive nature. Amy, on the other hand,
knew just how to handle the little girl, probably
because she and Emma were so much alike.

Footsteps sounded on the stairs and Dan's pulse
quickened. *Let the celebration begin.* He knew Amy
wouldn't sleep with him, not with Emma in the
house. But he might be able to steal a kiss or two…

The door to the parlor opened and Dan stood, a
welcoming smile already on his lips. But his smile
faded at Amy's tear-streaked face. It was obvious by
the bleak look in Amy's eyes that Emma hadn't taken
the news well.

Dan hurried across the room, knowing whatever
objections Emma had could be easily dealt with.
The last thing he wanted was for Amy to be discour-
aged.

"She'll come around." Dan reached for Amy, surprised when she jerked away. For Amy to be this
upset, Emma must have pitched an all-out fit. "I'll
talk to her."

"I think you better," Amy said, her voice cool and
measured. "But first *we* need to talk."

Dan wanted to pull her into his arms and
reassure her that this would all work out, but her

stiff body posture and crossed arms clearly said "hands off."

"I'm moving out," Amy said. "I know an older woman who's in between assignments who'll be happy to help you out while you look for someone permanent."

Dan's overstressed mind fought to make sense of what she was saying.

"Move out?" He pulled his brows together in puzzlement. "You mean until after the wedding?"

"There's not going to be a wedding," Amy said flatly.

Now she was talking crazy. Emma loved Amy. Whatever Emma had said to upset Amy, she couldn't have meant. "What did Emma say?"

"This doesn't have anything to do with her." Amy's voice rose. "It's about you and why you want to marry me."

Dan's blood turned to ice.

She'd overheard his conversation with Jake. That had to be the explanation. Dan tried to remember what Jake had said—and what he'd said—but, at the moment, his rioting emotions seemed to be short-circuiting his brain.

"I know about Emma's grandparents and your fear that if anything happened to you they might get custody," she said when he remained silent.

"That wasn't why I asked you to marry me." The words tumbled from his lips. "I admit that may have started me thinking about marriage, but that isn't why I asked you."

She opened her mouth, then shut it, the momentary indecision giving him hope. He gestured to the sofa. "Why don't we sit down and talk?"

But Amy didn't even glance in the sofa's direction. "I just have one question."

"Anything." He found himself encouraged by the continuing dialogue. If he could just keep her here and talking, he knew they could work things out.

"Do you love me, Dan?" Amy's gaze met his. "Not as a friend, but the way a man should love a woman he wants to marry."

Dan paused and tried to convince himself that he could say yes and have it not be a lie. He did care for Amy and compared to some of his friends, his feelings went far beyond what they appeared to feel for their wives.

Dan opened his mouth but Amy spoke first. "The way you loved Tess."

Damn.

Why did she have to bring up Tess? What he'd felt for his wife had been a once-in-a-lifetime thing.

"Amy, I—" Dan reached out to her, then let his hand drop. "You know how I felt about Tess."

A sad little smile touched Amy's lips. "I want that, too. I want someone who's crazy about me. Someone who can't live without me."

Her lips began to tremble. Swallowing a sob, Amy turned on her heel and ran down the hall.

"Don't go. Please." Dan hurried after her, his heart in his throat. His panic increased when he saw her bags sitting on the kitchen floor. "We can make this work."

"We could." Amy turned toward him, her eyes reflecting her pain. "But we're not. I'm not going to spend my life being second best to a dead woman."

"You're not—" He stopped himself.

"I have dreams, too," Amy said. "Things that are important to me."

"What are you talking about?"

"The job at Chez Gladines." Amy lifted her chin. "Did you even once stop to ask me what *I* wanted to do, what *I* thought would be best?"

The accusatory tone took Dan by surprise. His temper surged.

"I thought getting married was what you wanted." Hurt mingled with his anger. "I thought you liked taking care of our home and being with me. But you're just like Tess. Not content to be a wife and mother. Always wanting more."

The words came from his lips, but Dan couldn't believe he'd said them. Couldn't believe he'd *thought* them.

"I do want more." Amy met his gaze. "I want your love. I want your support. I don't have either. That's why the engagement's off."

Chapter Seventeen

Amy hadn't raised her voice above a normal conversational level but tension hung thick in the air. Though she'd done a good job of keeping her composure, Amy was a quivering mass of nerves inside.

She couldn't imagine walking out of the house that had been her home for the past three years. She couldn't imagine leaving Emma. And she couldn't imagine leaving Dan. Or at least the Dan she thought she loved. But she couldn't stay now. Her heart hardened against the pain. She'd respected Dan. She'd trusted him. It only made his betrayal the harder to bear.

"We can work this out." Dan shoved his hands in his pockets and rocked back on his heels.

Amy sighed. "How, Dan? Are you going to make yourself love me?"

After what he'd done, after what he'd left unsaid, pulling the ring off her finger and handing it to him should have been easy. But still she hesitated.

"I was afraid if anything happened to me, Tess's parents would fight for custody." A hint of desperation filled Dan's voice. "You know what they're like."

"I thought I was in your will as her guardian?"

"You are," Dan said. "But Gwen made it clear that she'd never let a nonrelative raise Emma."

"I have to hand it to you. Your plan almost worked." Slipping off the ring, Amy held it out to him. "Take it."

"I don't want it." He lifted his chin. "I gave it to you."

Amy glanced at the clock on the kitchen wall. Steven should be here any minute to pick her up. Not that she was rushing because of that. If she thought the wall between them could be scaled by simply talking, she'd stay all night.

But Dan didn't love her. There was nothing to discuss.

Amy placed the ring on the counter, then turned to Dan. "I left Aunt Verna's address, as well as the name of the woman I mentioned, on the dresser in my room. You can send my last paycheck to Verna's. I'll be staying with her until I find a place of my own."

Before the last of the words had left her mouth, Dan

was beside her, wrapping his arms around her, pulling her close. For a second Amy just stood there, absorbing the warmth from his body, breathing in the familiar spicy scent of his cologne, feeling his strength.

"I don't want you to leave." Dan whispered against her hair. "You're my best friend. Can't we build on that?"

A horn honked, but when Amy tried to slip from Dan's embrace, his arms remained tightly locked around her.

"It's too late," Amy said, her voice hardly above a whisper. "You know as well as I do that we can't go back to the way it was before."

Dan stood motionless, his heart beating a rapid rhythm against her. "What about Emma?"

Amy hesitated. A clean break might be the easiest for her but she knew that wouldn't be the best for Emma.

"I'd like to continue to be a part of her life," Amy said, the words coming out in a rush. "She never knew things had gotten…more intense between you and me…so it shouldn't be awkward. That is, if you don't mind."

"I'd like that." Dan cleared his throat. "She's going to miss you."

He loosened his hold and Amy stepped back.

"I know," Amy said. "But continuing to live here would never work."

A horn sounded again and Dan swore. "Who is making all that noise?"

"Steven."

Dan's gaze narrowed.

"I called him." Amy lifted her chin. "He's giving me a ride to my aunt's house."

She'd tried to reach Verna, but the call had gone straight to the recorder. Amy didn't want to spend another night under Dan's roof. If Verna wasn't home when she got there, she'd have Steven drop her at a motel.

"You didn't need to call him." A tiny muscle jumped in Dan's jaw. "You have the Saturn."

"You bought the car for Emma's nanny," Amy pointed out. "You'll need it for the woman who takes my place."

Dan's gaze met hers. "No one will ever take your place."

Amy didn't bother answering. Dan may not want to hire another nanny but he would. With his work commitments he couldn't take care of Emma by himself. So, he'd do what he had to do.

And she'd do the same. By walking out the door.

As they sat at the stoplight just down the street from Dan's house, Amy sensed Steven's gaze on her. Instead of looking in his direction, she kept her head back and her eyes half shut.

She knew it was rude but she didn't feel much like talking. Her emotions were too raw, too close to the surface.

When she'd called and asked Steven for a ride

he'd said yes without asking any questions. She'd known he was curious, but thankfully too polite to probe. Unfortunately Dan standing in the doorway watching them load the bags in the car appeared to have pushed his curiosity to the breaking point.

"What happened?" Steven asked. "What made you move out?"

Heaving a resigned sigh Amy opened her eyes and turned to face Steven. She owed him some sort of explanation. After all, he'd just gotten back into town, yet he'd dropped everything to pick her up.

"I have a new job," Amy said, forcing a smile and trying to drum up some enthusiasm. "Chez Gladines wants me full-time."

A startled look crossed Steven's face and she could tell it wasn't the answer he'd expected. Still, he quickly rallied, his lips curving up into a broad smile. "Congratulations. That's fabulous news."

Amy shifted her gaze, finding his joyousness almost painful. She picked at a loose thread on her coat. "Yes, I guess it is."

His brows drew together in puzzlement. "You don't seem very excited."

"It's a lot of responsibility," Amy said. "I'll be in charge of all the desserts, not just pastries."

She'd never doubted herself before but the experience with Dan had left her feeling unsettled.

"You'll do a great job." As if he could read her mind, Steven reached over and gave her hand a squeeze. "I knew it was just a matter of time. Once they got a taste of your talent, how could they not want more?"

His generous words acted as a soothing balm on her wounded spirit. Steven was such a great guy. He had so much to offer a woman. Life would be so much easier if only she could love him instead of Dan. Amy sighed.

"You're the best," Amy said. "Anyone ever tell you that?"

"Every day," Steven said, shooting her a wink before his gaze turned speculative. "How did Dan take the news?"

"Not well," Amy said. It was an understatement but she didn't feel like elaborating.

"Did he give you an ultimatum?" Steven probed. "Is that why you moved out in the middle of the night?"

Amy shrugged. "You know Dan. Everything has to be his way."

It wasn't completely true or for that matter, particularly fair. If Amy were feeling generous, she'd correct the mistaken impression. But she wasn't feeling kind *or* generous.

"It must have been hard to realize your dreams mattered so little," Steven said. "I know how much you like him."

Amy stared out the passenger window into the inky darkness. Tonight she'd been forced to face facts. To toss aside her rose-colored glasses and see Dan for who he was and not how she wished he could be.

A wave of sadness washed over Amy. The truth was Dan didn't love her. Heck, he probably didn't even like her all that much. Everything he'd done, everything he'd said, had been a means to an end.

Her heart hardened.

"I used to like Dan," Amy said finally. She closed her eyes and leaned back against the seat. "Not anymore."

"Daddy, is Amy coming home today?"

Dan's hand paused on the can of green beans. Pain stabbed him and the loneliness he'd fought to contain returned full force. He turned to find Emma staring at him over the top of the grocery cart.

"No." He kept his tone matter-of-fact. "Not today."

It had been four long weeks since Amy had moved out and the house seemed empty without her. Every day, Emma asked if Amy was coming home. At first, the question prompted long discussions. He'd emphasize that Amy still loved her and would be seeing her regularly. But she kept asking. After a while Dan just started saying no, not today.

Usually Emma went on to talk about Amy. But today, Dan wasn't in the mood to listen to his daughter go on and on about how wonderful Amy was.

The last time she'd stopped over to take Emma to the children's museum, she'd *looked* wonderful. Her hair had been layered, giving it a stylish windblown appearance and the coat she'd been wearing had been one of those fur-trimmed ones that was all the rage.

To his critical eye she'd looked thinner and he wondered if she'd been eating properly. Or maybe she'd been sick. But there'd been no time to ask because she'd whisked Emma out of the house without giving him a chance to say much more than hello and goodbye.

"…and Steven."

He blinked, the can of green beans still in his hand. "What did you say?"

"I climbed on the fire engine at the children's museum," Emma said. "And then Amy and Steven got me ice cream."

Dan dropped the can into the cart and counted to ten. He'd agreed to Amy spending time with Emma but that didn't include her boyfriend. "I didn't know Steven went with you to the children's museum."

"He didn't," Emma stood on her tiptoes and peered into the cart. She wrinkled her nose. "Green beans. Yuck."

"They're good for you," Dan said absently. "What do you mean Steven didn't come with you? I thought you said you all had ice cream."

"After the museum, me and Amy went to the mall." Emma's eyes brightened. "I like the mall. Will you take me there sometime, Daddy?"

"Sure," Dan said. "So you met Steven at the mall?"

He didn't know why he was pushing so hard for

details. After all, as long as Steven hadn't deliberately been part of the outing, it wasn't any of his
concern.

"He was at the store that had all the pretty
jew-ry," Emma said. "Buying Christmas presents."

Emma twirled in the aisle. "I want lots and lots of
pretty presents."

Dan tuned her out. He'd already heard too much.
Steven had been looking at jewelry. Buying presents.
Probably picking out *Amy's* Christmas gift.

Steven was a successful, eligible bachelor who
seemed genuinely interested in Amy. Dan knew he
should be happy for her. But all he felt was jealous.
He wanted to be the one buying her ice cream on a
Sunday afternoon. He wanted to be sitting across the
supper table from her, talking about the day and
laughing with her at Emma's knock-knock jokes. At
night he wanted to be the one in her bed. And, if
anyone was buying her jewelry, Dan wanted it to be
him.

His jaw tightened.

"Steven's taking Amy to a party Wednesday night,
so she can't come see me." Emma's smile turned to
a pout. "It's not fair. Wednesday night is *my* night."

Shortly after Amy moved out, they'd set up a visi-
tation schedule. She took Emma every Wednesday
night and every Sunday. This would be the first time
she'd canceled.

Not many women would have been so diligent.
Most of the ones he knew put career and their various

social obligations before children. Tess, he'd finally come to realize, had been no exception.

When Dan had married Tess, he hadn't thought much about the kind of wife and mother she'd be. All he knew was that they were happy and in love. But as time went on, he found himself wishing she didn't see the need to be so involved in everything. He'd gotten tired of eating out every night and always being on the run.

He'd hoped she'd slow down after Emma was born, but if anything, the pace only picked up. Maybe it was a good thing Amy had backed out of their engagement. When she'd talked about working fulltime at Chez Gladines he'd felt as if she'd taken a knife to the heart. The last thing he wanted was to come in a distant second to her career. Like he had with Tess.

Still, Dan missed Amy. Marjorie, the woman who Amy had recommended, kept the house clean and took good care of Emma. But without Amy, the house no longer felt like a home.

"I want to go to the party with Steven and Amy," Emma said. "Can I, Daddy? Can I go?"

Dan only wished he could grant Emma's wish. He'd love to send his daughter along as a chaperone. But he knew Amy needed to get on with her life, just as he did. He threw a box of cereal into the cart and shook his head, unruffled by Emma's pleading expression.

"The only place we're going is home," he said.

"Grandpa Phil and Grandma Gwen are coming tonight and they're bringing your presents."

Emma gave an excited squeal and Dan smiled. At least one of them was happy about the visit. But he couldn't complain because he was the one who'd invited them.

In preparation for tonight, he'd made a quick trip to his attorney's office and had gotten the information he'd needed, information he should have gotten a long time ago. After dinner, he'd send Emma up to her room to play with her toys. Then he would have a talk with Gwen and Phil. A long overdue talk.

Chapter Eighteen

Dan glanced around the grand ballroom of the Michigan Avenue hotel, which had been transformed into a Winter Wonderland. Fake snow and ice sculptures, red and white roses as well as the more traditional poinsettias and garlands of greenery were everywhere. The laughter of the festive holiday crowd filled the air.

With a resigned sigh, Dan snagged a glass of champagne from a passing waiter. He'd planned to spend the night playing board games with Emma, but at the last minute one of the other partners couldn't attend the mayor's Christmas Gala, and Dan had been roped into going.

Christmas.

The big day was less than a week away and Dan
hadn't bought a single gift or even put up the tree.
Christmas had always been his favorite holiday but
this year he hadn't been able to summon up much
enthusiasm.

The season was off to a great start. Amy had
moved out. Then, Phil and Gwen had left in a huff
barely twenty-four hours after they'd arrived. To top
it off, his mother and stepfather had decided at the
last minute to spend the holidays in Texas with his
aunt.

This year it would be just him and Emma. The fact
that his mother and Hal wouldn't be spending the
holidays with them didn't bother him. Not as much
as the knowledge that, for the first time in three years,
Amy wouldn't be at his side. He shoved the disturbing thought aside.

Mistletoe hung at discreet locations throughout
the room. Dan felt a tap on his shoulder and realized
with horror that he was standing under one of the
sprigs. One of the wives of a prominent city official
loved to kiss men she found standing under the
mistletoe and for a second Dan feared he'd been
caught.

He turned and breathed a sigh of relief. "Bree.
What a pleasant surprise."

Dressed in a clingy copper-colored dress with a
front that was cut almost as low as the back, Bree
looked more like a sexy chorus girl than a respected
tax attorney.

"Merry Christmas, Dan." Bree put her hands on his shoulders and brushed a friendly kiss across his lips. She took a step back and gazed up at him, as if waiting for his reaction.

"Merry Christmas to you, too." Dan glanced around. "Who'd you come with?"

"I'm alone," she said with a sigh. "Poor little Bree, doesn't have a date."

Her lips pulled together in a cute little pout.

"If it makes you feel better, I'm in the same boat," Dan said. "This was Harry's year to come but he got sick so I'm a last minute fill-in."

She rested a hand on his arm. "I'm so happy I ran into you."

She smiled warmly and sounded so genuinely pleased that Dan found himself relaxing for the first time since he'd walked into the ballroom. He'd been lonely since Amy left and it was nice to see a friendly face.

"Care to dance?" he asked impulsively. If he was forced to spend the evening mingling he might as well try to have a good time.

Bree's smile widened. "I thought you'd never ask."

"Are you still dating Jake?" Dan had been so furious with Jake—and with himself—that he hadn't seen much of the man during the past month.

"Good Lord, no." Bree laughed as if he'd made a joke. "We never did date. I just went to that one party with him. Actually I'd been seeing someone else. But we just broke up." She paused and cast him a speculative gaze. "I heard Amy moved out."

"Yes, she did." Thankfully they'd reached the dance floor and instead of saying more, Dan took Bree into his arms.

As she cuddled up against him, he realized she smelled as good as she looked. Dan inhaled the light citrus scent and let his hand caress the soft silky skin of her back.

He waited. Waited to feel a jolt of lust. Waited to experience the urge to pull her close. Waited for that rush of desire that would make him want to kiss her.

Instead he felt…nothing. If it were Amy, he'd be already kissing her and thinking of ways to ditch the party so he could get her back home and into his bed.

"…you might be interested."

Dan lifted his gaze and blinked. "Interested?"

"In a kitten," Bree said, a hint of exasperation in her tone. "Like I was saying, Kellycat, my Scottish Fold, had kittens six weeks ago and I'm looking for good homes."

"A cat is the last thing I want or need," Dan said absently. He wondered if Amy was going to be going home with Steven tonight. His hand clenched into a fist behind Bree's back.

"I was thinking of Emma," Bree said, a note of concern in her voice. "She lost her mother and now Amy. I was an only child and I know how lonely it can be."

Dan resisted the urge to tell her to mind her own

business and reminded himself that Bree was only being a concerned friend.

"Emma's not lonely," Dan said firmly through gritted teeth, hoping Bree would get the message and let the subject drop. "She's always had lots of friends."

"Friends are fine." Bree laid her head against his chest. "But they can't cuddle with you. And we all need someone to hold. Someone to love."

Dan's heart clenched as an image of Amy flitted across his consciousness. He'd had a best friend, someone to hold, someone to—

"I've got the prettiest black-and-white," Bree said. "Very nice markings."

Dan had finally had enough. "I don't like cats. I won't have one in my house."

Dan didn't know if it was his tone of voice or his flat dismissal of the feline species that raised Bree's ire. But her blue eyes flashed and she went rigid in his arms.

"Emma loves kittens." Bree lifted her chin. "But you won't even consider it."

"That's right." He breathed a sigh of relief. Finally he'd gotten through to her. "No cats."

"Because you say so."

"Yes, because I say so." Dan wondered where this belligerence was coming from. He'd dated Bree for months and had never seen this side of her.

"You haven't changed," she said.

Dan had a feeling he shouldn't ask but he couldn't help himself. "What in the world are you talking about?"

"You want to know why we didn't work out?"

There it was again, that argumentative tone. He almost wished he was back under the mistletoe worrying about the city official's wife. But he decided to play along. After all, the question was a no-brainer. They'd broken up because she'd wanted a more serious relationship. He didn't.

"Okay, Bree," he said. "Tell me. Why didn't we work out?"

"Because of your pigheadedness." Her blue eyes narrowed. "I'm sick of men who get mired in the past and refuse to move on."

Dan wasn't sure what had set Bree off, but he sensed she was just getting started. "I—"

"I, I, I," she snapped. "What? *I* can't let myself love you because I'm still in love with my dead wife?"

"Bree," he said in a low warning tone.

"At least be honest with yourself." Bree's voice trembled with emotion. "You're afraid to love again, afraid of getting hurt."

"You don't have any idea what it's like to lose a spouse."

"No, and I don't have any idea what it's like to get divorced, either. But I know when someone is letting the past screw up their future."

"Divorce?" Dan asked, now thoroughly confused.

"It doesn't concern you." Bree waved a dismissive hand. "A guy I'd been dating went through a bitter divorce. The problem is he's still letting his ex-wife's betrayal color his view of all women."

Now, Dan understood. Bree had really liked the guy. And once again things hadn't worked out for her.

"You'll find someone else."

"What about you?" Bree asked. "Will you find a woman to replace Amy?"

Dan stiffened. He didn't want to talk about Amy. Not with Bree. Not with anyone. "I have a temporary nanny."

"That's not what I'm talking about," Bree said. "You two were close. Now she's gone."

"She's got a full-time chef position at Chez Gladines," Dan said. "She had to make a choice."

"Emma's in school all day," Bree said. "You could have worked something out. But you weren't willing to work with her because it's all or nothing with you. Just like with Emma and the cat. I bet even if she wanted one you wouldn't consider it. Am I right?"

"You think you know so much." Dan's temper had reached the breaking point. "But I don't see *you* doing all that great in your personal life."

Bree's cheeks reddened as if she'd been slapped but her gaze remained steady and her chin up. "At least I'm open to love. And when I find the right one I'm not going to be rigid and insist on everything being my way. I'll look for ways to make it work."

"With that accommodating attitude I'm surprised you're still not with your divorced friend," Dan said, his tone slightly mocking.

"It takes two to make things work, Dan," Bree

said. "Kyle wasn't ready or able to get past his fear. The problem is once he is, I won't be around."

Dan shifted uncomfortably from one foot to another.

Bree met his gaze. "I know you really cared for Amy. I saw the way the two of you were together. Do you know that when we dated I was jealous of her?"

Dan frowned. "Of Amy?"

"Yes, of Amy," Bree said. "There was a chemistry between you two, a closeness that went far beyond friendship. When you'd talk about her, you'd get this look in your eye…sometimes I had the feeling I was dating a married man."

Dan swallowed hard against the sudden lump in his throat. But even if he could respond, he didn't know what to say. There *had* been something special between him and Amy. He couldn't deny it.

"You care for her. And, as your friend, I just want you to take a look at what you're losing. And for what? Because you can't let go of the past?"

"You make it sound so easy," Dan said. "Tess was my wife. I'd loved her since we were kids in school. She—"

"She's dead, Dan," Bree said. "And she'd want you to move on with your life. Fall in love again."

"I don't know if I can…"

"I think you already have," Bree said. "Now you just have to decide what you're going to do about it."

Chapter Nineteen

Amy leaned her cheek against Steven's chest and let the music wash over her, grateful she could enjoy the closeness without worrying her actions would be misconstrued.

When she'd made the break with Dan, Steven had seen the split as an opportunity to deepen their relationship. He'd been stunned when she'd told him she thought of him only as a friend. But in the end he'd appreciated her honesty. And when his date had canceled at the last minute, he'd called and asked her to accompany him to the mayor's Ball…as a friend.

She hadn't really wanted to go but she'd decided a night out might do her some good. She'd been in a funk for weeks. Some of it was living with Verna.

Her aunt had run her household a certain way for many years and having Amy around disrupted her schedule.

Some of it was her new job. While she was up to the challenge and learned something new every day, she missed being her own boss. She liked the flexibility she'd had being a nanny and doing small catering jobs on the side.

But most of her blue mood she knew could be directly tied to Dan Major. Her anger over his deception had diminished to a profound regret. If he'd had concerns about Emma's welfare, they could have talked about it, strategized. But to deliberately set out to make her fall in love with him...to deliberately seduce her...well, she'd expected better of him.

She knew he liked her. She had no doubt that he wanted her. Even now, when she picked Emma up she'd catch him looking at her and the longing in his eyes would take her breath away. Yes, he wanted her. He just didn't *love* her.

Tears momentarily blurred her vision. Amy blinked rapidly for several seconds until she could see clearly again.

"All this dancing is making me thirsty," Steven said. "How about we get some champagne and go for a stroll?"

They'd reached the edge of the dance floor when Amy stopped in her tracks. For a moment she felt light-headed.

"Dan." Her gaze widened to include the woman

standing next to him, a proprietary arm through his. "Bree. What a surprise."

The introductions went quickly. Bree's eyes brightened with interest when she heard Steven's name.

"Bree is an attorney, too, Steven," Amy added. "She works for Seim Anderson."

"I've known Jerry Seim since I first moved to Chicago," Steven said.

The comment started an animated conversation between the two lawyers, leaving Amy and Dan standing at the sidelines.

She gazed at Dan, her heart in her throat. She'd never known a man who looked so good in a tux— although she did notice his tie needed straightening. But for once she kept her fingers to herself.

"Would you care to dance?" Dan asked politely.

Amy said neither yes or no, but let him take her hand and lead her back onto the dance floor. The familiar scent of his cologne sent her senses into overdrive and the light touch of his hand made her pulse pound.

But when Dan placed a hand on her waist and drew her close, and with his other hand took hers in a warm clasp and began to move her in time to the music, Amy was unprepared for the intimacy of it.

"You're gorgeous," he whispered.

Amy's face warmed. She closed her eyes, trying to concentrate on the music, or the conversations surrounding them, on anything except how good his body felt pressed against hers.

"You're the most beautiful woman in the room."

She kept her eyes tightly closed and acted as if she hadn't heard.

Dan couldn't believe after four long weeks she was finally back in his arms where she belonged.

"I've missed you," Dan said, embarrassed at the breathless quality of his voice. But, oddly enough, he felt breathless.

The minute he'd touched her, he wanted nothing more than to take her home, lie naked beside her and touch her everywhere. He'd start with her breasts...

"Are you and Bree seeing each other again?" Amy tilted her head and gazed up at him.

Her words had the dousing effect of ice water, and the dream vanished.

"No, we're not. I ran into her just a few minutes before I saw you." He cleared his throat. "How about you and Steven? Are you exclusive?"

Amy shook her head. "We're just friends."

Relief rushed through him. When he'd seen them together...

"Anything new with Bree?"

The question took him by surprise. Until he felt Amy's hand tremble and realized she was nervous and merely making light conversation.

"Not really," he said. "Unless you count the fact that her Scotland cat just had kittens."

Scotland cat? It didn't sound right, but he must

have been close enough to be understood because Amy's eyes brightened. "Kellycat's a momma?"

"She had a whole bunch of kittens and apparently they're ready to be adopted." Dan couldn't believe he was having a conversation about *cats*. But he'd talk about them all night long if it would keep Amy in his arms.

"I'd love to see them." Amy's smile brightened then faded. "On second thought, I'd better not."

"Why not?" Dan tightened his arms around her. Dancing with her was heaven. Absolute paradise. There was no space between them, no way they could get any closer—at least not with their clothes on. He'd missed her so much…

"I'd want to take one home." Her voice sounded sad and wistful.

Dan opened his mouth then shut it. The last thing he wanted to do during this brief time together was hear himself talk.

"Didn't you used to have a cat?" Dan asked, moving his hand slowly down the bare skin exposed by the deep V of the back of her dress.

She quivered and his body responded immediately. But if she could feel his arousal, she gave no indication.

"Yes," she murmured. "His name was Mittens and he was black and white and very beautiful. My father got him for me as a birthday present. But when I went to live with my aunt, he had to go to the animal shelter. I'm sure someone nice adopted him."

Though her tone didn't vary, Dan knew her so well he heard the pain beneath the matter-of-fact words.

"Losing him had to have been hard," he said.

Amy's eyes took on a distant faraway look. "I promised myself that when I grew up and had a place of my own I'd get another Scottish Fold—that's the kind of cat Mittens was—but I've never lived anywhere that's allowed pets."

Dan had known she liked cats but he realized with sudden insight that if they'd married she'd still not have one. The knowledge filled him with shame. Too late, he realized he'd give Amy the sun and the moon if he could. Hell, he'd even give her a cat.

He stopped, startled. He'd never go to that extreme for someone he just liked. Only for someone he *loved.*

Was Bree right? Had he told himself he couldn't love anyone but Tess because he was *afraid?*

It hardly seemed possible. After all, he'd never been a man to make decisions based on fear. But if he didn't love Amy, why had he been so miserable without her? He'd tried to tell himself it was because he and Emma had grown to depend on her.

But her replacement did a wonderful job taking care of things around the house so it couldn't be that. It was *Amy* he missed. Amy who made the house a home.

I'm in love with Amy.

The words echoed through his head and he knew, without a doubt that they were true. With Tess, love had hit him like a lightning bolt. With Amy, love had come softly. It had crept into his heart and taken up residence without him even being aware it had happened.

Now, all he had to do was to let Amy know how he felt…and hope it wasn't too late.

"Emma." Amy opened the door and called out. She'd tried the doorbell but no one came. It was the Sunday before Christmas and she and Emma were going to the mall.

The house was strangely silent. Sunday was Marjorie's day off so she hadn't expected to see the housekeeper. But she had expected to find Dan and Emma at home, especially since she'd just confirmed the five o'clock pickup time with Dan earlier that afternoon.

The call had been the first time they'd talked since the party. She'd worried it might be awkward but Dan had been in good spirits—asking her about her job and seeming genuinely pleased when she reported things were going well.

Maintaining a positive relationship was a good thing, she told herself. It was important for Emma that they be cordial. Wednesday night had gone a little beyond cordial. For a moment on the dance floor Amy had felt as if Dan might try to kiss her. And even worse, the way her body had been responding to his closeness, she had the feeling she'd have let him.

When she and Dan had returned to Steven and Bree, the two attorneys were seated alone at a large round table totally engrossed in a conversation about some legal case.

Dan hadn't seemed to mind. He'd confiscated glasses of champagne from a passing waiter and pulled out a couple of chairs across the table from Bree and Steven.

Amy had been surprised when Dan brought up her job at Chez Gladines. It was the first time she'd discussed the position with him and, looking back, she was sure she'd bored him with way too many details. Sitting with him at that linen clad table had reminded her of all the times they'd talked over breakfast, all the discussions they'd had at the supper table.

It would be so easy to be drawn into the trap of equating interest with love. But she'd made that mistake once and she wasn't going down that road again.

"Emma," Amy called again, glancing at her watch. "We need to go. The mall closes early today."

Still no answer.

Amy left the kitchen and headed for the parlor, where Emma loved to sit and read. But Amy only got as far as the dining room before she stopped. Though there was no food yet on the table, there was crystal and china and candles. And a fresh flower center-piece.

Spider mums. Her favorite.

Amy's heart twisted.

It didn't take a genius to know that Dan had a romantic evening for two planned. Either he'd gotten back with Bree or there was someone new in his life. She wondered if he'd deliberately planned this date knowing Emma would be gone most of the evening? It wasn't any of her business, of course. She was simply...curious.

"The brisket is in the oven."

Amy jumped at the sound of the voice and turned to find Dan in the doorway. "It smells delicious," she said. "Brisket has always been one of my favorites."

It was a stupid thing to say and Amy regretted the comment the second it left her lips. After all, what did it matter what *she* liked. *She* wasn't the one who'd be eating it.

She swallowed hard past the sudden lump in her throat. "Is Emma upstairs?"

"Actually—" Dan shoved his hands into his pockets and rocked back on his heels "—there's been a slight change in plans. Emma is spending the night at Rehn's."

Amy's heart fell. "She was going to buy your Christmas gift tonight. I can't believe she forgot."

Emma had been excited about this day for weeks. Yet, she'd decided to spend the night with a neighbor? It didn't make sense.

"She didn't forget." A rueful smile lifted Dan's

lips. "The only way I could get her to go to Rehn's was to tell her you and I had plans for the evening."

Amy stiffened. She couldn't believe he'd lied to his daughter so that he could get together with his new girlfriend. "That's not fair, Dan. You shouldn't get her hopes up just because you want to spend an evening with—"

"With you," he said, finishing the sentence. "I want to spend the evening with you. There's so much I have to say."

Amy glanced at the table. It had seduction written all over it. Okay, so he was lonely. And he'd probably missed having her in his bed. Goodness knows she'd missed holding him tight. But as much as she'd like to share that intimacy again, the physical closeness was no longer enough.

"I don't think that'd be a good idea." Amy's fingers tightened around her purse. "Besides, what more is there to say? Everything's already been said."

Dan swallowed hard and took a step forward.

"I haven't said I love you before," he said softly. "But I do. Very much."

He was surprised, once the words were out, that he should feel so unmanned, and that tears should be stinging his eyes.

When she just kept staring at him, he turned away and continued.

"I know I haven't been good to you." He shook his

head. "I've been selfish. I only thought about myself."

"That's not true." A tiny catch sounded in her
voice.

"It is. When I think back on it now, I'm so
ashamed. I wish I could tell you how much I regret
the way I treated you, as if you were just an
employee."

"Dan," she said firmly. "I *was* your employee. If
anyone was at fault it was me for foolishly believing that I was different, that you could love me."

He felt her hand on his arm. "You were good to
me. You made me feel like a part of the family. But
that said, it was wrong of you to lead me on."

"I love you," Dan said.

"No." She shook her head. "You love Tess. She's
the only woman you'll ever love."

"I love you," he repeated emphatically.

"You don't," she insisted. "You told me over
and over again that Tess is the only woman you'll
ever love."

"I did love Tess," he admitted, "but I love you, too."

"Dan," Amy said patiently as if speaking to a
child. "I understand you need a mother for Emma
and someone to take care of you and your house, but
lying isn't the answer."

Amy turned to go but Dan grabbed her arm and
pulled her to him, hugging her tightly.

"I was such a fool," he murmured. "I know I hurt
you. But listen to me, please. I won't deny that I

loved Tess. I won't deny it because I did. But what I didn't realize is that I've been afraid. And I didn't understand anything about love. I thought I could decide my feelings—thought I could decide whether to love someone or not—but that isn't how love works. It happens all on its own. I kept telling myself that I couldn't love you, that I *didn't* love you, but I did."

Amy wanted to believe him. More than anything she wanted to believe his words.

"What about my career?" she asked.

"That's another thing I regret," Dan said. "I just assumed you'd want to start popping out babies. I didn't even ask what you wanted. I think I was afraid if you had a career, our home life would come in a distant second like it did with Tess."

"I'd never let that happen," Amy said. "You and Emma would always be the priority."

"I realize that now. And I know we can make it work," he murmured against her hair. "Just give me another chance. I'll show you how much I love you."

Amy wanted to believe him. But she couldn't forget his conversation with Jake. "How do I know you're not just saying this because you need a mother for Emma? Because you're afraid of Gwen and Phil getting her if something happens to you?"

Her words made Dan's heart ache with remorse and sorrow.

"I spoke with my attorney and he said they could fight all they want but the courts would uphold my wishes, I also spoke with Gwen and Phil and made It clear that I wanted you to raise Emma." Dan's lips lifted in a rueful smile. "It was never an issue. I just thought it would be."

Amy's brows pulled together. "Why didn't you check this out before?"

"I know it was stupid," Dan said, a sheepish look on his face. "The only explanation I've been able to come up with is that it gave me a reason to marry you without admitting to myself that I loved you."

Dan laced his fingers through her hair. "I'm not asking you to be my wife because I *need* to marry you. I *want* to marry you. Because I love you."

An ache of longing raged through Amy. She closed her eyes and let her head rest against his chest. Would she be making a mistake by saying yes?

"Mew."

Amy's eyelids popped open. She shifted in Dan's arms just in time to see a small furry head peer around the corner.

"What's that?"

Dan smiled. "Your Christmas present. From me to you with all my love."

He reached down and scooped the black and white kitten into his arms. "She's a Scottish Fold. See how her ears flop over. And her eyes are more round than oval."

Amy's heart melted. Tears filled her eyes. "You don't like cats."

"But *you* do," he said. "That's what matters."

She took the kitten from his arms and held it tight against her. "She even has four white feet, just like Mittens."

"I'll make you happy, Amy," Dan said. "Just give me the chance."

He appeared relaxed but she could see the tenseness in the set of his shoulders, in the tiny muscle that jumped in his jaw.

Amy leaned over and dropped the ball of fluff gently to the floor. While she loved her new kitten, she loved Dan more. And right now he needed her attention and reassurance.

"I love you, Dan," she said very softly, "and I know you love me."

He grabbed her, held her fast. "Thank you, God."

His voice was thick with emotion, with relief. He kissed her again, this time so fiercely they almost tumbled into the table. And he kept kissing her.

"Will you marry me, Amy? Will you be my wife?"

She lifted a finger to her lips and pretended to think, but inside her heart had already started to sing.

"Say yes," he said, kissing her. "Come on. Say yes."

When she didn't answer, he kissed her again, then again.

"Say yes," he whispered against her lips.

"Mew."

Tiny little claws dug into Amy's ankle. She yelped and jerked back from Dan's arms.

Dan's brows pulled together. His gaze dropped to the black and white kitten that now sat staring up at them. After a moment his frown eased. His lips twitched. He grinned.

"See," he said finally. "Even the cat thinks you should give me a chance."

Amy could only laugh.

"I love you, Amy," Dan said, taking her hands, his grin fading, his expression turning serious. "If you marry me, I'll spend the rest of my life making you happy."

Of that, Amy now had no doubt.

"Yes," she said, nodding her head emphatically.

"Yes, you know I'll spend the rest of my life making you happy?" he asked cautiously. "Or yes, you'll marry me?"

Amy's heart overflowed with joy. She placed her hands on his shoulders and kissed him full on the mouth. "Yes, to both questions."

And, as Dan pulled her close murmuring words of love, Amy knew the fairy-tale ending was finally hers.

A man to love.

A child to cherish.

A cat to litter train.

It was all she'd ever wanted and more.

Dan was already downstairs when Amy woke the next morning. She stared down at the sparkling diamond on her left hand. Today, they'd get their marriage license. Tomorrow would be their wedding day.

Just in time for Christmas.

She would be his Christmas present and he would be hers. Dan had told her last night that having her as his wife was the only gift he wanted. Then he'd proceeded to show her again just how much she was loved.

Amy showered and dressed quickly, happiness bubbling up inside her. She gave the kitten a quick pat and a treat but didn't linger. She wanted to be downstairs before Emma got home so that she and Dan could tell her the good news together.

She was outside the kitchen when she heard Emma talking to Dan. Amy paused to listen, her heart in her throat.

"Did Amy come over last night, Daddy?"

"Yes, she did."

"Did you two kiss and make up?"

Dan's cough sounded suspiciously like laughter. "Yes, we did."

Amy's skin warmed, remembering just how thoroughly they'd kissed and made up.

"Is Amy coming home today?" The childish hope in Emma's voice tore at Amy's heartstrings.

She couldn't bear to wait a second longer. Before Dan could answer Amy stepped around the corner. "I'm already here."

Emma squealed and ran into Amy's open arms, pressing her tiny body tight against her. After a moment, she lifted her head, her gaze anxiously searching Amy's. "How long are you staying?"

Amy lifted her gaze to meet Dan's, the promise in his eyes a reflection of what was in her heart. She smiled down at Emma. "Forever."

* * * * *

Welcome to your new-look
By Request series!

RELIVE THE ROMANCE WITH
THE BEST OF THE BEST

This series features stories from your favourite
authors that are back by popular demand—
and, now with brand new covers, they
look even better than before!

See the new covers now at:
www.millsandboon.co.uk/byrequest

A sneaky peek at next month…

By Request

RELIVE THE ROMANCE WITH THE BEST OF THE BEST

My wish list for next month's titles…

In stores from 16th May 2014:

❏ Misbehaving with the Millionaire –
Kimberly Lang, Margaret Mayo & Lee Wilkinson

❏ Hot Summer Nights! –
Kelly Hunter, Cara Summers & Emily McKay

In stores from 6th June 2014:

❏ Royal Seductions: Diamonds –
Michelle Celmer

❏ Wedding Wishes – Liz Fielding,
Christie Ridgway & Myrna Mackenzie

3 stories in each book - only £5.99!

Available at WHSmith, Tesco, Asda, Eason, Amazon and Apple

Just can't wait?

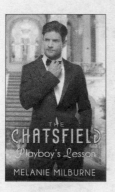

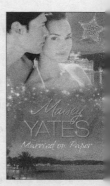

The World of Mills & Boon

There's a Mills & Boon® series that's perfect for you
There are ten different series to choose from and
new titles every month, so whether you're looking for
glamorous seduction, Regency rakes, homespun
heroes or sizzling erotica, we'll give you plenty of
inspiration for your next read.

By Request
Back by popular demand!
12 stories every month

Cherish
*Experience the ultimate rush
of falling in love.*
12 new stories every month

INTRIGUE...
*A seductive combination of
danger and desire...*
7 new stories every month

Desire
*Passionate and dramatic
love stories*
6 new stories every month

nocturne
*An exhilarating underworld
of dark desires*
3 new stories every month

For exclusive member offers go to
millsandboon.co.uk/subscribe